GOODY TWO SHOES

INVERTARY BOOK 2

JANET ELIZABETH HENDERSON

ISBN: 978-0-473-46130-0

Cover design by Janet Elizabeth Henderson

Editing by Liz Dempsey

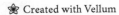 Created with Vellum

ACKNOWLEDGMENTS

A big thank you to the fabulous Scotland shop www.Scotland-Shop.com for letting me use a photo of their gorgeous tartan shoes on the cover of this book.

Thank you to the ladies of Romance Writers New Zealand for their support, humour and encouragement. I would feel like a nutty hermit without you!

Thank you to one of my best friends, Liz Dempsey, who is also my proofreader. As usually, you've done an amazing job. You get cake!

Thank you to my wonderful supportive husband, without you entertaining the kids, there would be no books. Although, there would be even more if you stopped constantly interrupting me to ask how the work was going! I love you very much and hope that one day you'll actually read more than the acknowledgement page and make it through a whole book!

And, last but not least, thank you to my readers. You lot are lovely! Your letters of encouragement and support have a huge impact on my life and I appreciate them ever so much. Thank you for reading my books.

PROLOGUE

Six Months Ago—Las Vegas

When Josh McInnes realised it was time to settle down and start a family, he did what any self-respecting celebrity would do and called his manager.

"This better be important," Mitch grumbled down the line. "It's four in the morning over here."

Josh glanced at the clock and winced. He hadn't thought about the time in New York. In his mind's eye he could see his best friend with his hair standing on end and a scowl on his face.

"I want to get married," Josh said instead of apologising.

There was silence for a beat.

"Thanks for the offer, Josh, but you're not my type."

"Not to you, fool, to a woman."

"Please tell me that you aren't planning a Vegas cliché? The world doesn't need another celebrity with a drive-through marriage license."

"You don't seriously think I'd do something that stupid?" There was no reply. Josh frowned at the phone. "No, dumbass, I've decided that it's time to start a family, before I'm too old to play football with the kids."

"You're only thirty-five." Mitch sounded fed up.

"And by the time I find a wife and start churning out the kids, I'll be older. I don't have time to sit around waiting for it to happen. That's why I'm calling. I need you to find me a wife."

The line went dead.

Josh's lips pursed as he listened to the dial tone. Then he hit redial.

"Go to sleep," Mitch said by way of hello. "Or at least let me go to sleep. I was in meetings all day; I'm beyond beat and don't have the energy for whatever the hell this is."

Sleep? Josh scoffed at the phone. It was barely one a.m.— Vegas was just getting started.

"Did you hear me? I need you to find me a wife."

"Yeah, I heard. Are you drunk? Why the hell would I find you a wife? Find your own woman."

"You're my manager." From his room high above the city, Josh watched lights flicker on the Vegas Strip.

"Exactly. I manage your career. Your life is your business."

"You're also my best friend."

"That doesn't mean I want to play matchmaker. Marry one of the many women who throw themselves at you." Mitch paused. "Just don't do it in Vegas."

"I don't want one of them. They're factory made. I feel like I'm a product tester for Mattel. One more Barbie lookalike and I'm going to lose it. I don't need another date. I need a wife. Someone different. Someone real. I want you to arrange a marriage for me. You know, like they do in India."

"Like they do in India?"

2

"Why are you repeating everything I say?" Josh was losing patience; Mitch was supposed to be the one with the brain.

"Seriously? You have to ask me that? You call me up in the middle of the night and ask me to get you married and you wonder why this is hard to follow?"

"Look," Josh said, "I thought this through."

"Yeah, that's what worries me."

"You know me better than anyone else, so you're the best person to find me a wife."

"What about romance, attraction, crap like that?"

Josh waved a dismissive hand, even though Mitch couldn't see him. "You know I don't believe in that stuff."

"You make millions from that stuff."

"Singing about romance is different from actually believing it exists. It's the same as singing about Santa. He doesn't exist either. There's no such thing as romantic love, only hormones and lust."

"That's a great quote," Mitch told him. "Should we put that on your next album cover?"

"Funny."

"So you don't want to love your wife, just bang her and get to the baby part?"

"I didn't say that." Josh kicked off his shoes. Dealing with Mitch was using all his energy. Suddenly the party he'd planned to attend didn't seem like such a great idea. "I believe in love. But love doesn't happen instantly. You start with commitment and then you get love. And what's more committed than marriage? The love will come later."

"Commitment my ass. You should be committed," Mitch mumbled.

"I know what I'm talking about. I've been around all that romance stuff since I was a teenager. I know every soppy ballad out there. I'm telling you, there's no such thing as romance. I want a wife."

"A non-romantic wife?"

"Exactly."

"A wife with family values who doesn't care about her career?"

"She can have a career, just not one that involves using me to get ahead."

"My mistake."

"Carry on." Josh grinned at his reflection in the window.

"Basically, you want a relationship from the fifties?"

"Yes!" He thought about it. "No! Wait a minute; you're putting words into my mouth again."

There was a long sigh in his ear. "Don't worry. I get it, buddy. You want me to vet some women and find you a wife, and"—there was a grin in Mitch's voice—"if she happens to be Doris Day, even better!"

CHAPTER 1

Present Day—Invertary Castle, Scotland

Caroline Patterson pursed her lips at Invertary Castle's main entrance. It made her sick to her stomach that a celebrity had bought the place. He would probably paint the interior gold and throw orgies in the grand room. She stepped back to look at the building and smiled. Not big by castle standards, it was more on the scale of a grand house. Caroline loved the pale grey stone; she was tempted to run her fingers over it while she waited for the lord of the manor to open the door. Instead she let her gaze follow the sleek lines of the building up over four floors to the twin turrets at the top. Gorgeous. Like a tall, lean sculpture, full of grace and life—and, unfortunately, Americans.

Her admiration of the building was interrupted when the heavy wooden door swung open. Standing before her was Josh McInnes, *People* magazine's sexiest man alive. He was taller than he'd looked in the photos she'd seen. His shoulders were broad, his hips slim and his legs long. Black hair flopped towards one of his brilliant blue eyes. They were electric. And they were amused. Caroline blinked hard. He was smiling at her—a lazy, confident smile. Caroline pushed back her shoulders, took a step forward on wobbly legs and thrust out her hand.

"Caroline Patterson." Her voice was a little huskier than usual. "I represent the Council. Your friend Mitch met me in my office at the community centre. I have the forms he asked me to drop off."

She cleared her throat and resisted the urge to fidget. She never fidgeted.

"Josh." He captured her hand in his.

He held it a moment longer than was polite, and Caroline could swear she felt the heat from his touch slide across her body like honey on warm toast.

"Come on in, Caroline Patterson." He flashed his award-winning grin. "We've got a lot to talk about."

Caroline followed him into the castle and promptly forgot all about him. It was worse than she'd imagined. Not only had the previous owners covered the beautiful wood panelling in the hallway with smooth board, and the marble floor with grey carpet—they'd lowered the ceiling to hide the plaster moulding that wound around the top of the walls.

"This way." Josh put his hand on the small of her back.

Caroline stepped away from his touch as her heart sank further. The grand room was no longer grand. The walls were cream, the old stone fireplace had been covered over, only to be replaced by the biggest TV screen she'd ever seen, and the chandelier was now a modern spotlight system.

"Please, sit down." Josh pointed to one of the twin blue sofas.

Caroline perched on the edge of an overstuffed cushion, holding her briefcase in her lap. She wanted to weep. From the inside of the castle, you wouldn't know it was a beautiful nineteenth-century building. The character of the place had been stripped away.

"Can I get you something to drink?" Josh said.

Caroline pulled her attention away from the utilitarian blinds on the bay window long enough to reply. "Tea, please."

"Ah." Josh scratched his head. "I'm not sure we have tea."

Then why ask?

"Don't worry." Mitch entered the room carrying a tray. "I have tea."

He put the tray on the monstrous modern coffee table.

"Nice to see you again, Caroline." Mitch handed her tea in a large mug with "Party Hearty" written on it. "Sorry." He winced. "Josh hasn't gotten around to stocking the place yet."

"It's perfectly okay."

She tried not to grimace as she sipped the tea. Basically, it was a delicious mug of hot, watered-down milk. She put it on the ugly glass table, before reaching into her briefcase.

"I have the paperwork that you need to fill in to obtain permission to renovate the castle."

She held the paperwork out towards Josh, who sat opposite her on a matching sofa. The ankle of one of his legs was perched on the knee of his other leg. He was watching her. No, studying her—in a way that was almost predatory.

"I'll take that." Mitch reached for the paperwork.

Caroline smiled gratefully. Out of the corner of her eye she could see that Josh was still staring at her. She wriggled uncomfortably before picking invisible fluff from her skirt.

"So, what do you plan to do to the place?" She flicked a glance at Josh before turning to Mitch for the answer.

"We're going to convert this room into a sound studio," Mitch said.

Caroline felt the blood drain from her face. "You're going to convert the grand room into a sound studio?"

Mitch shrugged. "It seems to be the best space for it."

Caroline bit her tongue as anger bubbled inside her. It made her feel sick to think that the castle was now in the hands of people who didn't recognise its value.

"Well, if that's all." Caroline stood. "I'll get back to work." *And start proceedings to stop you messing up the castle any further.* She flicked through her contact list in her mind, planning what strings she would pull to save the castle. "Thanks for the tea."

She took a step towards the door.

"Actually." Josh stood up. "There's one more thing I'd like to discuss."

Mitch shot him a pointed look. "Don't you want to think about that first, buddy?"

"Nope." Josh grinned widely. "I'm sure."

Caroline didn't know whether to sit or stand. Mitch sighed and rubbed his face. Caroline's stomach clenched tightly. Whatever was coming, she wasn't going to like it. If he told her he was going to replace the lead windows with aluminium, or paint the exterior pink, she'd have to resort to violence.

"It's like this," Josh said in that melodious voice of his, before peering out from under lashes that were thicker than hers. "I'm looking for a wife, and I think you might be it."

Caroline looked at both men in turn. Mitch shrugged, like this was out of his hands. Josh thrust his hands deep into the pockets of his worn jeans and rocked back and forth on the spot. He flashed his megawatt smile.

"So what do you say, Caroline Patterson. Do you want to marry me?"

Caroline swayed before sitting back down with a dull thud.

. . .

JOSH SHOT a worried glance at Mitch. His friend had one of those "I told you so" looks on his face. So maybe he'd rushed things a little? When he'd opened the door and saw her standing there looking like Grace Kelly in a Hitchcock film, it was as though he'd been punched in the gut. He knew she was the one—with a certainty that had shocked him. She was perfect. All buttoned up and proper in her grey polyester suit, without even a dab of makeup on her smooth, creamy skin. She was screaming out for someone to come along and ruffle her a little. And he itched to be the one. He'd made up his mind on the spot. He'd found his wife. Unfortunately, from the bewildered look on Caroline's face, it seemed she didn't agree.

"You want to marry me?" Her voice was barely a whisper.

She tucked a strand of her perfect blond bob behind her ear.

"Yes." Josh sat on the edge of the sofa opposite her.

She looked at Mitch, then back at Josh. "Is this a joke?"

"I'm dead serious."

She turned to Mitch, who sighed heavily. "He's telling the truth. He's serious."

Caroline swung back to Josh. "Why on earth would you want to marry me?"

Okay, so not the response he was looking for, but he could work with it.

"You're exactly what I'm looking for." He gave her his best charming smile. The one that usually made women swoon.

"You've been looking for an ordinary Scottish woman who works in a community centre?"

She reached for the mug of tea she'd obviously hated, and took a large gulp. Her nose screwed up.

"It's like this." Josh worked at keeping his tone soothing. "I don't believe in romance. I believe in commitment. I want an arranged marriage, like they do in India. So, Mitch here has been checking out potential wives for me. Up until now he's completely bombed out, but I think he's spot on with you. You're perfect. I think you should marry me."

Her jaw fell open. "You think I should marry you?"

Josh looked at Mitch. "Why does everyone insist on repeating what I say?"

"It's a mystery." Mitch's tone was droll.

"You don't know anything about me." Caroline's cheeks had turned the prettiest shade of pink. It made up for the boxy suit and sensible shoes his mother would love.

"I know you care about family. I know you quit college to help your sister when she got pregnant as a teenager." He smiled reassuringly. "I know you lost your parents when you were a kid, and your grandfather raised you. I know you live alone and aren't in a relationship. I know the whole town considers you to be the woman in charge around here."

The colour leeched out of her face. "You've been spying on me?"

Josh realised his mistake. "Not spying, just checking you out."

Caroline frowned at the two of them. "That is very…" She looked around the room. "Creepy," she said at last.

Josh rubbed his neck. This wasn't going how he'd planned it to go. Now she not only looked like she was going to run, but call the cops while she did it. He tried a different tack.

"Lots of people get married for practical purposes. It isn't always about falling in love. It's really quite simple. Think of it as a business arrangement, only with sex."

Mitch groaned and slapped a hand over his eyes.

"You mean like a prostitute?" Caroline's green eyes went wide.

"No!" Josh threw up his hands. "That came out wrong. It's a marriage."

"Between two people who don't know each other."

"But who will grow to care for each other." He infused his words with the absolute conviction he felt.

Caroline sat silently for a minute. At least she seemed slightly less stunned. She turned to Mitch.

"You picked me?" She pointed at Josh. "For him?"

"He needs a nice girl." Mitch shrugged. "Someone down to earth who can balance out the nuttiness."

Caroline shook her head. "I'm sorry." She spread her elegant hands. "I don't understand this at all. Don't people like you usually marry models, or film stars? Isn't there someone more appropriate who fits your bill?"

"Uh-uh. Not going to happen. I've been down that road. I don't want a famous wife."

"No," Mitch said. "There's only room in his life for one ego."

"You're not helping," Josh told his friend.

Mitch grinned and settled into one of the cream-coloured armchairs.

"This is ridiculous." Caroline's voice had a slightly hysterical edge to it. "Why would I marry you?"

Josh spread his hands wide. He thought it was self-evident. Apparently not.

"Because you'll have a great life with me. We'll travel the world, meet interesting people, have loads of fun and you'll get to live in a castle." He leaned towards her and lowered his tone. "And trust me, I *will* make you feel good. Very, very good."

Her cheeks turned a deeper shade of pink. They stared into each other's eyes for a minute before she blinked and looked away.

"It wouldn't be a hardship. I'm easy to be around. Ask anyone."

She looked at Mitch.

"It's true. You get to live in a castle, and if you can deal

11

with whatever mad idea he has going next, then he's easy to live with."

Caroline's brow wrinkled in confusion. It was cute.

"Is this like a job position? You'd pay me to live with you and have your children? Are we talking something Michael Jackson would have done?"

Josh almost laughed, but she was deadly serious.

"We're talking about a marriage. An equal partnership. Everything I have will be yours, and vice versa. We'll make decisions together and get to know each other as we grow old. It's simple. It's how marriage used to be. People have been doing this for centuries. It isn't a big deal. Don't over-think it. It'll be great. Instead, focus on all the fun we'll have down the years."

"But I don't know you. I don't know anything about you. Other than you sing Sinatra songs and middle-aged women throw underwear at you."

"I don't just sing Sinatra," Josh informed her. "And there's nothing I can do about the underwear. Believe me, I've tried. Who knows what goes through a woman's head that makes her think I want her used nylon underpants."

Caroline blinked several times.

"She wants to know more about you," Mitch said help-fully. "Not the underpants."

"Sure." Josh nodded. "What do you want to know? Ask away."

She seemed blank. Her gaze darted about the room as she searched for something to say. Josh took pity on her.

"Fine," he said when no questions were forthcoming. "I come from a decent family. My dad is Scottish, my mom is American. They met in Atlantic City when my dad was on shore leave from the merchant navy. They were married fast and settled in Atlantic City, where they ran a miniature golf course together. I had a normal childhood. Wasn't brilliant in school and wasn't dumb either; mainly I just wanted to sing. I started doing gigs when I was thirteen, then as soon as I was legal I worked the clubs. I got my first big break playing Caesars. Apart from that, I don't have any brothers or sisters, and this idiot"—he pointed at Mitch —"has been my best friend since I was six. What else is there to know?"

She took a deep breath. "Any history of mental illness?"

"You mean me?" Josh pointed at himself. He couldn't hold in a laugh, the question was so ludicrous.

"Don't worry," Mitch said. "I know where you're going with this. Unfortunately, he's sane. We have the paperwork to prove it."

She turned back to Josh, who was trying his hardest to appear serious and sane.

"Are you dying and desperate to reproduce before you go?"

"What? No!"

Caroline's green eyes stared at him, while she pursed her luscious pink lips. His eyes wandered over her delicate cheekbones down to the beauty spot on the curve of her chin. That spot was begging to be kissed.

"You're homosexual, aren't you?"

Mitch spat coffee all over the carpet.

"No," Josh told her. "I'm not gay. Not even remotely."

Mitch was struggling to hold in his laughter, which wasn't helping.

"Don't you need to be somewhere else?" Josh asked him.

"No way." Mitch grinned with delight. "I'm not missing this.

"Look," Josh said. "I'm offering you everything I have. You won't regret this—trust me, I'll make sure you're happy."

"You don't know that. You can't promise something like that."

13

"Yes. I can and I will. You'll be so damn happy you won't know what to do with yourself."

Her cute little brows frowned with confusion, and Josh wondered when the last time was that he saw a woman frown. Every other woman he knew had been paralysed with Botox. There was silence in the room. Caroline looked around, giving every item her full consideration. Only the pulse throbbing at the curve of her jaw gave away the fact that this was anything but a normal conversation.

CAROLINE'S BLOOD was pumping so fast that it made her feel dizzy.

"Is this real?" she said.

Josh laughed. He had a good laugh. It was deep and full of joy. From the sparkle in his eyes and his easy, laid-back attitude, she bet he was a man who laughed a lot. She almost envied his ease, and wondered what it would be like to be so relaxed about life.

"I'm afraid so," he told her.

He leaned forward to put his elbows on his knees. He clasped his hands as he stared her in the eye. Her heart thudded loudly under the spotlight attention. She licked her lips.

"What do you say, Caroline Patterson," he drawled. "Want to marry me?"

Caroline swallowed hard as a cool sweat broke out on the small of her back.

Mitch lobbed a small blue cushion at Josh. "How about you give the girl some time to think about it?"

Josh tossed the cushion back. "Why don't we let her decide what she wants to do?"

The two men stared at her. Josh all shoulders, blue-black hair and luminous blue eyes. And Mitch with his wavy golden hair, hazel eyes and tall, lean frame. You didn't see many men like these in Invertary. There was more testosterone in the room than in all of Scotland.

She studied Josh, hoping for some clue as to whether this was some sort of joke. But all she saw was complete conviction and determination. His full lips softened into a mischievous smile.

"I promise." His voice was a low vibration that worked its way across her skin. "You won't regret it."

Caroline knew, from scanning the tabloid magazines in the library, that there were women queueing up for a chance to marry Josh. Women who fancied themselves already in love with him. Or women who wanted his money and fame. Caroline wanted neither, and she definitely wasn't in love with him. In all her thirty-one years she'd never been in love. And, as far as she was aware, no one had been in love with her. She'd been waiting to be swept off her feet. She was still waiting. She clasped her hands tightly as they began to shake. What if this was her only chance at a family? She glanced at Josh. His children would be beautiful. No, *their* children would be beautiful. Her heart stuttered and her mouth dried. Children. She'd given up all hope of ever having any.

Avoiding Josh's eyes, Caroline worked at steadying her breathing. Her gaze roamed around the grand room, and she automatically detailed every missing feature and hidden piece of history. His words rang in her ears—they would be partners, what was his would be hers, she'd get to live in the castle. Her palms began to sweat. She eyed the cracked single-pane windows that he'd no doubt replace with aluminium double glazing. She shuddered. What if this was her only chance to save the castle?

She shook her head to clear it. It didn't help. What she was thinking—what she was considering—was wrong. So very wrong. She looked at Josh's smiling face, and then at the

TV where the fireplace should be. That beautiful old fireplace. Knowing it was hidden tipped her over the edge. She felt her decision rush at her like a high-speed train. There was no avoiding it. She'd decided subconsciously. The deed was done.

"I have some conditions." Her voice was a croak. She cleared her throat.

Her heart was beating so loudly she could hardly hear anything else. Part of her brain was screaming for her to shut up. The other part was cheering her on. Josh shot Mitch an excited look. He beamed at her while his friend slumped down into his chair in resignation.

"Shoot." Josh spread his hands wide.

"If I agree, I want to be in charge of the castle restoration. I don't want any complaints. I want to be able to restore the place without interference. What I say goes."

"Done. The castle is yours."

Adrenalin shot through her. *The castle was hers*. She took a deep but shaky breath. She'd just sold herself—and the price was a castle. The room blurred in front of her as her heart pounded hard enough to be painful.

"I want to get married here, in Invertary." She was pleased her voice didn't waver.

"Fine by me." He was practically bursting with enthusiasm. "But I don't want to hang around. We'll go to the registrar tomorrow and get it done."

Caroline swallowed hard. "No. I want a proper wedding. With friends and family. In a church."

Josh stared at her for a moment. "Fine. You have three weeks."

"My sister is eight months pregnant. If it's in three weeks, she won't be able to attend."

"We'll do something else for her later. If we're going to do this, I want to do it fast. I'm done waiting. I want to be married. Three weeks is long enough."

Caroline stared at his determined expression. He smiled softly. Something inside of her calmed. "Okay."

Caroline stood unsteadily. Josh and Mitch stood too, making the vast room seem a whole lot smaller.

"Then"—she cleared her throat—"the answer to your question is yes." She looked up into the mischievous eyes of a stranger. "I will marry you, Josh McInnes."

She held out her hand to him, to seal the deal. With a wicked smile, he engulfed her hand in his. A bolt of pure electricity shot up her arm and through her body. She tingled from head to toe. Josh's eyes darkened.

"Good decision," he told her. "You won't regret it."

CHAPTER 2

"You know." Mitch chugged on his bottle of beer while he sat at the kitchen counter. "I thought that your most embarrassing moment was in Italy, when you were serenading that chick you were drooling over and fell off the stage." He shook his head slowly. "But this tops anything you've done in the twenty-nine years I've known you."

"What?" Josh shrugged. "This is great. The hunt is over. I'm getting married. Why is this embarrassing?"

"The fact you don't know the answer to that question is what worries me the most."

Josh ignored him and padded over to the freezer. There had to be something he could zap and eat. Adrenalin always made him hungry.

"You should be happy." Josh pulled two trays of lasagne out of the deep freeze. "This is what we've been working towards for months." He grinned as he stabbed the plastic lid with a fork. "I have to be honest with you. There was a minute where I thought you weren't going to pull it off. I thought I'd have to bring in the professionals."

"And I have to be honest with you. I thought you'd get

bored of this and move on to something more productive and slightly less insane—like the new album."

Josh plonked the food in the microwave and pressed the button that said *dinner*. Nothing happened. He randomly pressed a whole lot of other buttons until the machine started to work.

"Look." Josh grabbed two root beers from the fridge. "You know me. When I make up my mind about something, it's a done deal."

"Yeah, but that's business. Not finding a wife."

"Apparently it works for everything."

Mitch rubbed his hand over his face. "There's no talking to you. You're determined to ride this insanity train wherever it leads, aren't you?"

Josh pulled the trays out of the microwave to see if anything was happening. They were still ice. He put them back in and pressed random buttons again.

"This isn't insane. It's logical. Practical. You're just jealous because you didn't think of it first. I'm not possessive. You can have my idea. I'll even find you a wife if you want."

"I'll take you up on that"—Mitch paused as if in thought —"the minute hell freezes over."

Josh grinned at him.

"You do realise," Mitch said, "that you've just told a woman you don't know that you're going to have sex with her, and only her, for the rest of your life."

Huh? Josh leaned against the counter.

Mitch pointed at him. "You didn't think about that, did you?"

Josh bristled. "I can do commitment. I'm looking for commitment."

"Well, you better hope she's good in bed."

Josh felt a momentary pang of doubt. He narrowed his eyes at his friend. "You're not going to make me second-guess this. I know I'm doing the right thing. And I'm not going to discuss my marital sex life with you."

"What sex life? You proposed. You shook hands. She practically jumped out of her skin and then she left. I'm still burning from the heat of the exchange."

"I'm not listening to you." Josh reached for the phone. "You can't talk me out of this. I know it's a great idea."

Mitch shook his head as he looked at the ceiling. Josh dialled his parents' number in Florida.

"It's Josh," his dad shouted through the house.

A moment later, his mother was on the other phone. Josh grinned over her endless questions about his health. This was what he wanted: exactly the kind of comfortable relationship his parents had. Something that was stable and built on strong foundations, not on hormones. He glared at Mitch. Like he was going to take advice from a guy whose social life was dead and whose last serious relationship was in high school.

"I've got news." Josh squeezed the words in when his mother paused for breath. There was silence. He chuckled. "Don't worry, it's good."

"Do you want to spit it out, son?" his dad said. "Or do we have to guess?"

Josh took a deep breath. "I'm getting married."

More silence.

"We didn't know you were dating anyone." His mother sounded confused.

"It's been a fast process. I haven't known her long, but you're going to love her. We're getting married in a few weeks." He checked the calendar stuck to the fridge. "Mid-August. In Scotland."

There was silence.

"Hello?" Josh called.

"You got a girl pregnant, didn't you?" His mother's tone oozed disappointment.

"You better not have," his father threatened—like he could influence the situation in some way. Josh almost laughed.

"I didn't get anyone pregnant." How was it possible he was thirty-five and his parents still made him feel like a teenager?

"I don't understand," his mother said. "Was it love at first sight?"

"Not exactly," Josh hedged.

"If there's no baby on the way, then why the rush?" his father said. "Marriage isn't something you jump into quickly."

"You two did," Josh pointed out.

"Those were different circumstances," his father said.

"Yeah, but you don't regret it," Josh said.

More silence. He heard his mother take a deep breath.

"What's she like?" his mother said at the same time as his father said, "How long have you known her?"

Josh answered his mother. "She's great—she's sensible and sweet and really organised."

He could almost hear their stunned expressions.

"She's not like your usual girlfriends," his mother said anxiously.

"And that's a good thing, right?"

"How long have you known her?" his dad asked again.

Josh ignored him. "I'll send you some plane tickets for the wedding. It's going to be great."

"How long have you known her, son?" His dad used the voice that used to scare him witless as a kid.

But he wasn't a kid any longer. He glanced at the clock. "About an hour."

"What the hell?" his father barked in his ear.

"Well, great. Good talk," Josh said. "I'll see you both at the wedding." He doubted they could hear him. "I'll call another time." He hung up.

"That went well," Mitch said from behind him.

Josh turned to see that Mitch had eaten both portions of lasagne. His stomach grumbled.

"They'll come around." He opened the freezer and started his hunt for food all over again.

CAROLINE WALKED STRAIGHT past the community centre and into the Presbyterian church on the corner of Dewar Street. She wasn't sure how she'd gotten out of the castle. All she remembered was agreeing to marry Josh, and the next thing she knew she was walking back to work. They'd shaken hands to seal the deal.

She shook her head slightly. When she'd imagined a proposal as a child, it hadn't included a handshake. But, in saying that, back then her proposal fantasy had included a unicorn, a flowing pink dress and a real-life prince.

She pushed open the heavy wooden doors and went searching for the minister. She found him in his office.

"Caroline," the old man grumbled. "If this is more hassle about the roof fundraiser, you can turn around and leave now."

Caroline sat down hard in the rickety wooden chair facing his desk. She held her briefcase tightly in her lap. "I have a confession," she said.

He looked confused. "You know we're not Catholic, right?"

"Of course I know that, but I need to confess. I've done something terrible."

"Okay." He took off his bifocal glasses and linked his hands on the blotter in front of him. "I'm all ears. What do you need to confess?"

Caroline took a deep breath. "I've agreed to marry a man I don't love." The words rushed out in a gust of air.

Reverend Morrison frowned at her. "Why are you bothering me with this? We both know that isn't a sin. If it was, half the town would be in here complaining."

"But it's wrong. Isn't it? It has to be wrong." She glanced around the room, taking in the battered desk and the wall full of photos from his years running the parish. "I only did it to get my hands on the castle."

"The castle?" He thought for a minute. His eyes went wide. "Did you agree to marry that singing American?"

She nodded as her cheeks burned.

"Caroline, I don't know what to tell you. I don't know why you're asking me if this is okay. You have a better grasp of life's moral issues than I have. Does this man know you don't love him?"

She nodded again.

"Then you aren't lying." He sighed. "Does he know you want the castle?"

"I made it a condition of agreeing."

"Then you've been up front. I guess now all you need to decide is whether or not you're going through with it."

She sat up straight. "Of course I'm going through with it. I made a promise."

He spread his hands wide. "What do you want from me, then?"

It was on the tip of her tongue to say *reassurance*.

The minister let out a long-suffering sigh. His shoulders relaxed.

"Look, lassie, if your conscience is clear and you think you can live with the man, then I don't see what's to stop you."

In an uncharacteristic gesture, Caroline gnawed her bottom lip. "I don't really know him," she confessed.

"Maybe you should get to know him."

"The wedding is in three weeks."

"Who's doing the service?"

She smiled apologetically. With a grump, the minister reached into his desk drawer and pulled out an old, battered calendar.

"Let me see. It's Monday now, so how do Thursday afternoons suit you?"

She looked at him blankly.

"Wedding counselling. Looks like you two need the full package."

Caroline's shoulders slumped slightly. "Thursday will be fine. Will you tell Josh or will I?"

At last the old man grinned. "Oh, I think that should be your job."

"I'VE BOOKED THE FLIGHTS." Andrew McInnes stood in the doorway to the bedroom. "We leave in a couple of hours. Is that enough time to pack?"

Helen McInnes didn't look at her husband as she pulled clothes from the drawers. "It will have to be."

There was silence. She gritted her teeth. Andrew McInnes was a man of few words. It had been charming when she'd met him as a girl, but now it was lonely. All those conversations she had with herself. All those years spent trying to guess what was going on in his head. She was tired of it. All of it.

She heard him shuffle his feet. "Are we going to tell him?"

Helen turned to look at her husband of thirty-five years. Logically, she knew he was older. His hair was greying and there were wrinkles round his eyes, but he still looked like the man she'd met all those years ago. He was tall, with broad shoulders, and deep-set eyes that were always so intense.

She'd loved those intense blue eyes of his, especially when they were focused on her. It'd been a long time since his scrutiny had made her tingle. Now it only made her sad.

"I guess we have to."

He nodded. No wasted words for Andrew McInnes. He pushed his hands into the pockets of the ugly tartan trousers he insisted on wearing, and looked at her. Just looked.

"I better pack, then." He turned and headed to the spare bedroom, where he'd been sleeping for almost a year.

Helen let out the breath she hadn't been aware she was holding, and stared out of the window to the golf course behind their house. A house she hated. She felt guilty as she looked down onto their pool—guilty because she missed her friends in Atlantic City; she missed working all day long beside her husband. At least back then they'd had something to talk about. Now there was nothing.

With a sigh, she packed summer dresses into her bag, wondering how warm it got in Scotland in July. She could have asked Andrew, he would have known, but somehow along the years of enduring his silence she'd grown weary of hearing her own voice. She threw in a couple of sweaters. That should tide her over. If she needed anything else, she'd go shopping. It wasn't like money was a problem anymore. Josh had been very generous to them, and the sale of the business had made them a tidy profit.

"I'm all done." Andrew was back in the doorway. It was as though he was scared of entering the room.

"I won't be long."

"I'll make us a sandwich." He disappeared downstairs.

Helen patted her rounded belly and wondered if bread was a good idea. She'd been struggling through a low-carb diet for months now, but didn't seem to be losing the last flabby spots on her body. She sucked in her belly and looked at herself in the mirror. Her hair was the same bleach-blond bob she'd worn for almost forty years. Her breasts had long ago given into gravity, and now she couldn't bear looking at them without a bra. And her hips—great child-bearing hips, Andrew had called them…well, her child-bearing years were over and now her hips were just wide.

She looked at the door where Andrew had stood. She couldn't put off going downstairs much longer. She'd make it through another silent meal together. And after they'd dealt with Josh, they'd go their separate ways.

She wondered if she would feel lighter, or if she would die a little more inside.

CHAPTER 3

By eleven o'clock on Tuesday morning, the castle was full of workmen. There were guys stripping boards off the walls in the hall. A team were ripping up the carpet, and a group of teenagers were removing the TV from the living room wall and hacking at the spot where it used to be. Josh dragged the foreman into the kitchen as Mitch came down from the fourth floor with bags under his eyes the size of suitcases.

"What the hell is going on?" Mitch demanded.

"I'm about to find out." Josh perched on a stool at the kitchen counter. "This here is Mr. Buchanan; he's in charge and he's going to fill me in on what everyone is doing." He turned to the foreman. "When I let you in, I thought you were here to work on the sound studio."

The old man pulled his cap from his head and scratched the bald spot in amongst his thinning grey hair. "This is your house, Mr. McInnes—if you don't know what's going on, I'm not sure how I can help."

"I need coffee." Mitch headed for the espresso machine.

"I spoke to Caroline yesterday." Josh folded his arms over his Scooby-Doo T-shirt. "She said it'd take weeks to get permission for the renovation. How come you guys are here this morning?"

"Ah." The old man shuffled his work boots. "You don't know our Caroline. It may take *you* weeks to get the permits you need, but Caroline has a way of getting things done on her schedule. And she wants the work to start today."

"Why are you ripping up the hall carpet?" Mitch was banging around with the coffee machine. "We only want to renovate the main room. That's where the building should be taking place."

The small man dug around in the pocket of his shabby white overalls and came out with a crumpled piece of paper.

"It doesn't say anything here about renovation. This is a restoration job. Caroline herself told me that we're to get the castle back into its natural state as fast as possible. She said, 'Get rid of the ugly carpet and unearth the mouldings, and while you're at it find a rubbish dump for the TV.' I'm just following orders." He shoved the paper back into his pocket. "Don't worry. We know what we're doing. We're the crew that helped Caroline restore Macgregor's folly a while back. You don't need to worry; the place will soon look like a proper castle."

Josh stared at the man. "But I like it the way it is. All I need is a sound room."

The old man chuckled. "You'd best be taking that up with Caroline. She said she was in charge of the project and we take our orders from her."

"I own the damn castle," Josh pointed out.

"Ah." The old man nodded. "But you don't own Caroline. No offence, but I'm more scared of her than I am of you, so I'll be following her orders until I hear otherwise."

With that, he put his cap back on and went off down the hall. Josh stared after him.

"She's restoring the castle," he said, more to himself than anyone else.

Mitch came round to sit beside him. "I recall her saying, 'I'll do it for the castle, what I say goes, you can't interfere.' And you said, 'Done.'" Mitch took a long gulp of scalding coffee. "As your friend, manager and lawyer, I'd like to point out yet again that this is one of your more insane ideas."

"Can she do this?" Josh felt bewildered.

Somebody shouted "timber" and there was a loud crash.

"She *is* doing this," Mitch pointed out.

Josh frowned in the direction of the noise. "We might have to sort out some of the details in this arrangement."

"You think?" Mitch mumbled before finishing his coffee.

CAROLINE COULDN'T ABIDE it when things didn't run according to plan, and she abhorred rudeness. She looked at her watch for the third time. Making people wait was extremely rude. Her assistant, Beth, was seven minutes late, which made Caroline seven minutes late for her meeting with the vicar. And Caroline Patterson was *never* late.

"You need to calm down, girl," Archie McPherson told her again. "Something is going to pop in that pretty head of yours and you'll spend the rest of your life in a nice white jacket that buttons up the back."

"I am calm. I'm always calm."

"No, you're controlled. That's something else entirely."

Caroline pursed her lips at the man who had been her grandfather's best friend. "I'm not controlled. I'm in control. There's a subtle difference."

She pushed back her shoulders and picked a piece of lint from the front of her grey A-line skirt. She loved this skirt. She wasn't sure what the material was, but it was indestructible. It never needed ironing and liquids seemed to roll off it. It was the best second-hand bargain she'd ever picked up.

Archie sat back in his chair and smiled at her, making Caroline wonder why she'd bothered to leave her office to say hello to the domino boys. The other three men at the table watched with amusement. They'd been present at many of these discussions, and their game of dominoes was forgotten now that there was better entertainment on offer.

"When I was working in the shipyards," Archie said, "there was a boiler in the steam room and one of the new boys tightened that thing to within an inch of its life. There was no give. One day a bolt popped and the whole thing blew. That's you. You spend so much energy controlling everything that one day one of your bolts will pop and then kablooey."

"Thank you for the advice, Archie. But I'm perfectly fine. There's nothing wrong with wanting life to be orderly."

"There is when you want everyone around you to be orderly too," Brian grumbled.

Caroline tuned them out as they went into yet another discussion of their various ailments, which was even worse now that Findlay's nephew had taught him how to use the internet. He'd printed off everything he could find on all of their problems and brought it into the community centre in a wheelbarrow. For over a week their afternoon domino game was forgotten while they terrified each other with medical knowledge they barely understood. In the end Caroline had stepped in, confiscated the paperwork and strong-armed the town doctor into spending a few hours answering their questions.

The door to the community centre banged open and Beth barrelled in.

"Caroline," Beth gasped. "I'm sorry. There was a huge line at the bakery."

Caroline was not happy with that. At. All. "You're late because you were at the bakery?"

There was silence behind her as the four old men tuned into their conversation.

"Morag's mince pies were on sale." Beth held up a bag. "I got some for everyone. My treat."

There were cheers from the domino players. Caroline scowled at them.

"Beth, I expect you to be at work on time. I have other commitments that mean you have to be here for the hours that you are paid to be here. If you're late, then I'm late. That isn't professional, or polite. And stopping to buy pies isn't a reason to shirk your responsibilities."

Beth's face fell and her eyes welled up. "I won't do it again. I promise."

At twenty-two, it didn't take much to make Beth cry, and Caroline was beginning to suspect that the woman used her ability to get out of trouble.

"Don't you have to rush off somewhere?" Archie barrelled past Caroline to get to the pies. The old man grinned widely and smacked his lips at the aroma coming from the bag. "Boys, time for a tea break."

"We'll talk about this later," Caroline promised Beth. "Right now I have to go. Make sure you organise the children's section in the library. It looks like a tornado went through it. The Weight Watchers group have booked the green room for two o'clock. You'll need to air the place before they get here or the smell of pies will sabotage them. We can't have another disaster like the day they were double-booked with the cake-baking society."

"That was a great day." Archie sounded wistful.

Brian nodded. "Cake and needy women. I didn't realise until then how much comforting a woman who broke a diet needed. Plus those cakes were damn good."

"Behave yourselves," Caroline warned as she fought a smile. They were four teenage boys trapped in wrinkled packaging, and she loved them dearly.

"Yes, miss." The domino boys saluted like boy scouts.

Caroline shook her head with resigned amusement.

"Where are you off to in such a hurry, anyway?" Findlay asked.

"I have a meeting with the vicar." She picked up her brown briefcase.

"Church roof fundraiser?" Archie asked.

"Something like that." Caroline felt her cheeks begin to burn.

Archie's sharp grey eyes zoomed in on her. "Is it a committee meeting or not?"

Caroline pretended she didn't hear him, but her face burned hotter. "Make sure you remember to air the place out. I don't want to smell any pie fumes. I'll be back in an hour or so." *As soon as I've organised a wedding ceremony.*

"Now wait a minute, lassie." Archie trailed behind Caroline as she marched to the door. "Something fishy is going on here and I want to get to the bottom of it."

"No time. We'll talk later."

She yanked open the door and walked straight into Josh McInnes.

"Hi, GORGEOUS." Josh wrapped his arms around Caroline.

She put her palms on his chest and tried to push away. Josh held her tight against him, a second longer than was necessary, before releasing her. She smoothed her hair and straightened her skirt before casting a nervous glance behind her. Josh dragged his attention away from Caroline to survey their audience—four old guys, who seemed bewildered, and a wide-eyed young woman who was mouthing him name silently.

"What are you doing here?" Caroline snapped at him, bringing him back to the reason for the visit.

"Well." He put his hands in his jeans pockets. "My house is full of workmen and none of them know about the studio I need."

She bit her bottom lip. "Maybe we should talk about this in my office."

Josh was the first to admit that he wasn't the most sensitive of people, but he was picking up her signals loud and clear. If he wasn't mistaken, she was embarrassed by him.

One of the old guys walked towards them. "Aren't you going to introduce us to your friend, lass?"

"Sorry." Caroline drew back her shoulders. "Archie McPherson, this is Josh McInnes."

The short brunette behind them squealed as she pushed past Archie. "I love your music," the woman gushed. "I love everything you do. I have all your albums and I saw you perform in Glasgow two years ago." She sighed. "You're wonderful."

Everyone stared at her.

"It's always great to meet a fan." Josh smiled as he gave his standard answer.

She beamed at him, batted her eyelashes and reached out to pat his chest.

"Beth." Caroline's tone snapped the younger woman out of it. "Kindly keep your hands off Mr. McInnes."

The woman sprang back as though she'd been smacked. She pouted as tears pooled in her eyes.

"Here we go again," muttered Archie.

"Please go and sort the children's section of the library," Caroline told Beth.

With one last longing glance at Josh, Beth dragged her feet towards the library room.

"As I was saying"—Caroline's attitude was businesslike and efficient—"these are the domino boys—Archie, James, Brian and Findlay. Boys, this is Josh." There was a round of hellos. "Now let's go to my office."

"I'm happy to talk here." Josh wanted to see what happened when he didn't follow her orders.

Caroline tapped her toe on the linoleum floor impatiently. She wasn't amused. For some reason, that delighted him.

"You'll be wanting a cup of tea," one of the old guys said.

Josh would rather drink water from a puddle. "Tea sounds great." He ignored the frown of disapproval on Caroline's face and followed the old guys.

"I need to make a quick phone call," Caroline said. "Reschedule my appointment."

"Don't worry"—Archie flashed a wicked smile—"we'll take good care of him."

"That's exactly what worries me." Caroline disappeared through a door in the foyer marked "Manager."

Josh followed the guys into a room with blue walls, and over to a large brown Formica table near the window. There were four tables in the room, all large and well worn, surrounded by an assortment of wooden chairs. At the end of the room, farthest away from the door, someone had put in an old gas fire and arranged some high-back armchairs around it. It looked like one of the retirement homes Josh had sung in as a kid.

One of the guys placed a plate of cookies and a mug of tea in front of him. They stared at him while he wolfed down the cookies.

"So, you're the singer." Archie eyed him speculatively.

"Guilty as charged." The tea was revolting.

"I saw Sinatra play in '62," Archie said. "You've got nothing on him."

Josh barked out a laugh. "Who does?"

The old man grinned.

"I hear you have sex with all your groupies," Brian said.

Josh forced himself to take a sip of the tea. "I've made my fair share of mistakes. But I eventually grew up."

The guy looked disappointed. "So there's no groupie sex, then?"

"Not for a long time."

"Pity," Brian muttered. "I was trying to live vicariously. It's not like there's a lot of action in this town."

One of the other men cleared his throat and nodded at the door. A second later, Caroline swept through.

"Okay." She stood beside him. Her back straight as a board. "I've cancelled my appointment. Let's go to my office and talk."

The men's shoulders slumped with disappointment. Caroline glanced pointedly at her watch. Josh smothered a chuckle. Everything about her made him want to mess with her. "Pull up a chair, baby. I'm happy here."

He thought he saw her jaw clench. She stared at him for a moment, as though trying to figure out the best way to get him to comply. He winked at her. Her eyes went wide, then she blinked hard. Without a word, she turned a chair from the table beside them and perched on the edge of it. She folded her hands in her lap and waited. The domino boys were astonished, and Josh felt kind of smug. It was then he caught her thin smile and realised his actions would have consequences. It sent a thrill right through him.

"As I was saying before…" Josh gave Caroline his best dazzling smile. She was unimpressed. "There's a work crew in my house and none of them are there to build a studio. Want to explain it to me?"

35

The men leaned in towards them.

"And explain loudly," James said. "I don't have my hearing aids."

Caroline frowned at Josh. "You agreed that I could do whatever I liked with the castle. Did you not?"

"Yes, I did. But I also remember telling you I needed a sound studio."

"You can build one in the grounds, or rent a portable one, or something."

"Or you could put one in the room where I want it to be."

"That wasn't our agreement. You said I could do what I want without interference. I want to restore the castle." She gave him a frosty look.

"I like the castle the way it is. It's comfortable."

"It looks like a city apartment. All the period details have been wiped out. I'm putting them back."

"I didn't want a restoration. I wanted a renovation. I need somewhere to work on my next album."

Her eyes narrowed. "How about New York?"

Josh burst out laughing. She glared at him. Her perfect little nose thrust in the air and her pink lips were in a tight line.

"You can't get rid of me that easy," he said. "We have an agreement."

"Yes. We agreed that I get the castle."

"Yep, you get the castle." Josh grinned wide and slow. "And I get you."

CHAPTER 4

Caroline wanted to melt into the ugly brown carpet—straight after she wiped the smug smile off of Mr. America's face.

"Caroline." Archie folded his arms and frowned. "What's the Yank talking about?"

Josh folded his arms and raised an eyebrow in her direction. His eyes twinkled with amusement. The message was clear. She was on her own.

She took a slow, steadying breath. "Josh and I have agreed to get married."

There was a stunned silence.

"To each other?" Findlay said.

Josh burst out laughing, and Caroline had the uncharacteristic urge to kick him.

She fought for patience. "Of course to each other. What else would I mean?"

"But you don't even know each other," Brian said.

Josh was being no help at all. Worse still, he seemed to be enjoying himself.

"Apparently this is the in thing for celebrities. You choose a woman at random and propose."

"But you're not the marrying kind," James boomed. The other men shushed him. "We all thought you'd come to terms with being a spinster."

Anger fought with humiliation as Caroline watched the men's faces.

"It's a bit confusing, lass." Archie leaned forward and gently patted her hand. "We assumed you weren't interested in all that stuff."

"All what stuff?" Caroline hoped they would note her icy tone.

They didn't. "You know," Brian said. "Husband, kids, S-E-X."

Her jaw dropped. "You do know I can spell, right?"

Brian at least had the good grace to look embarrassed.

Caroline wished she had the power to turn invisible at will. Instead she had to sit there pretending she wasn't humiliated, while the boys informed the man she was going to marry that she was an asexual spinster. She had absolutely no doubt that Josh was rethinking his decision to wed her. She only hoped she'd get the castle restored before he found another woman to take her place.

"You've got this all wrong." There was a smile in Josh's voice.

Here it comes, the rejection. She sat up straighter and made sure her face was carefully blank. Suddenly, she felt a strong hand curl around hers. Startled, she looked down to see Josh's fingers linked with hers.

"Caroline here has a very healthy interest in S-E-X." Josh winked at her. "Seems like we know two different people."

Caroline blinked hard. Was he defending her? Josh squeezed her hand. She tried to pull it away. He held tight. It was on the tip of her tongue to point out that she could look after herself. When she turned to tell him so, the soft look in his eyes made the words stick in her throat.

Archie dragged her attention back to the domino boys. "When's the wedding?"

"Three weeks." Josh's fingertips caressed the palm of her hand. "I have a wedding planner flying up from London to help sort things out."

Caroline tried to hide her disappointment. "I was going to organise it. I made a list."

"She's working for you, baby. You can use her any way you like."

There was an awkward silence. Caroline tried again to pry her hand from out of Josh's grip, but it was impossible. Worse still, he seemed amused by her efforts.

Josh turned to the domino boys. "We'd be grateful if you could keep this information to yourselves. We don't want the town overrun with press."

The boys shared a look that Caroline didn't like one bit.

"It's going to cost you," Archie said at last.

"Archie Mcpherson!" Caroline started to lay into him, but Josh held up a hand.

"I want to hear this." He turned back to the boys, who were looking craftier than ever. "What's it going to cost?"

"Oh, we don't want money," Archie said as the other men nodded.

"No"—Brian grinned widely—"we want something much better than that."

Caroline had an awful sense of foreboding.

James leaned across the table towards Josh. "We want in." The boys nodded in unison.

Josh just grinned. "And by 'in,' you mean?"

"We want to work on the wedding," James said. "You have your namby-pamby English planner coming in, but we want to be wedding planners too. Caroline needs someone looking out for her interests, so that she doesn't get overlooked in this whole celebrity shindig."

"Yeah," Josh drawled. "Because we all know that Caroline has a problem standing up for herself."

They all laughed.

"Sitting here," Caroline snapped at them. "Sitting right here and planning to check out the book on poisons we have in the library. Remember that the next time I make you a pot of tea. Also remember that I know where to hide the bodies."

Josh seemed impressed. The rest of the men paled.

"Caroline Patterson," Archie said. "Don't go telling lies. We all know you're far too moral to break the law. You'd no more murder us than you would steal from the post office."

"Fine." Caroline glared at him. "But I have no problem lacing everything you eat and drink with laxatives."

Josh put up his hands. "There's no need for that." He winked at Caroline, making her even madder. "Why the hell would you guys want to plan a wedding?"

All four answered as one: "Boredom."

"And if we don't get to help, we'll entertain ourselves with the only other option we have available," Archie said with calculation in his eyes.

"Aye," Brian said, "with talking to the press."

Caroline was gritting her teeth so hard she was sure she'd pulverised a few. "I won't be blackmailed."

"Maybe not." James smirked. "But I bet he will." He pointed at Josh.

"Sorry, honey," Josh told her. "The man has a point. We need this kept under the radar more than we need these guys to butt out."

"One." Caroline held up a finger. "I am *not* your baby, honey, sweetheart or darling. Two." She pointed at each of the men in turn. "You will all be sorry about this. Not one of you knows anything about weddings. What makes you think you can 'help'?"

"Between us we've been married seven times," Archie said. "Not to mention we know everyone and everything in Invertary. And"—he gave her a smug look—"as you keep telling us, we're in a library—what we don't know, there's bound to be a book on it somewhere." The four men cackled like Macbeth's witches. "Let's face it. You need us. Without us you'd plan something so uptight that no one would have any fun."

Caroline stood before taking a slow, measured breath. "You have one chance. If you screw up, that's it. I don't give a flying fig if you run to the press or not."

"We'll make you proud." James nodded to his friends, and they all made the sign of the boy scout's promise.

Caroline rolled her eyes in disgust before striding out of the room and into her office.

A FEW MINUTES LATER, the boys were sitting at a table in the library room surrounded by bridal magazines. At least they were occupied and had stopped annoying her. Caroline shut the large windows in her office. There were two: one that faced into the library room and another into the reception area. Normally she liked being able to see everything that went on in the centre. Today it felt a little bit too much like a goldfish bowl. She turned to Josh, who was perched on the edge of her desk. He wore faded jeans, a blue T-shirt with Scooby-Doo on it and a pair of grey Converse. Everything he had on was worn, yet he looked more put together than Caroline did on her best day.

"You're taking up too much space." She wanted to push him out of her office into the foyer, but instead she sat behind her desk and scowled at him.

"There's not a lot I can do about that, baby."

"Stop calling me baby. Do I look like an infant?"

"Would you prefer 'sweetheart'?"

"I prefer Caroline."

Josh sauntered around to sit closer to her. Caroline tried to put some space between them, but the wall blocked her retreat.

"We need to clear up a few things." Josh's laid-back attitude irritated her.

"I'm not putting a studio in the castle." A deal was a deal. She was restoring the place, not converting it into a musician's playground.

He reached for her hair, making Caroline jerk away from him.

"I need to work."

"Well do it somewhere else."

"I also need to live. You're ripping out all the comfort in the place."

"I'm putting the character back in."

"Character is a pain in the ass. I want to be able to relax."

"Relax somewhere else."

He studied her for a moment, his blue eyes sparkling with mischief. "You want me out of the castle, don't you?"

Caroline thought about it. "No. I just want it to be perfect. You can stay there as long as you don't interfere."

With an amused smile, he shook his head. "There needs to be compromise in a marriage. Your husband needs to be able to work and relax."

"My *husband* should have thought of that before he proposed to *me*."

Josh threw back his head and laughed. The sound rumbled through her as a wave of vibrations, setting off sensations she wasn't used to dealing with. Caroline stood and inched around the desk to get away from him.

She positioned herself beside the door to her office, and folded her arms. Josh took the hint and walked towards her. He stopped between her and the door, standing far too close for comfort.

"You need to stop jumping every time I come near you." His words were a whisper against her hair.

Caroline's head shot up to look at him. "I do not jump when you're near."

He quirked an eyebrow. Slowly, he reached out and ran his fingers gently down her upper arm. Caroline jerked away from him. Her whole body flushed with embarrassment. The man was right. She did jump when he touched her.

Josh took a step closer to her. "Close your eyes." His voice was barely a whisper.

Caroline looked up at him and shook her head. What? Did he think she was crazy? She barely knew him.

"Trust me. The building is full of people. You're safe here. Now close your eyes."

Trembling, Caroline wrapped her arms tightly around herself and reluctantly did as she was told. She stopped breathing. Even though he wasn't touching her, she was completely aware of him. She felt his body heat engulf her, and the musky scent she'd come to know as uniquely his toyed with her senses.

"You need to remind yourself"—his voice was a vibration against her cheek—"that I'm not a stranger." His breath brushed her ear. She felt herself sway. "I'm the man you're going to marry." Gently, slowly, his fingers brushed her hair back behind her ear. "I plan to touch you." His words were a warm breath against the curve of her neck. "And taste you." His lips gently nipped at her skin. A tiny whimper stole through her lips. "Trust me." He whispered in her ear, "You won't want to run away. You'll want to experience every single second."

Suddenly his presence was gone, and Caroline felt cold. She heard her office door click shut. Her eyes fluttered open. She put out a hand to steady herself against the bookcase beside her. For a moment she just blinked, then she threw open the door. Josh was halfway out of the building.

"You're still not getting a studio," she called after him.

He flashed a knowing smile before disappearing into the sunlight.

Caroline leaned against the doorjamb and tried to breathe steadily. She had an uneasy feeling in the pit of her stomach that Josh wasn't playing by her rules. Unlike everyone else around her, he didn't seem to realise that she was in charge.

With a deep breath, she turned back to her office, only to see Beth standing in the doorway to the library, glaring at her.

"Can I help you with something?" Caroline asked her assistant.

"Ha!" was all Beth said before storming back into the library. She slammed the door behind her.

As soon as Caroline entered her office, there was a knock at the library window. James was on the other side.

"What colour do you want for your wedding?" He waved a magazine at Caroline. "It says in here that you need a colour scheme. Going by what you usually wear, we're thinking grey. Is that right?"

Caroline shut the window and went in search of some aspirin.

CHAPTER 5

On Wednesday morning Caroline was summoned to the castle—by Mitch. Josh was caught up in a conference call but wanted her to know that the wedding planner had arrived from London. The lord of the manor had used his minion to request her presence. Once again he was confused at his place in the hierarchy. People did *not* summon Caroline. Ever. Still, she was curious enough to do as she was told. This time, at least.

There was a note on the castle door for Caroline, saying that she should let herself in. As soon as she entered the foyer, her jaw dropped. The carpet that had once hidden Italian marble flooring was now gone. The rich walnut panelling had been unearthed from beneath the generic plasterboard. And snaking its way around the top of the wall was the decorative moulding that Caroline loved. It was wonderful.

"I hope you're pleased with yourself." Josh stood in the doorway of the grand room.

He leaned against the doorjamb, ankles crossed and arms folded. Today's T-shirt had the Cookie Monster on it.

Although he was trying his best to appear annoyed, the sparkle in his eyes undermined his efforts.

"I'm suffering here. The floors are cold, the hall is dark and someone's got to dust all that crap up there." He pointed at the cornices.

Caroline rolled her eyes at him. "I wouldn't worry. It won't be you."

He smiled at her, and her stomach tried to climb up her oesophagus.

"At least let me get some rugs. Marble would be great if we lived in the Mediterranean. But this is Scotland. It's like walking on an ice block."

"Fine. You can have rugs." He opened his mouth to speak, but Caroline got in first. "But I'm choosing them."

He grimaced. "Make sure you don't get those thin Persian things. I want something with depth." He thought about it for a minute. "Maybe we can get rugs that are heated. Like electric blankets for your feet. If they don't have something like that, I'm inventing it." He grinned at her, clearly pleased with himself. "I invented something."

"Well done. You're a genius. Now where is this meeting?"

Josh threw an arm around her shoulder, which she promptly tried to shrug off. He held her tighter. "Did you wake up on the wrong side of the bed this morning? Or are you just tired from dreaming about me all night long?"

She wriggled to free herself. As usual, her effort was wasted.

Josh leaned in towards her ear and murmured, "Caroline, Caroline. This marriage will be no fun at all if you can't get used to me touching you."

"It feels strange. I hardly know you."

"We'll have to work on that." He waggled his eyebrows mischievously as he pushed open the door to the kitchen.

"We were thinking a grey colour theme," Archie was telling the wedding planner.

Great. Things just kept getting better. The domino boys had been informed of the meeting.

Archie waved at her as he kept right on talking. "We're thinking of something like the colour of a submarine. You know, from a naval base."

Caroline strode past Archie and held out her hand to the pristinely dressed woman with a stunned expression on her face. Her chestnut hair was in a chignon, her makeup was understated in its perfection and her black suit screamed money. Caroline suddenly felt grubby.

"Caroline Patterson. I'm marrying Josh." She stumbled over the words. They sounded completely ludicrous. To her credit, if the woman had any thoughts on the mismatch between Caroline and Josh, it didn't show on her face.

"Millicent Price. Wedding planner and event coordinator."

"We're planning the wedding's theme," Archie told Caroline. "We figured that 'grey' and 'orderly' were the two words that summed you up most. And what's more grey and orderly than the navy? So how about a naval-themed wedding?"

He looked so proud of himself that Caroline almost agreed to avoid disappointing him.

"I made a collage." James held up a large piece of grey paper. "My grandson helped me." There were pictures of naval boats and submarines, grey balloons, a cake in the shape of a naval destroyer and several suggestions for music —all of which seemed to centre around the war music of Glen Miller's band.

Caroline took a deep breath. "I don't know what to say."

The men patted each other on the back.

"Told you she'd be impressed," James said.

"I still say we need something more girly. Weddings are girly," Brian said.

"We can girly it up," James said. "Anyone know any grey flowers?"

Caroline had to put a stop to this before they'd ordered the flowers and hired a boat. "As much as I appreciate the work you've put in, I don't really want a naval-themed wedding. And I would like to hear what Millicent has to say."

They looked like she'd shot their puppy. Caroline ignored them. They got the same expressions when she filled the biscuit tin with biscuits that weren't chocolate coated.

Millicent flicked on her iPad. "Let's start with the basics. Where would you like to get married?"

"Church," Caroline said at the same time as Josh said, "Here."

He was leaning against the kitchen counter sipping coffee out of a mug shaped like Mickey Mouse's head.

"You want to get married in the castle?" Caroline wasn't sure what she thought of that.

He shrugged. "I thought it would be fun."

She chewed her lip. "The restoration won't be done in time."

"We could postpone the work until after the wedding."

Her eyes narrowed. "Nice try, but I don't think so."

"How about a church ceremony followed by a reception in the castle garden?" Millicent said. "We can set up a glorious marquee. That way we can control which aspects the guests see of the castle, and you both get the venue you want."

Josh shrugged. "Works for me."

Caroline nodded.

"I think you should get married beside the loch," Archie told them.

Caroline helped herself to a cup of tea from the pot on the table in front of her. "The loch will be full of midges."

James bit into a biscuit and spoke with his mouth full. "With any luck they'll only bite the foreigners."

Millicent blinked at the man before turning back to Caroline. "How about photos at the loch? That way you can have loch, castle and church."

"Sounds great to me." Caroline took a sip of her tea. "Josh, what do you think?"

"Whatever you decide is fine."

He couldn't have come across less interested if he'd tried.

"Now, the gentlemen were talking about having a grey colour scheme." Millicent was clearly horrified by the idea. "What do you think?"

They all looked at Caroline, who was wearing yet another second-hand grey skirt suit. Although Caroline had never bothered with fashion, she was beginning to think she might have to wear some other colours.

"No, I don't want grey," Caroline sighed. "I like lavender."

"Lavender it is," Millicent said. "Any thoughts on flowers?"

"Heather," Caroline said.

Archie threw up his hands in disgust. "You can get heather on the damn hill. Pick something he has to pay for. The man is a gazillionaire. What's the point in marrying him if you can't splash out?"

Caroline looked at Josh. "What kind of flowers do you want?"

Josh was munching his way through a giant bag of chips. "I really don't care about flowers."

Caroline felt her blood pressure rise. "Do you care about the wedding at all?"

"Of course I do."

"Well, what ideas do you have for it?"

"Fine." He pushed himself away from the counter and sauntered towards them.

Caroline bit the inside of her cheek to stop from commenting. Everything the man did was so unhurried. It was beyond irritating.

He pulled up a chair, swung it around, straddled it and leaned on the back with his forearms. He was so close Caroline could feel the heat coming off him.

"Okay, this is what I think." Josh spread his hands wide. "I'm thinking a couple of hundred of our closest friends, large dance floor, great band. I might sing, but we can get someone else in too. Lots of food. I want steak. Apart from that, I don't care what colour the thing is or what type of flowers we have."

"So, you're going to leave the details up to me?"

"Isn't this what women do?"

The men gasped. "Ooh, you're in trouble now," Brian sang.

"I need a word in private." Caroline's voice was ice. She stood and tugged down her suit jacket. "In the hall. Now."

"Yes, ma'am." Josh saluted her.

As soon as they were outside the kitchen door, Caroline confronted Josh. "This wedding is your idea. You need to be more involved. I have a lot on my plate right now, what with the community centre, the committees I'm involved with and the restoration of the castle. You need to pull your weight."

Josh scratched his head as though the idea of planning a wedding was a bewildering one. "I thought women dreamed about this sort of thing. Don't you have a plan somewhere? A list of stuff you want at your wedding? Don't you have a scrapbook?"

"You've been watching too many romantic comedies. I haven't spared a thought about getting married since I was nine, and back then my fantasy wedding involved riding on a unicorn and having a bubble machine at the ceremony."

"We can do the bubbles, but the unicorn might be hard."

"You're not taking this seriously." She folded her arms. "I'm beginning to think that you don't take anything seriously. Do you have any idea how maddening that is? We have less than three weeks to organise a wedding. People need to be invited. Accommodation needs to be sorted. Where will two hundred guests stay? Have you thought about that? Would your Hollywood friends like to spend the night in the local B&B? I need to find a dress. I don't even know where to look for a dress. Then there's registering for gifts. Where would we do that? Here? America? Do we even want gifts? Not to mention the other little things that need to be sorted, like the ceremony, the best man, maid of honour, rings. There isn't enough time to do everything and I have no idea how you expect this wedding to go."

Josh took a step towards her, crowding her space. "You're really cute when you're panicking."

"I am not panicking. I'm trying to organise a wedding. A wedding you have to help with—"

Before she could continue her lecture, she saw a flicker of desire in his eyes. He moved towards her like a cat on the prowl. Without thinking, Caroline stepped back and felt the wall behind her.

"We need to sort this out." She was ashamed of the tremor in her voice. "I'm serious here."

"I know." Josh closed the distance between them. "You spend far too much time being serious."

Caroline grew anxious as he put his hand on the wall beside her head. "What are you doing?"

His free hand cupped her cheek. Far too gently for a man who towered over her, making her feel small at five foot six.

"I don't know you well enough for this." Caroline's

breathless words were at odds with the nervous flutter in her stomach.

His impossibly blue eyes smiled at her. "About time you did, then." His words were a breath on her lips.

"Did what?" Caroline's voice was a whisper.

He smiled a slow, knowing smile. "Get to know me, of course."

And then his lips were on hers.

CHAPTER 6

Fireworks went off in Josh's head. He was pretty sure it was his synapses frying from the sensation of Caroline's lips on his. She tasted exactly how he'd imagined her to taste. Like peach cobbler and something else. Something uniquely Caroline.

He ran his tongue along the seam of her lips and felt, rather than heard, a gasp escape her. He gently bit at her bottom lip, and her rigid posture crumbled. Josh moved the hand he'd placed on the wall down to the small of her back. He sucked on her bottom lip. Slow. Gentle. Caroline trembled. She tentatively grasped the cotton of his T-shirt above his heart.

"Yum," Josh murmured against her lips.

He leaned back to look at her, holding her tightly lest she escape. Heavy eyelids blinked open as she turned her face up him. What he saw made his breath stutter. Gone was the woman who delighted in ruling the universe. She'd been replaced by someone softer. Someone more vulnerable. Someone who knew desire. And that desire was directed at him. Before she could wake from her daze entirely, he captured her mouth again.

He clasped the back of her head. Gently, but firmly angling her mouth against his. This time, his tongue met no resistance as he slid into her mouth. He sighed against her. Delicious. Caroline's fingers clung to his shirt. Her nails scraped his chest. Josh pressed into her, holding her in place against the wall.

He felt the shivers of need rack through her body as her tongue tentatively found his. Josh's hand slid to her hip as one of his knees made space between her legs. Josh's senses were being consumed by her. He didn't know if it was the lack of sophistication in her touch, or the fact she'd metamorphosed in his arms, but he'd never felt anything like this before. It was mind-blowing. Addictive. And he wanted more.

He wanted all of her.

CAROLINE HAD LOST HER MIND. No. Josh had stolen it. With his touch. With his kiss. With the heat and the strength of him. She was drowning in the man, and there was nothing to hold on to except him. She didn't know if she could take much more. At the same time, she didn't know if she could bear for him to stop.

As his tongue traced lazy circles around hers, she flattened a palm against the wall of his chest. His muscles clenched beneath her touch. It was overwhelming to be that close to so much power. To have it tremble for her. Because of her. The musky scent of him was heady. It enveloped her. She was cocooned in him. In his arms. In his scent. In his heat. There was only Josh. Everything else had disappeared as if by magic.

Something creaked in the corner of her mind. A noise intruded.

"Oh for Pete's sake," someone said.

Caroline blinked out of her dream.

Josh muttered a curse against her lips.

"Get a bucket of water," James shouted. "The cats are in heat."

As if someone had waved a magic wand, Caroline's back snapped straight.

"This isn't over," Josh rumbled in her ear before stepping away from her.

Caroline realised her fingers were woven into his T-shirt. She snapped her hands away as though burned. Josh raised an eyebrow at her. She cleared her throat, resisting the urge to touch her lips. Self-consciously, she tugged at her grey suit jacket.

James cackled. "Why bother with a wedding? Why not go straight to the honeymoon? That's what I'd do if I was getting hitched again."

"I'll just go find the bathroom," Caroline mumbled.

She couldn't look at Josh as she passed him. Her cheeks were burning from more than lust as she walked down the hall to the powder room. Once inside, she ran icy-cold water into the porcelain sink and splashed her face with it. Shaky fingers reached for a towel. Patting her skin, she examined her reflection in the mirror above the sink. She was wanton. Lips swollen. Cheeks flushed. Her skin still tingled from Josh's touch. And every inch of her body resented being away from him. If he'd been behind her she would have sunk into his embrace without a second's hesitation.

She took a deep, shaky breath. She thought she'd be able to control everything about this wedding pact. Now, she had a niggling feeling that she may be out of her depth. So far out that she couldn't even see the shore.

· · ·

ANDREW HAD BEEN silent during the whole drive up from Glasgow. Helen had spent years monitoring his moods like the weather, and she knew something was bothering him. Fortunately, his moods weren't her responsibility anymore. So instead of trying to coax the problem out of him, she spent the time soaking up the scenery.

According to her guidebook, they were in the Trossachs. It claimed to be one of the most beautiful areas in the world. Helen thought they'd undersold it. From the crystal-clear lochs to the rolling hills that burst with colour, it took her breath away.

"You didn't need to shove it in my face."

It took Helen a minute to come to terms with the fact Andrew had spoken. Without being coerced, no less.

"Shove your face in what?"

He frowned at her before snapping his eyes back to the winding single-lane road. "You know fine well."

There was a time Helen would have felt distress at his words. A time when she would have spent hours trying to figure out what he meant. Not anymore. In fact, being away from the US had made her feel freer than she'd felt in years. Her need to tiptoe around her husband's moods wasn't as strong as it once was. She smiled at the thought.

"I don't have a clue what you're talking about," she said. "And frankly, I don't really care."

His knuckles went white on the wheel. Helen turned back to the view. Andrew's anger never bothered her. He wasn't the type to strike out.

They rode in silence for a few miles. Helen had thought the conversation was over, but he shocked her by speaking again.

"The guy on the plane. You flirted with him for almost eight hours. Under my nose."

Helen felt her heart lurch inside of her. Was that jealousy?

No. It couldn't be. "I wasn't flirting. I was having a conversation. A very pleasant conversation with someone who actually thought I was interesting."

"What's that supposed to mean?"

"You can work it out yourself, Andrew McInnes." She turned back to the glorious view. "Now if you don't mind, I want to enjoy being here. In fact, stop at the next hotel you see. I want to spend a night here before we go to Invertary."

"And if I don't want to spend the night?"

"You can drop me off and I'll see you at the castle tomorrow."

She thought she heard a growl, but when she looked back at him he was still staring at the road. Helen felt a zing of exhilaration course through her. This was the person she remembered being. The person she'd been years ago. She wasn't sure if it was the scenery or the attention of the man on the plane, but she felt more like herself than she had in years.

A few more miles and Helen relaxed back into her seat, letting the blues and purples of the Scottish highlands wash over her. She wished she'd made Andrew take her to Scotland years ago. It should have been something they'd enjoyed together.

"It isn't right to flirt in front of your husband." His low voice rumbled through the interior of the car.

Helen smiled as she looked out over a picture-perfect loch. And for the first time in her life, she was the one who stayed silent.

"WHERE'S THE BRIDE?" Mitch said to Josh as he came into the kitchen.

"Around," Josh snapped. *Hiding*. The coward. One little kiss and she'd fled like the hounds of hell were on her tail.

Mitch grabbed some chips from the cabinet.

"What's with the group meeting?" Mitch pointed at the wedding planner and the domino boys.

"Would you believe we're planning the wedding?"

"By committee?"

Millicent snorted, then covered her mouth as she pretended to cough. Josh frowned at her. At all of them. His famous sense of humour absent for once.

"Right." Caroline swept into the room and took the chair opposite him at the table—as far away from his as she could get. "Let's get on with this."

Her back was rigid again. Her chin was in the air and her tone was icy. She was back in control. If it weren't for the fact she wouldn't make eye contact with him, Josh would have wondered if the whole episode in the hall had actually happened.

"We need to decide on the submarine," James said.

Mitch almost choked on his chips. Josh shot him a glare.

Caroline turned to the domino boys. "Not. One. Word. I already told you that this would not be a naval-themed wedding." Her tone cold enough to freeze alcohol. They visibly swallowed and, one at a time, lowered their eyes.

There was a moment of heavy silence. Josh glanced at Mitch, whose eyebrows had travelled up his forehead.

"Now"—Caroline spread her hands on the table—"we are going to sort this wedding. Anyone have a problem with that?"

"Not me," Mitch said as Millicent and the boys shook their heads.

At last, Caroline looked directly at Josh. The air sizzled between them. Josh wanted nothing more than to clear the room and carry on where they'd left off. Instead he gave her a lazy smile imbued with promise. He took great delight in the fact her breath hitched and her cheeks warmed. "You've got my attention, baby."

Her eyes went wide and she frowned. "Don't call me baby."

Caroline turned her attention on Millicent. "Order a marquee. I want heather and snowdrops as flowers. Book any band Josh thinks is good. I want a wooden dance floor. Lavender and silver are the colour scheme. I want everything to be simple, tasteful and elegant. You are in charge. No one else. I want menu ideas by end of day tomorrow. I need a recommendation for a dress. And you will have to organise mobile accommodation for the guests. I'm thinking luxury trailers in the castle grounds. That is unless the guests wish to stay in Glasgow or Edinburgh and travel up for the ceremony. We don't want gifts; suggest that the guests make a donation to a charity instead. I'll send you a list for them to choose from. I'll sort out my maid of honour. I'm assuming Mitch will be best man." Mitch nodded. Her attention moved back to the wedding planner. "I'll talk to the minister about the ceremony. Josh?"

He quirked one eyebrow at her. "Yes, ma'am," he drawled, just to get under her skin.

She ignored him. "You are in charge of getting the rings."

"Are you sure I can handle that?"

"No." Caroline gave him a haughty glare.

Mitch didn't even try to cover his laugh.

"As for you lot." Caroline focused on the domino boys. "You will no longer be involved in wedding planning. You can help with the security for the event instead." The men gave each other a round of high-fives, obviously pleased to be doing something more manly. Caroline swept a prim glance around the group. "Anything else?"

"No." Millicent smiled for the first time since she'd

arrived at the castle. "That's perfect. I'll get right on it."

"Good." Caroline stood up and smoothed down her skirt. "In that case, I need to talk to the foreman about the restoration, and then I have to get back to the library to look after the Grayson toddlers."

And she sailed out of the room without so much as a glance at Josh.

"I want her." There was awe in Mitch's words. "I could rule the world if she worked for me."

"Absolutely," Millicent said. "That was impressive."

"She's babysitting some kids at the library?" Josh looked to Archie.

"She turns it into a day-care every Wednesday, just for Sheila Grayson."

"Never charges her a thing," James added. "And those little buggers always eat all the chocolate biscuits."

"Huh." There was a lot more to Caroline Patterson than met the eye. Josh stared at the door she'd disappeared through.

Mitch's eyes were also on the door. "That woman has organisational skills people would kill for. Maybe she'd be open to a job offer," he mused.

"She'd be great in event planning too," Millicent agreed.

Josh headed to the counter for some much-needed coffee.

"Back off, people," he told them. "The ice queen is mine."

CHAPTER 7

"Explain to me again why we have to do this," Josh grumbled the following afternoon as they headed towards the Presbyterian church.

Caroline sigh was long-suffering. "If we want Reverend Morrison to perform the ceremony, then we need to do what he requires." She stopped suddenly, making him pull up short against her. "And he requires that he counsels us and that we get to know each other. We should be thankful that's all he wants—the man wouldn't have been out of order if he'd demanded we get a psychiatric evaluation."

"I keep telling you, Caroline. I'm as sane as you are."

"Right now, that isn't much of a comparison, is it?"

Josh reached out and snatched her hand, holding tight in case she pulled away. Slowly, he caressed the soft, fleshy part of her palm with his thumb. "I can think of better ways to spend our time." He waited for the pink dots to appear on her cheeks, and smiled when he saw them. "Come on." He stepped towards her. "Let's blow this off."

She stared up at him. For a second he thought he saw desire flash in her eyes. He smiled knowingly. She snatched her hand away and curled it around the handle of her over-sized brown leather bag.

"We're in public." Her tone was a reprimand.

"Alert the media. Josh McInnes was seen holding hands with his fiancée on an Invertary street."

She blew out an exasperated breath. "We're going to be late. Get a move on. I hate being late."

"Why am I not surprised?"

Her haughty look made him want to do wicked things to her body. The more superior Caroline behaved, the more he wanted to make her pant. And after yester-day's kiss, Josh couldn't wait to get his hands on her again. He'd pin her down and tease her until she made those little whimpering noises that drove him out of his mind.

"There's the minister." Caroline distracted him from his plans.

"Good, you're here." The guy was the double of Ed Asner. "I thought you'd chicken out and run."

"You know better than that," Caroline told him.

"Not you." The minister pointed a knobbly finger at Josh. "Him."

"You know you look exactly like that editor in *The Mary Tyler Moore Show*, right?" They stared at him blankly. "Cultural differences. I get it. Lead on, *Ed*, we're eager to get started.

"And get it over with," he mumbled.

They traipsed through the old stone church and into a small room lined with dog-eared books. There was a circle of mismatched wooden chairs placed on the faded purple carpet. The vicar sat on the only chair with a cushion. Caroline and Josh sat side by side opposite him, on chairs that creaked when they moved.

"So..." Reverend Morrison studied them. "You two want

to get married. Tell me, Josh McInnes, famous singer and American playboy, what's in it for you?"

"I resent the playboy label. I only ran around when I was a kid."

The minister smiled like he knew better.

Josh resisted the urge to roll his eyes. "What's in it for me? A great wife. A family. What else is there?"

The minister grunted. "Do you two know anything about each other?"

"We know the basics." Caroline glanced at Josh for confirmation. "Josh had his friend investigate me, and I looked him up in the library database."

"I'm sure that was very informative. Next you'll be telling me you did one of those personality tests they have in women's magazines." He glared at them for a moment, and Josh felt like he was back in kindergarten. "You two don't know each other at all. It's time to rectify that. Tell me, where do you plan to live after the wedding?"

"LA," Josh said at the same time as Caroline said, "Here."

"See what I mean?" The minister took his glasses off the end of his nose and polished them.

Caroline frowned as she folded her hands in her lap. Her back got even straighter. Josh saw a flicker of determination in her eyes that worried him.

"How many kids do you want?" The vicar perched his glasses back on his nose.

"Four," Josh said as Caroline said, "Two."

"This is more fun than I thought it would be." Reverend Morrison chuckled. "Okay, try this one. Will Caroline keep her job after the marriage?"

"I don't think so," Josh said as Caroline said, "Of course."

She turned towards him. "What do you mean you don't think so?"

Josh knew enough about women to recognise an open

can of worms when he saw it. He tried to come up with the most diplomatic answer.

"It might be a bit far to commute when we're living in LA."

"I don't want to live in LA. We have a nice castle here. I don't see why we can't stay here."

"My work is mainly in the States." He used his most conciliatory tone.

The minister sat back, stretched his legs out in front of him and folded his arms. He looked like he was enjoying the show.

"And my work is here," Caroline told Josh.

"Yes, but..." Josh had the good sense to stop talking.

Caroline's eyes narrowed. "Yes, but what? Your job is more important than mine?"

"I didn't say that."

"You were thinking it, weren't you?"

He couldn't argue with that.

"Why?" Caroline looked like she wanted to smack him. "Because you earn more money that I do?"

"This isn't about money." He ran a hand over his head. This was not going well at all. "We can look into making Invertary our main base. But we'll have to be gone some of the time. I have work in the US; I have family there. And I spend a huge chunk of my time touring."

"Do you expect me to go with you? How am I supposed to keep my job when I'm bouncing in and out of the country all the time?"

"I'd hoped you'd want to go with me." He covered her clasped hands with one of his. She didn't pull away from him, and he almost cheered in victory. "We can work this out. It's only geography." He took a deep breath. "But if you stay working at the community centre, you need to know that it won't be the same as it is now. Photographers will have access to you. Reporters will turn up to talk to you. Your life will make international news."

She rolled her eyes, and her shoulders relaxed slightly. "That's your ego talking. You aren't Prince William. No one cares what your wife does."

"Someone will. Someone always does." He ran a hand over his face. "I'm not saying this to make you do what I want. I'm just telling you how it is."

"I'm not sure I like how it is."

"We made a deal, baby. No backing out now."

She glowered. "Don't call me baby."

Feisty. He loved it. Josh resisted the urge to kiss her then and there.

"Great." Reverend Morrison clapped his hands. "I don't know about you two, but I've had enough. I'll see you both next week. In the meantime, I have homework for you to do." He walked to one of the bookcases and came away with two red folders. "Fill these in and bring them next time." He looked straight at Josh. "No homework, no wedding."

"There are other places we can get married." Josh seriously wanted another minister to marry them. This one was a pain in his ass.

The vicar cocked his head towards Caroline.

"I want to get married here," she said.

Josh sighed in defeat. "Fine. Then I guess we're going back to your place to do homework, *baby*."

"We can't." Caroline's smug smile was priceless. "I have a meeting to attend."

If she thought it would be that easy to avoid him, she had another think coming. "That's okay. I'll come with you and we'll do the homework after it."

Caroline's mouth opened and shut. No sound came out. It was Josh's turn to smile smugly.

. . .

"Josh isn't here," Mitch said as he hugged Helen. "He's going to be pleased you came early."

"I'll bet." Helen knew her son. The last thing he'd want right now would be his parents. As far as she could tell, only three people ever questioned his common sense. And one of them had failed. She gave the failure her "you're in trouble now" look. He swallowed loud enough to be heard. "What's going on with this wedding? Why haven't you stopped Josh?"

Mitch turned away quickly. He led them through a building site to a kitchen large enough to have swallowed her first apartment.

"Mitch?" Helen pressed. It was like they were teenagers. Always covering for each other.

"Josh will be home soon. You can ask him all about it. How was your flight?"

She put her hands on her hips. "You helped him do this, didn't you?" He grimaced, and she knew she was right. "What the heck have you two been cooking up?"

Behind her she felt the air shift as Andrew brought the gargantuan chip on his shoulder into the room. He hadn't said a word to her since telling her off about flirting. Not one word.

She ignored her husband. "Mitch, tell me everything."

"Fine. Josh wanted an arranged marriage. So I arranged one for him."

Andrew let out one of the creative curses he'd learned as a boy in the Glasgow shipyards.

"An arranged marriage?" Helen could hardly believe her ears.

"Yeah." Mitch cringed. Evidently it made as much sense to him as it did to her. "He wants what you guys have. Long-term commitment. Friendship. He thought romance would get in the way."

Helen shrugged out of her cardigan. "He wants what we

have?" She glanced at Andrew. "If he doesn't watch himself, he'll get exactly what we have." Her husband's face was unreadable. Helen took a deep breath. "Show me to my room," she told Mitch. "I'll deal with Josh and his arranged marriage in the morning. Right now all I want to do is grab some dinner, shower and crawl into bed."

Mitch breathed a sigh of relief and practically ran up the stairwell. Andrew grabbed the suitcases and followed. On the second floor, Mitch pushed open a door to a light and airy room.

"This is the only guest room that's made up right now. I hope it's okay."

Helen almost sighed with delight. There was a vast brass bed made up with crisp white linen. A small blue and cream sofa in the curved window—not much bigger than an armchair, but perfect for reading. An antique dresser and wardrobe completed the furniture.

"Perfect."

"Great." Mitch backed away. "I've got work to do. Josh will be back soon." And then he was gone. Running from further interrogation. Some things never changed.

Without thinking, Helen turned to Andrew and smiled in delight.

"Can you believe it? We're sleeping in an honest-to-goodness castle."

His face was inscrutable. But stupidly, Helen kept smiling at him, hoping for something in return.

"I'll sleep on the couch," he said at last.

And just like that, her perfect moment shattered.

THE MEETING JOSH had invited himself to was beyond boring. It was the most mind-numbing meeting in the history of the universe. Fifteen people droning on about how to finance a new roof for the church. Hell, for the first half-hour one guy lectured everyone else on why a roof was necessary. Josh could have knocked that discussion on the head in three seconds—we need a roof to keep the rain out. Seriously? Why was that hard? The guy loved the sound of his own voice. How Caroline sat through this crap without killing someone, he didn't know. Josh noticed the pain-in-the-ass preacher wasn't at the meeting, and his opinion of him rose infinitely. Anyone with any sense would run from this committee. No woman was worth enduring this agony. He eyed Caroline as she took notes for the group. Fine. One woman was worth it. Josh turned his eyes towards the community centre ceiling and begged God to make it end.

At last, talking stopped and people left. Caroline came over to where Josh was dozing on one of the blue room's old armchairs.

"I told you, you didn't want to be here."

He opened one eye. "You didn't tell me I'd want to kill myself while I was here. Seriously. I was one step away from finding that book on poisons you keep going on about, and putting myself and everyone else out of our misery. Baby, this is hell."

Caroline rolled her pretty green eyes. "A slight exaggeration, Josh McInnes. But I will concede that this committee is one of the more trying ones I sit on."

"Hell, Caroline, how many of these things are you on?"

She tugged at her grey suit jacket. "A few."

When she didn't look him in the eye, he guessed it was more than a few. He had a horrible feeling Caroline was in the thick of it with every damn committee in Invertary.

It took an embarrassingly long time to get out of the chair. The cushions had sucked him in. It was as though it was trying to eat him. Speaking of food, Josh's stomach rumbled. "Can we leave now? I'm starving to death."

"Yes. I can see that."

"Are you saying I'm fat?" Josh tugged up his T-shirt and examined his abs. Okay, so they weren't as tight as they'd been at the end of his last tour, but he was on his downtime, damn it.

He glanced up to see what Caroline thought, and caught her staring at his stomach. Her cheeks were pink and her little tongue darted out to lick her lips. Josh smiled wickedly. He ran his fingers over his abs. "Maybe I could work out a bit more." He grinned wider as Caroline's eyes ate up his movement. Nope. There was nothing wrong with him. He reluctantly dropped his shirt, and Caroline snapped out of her daze. Pity.

"Right. Okay." She seemed flustered. "Let's pick up some food and get this homework done."

"Great. This night never ends."

Her back snapped straight. "No one is keeping you. You can go home any time you like. As I recall, you forced your way into coming with me."

Josh took her hand and dragged her towards the door. "Feed me, Caroline. There's a limit to what I can suffer, and all I've had since lunch was whatever was in the domino boys' cookie tin."

"You ate their biscuits?"

The community centre door slammed behind them, and Caroline turned to lock it.

"It was either that or eat the guy who wouldn't shut up. I thought I made the right choice."

Caroline stifled a giggle. "Fine. We'll pick up some food at the pub and eat it at my place while we work."

Josh didn't hear anything past the word *food*. He grabbed Caroline's hand and practically ran to the pub.

CHAPTER 8

"What's your favourite food?" Josh looked up from the work-book the vicar had given him, and grimaced at Caroline. She tried not to smile at the sight of him sitting at her tiny table. He was far too big for the furniture she'd inherited. In fact, he was too big for her whole house. It made her feel like they were in a Wendy house, playing at being adults. "Seriously? He wants to know what my favourite food is? What does this have to do with the wedding?"

Caroline resisted the urge to smack him upside his head. "He doesn't care what your favourite food is. He's trying to fast-track the 'getting to know you' part of our courtship. He's helping us."

"Yeah. Right." Josh ate another fry. He'd already polished off two massive burgers. "I know a better way to fast-track getting to know each other." He waggled his eyebrows at her and gave her a fake leer.

"Do you only think about sex?" She was pleased that she didn't blush when she said the word.

Josh shrugged. "I think about food too." He gave her a

sexy smile that made her toes curl. "Come on, Caroline, let's do something that's way more fun."

Caroline ignored him and stepped over to flick on the kettle.

He sighed dramatically. "So what's your favourite food, then?"

"Bacon and eggs."

His eyebrows shot up. "Not chocolate? I thought every woman loved chocolate."

"Do you actually need me here to answer the questions? Or will you just use your extensive knowledge of women to come up with an average?"

"Snippy, Caroline. Very snippy." He seemed proud of her.

She tried not to smile. "What's your favourite food, then?"

"Steak. No. Pizza." He grinned. "Steak pizza." His triumphant smile made her laugh.

"Maybe we should have that at our wedding?"

"Now that's a great idea." Josh shook the pen in his hand before looking at it with disgust. "This isn't working."

"There are some more on the desk next door."

Grumbling about the fact he was never going to have any fun, Josh squeezed his frame through her kitchen door and into the hallway.

"Holy crap, Caroline, you got enough books?"

She grinned in spite of herself. She was very proud of her fiction collection. Even though she was running out of space to put bookcases.

"They're in alphabetical order." He sounded shocked. "And topic. Historical romance. Paranormal romance. Contemporary romance." He paused. "I'm picking up on a theme here. Where are the really kinky ones?"

Trust Josh's mind to go straight back to sex.

"Are you coming back?" Caroline made a cup of tea. "Or are you going to entertain yourself in there forever?"

She wondered what Josh thought of her minuscule terraced house. It was nothing compared to the castle, but Caroline had been overjoyed when her grandfather had left the former miner's cottage to her in his will. With two small bedrooms and a bath upstairs, and just the kitchen and living room downstairs, you could have fit the whole house into the grand room at the castle.

Josh sauntered back into the kitchen, ducking to avoid hitting his head on the doorjamb.

"I don't get it. When do you have time to read?" He pointed to the wall planner pinned above the kitchen table. "You've got meetings coming out of your ears. I don't see how you can read that many books as well."

"I'm a fast reader." Plus she lived alone and didn't have a social life. Sometimes she wished she *didn't* have so much time to read.

Josh's face fell when his attention turned back to the workbook. She almost felt sorry for him. Almost. Caroline placed her mug of tea on the table beside him and turned to get the cookies she'd been hiding in the back of the cupboard. She didn't question the logic of trying to hide cookies from herself. After all, she clearly knew the hiding place.

As she stepped past Josh, an arm snaked out and wrapped around her waist. Caroline yelped as Josh pulled her against him.

"What are you doing?" Her voice quavered.

"Exactly what the minister intended. Getting to know you."

She thought he sniffed her hair. Was that normal? "We need to fill in the book."

"Later, baby. I've been around you for hours and I've been well behaved. Now my belly is full and my other needs are rearing their head."

Caroline pushed at his arm, but she may as well have been trying to unhinge an anaconda. "Other needs?" She was almost afraid to ask.

"The need to be close to you," he murmured against her hair. "The need to hold you. The need to breathe you in."

"Let go of me." She pushed to get away from him, but he held her fast.

"No way."

She snarled at him. Wanting him to release her and hold her tighter all at the same time.

"You're holding me against my will."

"No, baby, I'm holding you against my body."

He leaned over and gently nipped the curve where her neck met her shoulder. A shiver ran up her spine.

"You feel good. You smell good too," he whispered against her skin. "What is that fragrance? I love it. It's going to drive me crazy if you don't tell me." Josh ran his lips up to her ear.

Caroline was overwhelmed by sensations. His breath on her skin. His arms holding her tight. His body, so solid against hers.

"Caroline?"

She cleared her throat. "It's soap. Dove soap."

"Seriously?" He nuzzled in her hair behind her ear. "It can't be soap, it must be you."

He inhaled her deeply. "Yeah. It's you. You smell like Christmas." He buried his nose into her hair. Caroline wrapped her fingers around his arm, holding tight. "Do you taste like Christmas too?"

His voice sent vibrations racing through her body. And then his tongue trailed down from her ear to her shoulder. He playfully bit the muscle in the curve of her neck, and a little moan escaped her.

"I'm not sure we should be doing this. Maybe we should wait until after the wedding to...you know?"

His arms wrapped tight around her, and he pulled back from her to look her in the eyes. The twinkle in his eye was back. She was amusing him. Again.

"No, I don't know. Explain it to me."

His full lips curled into a slow, sexy smile. Caroline half expected a flash of sparkling light to twinkle off his teeth.

"Maybe we shouldn't be, ah, physical until after the wedding?" Her voice was embarrassingly breathless.

"Are we talking all physical contact or just the good kind?"

She wasn't sure. She wanted to ask what he meant by the good kind, but she was too scared of the answer. "Why don't we keep all touching to a minimum until after the wedding? That way we can get to know each other a little before we..."

"Get physical?"

"Yes." She sagged with relief. "What do you say?"

"Well, we can't *not* touch. That would be unnatural. Maybe we should set a limit instead. Tell me when I step over the line."

He was laughing at her. She opened her mouth to tell him so, but instead he deftly turned her to face him, and his lips met hers. She forgot her complaint. His tongue traced a lazy trail around her lips, tasting, teasing, before dipping into her mouth. Tiny little lights flashed inside Caroline's eyelids as Josh seduced her with his kiss. One minute it was soft and slow, the next intense and demanding. She clutched his shoulders and held on tight as her mind soared.

"Was that too much touching?" he purred against her lips. His voice was a soft seduction. Caroline found it hard to think.

He trailed his lips over to her ear before tugging her earlobe between his teeth. His breath made her heartbeat race.

"Tell me when it's too much," he whispered.

In the back of her mind Caroline got the feeling they were talking about two different things. He peppered tiny kisses along her jaw to her mouth, before biting her bottom lip. Caroline panted. She wrapped her arms tight around his shoulders as his left hand splayed across her waist. His thumb traced lazy circles on her stomach.

"Remember," he said against her mouth, "cry uncle."

His words may as well have been German. She was way past thought. She was lost in a place where only sensation mattered. Her breasts pushed against his chest. They felt uncomfortably heavy, and ached to be soothed. As though he were reading her mind, his hand skimmed the underside of her breast. Caroline pressed against him as his tongue teased her upper lip. Suddenly she was in his hand. She felt his touch graze her nipple. She whimpered. More. She needed more.

She felt him tug at the clasp of her bra; there was a ping and she was free. A momentary panic dulled her desire. The hand on her breast disappeared, only to return under her shirt. Skin on skin. Moving achingly slowly towards her breast. She felt him push the lace of her cup out of the way. Her spine went stiff as anxiety rimmed the edge of her passion. A warm hand engulfed her, and something snapped in her mind. She wasn't even aware she'd moved. The next thing she knew, she was standing on the other side of the room with her arms folded over her chest.

Josh's blue eyes were dark. He stared at her for a moment before running a hand through his hair.

"What's wrong, baby?"

Caroline's eyes flicked to the door. Part of her wanted to run. The other part wanted to drag him upstairs to her bedroom. She needed to get things under control. She looked at his worried blue eyes. She needed to tell Josh the truth. She needed to explain to him exactly how minuscule her experience really was. Her shoulders slumped. This was going to be a fun experience.

"I'll be back in a minute." Caroline fled for the bathroom. This wasn't a conversation she wanted to have with her boobs hanging out.

As she passed her bedroom door, another idea popped into her head—if Josh was called away, she wouldn't need to have the conversation at all. Looking down the stairs, she checked to make sure Josh couldn't see her. He was still in the kitchen. She turned the tap on in the bathroom, then tiptoed into her bedroom and picked up the phone. She felt sick at what she was about to do. It went against her nature to lie. Before she could stop herself, she dialled the local police station.

"Caroline, is that you?" Agnes barked into her ear.

Blast. Caroline had planned to do this anonymously. She forgot the police station would have caller ID.

"Yes." She cleared her throat. "Yes it is. You need to send a police car to the castle. I thought I saw someone breaking in. You had better call Josh McInnes too. I know he has problems with troublesome fans."

She had lied to the police. She never lied. And she'd lied to the police. She was going straight to jail. Do not pass go. Do not collect two hundred dollars. And never, ever get a chance to roll the dice and break free.

"We'll get right on it." There was a pause. "Why did you wait until you got home to call?"

"You know I don't have a mobile phone, Agnes." At least that wasn't a lie.

"Right. I forgot. Thanks for calling."

A moment later, she heard Josh's phone ring downstairs and dashed back into the bathroom. As feet pounded up the stairs, she refastened her bra and tucked her shirt back into her skirt. She was patting her cheeks with a towel as Josh appeared in the doorway.

"Sorry, baby, I have to go. There's been a break-in at the castle. It's probably nothing, but I should be there."

"Of course. You go on. We can talk another time."

Josh wrapped his hand around the back of her neck and kissed her hard on the lips. "We're okay, yeah?"

"Of course. Now go." She dazzled him with her best fake smile. He didn't seem to notice it wasn't real. He turned and ran down the stairs. The best sound Caroline had heard all day was the slam of her front door behind him.

Caroline dragged herself through to the bedroom and fell on her back on the bed. Her hands covered her face as she let out a long, mournful groan. Forget jail.

Her lying backside was going straight to hell.

"You don't need to sleep on the couch." Helen eyed the king-sized bed. "We can make this work for the next few weeks."

"I'm taking the couch." Andrew nodded to the tiny two-seater sofa by the window.

Helen felt her throat tighten. Did he hate her so much that he'd rather sleep upright than share a bed with her again?

"I'm sure we can manage in the bed."

"I'll find another room if you don't want me on the couch."

"Mitch said the other rooms were full of junk."

He grunted. She wasn't sure what that meant. She felt tension wind its way up her spine to her neck. She bit the inside of her cheek to stop from talking. Years of asking questions and getting no reply had taught her that it was pointless. But she felt angry. Angrier than she had in years. She turned to her husband, the stranger she'd married. He was standing inside the doorway, looking at the bed as though it would bite him. His hands were wedged deep into those awful tartan pants of his, and he was hunched over as though he was trying not to be there at all.

Something inside Helen snapped, and she opened her mouth. "What does that mean?" His eyebrows shot up. "What did that grunt mean? I don't speak grunting. I speak American. You need to translate. Does it mean you're sleeping in the bed or not?"

He took a slight step back towards the door. She was pretty sure he wasn't even aware that he'd done it. Subconsciously, the man was retreating. Running. As he usually did. She put her hands on the hips of her yellow flowered sundress, the one that clashed with her hair, and waited.

"Well?"

He shuffled on the spot. "I don't think it's a good idea to share the bed."

The look he gave her was unfathomable. Helen felt bile bite at the back of her throat. After thirty-five years, he couldn't even share a bed with her for one more month.

"Fine. Take the couch." She stomped towards him and picked up his bag, which was beside the bed. "But you're not taking this one." She swung her arm and launched the bag out of the room and down the stairs. "Sleep downstairs. That way you won't have to look at me at all." Then she shoved him hard, making him stumble into the hallway, before slamming the door behind him.

For a minute or more, she stared at the door while tears welled in her eyes. She couldn't believe she'd shouted. Ever since boarding the plane to Scotland, things had been bubbling out of her. Things she'd tried to contain for too many long years. At last she heard him make his way down the stairs after his bag. Helen sniffed and blinked away the tears. She wasn't going to cry. Not again.

She slipped into the en suite bathroom and splashed her face with cold water. In the mirror she saw a face changed with age that she didn't recognise. She felt her chest tighten. Something had to give. Something had to change. She rooted around in her makeup bag and came out with a pair of scissors. Without giving it a second thought, she started to snip off her shoulder-length hair.

THERE WAS no break-in at the castle. The person who'd made the call had either been mistaken, or it was a prank. The cop who'd walked around the exterior with Josh and Mitch was not pleased that it had turned out to be nothing. He'd been in the middle of watching a football game and wanted to get back to it. He left muttering about locking up the moron who'd interrupted his viewing.

"Your parents are here." Mitch ran his fingers through his hair.

"That explains the look." Josh pointed at Mitch's face.

They walked to the back of the castle and through the door into the kitchen. Without asking, Mitch opened the fridge and got beers for both of them. Josh was hungry again, so he went poking around in the cupboards for snacks.

"Your parents are pissed." Mitch sat sprawled in an armchair by the windows. He looked frazzled. Josh could identify with that.

"Figures." Josh threw his friend a bag of chips. Mitch snatched them out of the air. "They weren't too impressed with the marriage plan when I called them."

"They're fighting as well. Your dad is asleep on the couch."

Josh cocked an eyebrow. That was new. "They fighting about the wedding?"

Mitch shook his head. He took a swallow of beer. "I heard something about them sleeping in separate beds and your dad not talking. Then I ran. I do *not* want to get in the middle of a McInnes meltdown."

"It's probably nothing. You know what Dad is like. Mom's probably fed up listening to her own voice. It'll pass."

Mitch didn't look so sure. "What about you and the delectable Caroline? How are things going there? No regrets?"

Josh grinned. "None. She's perfect. We made the right choice. In fact, I was just getting to know her a little better when I got the call to come home." He felt a tingling in his spine. His eyes widened. "Now that I think about it. Caroline freaked out a bit at us getting physical. She ran to the bathroom, and the next thing I knew I was being called away." He looked at Mitch, whose eyebrows had shot up his head. "You don't think she was the one who called?"

"She wouldn't. Would she?"

"Caroline is capable of anything." He didn't know whether to be proud or angry.

They stared at each other until Mitch burst out laughing. "I love that woman. You are so not getting any until you're married. I bet she's keeping you at arm's length until she makes sure the wedding goes through. You are so screwed. Or not, as the case may be." Mitch snorted beer.

"Funny. You're funny." Josh thought about it. There was something off. Surely Caroline didn't want him to stop touching her so badly that she called the cops. "Caroline wouldn't lie. She's got that whole moral code thing going on." He didn't sound convinced.

"Or maybe she just doesn't find you attractive? Maybe this whole wedding thing is more of a chore to her than you thought? You've been so busy thinking about whether or not you're attracted to her, you never figured that your woman might not want you."

"Naw." The thought horrified him. "No. It can't be. I've never had any problems. Hell, I'm fighting women off."

"Not this time, buddy." Mitch was laughing so hard he started to choke.

No. Mitch had to be wrong. Caroline had responded to his touch. She was definitely as attracted to him as he was to her. He relaxed slightly. He was being an idiot, letting Mitch wind him up. He should know better. Nope. Everything was fine. Caroline wanted him just as much as he wanted her.

Didn't she?

CHAPTER 9

"Want to tell me why you're sleeping on the couch?" Josh asked his dad the following morning, over a late breakfast.

Bacon and eggs. It made him think of Caroline. He bet she wasn't indulging in her favourite food. She was probably eating some healthy granola crap that tasted like cardboard.

"Hello to you too, son. Good to see you."

"Yeah, it's great. So what's with the couch?"

"It's between your mother and me," his dad grumbled into his coffee.

"You must have done something really dumb. It takes a lot to piss Mom off."

His dad grunted.

"Are you going to be this cheery right up to the wedding?"

"This wedding is a farce."

That answered that question. Josh turned his focus back to his food. But looked up when his dad made a strangled noise.

"What the hell happened to you?" His dad's attention was on the doorway.

Josh followed his father's gaze to where his mother stood

stiffly. Her hair was short, and stuck out from her head. It looked like she'd been assaulted by Edward Scissorhands.

She touched her choppy hair self-consciously. "What do you care, Andrew McInnes?"

She smiled at Josh, who had to work at closing his mouth. His mother had worn the same hairstyle his entire life, and now she looked like an abused version of herself.

"Hello, sweetheart." His mom pulled him into a hug.

Josh swallowed his shock. "Good to see you, Mom."

"Even when she looks like that?" His father's words made him cringe. No wonder the fool was sleeping on the couch.

"We'll catch up later." She patted his cheek like he was five years old. "I'm going out right now."

"Wear a hat," his father said.

Josh willed him to shut his mouth. The man barely spoke. Surely he had enough sense to know that now wasn't the time to start talking.

"Why on earth did you do that to yourself, woman?"

Josh groaned quietly. Apparently the family skill for dealing with women had skipped a generation.

"What I do and don't do is none of your business anymore. Now why don't you concentrate on what you do best and keep quiet."

Josh let out a low whistle. He took a step back towards the door. If things got ugly, he'd make a break for it.

"I know you're upset." His father just didn't know when to quit. Josh kept inching his way towards freedom. "But that's no reason to mutilate yourself."

"You know I'm upset?" His mother's voice rose higher with every word. "You know I'm upset?" She marched towards his father. Josh stopped his retreat, wondering if he should stay and referee. "How would you know I'm upset? We don't talk. We never talk."

"And what do you want me to do about that?"

His mother let out a strangled groan before grabbing Josh's half-empty cup of coffee off the table. She held her hand high and tipped it over his dad's head. "Why don't you do something about this instead?" She stormed out of the kitchen.

Josh stared after her for a moment before turning to his dad. The man was wiping coffee out of his eyes with his sleeve.

"Want to tell me what's going on?" Josh handed him a dishtowel.

"If I knew, I'd tell you. Everything has gone to hell, and I'll be damned if I understand any of it."

With that, his father stalked from the room, leaving Josh with cold bacon and eggs and a deep regret that his house had guest rooms.

CAROLINE WAS up to her ears organising a wedding. Add to that liaising with the castle restoration team, her duties at the community centre and the many committees she was on, and there was no time to think about Josh. Which was perfect, because she figured the only way she'd make it to the wedding without freaking out completely was to avoid him.

She knew it was stupid to be scared of your fiancé touching you. She resisted the urge to bang her head on her desk. It wouldn't knock any sense into her anyway. Intellectually, she knew she had to touch him. Physically, she wanted to touch him. But emotionally, she wasn't ready. It was all going too fast. And she was scared. Scared she wouldn't be good enough. Scared he'd expect more than she was willing to give. Scared that he would be repulsed by how little experience she had and wouldn't want her anymore.

She needed to become more knowledgeable about sex. And fast. There was only one thing for it—research. She checked that no one was looking and sneaked into the library. There was exactly half a shelf dedicated to helping couples with their sex lives. With her cheeks burning, she scooped up all the books and practically ran back to her office. She dumped them into a shopping bag beside her desk, quickly turning over The Joy of Sex so that no one could see the title. And then she did something she'd never done before—she didn't check any of the books out in her name.

She was on a slippery slope. First she was lying to the police. Now she was borrowing books without telling anyone. Who knew what depths she'd sink to next? Guilt gnawed at Caroline long into the afternoon, and overflowed into her meeting with the wedding planner.

"So we're agreed, then?" Millicent Price's question jarred her back to the present.

"Yes." Caroline looked at the proof for the wedding invitation on her computer screen. "They look perfect."

"Good." The wedding planner made a note on her iPad. "I'll make sure they get posted today. I've also made appointments for you with Pronovias and Browns in London."

Caroline tucked her hair behind her ears. "I'm sorry, I have no idea what you're talking about."

Millicent's smile was kind. "They are prestigious bridal wear boutiques. Pronovias is at Harrods and Browns is a legend. We don't have the time frame to get you into something bespoke, but we can at least get you a dress that you'll love and make sure it's fitted perfectly."

"I guess I should look into flights, then." The thought of going wedding-dress shopping in Harrods made her weak at the knees. She was a girl who bought her work clothes in her local charity shop. Harrods was so far out of her league it was on another planet.

Millicent seemed to read her mind. "Perhaps you should take someone with you. For a second opinion."

The compassion in her eyes made it clear that she thought Caroline needed way more than a second opinion. She needed someone to hold her up.

"That's a good idea." Caroline swallowed hard.

The question was who to take. Her sister was in Dubai. And she still hadn't managed to marshal her courage enough to tell her best friend Kirsty that she was getting married.

"I'll go with you," said a deep, masculine voice.

Caroline's head shot to her office doorway, where Josh was filling the frame.

"What are you doing here?" She flushed at her rudeness. See? Slippery slope.

"My house is a building site, so I can't work there. Looks like you're stuck with me." He cocked an eyebrow. "Unless you want to talk some more about a studio."

Caroline stuck her nose in the air.

"I didn't think so." He flashed a mischievous smile that made her stomach flip.

"You can't go with me to choose a wedding gown. Bridegrooms don't shop for wedding dresses. I don't believe in bad luck, but I do believe in tradition, and shopping together just isn't done."

Today's T-shirt had Elmo on it. He folded his arms over Elmo's face and leaned against the doorframe. "Nothing about this wedding is traditional. We'll go together."

His tone seemed to indicate that the conversation was over. Caroline opened her mouth to speak, but Millicent intervened. "That might not be a bad idea. Josh has to get fitted for a morning suit too."

Josh grimaced. "I have a closet full of suits. How about I wear one of those?"

"In Scotland, it's traditional for the groom to wear a morning suit to his wedding."

"I'm American. Does it really matter?"

"Why don't you get married in your Cookie Monster T-shirt?" Caroline snapped at him. Why was he making such a fuss? He wasn't the one who had to parade about dressed like a meringue.

"Don't tempt me, baby." He turned back to Millicent. "Make the appointments. We'll go together."

"Lovely. If that's all for now"—Millicent stood—"I'll get on with things."

Millicent passed Josh, and as soon as she was gone Caroline felt the room shrink. She shifted uncomfortably in her chair. With a little over two weeks to the wedding, she still had the urge to be wherever Josh wasn't.

"About last night." Josh took a step towards her.

"Caroline." Beth popped her head around the door and almost fainted at the sight of Josh. "You need to get into the blue room. There's a problem."

Saved by the bell. With relief, Caroline headed out of her office and away from a frowning Josh. Who, much to her disgust, just followed her. She heard the domino boys before she saw them.

"What's going on here?" Caroline put her hands on her hips.

The men growled at each other.

"Numb-nuts over there"—Brian pointed at James—"ordered electric fencing for the perimeter of the castle, and cattle prods in case anyone gets out of line at the wedding." He faced James. "You can't use cattle prods on people."

"Why the hell not?"

"Because, you old fart, you use Tasers on people."

"What the hell is a Taser?"

Brian threw his hands in the air. "I'm dealing with idiots."

Caroline massaged her temples. There wasn't enough aspirin in the world to deal with the headaches this wedding caused. By the time the day came around, she'd be hooked up to a morphine IV.

"Look." Caroline held her hands up to quieten the boys. "I told you that you could help with security. That means liaising with whomever Josh has hired to police the event." She turned to Josh, hoping he had something sensible to say.

He shuffled his feet. "I thought Mitch was organising security."

Caroline clenched her jaw and counted to ten. "Someone better organise something, don't you think?"

"Why?" Archie demanded. "We're sorting it out. The wedding is in good hands."

"What wedding?" Beth said from behind her.

Caroline was about to tell her to mind her own business and take care of the library, but James spoke first. "Caroline and Josh. It's the wedding of the year. And we're helping."

The men grinned. Caroline groaned. Josh sauntered into the room and sat beside the domino boys.

"You are marrying him?" Beth pointed at Josh. No one answered. "No!" Beth wailed. "You can't marry her. She doesn't even like your music."

His lips quirked, but he didn't say anything.

"That's enough, Beth. Go and sort the library," Caroline told her.

"This is wrong. You can't marry Josh. You're too uptight and mean for him. You don't even know how to dress properly."

"Beth." Josh's tone was a warning rumble. Caroline's eyes darted to him. His displeasure was soundly focused on Beth. "Watch what you say about my fiancée."

Caroline felt something surge under her ribcage. She thought it might be her heart.

"I've had enough." Beth stamped her foot like a two-year-old. "I can't work here anymore."

She spun on her heels and stormed out of the centre. Josh frowned after her. The domino boys, for once, were too shocked to speak. Caroline sat down in the free chair beside Archie.

"You stood up for me," she said to Josh. "People don't do that."

He shrugged like it wasn't a big deal.

"It's true," Archie said. "She's so damn scary, most folk assume she can take care of herself."

"And I can." She scowled at Archie, and he patted her hand patronisingly.

"Up for a game of dominoes?" Brian asked Josh.

"Sure." Josh pulled his chair over beside Caroline and stretched his arm across the back of her chair. Caroline found herself leaning in to him. Archie watched every move with rapt fascination. Josh bent towards Caroline. She held her breath. "Just for the record." His words were soft against her ear. "There's nothing mean about you, baby, and I don't have a problem with anything you wear."

Her breath hitched as her heart beat faster.

"We playing or what?" Archie demanded.

"We're playing." Josh used his thumb to trace little circles on Caroline's shoulder. "We betting on the game?"

Brian thumped his elbows onto the table. "Pies and cakes. Winner visits Morag's bakery."

"Done." Josh's hand slid to the back of Caroline's neck and gently held her.

She felt his touch shoot through her body like a ball in a pinball machine. She didn't dare glance at him. She wasn't sure what her face would betray.

"While I remember." Josh turned to her with his dominoes in hand. "My parents are in town. We're having dinner with them Sunday night."

Caroline felt her eye begin to twitch. She put a finger up to stop it. Josh gave her a questioning look.

"Your parents are in town? From America?" Caroline tried to keep her tone calm. She wasn't sure it was working. "And you didn't tell me?"

"I was about to tell you, then you bolted from your office."

It was all a bit much. "I need a cup of tea." Caroline jerked up from the table.

As though she didn't have enough to deal with, now she had to spend an evening explaining their wedding to Josh's parents.

HELEN HAD BORROWED a car from Mitch and driven to Fort William to go shopping. She needed new clothes. Something brighter and more modern. She also needed someone to fix the mess she'd made of her hair. She'd managed to stay away from Andrew for the whole day, and almost felt calm when she sneaked into the castle a little after ten o'clock that night. The place was dark. Josh had sent her a text saying he was at the pub with Mitch. And experience told her that Andrew was probably already asleep. Helen tiptoed past the living room, so as not to wake him, and headed for the stairs.

She patted her new cropped hair. It feathered over one eye and curved around to the base of her skull. It was young, it was chic and for the first time in forty years it was her natural colour—or as close as she could remember her natural colour to be. It was a warm honey shade, too dark to be blond but too light to be brown. She liked it. A lot.

"I liked your hair better the way it was," a voice said from the TV room.

Helen spun to find Andrew standing in the doorway.

"I don't care what you think."

"I don't know who you are anymore."

Helen scoffed. "You haven't known me for years. And I don't understand why it's bothering you now. As soon as we've told Josh all about the divorce, we'll go our separate ways and you won't have to puzzle over me any more."

As usual, he didn't say anything. Helen made herself shrug like she didn't care, and continued to walk up the stairs.

"It's just..."

Helen looked down at him. "Just what?"

He thrust his hands into his pockets and scowled. Helen waited longer than she probably should have for him to make up his mind to talk. At last she shook her head. "I'm going to bed."

She was done waiting for Andrew to speak. She was starting afresh and she didn't need his permission to do it. She turned at the top of the stairs, ready to climb the next flight.

"I never meant to hurt you." Andrew's voice floated up to her.

Helen stopped dead. Her heart thumped in her chest. "You should have thought of that when you started to shut me out."

Although she couldn't see him, she could imagine how uncomfortable he felt. Good. It was time he felt it too.

"I don't know what to do." He sounded lost.

Helen let out a deep breath. She walked back down enough of the stairs to see him. "About what?"

He looked her in the eye, the way he used to do. She felt his gaze zing straight through her body to her toes. She staggered back a step from the shock of it.

"Us. I don't know what to do about us."

She drew a sharp breath. "There is no us. That died a long time ago."

There was silence. She turned back to the stairs.

"What if it isn't dead for me?"

She closed her eyes briefly. Not now. Not when she'd let go of the man. She looked down at him and felt pity. But she didn't feel any urge to throw herself back into a life of silence and dread.

"It's dead for me. I'm tired of living in silence and tired of being invisible."

"I can fix this." She heard some of the same stubborn streak she'd once loved in him.

"Can you?" Helen turned away from him and dragged herself up the stairs to bed.

She was starting a new life. She was becoming a new person. And it didn't matter how much Andrew protested, there was one thing she was certain of—he didn't want to take the journey with her.

CHAPTER 10

By Sunday afternoon, Josh was convinced Caroline was avoiding him. He'd tried calling but couldn't pin her down. He was fed up with being ignored. It was time to track his reluctant fiancée down. After trying her house, where there was no answer, Josh worked his way down through town asking people if they'd seen Caroline. It was no surprise that everybody knew exactly who he was talking about. But no one had seen her. When he reached the pub at the bottom of the high street, he found Dougal behind the bar.

"I'm looking for Caroline." Josh ordered a Coke and a burger. Might as well kill two birds.

"Didn't you see her at church this morning?" Dougal placed a tall glass of ice-cold Coke in front of him.

"I don't go to church."

Dougal nodded as though that made perfect sense. "Of course, you're a heathen."

Josh spluttered out a mouth full of Coke. "I'm not a heathen, I was brought up Catholic. I just don't do church."

Dougal leaned across the bar. "So you're one of those

agnostic people, then?" He scratched his beard. "I'm not sure we have any of those in town. You might be the first."

Josh resisted the urge to thump his forehead on the bar. Apart from the fact he would have to look up the word agnostic when he got home, he really didn't want to talk about church. "Have you seen Caroline or not?"

Dougal looked around to make sure no one was listening. The action made the hairs on Josh's arms stand to attention. Dougal leaned towards him and lowered his voice. "You've only just missed her. She came in not ten minutes ago to pick up her order. If you hurry you can catch her at Patrick's house."

Josh stilled. *Order? Patrick?* "Caroline is with a guy?"

Dougal nodded. "Every Sunday afternoon, regular as clockwork. But keep it to yourself; she doesn't want anyone to know."

Josh felt the muscle at the corner of his jaw tick. She accepted his proposal when she had a standing date with some other guy? He couldn't keep the growl out of his voice. "How do I find this Patrick?"

Dougal considered him for a moment before nodding to himself. With a twinkle in his eye, the bar owner gave the directions he needed, and Josh shot out of the pub. Forgetting all about paying the man or eating the food he'd ordered.

Ten minutes later, Josh was confused. Dougal's directions had led straight to Shady Pines nursing home. Someone with a sense of humour had named the place, because it was nowhere near shade or pines. The building looked a lot like the community centre, the same utilitarian cube structure from the seventies. The same grey walls. And the same complete lack of character.

The woman at the front desk seemed to be expecting him. "Dougal called. She's in room five." She pointed down a puke-green corridor.

Josh followed her direction, passing several open doors along the way. Families were visiting the people in hospital beds. There was laughter and light. But it didn't make up for the stink of hospital disinfectant and the underlying aroma of urine. The door to room five was open too, and Josh heard Caroline before he saw her. She sounded indignant.

"You did this on purpose, Patrick Harris."

There was a croaky chuckle. "That book came highly recommended, Caroline. They even made it into a TV show. Not that I can watch it, mind you."

Josh peeked in the door. He found Caroline standing with her back to him, hands on hips. She was giving hell to a tiny, wrinkled blind man who was lying in bed—with a huge grin on his face.

Caroline picked up a copy of *Game of Thrones*, which was on the bed in front of her. "This book is full of violence and sex. You chose it just so you could make me read those scenes."

She turned slightly, and Josh saw she was smiling.

The man in the bed held up a hand. "Come on, Caroline, you come here to read to people. This is what I want to hear."

"I bet you do, you dirty old man. Well, next time I'm bringing some Jane Austen with me. Let's see how funny you find that when I read it to you."

His face fell. "You're not serious, are you? That's a women's book. Come on. I'll be good. I won't laugh when you stutter through the sex scenes or sound disgusted in the fight scenes." He put a palm over his heart. "Promise."

Caroline struggled to hide her laughter. "We'll see. I'll think about it. Right now I have to go see if Elsie needs any more wool. You behave yourself until I see you next week."

The man's whole face lit up. "Now why would I want to do that?"

With a shake of her head, Caroline turned to leave the

room. She didn't see Josh until she had stepped into the corridor, and the smile dropped from her face.

"What are you doing here?" She folded her arms over the pretty pink shift dress she was wearing.

"Looking for you. You've been avoiding me."

She rolled her eyes. "No. I haven't. I've been busy."

She strode past him and down the corridor. Josh jogged to catch up. "Every time I call I'm told you're in a meeting, or have gone off to sit on some committee somewhere."

She stopped short, making him trip over her. "That's because I *am* doing those things. Just because you waltzed into my life and disrupted everything, doesn't mean I don't still have responsibilities."

He folded his arms and pinned her with his stare. "Are you sure you aren't avoiding me after we got a little physical the other night?"

"Get over yourself, Josh McInnes. Not everything is about you. Stick a pin in that ego of yours and deflate it a little."

He frowned. "So what are you doing here, if not avoiding me?"

"I'm doing what I usually do: reading to Patrick, helping out with anyone else who doesn't have a visitor. Which I need to get back to." She headed towards another open door. Josh followed her.

The woman inside was tucked up in an armchair, knitting. She grinned when she saw them. "Oh good, you brought company."

"No," Caroline told her. "I didn't. He's leaving." She gave him a pointed look.

Caroline stood in the doorway to block his entrance. Josh glanced around the room and did a double take when he saw the place was filled with hand-knitted bears. All the same size and shape; only the colours varied. He blinked a couple of times before turning back to Caroline. "I'll wait for you. We've got dinner with my parents tonight."

"No. You won't. I have things to do after my visit here. Don't worry. I'll be at dinner on time." She didn't seem pleased by the thought.

"I'm happy to wait. I haven't seen you for days."

She let out a long sigh. "Josh, don't take this the wrong way, but I am a very busy person and I can't deal with you right now. I promise to make time for you after the wedding. Okay?" She patted him on the chest, patronisingly, then took a step back into the room. A second later, the door slammed in his face.

Josh stared at the door. "Is there a right way to take that?" he shouted.

People in the corridor stopped to stare at him. The woman behind the front desk was laughing hard.

"Fine." Josh struggled to regain his dignity. "I'll see you later, then." There was silence from the room.

Having no other option, Josh turned on his heels and went back to the castle.

CAROLINE WAITED until she was certain Josh had left the building, before she peeked out of the door.

"Don't worry," Grace called from the reception desk. "He's gone."

"Why are you hiding from this man anyway?" Elsie wanted to know. "If I had a boy chasing me with a bum like that, I wouldn't be hiding. If you don't want him, send him in here. I can think of some things to keep him busy."

Caroline took a deep breath. "What is it with the seniors in this centre? They have sex on the brain."

Elsie gave her a wicked smile. "When you're my age and as bored as I am, you'll be just the same."

Caroline didn't think so. "Right. I have to go. I have things to do before I meet Josh's parents." She inwardly cringed at the thought. "I'll get Kirsty's mum to drop off your wool. If you need anything else let her know."

"I'll be fine. You concentrate on the sex god who's following you around." She winked. "And don't forget to fill me in about it next time you come."

Caroline sighed and left Elsie to her knitting.

To make sure that she didn't bump into Josh, she followed the back roads and lanes up the hill to the graveyard. The cobblestone road was hot beneath the soles of her shoes, and the sun was heavy on her head. There was something about summer in Invertary that enticed a person to laziness. All around you meadows full of wild flowers and fragrant heather called out, demanding that you lie in the shade with a book. Or doze in the warmth of the sun. It took all of Caroline's formidable will to resist the call. There were things to do. There were always things to do and the summer season was no exception.

She let herself through the old wrought iron gate and into the graveyard. She negotiated her way around the myriad of old headstones, some covered with ivy, others so worn that you couldn't read the writing on them. In the corner, under the oak tree, Caroline stopped at the graves of her parents. She knelt down in the lush grass between the two graves. Her chest constricted at the sight of her parents' names. Even though she long ago stopped wishing they were still with her, the pain of seeing them there made her ache.

"I know you're not really here," she said to the stones. "I know you're in heaven and you can't hear me. But I still needed to talk to you." She pulled the skirt of her pink dress over her knees. This was silly. She knew that. But now, more than ever, she felt their absence. "Anyway." She felt her eyes beginning to sting and blinked several times to clear them. "I wanted to tell you that I'm getting married. His name is Josh and he's American."

She took a deep shuddering breath and brushed her fingertips over the stone of her mother's grave. "I know you wanted me to marry a nice local boy, but it seems that the men in Scotland aren't interested in me." She lowered her eyes. "I probably didn't turn out the way you wanted me to. I'm not as easy to get on with as you might have liked. And I'm not as pretty as you were." She straightened her back. "You should probably know that this isn't a love match. It's an arrangement. Josh wants a wife that isn't famous and a non-romantic relationship. And I want a family."

It became hard to swallow. Caroline watched the breeze play with the leaves above her head until she could speak again. "I miss being part of a family. I miss you both so much. And now that Elaine and Emma have moved away, and Granddad is with you, it's just me here. Alone in Granddad's house. And I'm fine with that. Really I am. I just want a family of my own. Children to take care of. People to love." She smiled at her father's headstone. "Dad, you would under-stand, you were always the practical one. You'd see the sense in accepting this deal from Josh. Mum," she turned back to her mother's grave, "you might have struggled. I know how romantic you were. I know you would worry that I'm not going to have the same sort of relationship you and dad had."

She chuckled. She wasn't sure anyone could have the same sort of relationship her parents had. The way they loved each other made them glow. She remembered their stolen kisses and the looks filled with longing that they'd shared. She cleared her throat and picked a daisy from the grass beside her.

"So, I'm meeting Josh's parents tonight and wanted to include you too. If you were here, we would be facing this together. But you're not." She paused for a moment. "I don't think they'll like me. I'm trying to be practical about that. They probably imagined Josh with some glamorous American woman, someone who knows how to dress and how to behave in public. Someone who isn't socially awkward, and who doesn't order people around when she feels nervous. Instead, they're getting me."

She turned her face towards the sun that flickered through the trees and closed her eyes. "I hope." She swallowed hard. "I hope that you aren't too disappointed in me. I hope you understand why I'm doing this. I'm sure if you were here that you would like Josh. He can be very funny and sweet." She stood and brushed some grass from her legs. "So that's it. I'm going to dinner with Josh's parents and I'm taking you with me. In my heart." She touched each stone in turn. "I love you both," she whispered, before turning away from them.

She sniffed, wiped her eyes and straightened her shoulders. It was time to get home and change into her only other dress. It was time to head to the castle and meet Josh's parents.

HELEN DIDN'T KNOW what she'd expected of Josh's fiancée, but Caroline Patterson wasn't it. She was tall, slender, with golden hair cut into a sleek bob that skimmed her shoulders. Her dress was plain, but pretty and, by the looks of it, an original piece from the fifties. It sat at mid-calf, just above dainty flat pumps. She didn't have any jewellery on, and barely any makeup.

Josh had walked her into the kitchen, holding her hand as though he was clinging on to a prize. Maybe he was. Josh stepped forward. He put an arm around Caroline's shoulder. She tensed slightly before relaxing into his touch.

"Mom, Dad, this is my fiancée. Caroline, this is Andrew and Helen."

Caroline held out her hand to Helen. She managed a weak smile. She thought she saw a flicker of insecurity in Caroline's eyes before she turned to Andrew.

"Pleased to meet you." Caroline held out her hand.

"I don't think so." Andrew folded his arms.

"Dad," Josh said in a tone Helen hadn't heard before. It made the hairs on her neck stand to attention.

For a moment Caroline stood there, hand untaken in midair. Then she dropped it to hold on to her clutch bag. "I understand. You're angry. You don't know me and you don't trust me. If I were in your position I'd be livid too."

And Helen felt herself give the girl a genuine smile.

"Sit here." Josh put a hand on Caroline's arm while he scowled at his dad.

Josh sat at the head of the table with Caroline by his side. Helen was on the other side of Josh, facing Caroline. While Andrew sat like a disgruntled king at the other end of the table.

"This is pretty." Caroline smoothed her hand on the white linen tablecloth.

"Don't get any ideas." Josh had a mischievous twinkle in his eye. "I hired the pub to cater."

Caroline's eyes darted to the kitchen area behind her, noticing the staff for the first time. The staff who were riveted to the action, as though it was an episode of *The Bachelor*. Her cheeks flamed red.

"Hello, Caroline, love," the man who looked like Santa Claus boomed.

"Dougal." Caroline stumbled over her words. "It's lovely to see you. The food smells wonderful."

"Only the best for our new wee bride to be." Dougal

wagged a finger at her. "You've been keeping secrets, lassie." He cast a mischievous glance in Josh's direction. "That explains why he shot out of the pub this afternoon looking for you. He was moving so fast I thought the devil was on his tail."

Josh shot Caroline a sheepish look, and she pursed her lips at him. Her son was in trouble already. No surprise there.

"So." Helen found her voice and turned to Caroline. "Tell me, Caroline, do you have family in Invertary?"

She shook her head. "My sister lives in Dubai with her husband. She's about to have a baby. Her second. She already has a ten-year-old girl. But there's no one in town."

Dougal and his servers approached with the food. "Caroline's parents died in a car accident when she was just a wee lass. Terribly tragic. They lost control on the road to Fort William."

Caroline studied the tablecloth in front of her. Dougal seemed to cotton on to the fact he'd said something out of turn. His voice grew louder as he changed the subject. "Our new chef trained in France. Tonight we have coq au vin."

Andrew muttered about pretentious food, but everyone else praised the meal.

"Caroline." Helen speared some chicken. "What do you do for a living?"

"I run the community centre. It houses the town library and the local council office."

"That's impressive," Helen said.

Andrew snorted. Caroline flicked a glance in his direction while Josh scowled. Dougal was back in the kitchen area, but cleared his throat loudly and gave Andrew a disapproving look.

"Caroline and I are going to London next week." Josh smiled at Caroline. "We're shopping for a wedding dress."

"With whose money?" Andrew demanded.

"Mine." Josh gave his father a steely stare.

Caroline played with her food as her face paled. "I can afford my own wedding dress."

Helen felt her heart ache for the girl.

"I'm paying." Josh's tone softened. His hand went over hers on top of the table. "This is my idea. I'm paying for everything. I already added you to my bank account; we can pick up your bank cards while we're in London."

Her eyes went wide. "I can't take your money."

"Yes. You can. Married couples share."

"I have my own money. I work."

"Then we'll share that too."

Helen couldn't help but grin at her son. She wanted to cheer him on, but instead she sipped her wine quietly.

Andrew smacked the table in front of him, making everyone jump. "Why don't you hand your money over to her now? She'll just take it all in the divorce anyway."

Caroline looked horrified. "I wouldn't. I don't want it." She turned to Josh. "We should get a prenup."

"That's not a bad idea," Mitch said as he entered the room. "Sorry for gate crashing, but I thought Caroline could use some moral support."

"She has me, dumbass." Josh glared at his best friend.

"Yeah." Mitch pulled up a chair on the other side of Caroline. "I factored that into my decision making." He grinned at Josh.

Helen tutted at them. They'd still be winding each other up when they were eighty and living in the same rest home.

"Back to Caroline's wise suggestion," Mitch said. The servers put a place setting and a full plate of food in front of him. "As your lawyer, I'd say a prenup was a great idea."

"No." Josh met each person's eyes in turn. "No prenup. You only need that if you are going to get divorced. We're not getting divorced."

"I raised a bloody idiot." Andrew pointed a finger at his son. "She's taking you for a ride."

"Andrew!" Helen wanted to smack the stupid man.

Josh's voice became dangerously low. "You will have some respect for my fiancée."

"Why should I bother? This whole thing is a sham."

"I'm serious." The look Josh gave his father made Helen worry. She flicked a glance at Andrew and wondered if she was going to see her son hit her husband. A sight she'd never thought to see.

Caroline shifted uncomfortably in her seat. "I can sign a prenup. I really don't mind. And I don't need, or want, your bank cards."

Josh's face softened as he turned to her. "You are going to be my wife. This is a lifelong commitment. We share everything. Including our money."

Caroline gave him a long-suffering smile. "That's not how couples do things anymore."

"It's how I do things." Josh sounded immovable.

Helen felt inordinately proud of him.

Caroline would not be dissuaded. "You're putting yourself at risk. All you have is my word that I won't go after your money if this doesn't work out. You can't know for certain that we won't get divorced." From the tilt of Caroline's chin and the determined glint in Josh's eyes, Helen would bet this wasn't the first time he'd butted heads with his stubborn little bride.

"Yes. I can. I'm sure we won't get divorced." Josh rubbed a thumb over her knuckles, and Helen watched Caroline's eyes widen in awareness of him. "I trust you," Josh said. "I know you don't care about the money." He paused. "I also know you'd fight me for the castle."

Mitch barked out a laugh. "He's got you there."

To Helen's surprise, Caroline beamed at Josh. "You are absolutely right, and you're unreasonably stubborn."

Josh's mouth quirked into a smile as the tension in the room eased.

"He gets it from his father," Helen told them with a smile of her own.

Andrew thumped his napkin on the table. "I'm having nothing to do with this." He stalked out of the room in disgust.

"Don't worry about him. He'll calm down," Helen said.

"In a year or two," Mitch muttered.

"I wouldn't worry," Dougal said. "It's not like you need him to walk you down the aisle. What does the father of the groom do, anyway? Nothing. The wedding will be fine."

For a second people were stunned, before they started to laugh. Josh winked at Caroline, who blushed in reply.

Without thinking, Helen leaned over the table and held Caroline's hand. "I like you, Caroline Patterson. I like you a lot."

She watched as Caroline blinked back tears before straightening her shoulders and nodding her thanks.

Helen patted her son's cheek. "Looks like you knew what you were doing after all."

"I'm disgusted that you ever doubted me." He signalled to the waitress for seconds.

CHAPTER 11

After dinner, Josh insisted on walking Caroline home. Considering his mother and best friend were there to witness his offer, Caroline didn't think she could refuse. That was how she ended up in her kitchen making Josh a cup of tea at eleven o'clock on a Sunday night.

"I really should get to bed." Caroline banged the mugs down on the counter a little harder than she'd intended.

"We can go to bed, baby."

Josh was sitting at her kitchen table. He wore a pair of faded jeans and a pale blue T-shirt that was tight across his shoulders. His very broad shoulders. Caroline licked her lips as she watched the muscles move beneath his shirt. She caught what she was doing and jerked her gaze up to his face. Josh smiled wickedly. It made her stomach tighten.

"That's not what I meant and you know it." Why wouldn't the man go home? Caroline had been doing her best to avoid him since they'd gotten physical on Thursday evening. It was working fine. So fine, in fact, that she wouldn't mind avoiding him totally until the wedding. Then they could have all those awkward conversations when they absolutely had to. And not a minute before.

She plonked his mug in front of him.

"No cookies?" His blue eyes sparkled under lashes so thick they made her mouth water.

Caroline sat facing him, and cradled her mug in her palms. "I'm sure there are cookies at your place. Why not go there?"

His laugh seemed to echo throughout her house. She gulped her tea. It burned her tongue. She didn't care. It was something else to focus on other than the man facing her. The man with soft, full lips. The man with firm muscles under soft skin. She wondered what that skin tasted like. Would it be salty? Would it be sweet? She blinked her thoughts away. She needed to go to bed. Her eyes flew open. Alone! She needed to go to bed alone. She took another large gulp of her tea. Forgetting yet again that it was hot. Hopefully, the sooner she finished, the sooner she could send Josh home.

"Dinner went well, I thought." Caroline could do small talk. Small talk was good. Small talk would keep her mind off of his thick thighs and long legs.

"Yeah, Dad was about normal. Mom likes you."

"That's good." What else was she supposed to say? She shifted in her chair. It felt as though her skin was on high alert. Even the air around her made it tingle. The soft linen of her dress felt abrasive. Her underwear felt like bondage. It was constraining her. "Are you done yet?" Okay, so it came out a little ruder than she'd intended.

"I'm savouring it." Josh took a sip. His eyes on Caroline. "I like savouring things. I like letting the taste rest on my tongue until it overwhelms me."

Caroline blinked hard. "Are you making sexual innuendo?"

Josh's eyes sparkled. "I was trying to."

"It was really bad. Cheesy, even."

"Good to know."

He placed his mug on the table in front of him, and Caroline peeked into it hopefully. It was still full. She narrowed her eyes at him. "You're not even drinking it, are you?"

He shrugged. "I hate tea."

"Then why on earth did you ask for it?"

Josh reached across the table to take her hand. "I wanted to come in."

Caroline pulled her hand from his. The air in the room seemed thicker somehow, and she felt like she was swallowing each breath rather than inhaling it. "I think it's time for you to go. I have work in the morning and it's getting really late."

She snatched the two mugs and took them to the sink, tipping the contents down the drain.

Her breath stuck in her throat as she felt strong hands at her waist. "Dance with me," Josh whispered against her neck, making her shiver. *Yes*, her body screamed. *No*, her mind answered. Too risky. Touching led to talking. And she really didn't want to talk. Not tonight. Maybe never.

"There isn't any music." Her words were a rasp.

She felt him smile against her skin. It was a tease to her senses. Her eyelids were heavy, and the urge to sink into him was so strong she almost couldn't resist.

They couldn't dance. He had to leave. She had an excuse. What was it? Oh yeah. "We can't dance without music."

"I can fix that."

He turned her in his arms, curving one hand around her shoulder and spanning the other across the small of her back. He pressed his cheek to her temple and started to sing. His voice reverberated through her body; it melted her anxieties and soothed her fears. The sound wove a cocoon around them. Caroline's hands trailed up Josh's sides and around to his chest. Her eyelids fluttered closed, and she let out a breath she hadn't realised she was holding. She felt hidden. Sheltered. Precious. It was heady.

They swayed together. Caroline didn't know the song. It didn't matter. She barely heard the words. It was the melody and his deep voice that undid her. There was only Josh. Only them. Nothing else mattered but the two of them together. The delicious sensation of their bodies moving as one. Josh's musky scent mingled with her floral one, making her mouth water. She pressed her cheek against his chest and felt the vibrations of the song work through her. His hand stroked her hair, and Caroline was floating.

She didn't know how long they stayed like that. One song bled into another. With each note Caroline fell deeper into Josh. With each word her need for him grew. When there was suddenly silence, Caroline felt like she was waking from a deep sleep. A beautiful dream. Her eyes flickered open. She was surprised to see that it was dark and they were no longer in the kitchen. Josh had danced them into the living room. The moonlight filtered through the trees outside, creating soft shadows and an intimate longing within Caroline.

Gently, Josh tipped her chin up towards him. His eyes were dark. The desire in them raw and intense. "Stunning," he whispered before his lips touched hers.

It all flowed together in one perfect harmony. His touch, his taste, the scent that was just Josh. Caroline whimpered as his kiss deepened. He clasped her face in his hands and angled her mouth, making it easier for him to control the kiss.

She groaned in complaint as his lips left hers. He kissed and licked and nipped his way down her throat to her shoulder. She let her head fall back, allowing him better access.

The room shifted and spun around her. She clung to Josh. Her anchor.

When Josh led her to the sofa, Caroline pulled back to look at him. His eyes had turned black with need. She licked her lips. He let out a tiny strangled groan.

"I'm not ready to go further." Her tone bled desire; she hoped Josh listened to the words instead, because she didn't have any defences against the man.

"That's okay, baby. Let's sit a while and I'll hold you."

Caroline found herself snuggled in Josh's lap. Her head drifted to his shoulder as he gently caressed her thigh.

The shadows of the room lulled her into a dreamlike state. Josh's heartbeat pulled her further under. She rubbed her nose against the curve of his neck and breathed him deeply. Everything within her melted as she sank into him. Josh's strong arms gave her a safe place to just be. There were no expectations of her here. No responsibilities. No condemnation. It was paradise.

Her eyes fluttered shut as Josh began to sing. She heard and felt the song as it worked its way through her. She didn't know how long she sat there wrapped in Josh, lulled into a state of bliss by his voice and his wickedly sensual kisses, but it was a time she never wanted to end.

CHAPTER 12

Caroline woke the following morning to find herself fully dressed and wedged into the back of her sagging old couch. The first thing she noticed was that her body ached from sleeping on the sofa instead of her lovely, soft bed. The second thing she noticed was that Josh was nowhere in sight. Tingles raced through her body at the thought of the night before. He'd transported her to another world. One where she didn't have to be strong, or in control. And Caroline had loved every single minute of it.

She rolled over to find a note on the floor beside the couch. *Have a meeting with Mitch that I can't blow off. Otherwise I'd be here with you, beautiful.* Caroline felt her heart stutter at his words. She glanced to the clock on the mantel and squealed. She was late. Very late. Damn Josh for not waking her. She set out at a run for the stairs and the bathroom.

When Caroline arrived at the community centre, the local newspaper editor was waiting for her.

"Malcolm, you're keen to get into the library this morning."

He patted his ample belly and frowned. "I'm not here for the library, Caroline. I need to talk to you."

"Okay." The insides of Caroline's eyelids were lined with sandpaper. The last thing she felt like was a chat. "Just let me open up and we'll go into my office."

He nodded solemnly.

Once in her office, Caroline sat behind her desk and Malcolm took the only other chair in the room. She wished she'd had time to make some strong tea before dealing with the local newspaper editor, but, from the look on his face, caffeine wasn't going to help her anyway.

"I had a phone call this morning." Malcolm curled his lip in disgust. "An anonymous tip." He sucked in a breath. "It was a woman. She told me that you and Josh McInnes are getting married."

Caroline felt everything within her still as her head throbbed furiously.

"I'm sorry to bring this to you, but I have to check everything that comes over my desk. Plus, the woman became angry when I said I didn't believe her. She said she was going to call the Glasgow press."

To stop them shaking, Caroline folded her fingers on the desk in front of her. "Do you think she did?" Caroline was pleased her voice sounded a whole lot calmer than she felt.

"She was pretty angry with you, so I'm guessing that she did."

"Do you think they took her seriously?"

"They don't know you as well as I do, so they won't realise it's a silly story made up by someone who has a grudge to bear. But there's a good chance they'll send someone to check out the tip."

Caroline pulled a notebook and pen towards her. She needed to make a list. Things were always easier to handle when she had a list. "How quickly will they do that?"

Malcolm stilled with his hand halfway through a belly rub. His keen eyes focused in on her.

Caroline kept her face blank. "You worked in Glasgow for years. You must have an idea how fast they will get here?"

"Tomorrow would be my guess." He studied her for a moment. "First they'll make some phone calls to see if Josh is actually here, then they'll check you out, and if they think the story has merit they'll send someone up here." He leaned forward in his seat. "It's not true, is it, Caroline? Are you really going to marry Josh McInnes?"

Caroline took a deep breath. "Yes. It's true."

"Holy smoke." Malcolm's mouth fell open.

"Indeed." She rubbed her temple.

The editor's expression was apologetic. "You know I can't sit on this. I have a business to take care of, and this is the biggest story we've had in Invertary since the Battle of the Bras." His face softened towards her. "I'm really sorry, Caroline. I'll have to run with the story."

"I know. But there must be something we can do about the rest of the press. We don't want the town overrun, do we?"

"Well..." He scratched his unruly hair, making it look much worse. "I wouldn't say no to an exclusive, but I don't see how we can keep the press out of town."

Caroline pursed her lips. "Leave that to me. Would you mind spreading the word? Emergency town meeting in the church hall tonight."

Malcolm seemed confused, but nodded. "Sure, but I don't see how even you can stop this."

"You'd be surprised what I can do when I put my mind to it."

The editor shook his head. A knowing smile curled his lips. "No, I really wouldn't."

. . .

"WE HAVE A PROBLEM," Caroline said in Josh's ear.

Josh tucked the phone between his shoulder and ear while he grabbed a coffee mug from the cupboard. Her lilting accent sent shivers down his spine. His brain flashed a replay of the night before on the inside of his eyelids. He wanted to let out a growl. But he didn't. Caroline was nervous enough around him without him channelling his inner animal. Instead he aimed for casual. "I know we have a problem. I'm here in the castle and you're not with me."

She ignored him. No surprise there. "The press know about the wedding."

Josh shrugged as he reached for the coffee pot, which his dad had been hoarding at the dining table. He was surprised the press had taken this long.

"You need to expect this sort of thing, babe. You're marrying a superstar."

His dad grunted into his coffee. Josh could practically hear Caroline roll her eyes on the other end of the line. He grinned.

"I won't have the town overrun with press." She sounded like she had some say in the matter.

"There's nothing you can do about it. I know it's a pain in the ass, but you'll get used to it, and after the wedding they'll move on to something else."

"I don't accept that. This is my life, and no matter what you or anyone else thinks, I will have control over it."

Yeah, good luck with that.

"There's a town meeting tonight at 7:30, in the church hall. I need you to be there."

"Won't that cause more problems?"

She sighed heavily, taking him right back to the sounds she'd made the night before. He shuddered. She was definitely too far away from him.

"You aren't going to be mobbed, Josh. I know you think

everyone in Invertary is dying to get close to you, but you have to trust me when I tell you that you aren't that big of a deal."

"Whatever you want to believe, baby. Whatever you want to believe."

"Just be at the meeting," Caroline ordered, then hung up.

He shook his head at the phone. His woman had some serious control issues. As he lifted his coffee to his lips, the drilling started.

His dad moaned. "Please tell me that isn't in my head."

Josh frowned at him—he'd spotted the empty whiskey bottle on the floor beside the sofa this morning. "No it isn't. But you'd deserve it if it was. You made an ass of yourself at dinner last night. You could have made an effort with Caroline. You embarrassed the family."

"This sham of a wedding is embarrassing me."

"Dad." Josh tried to soften his voice. It was obvious from the fact his father was living in the TV room that the guy had his own problems. "Caroline is a good woman. I'm marrying her. If you can't support us that's your problem, but you need to keep your mouth shut about it."

"As your father—"

"I'm thirty-five. I don't need or want your approval. But I would like to have you involved."

"I can't do that. You're being a fool."

"Seems to me I'm not the only one." He put his hand on his dad's shoulder. "Do us all a favour. Stop worrying about my love life and sort out your own."

He left his dad grumbling into his coffee and went to the study to make some calls—if he could manage to hear anything over the drilling, hammering and sawing.

CAROLINE CLOSED THE LIBRARY EARLY, again. She was beginning to spend more time out of the centre than working in it. At this rate she'd have to refund a percentage of her wages for the time she was missing. Not to mention she could add being irresponsible to her list of sins. Lying. Stealing books. Taking care of personal business on work time. She didn't recognise herself anymore.

She pushed open the door to her best friend's lingerie shop, and was ashamed that part of her was hoping Kirsty wasn't there. No such luck. Kirsty grinned at her from behind the counter. As usual she was stunning, in a long green dress with spaghetti straps. After years of watching her cover her scars, it still surprised Caroline to see Kirsty wearing clothes that revealed them. She was proud of her friend.

"Hey," Kirsty said. "You shopping?"

Caroline shook her head. She took a deep breath.

"I need to talk to you about the town meeting tonight."

Kirsty folded her arms over her chest, flashing the huge engagement ring Lake had bought her for Valentine's day.

"I heard about that. Do you know what it's about?"

Caroline looked around the shop. She was the only one there. Kirsty watched her closely. "Magenta is on her break. It's just us."

Caroline took a deep breath. "I'm getting married to Josh McInnes." The words came out on a rush of air. "He isn't into romantic relationships. He thinks marriage should be arranged for mutual benefit, like they did in the past. Apparently he's been looking for a wife for some time and thinks I fit the bill."

Kirsty didn't move a muscle. Caroline began to fidget with the strap of her handbag.

"The wedding is in two weeks and I'd like you to be my maid of honour."

Kirsty continued to stare. Caroline's mouth went dry.

"So, the press have gotten wind of the wedding and the fact Josh is here. The meeting tonight is to discuss how we're going to handle everything. We'd like to keep them away from the wedding if possible."

Nothing from Kirsty. In fact, she looked more like one of the mannequins in her shop than the famous model she used to be. Caroline let out an exasperated sigh.

"Oh for goodness' sake, say something. It's not that shocking. It's not like I've outlined a plan for world domination."

Kirsty shook herself. "You may as well have." She threw up her hands in exasperation. "What are you thinking? You can't marry a man you don't know and don't love. An arrangement for mutual benefit? What the heck does that even mean? Have you lost your mind?"

"Keep your voice down." Even though they were the only two in the shop, Caroline didn't want to take any chances.

"Keep my voice down?" Kirsty's voice rose an octave. "My best friend has lost the plot and you want me to keep my voice down?"

The door pinged as a customer came in.

"Sorry." Kirsty rushed towards the woman. "I have to close. Family emergency. Someone is having a mental breakdown."

She ushered the poor woman out of the shop, locked the door and flipped the sign to *closed*. Turning back to Caroline, she put her hands on her hips and glared. "Explain, Caroline Patterson. Right now."

Caroline flopped down onto the stool beside the counter. "There's nothing to explain. He asked me to marry him last Monday. I said yes. We're getting married the Saturday after next."

"Have you been dating? When did you meet him?"

"No, we haven't been dating. I met him for the first time about an hour before he proposed."

"Tell me it was love at first sight? That there were fireworks?"

"More like a business contract. We shook hands." She found it hard to look Kirsty in the eyes.

"What have you gotten yourself into?" Kirsty let out a heavy sigh.

"You know me, Kirsty—when was the last time some guy asked me out, let alone proposed? Opportunities like this don't just fall in my lap."

The look of pity in Kirsty's eyes made Caroline blush. "No, they don't, but this isn't you. You're the romantic one. You've got a house full of romance stories all about women being swept off their feet. You, more than anyone, should wait until you fall in love. You deserve that."

"And how long do I wait? I'm thirty-one. I've met pretty much every man in Invertary now. Surely if Prince Charming was here I'd have found him? This is a good opportunity for me. It's a chance at having a family of my own. How could I pass that up?"

Kirsty crouched down in front of her and put her hands over Caroline's. "You were always the one with dreams about weddings and falling in love. I was the one who didn't believe."

"And now you have Lake and you're happy. And I have Josh. It may not be hearts and roses, but it's not exactly a hardship. There are women all over the world who would kill to be in my shoes."

"It doesn't matter how many women would like to be in your place. It doesn't matter how he looks or how wealthy he is. All that matters is that you make a life with a man you love. A man who loves you. And you're not doing that. Caroline, can't you see how wrong this is?"

Caroline felt her stomach turn over. "I want a family before it's too late. Josh seems nice enough and he wants to be with me. He seems committed. He's in it for the long haul." She tried for a light-hearted grin. "Plus, he's letting me restore the castle."

Kirsty sighed, but returned the smile. "You deserve better than this."

"You're the only one who thinks so."

"Fine." Kirsty stood and straightened the skirt of her dress. "So what do you want me to wear as maid of honour?"

Caroline felt her shoulders sag with relief. "I'm going to London next week and I'll have them send a couple of options to you." She smiled sheepishly. "I have a dress fitting at Harrods."

Her best friend grinned. "Now there's a sentence I never thought you would say."

"Yeah, it's right up there with 'I'm marrying a world-famous singer.'"

The women looked at each other and burst out laughing.

By 7:28 p.m. the church hall was packed to capacity. Every seat was taken. People were crammed into the aisles, and the double doors were wide open so that those in the corridor could take part in the meeting. Caroline nodded to the domino boys, who were on door duty. She signalled to her watch. It was time to close the main doors and get ready for the meeting.

Josh bumped his shoulder into hers. "Don't you think it was a bit over the top to confiscate everyone's phones?"

He was sprawled out in one of the wooden chairs that had been set out in a row on the platform at the front of the room. His legs were straight out in front of him, ankles crossed, his arms folded. He looked about five seconds away from taking a nap. It made Caroline sit even straighter in her chair as she ground her teeth together.

"I don't want any pictures or videos."

He had on jeans and grey sneakers, but in deference to the occasion he was wearing a plain black T-shirt and black suit jacket. Yet again he made her look like she shopped at Goodwill, which she couldn't complain about as it was pretty much true.

"You should let people take their pictures. It makes them happy."

"Are you upset because you aren't getting your photo taken, Josh? Is this about your poor wee ego?"

"I don't have a poor wee ego."

"You can say that again. There's nothing wee about your ego."

She looked at her watch. 7:30. Dougal, the unofficial town mayor, gave her a thumbs-up as Caroline took her position behind the lectern.

"Thank you all for coming." Caroline shuffled her notes in front of her. "We have a bit of a situation that will affect everyone in town, and I need your help with it." She took a quiet breath; she didn't want anyone to know that she felt nervous. "First of all, Josh McInnes." She pointed at Josh, just in case they weren't sure whom she was talking about. He waved. "Josh and I are getting married." There was a stunned silence. Caroline leaned closer to the microphone. "To each other," she clarified.

Everyone started talking at once. Caroline waited patiently for calm to resume, watching the amazement pass through the room like a Mexican wave at a football match.

Dougal came up beside her and angled the mic towards himself. "Settle down! We've got a lot to get through. You can all gossip later." He turned to Caroline. "Carry on, lass."

"Thanks, Dougal." Caroline was confident she could have

managed the noise in the room by herself. "As I was saying, we're getting married two weeks from now, here in Invertary."

"We didn't even know you were seeing each other," a man at the back shouted.

"We weren't."

"So you just decided to get wed," someone else called out.

"Yes." The noise level grew. Caroline tapped the microphone. "I'm not finished. Sit down and listen." As usual, everyone did as they were told. "Josh and I had planned on keeping this a secret until closer to the wedding day. Unfortunately, an unscrupulous individual has contacted the press here, and in Glasgow, to tip them off about the wedding."

"Betty!" Several peopled shouted.

Betty McCloud climbed up onto the chair she'd been sitting on and glared around the room. The eighty-six-year-old was wearing one of her tartan tent dresses and, as usual, she'd forgotten her false teeth. "I did not tell the press about the wedding." She rummaged around in her pocket. She gave a triumphant look when she came out with her teeth and popped them in her mouth.

"Yeah, right," Archie called out. "If there's trouble around here, you're always behind it."

Betty looked quite proud of that before she growled at the domino boy. "If I was going to call the press, I wouldn't have rung the local rag. I'd have gone straight to the entertainment section at the BBC. What do you think I am? An amateur? If I wanted the press here, they'd be here already. Plus, I only just found out about the wedding, same as you. And I'll be having a word with Kirsty and Lake about that oversight as soon as this meeting is done."

"She's got a point," someone said. "Betty would have had the national press out before anyone noticed it'd happened. It can't have been her."

There were quite a lot of nodding heads.

"On the other hand." Betty flashed a wicked smile. "I am responsible for the ad in last week's paper that said Morag's pies were on sale."

"I knew it!" Morag jumped to her feet. "My bakery lost a lot of money because of that stunt. Lake Benson, can't you keep a leash on your monkey?"

Lake was leaning against the wall at the back of the room. "I keep telling you lot. Just because she came with the shop I bought, doesn't mean I'm responsible for her."

"And we keep telling you that you are!" Morag shot back.

"That's enough." Caroline smacked the microphone.

Betty climbed down from her seat, gave Morag a finger wave and howled with laughter.

"We'll deal with your pie problem later," Caroline told Morag.

Morag pointed at Betty. "She owes me the money I would have made if I hadn't been forced to sell cut-price pies."

"As I said"—Caroline eyed Morag—"we'll deal with that later. Right now we have more pressing matters, like the problem of the press."

"I don't see how that's our problem," a man at the back of the room called out.

Caroline scowled at him. "It's your problem because I'm making it yours. I've promised Malcolm at the *Invertary Standard* that he'll have an exclusive on the wedding. It's in everyone's best interest to make sure that happens."

"Why?" Morag shouted. "Won't the press bring business? We could use the business. Especially with Betty sabotaging everybody."

"Yes." Caroline felt her patience beginning to slip. "The press would bring business, but not as much business as our wedding is going to generate. We're making sure everything stays as local as possible. Plus the town will have celebrities and tourists. There will be plenty of interest." She leaned closer to the microphone. "But if this story breaks before I want it to, if this town is overrun by paparazzi and journalists, Josh and I will be forced to have our wedding somewhere else. Then there will be no new business for anyone." She gave Morag a pointed look.

There was silence.

"This is what I want," Caroline told the stunned crowd. "We will keep the press out of town. No one is to deal with them. We want to keep everything about this wedding top secret."

"How are we supposed to keep the kids off Facebook?" someone moaned.

"I'm sure you can think of a way. It's in your best interest to control them. This wedding will bring a lot of business to the town and will promote tourism for the future. Invertary will be talked about around the world."

"It will put us on the map," Dougal shouted.

"The teenagers don't care about the map," someone shouted back.

"You're off your head," one of the men said. "You're asking for the impossible."

The crowd descended into unhappy grumbling. Caroline held up her hand to quieten everyone. Out of the corner of her eye she could see Josh shaking his head at her.

"Settle down, right now," Caroline told the crowd.

It got slightly quieter. She folded her arms and waited. She would not tolerate being disobeyed.

JOSH WATCHED Caroline stare at the crowd like some misguided army drill sergeant. Any minute now she was going to order them all to get down and give her twenty for insubordination. He agreed with the grumpy guy with orange hair—she was out of her mind.

"I don't see why we should do this," a woman called out.

"I told you, it's for the good of the town." Caroline stuck her nose in the air. "And it's the right thing to do."

There was a collective groan. It was time to intervene. If there was one thing he knew, it was how to work a crowd. He sauntered to the mic, smiling at the people in the room. Slowly, quiet descended. It took Caroline a minute to notice she wasn't the reason for the silence. When she turned to him, she frowned.

"What are you doing out of your seat?"

Josh grinned at her. "When we're alone we're going to deal with this teacher fantasy of yours."

There were giggles. Caroline's face turned a lovely shade of pink, and she was speechless for once. Josh put a hand on each of her hips and moved her away from the mic.

"Hi, folks. Good to see you all. What my lovely fiancée forgot to say was that if everyone helps us out, I'll put on an extra show and donate the proceeds to the town." Caroline gasped. He gave her a lazy smile. "I don't know exactly how this town works. Maybe your mayor can help me out here."

Dougal bustled over to the lectern. "Unofficial mayor," he corrected.

Josh shook his head a little. Where the hell was the official mayor? Never mind.

"I'm thinking," Josh said into the mic, "that the proceeds from the concert can be held by the council and used for things the teenagers might appreciate. Things they want more than they want to post photos online."

Dougal patted him on the back. "Ah, I like the way you think, young man. A bribe. Well, we do need a new computer suite at the community centre, or a new football pitch on the edge of town. Who knows, maybe we could even stretch to a small recording studio for budding artists. I'm pretty sure we could cover all the interests represented by our teenagers."

Josh gave him an encouraging nod. Caroline folded her arms and glared at him. Josh swallowed a laugh.

"So there it is, folks—if you guys can help us out, we can do something for everyone in town. Your business will get a boost. Your kids will get a bribe. What do you say? Want to help us keep our wedding private?"

There was a roar of approval. Josh led Caroline back to their seats. She was stiff as a board. Mad at his interference.

"We're setting up roadblocks on the main road out of town," Dougal was saying as Josh finger walked up Caroline's spine to the base of her neck. She tried to shake him off. "It's our town. We can decide who comes and goes, and if we don't want the press in here, then we don't need to let them in. The domino boys have offered to man the barricades."

"I'll help," shouted Betty. "Lake's been teaching me interrogation techniques. They might come in handy."

When everyone turned towards Lake, he shrugged. "You want her to be bored?"

"The man has a point," Dougal said.

"I love this town," Josh whispered to Caroline, who gave an unladylike snort.

Josh rubbed the tense spot in Caroline's neck. She very slightly shrugged, trying to make him stop.

"Stop it," she snapped at him. "We're in public. And I'm annoyed with you. I had everything under control. You didn't need to butt in and bribe everyone. People would have done the right thing, because it was the right thing to do." She gave him a look that might have turned him to stone—if she'd possessed any sort of power over him. Instead, it made his mouth water.

She shuffled in her seat to get away from him. Josh

wrapped his hand around her hip and tugged her back, snug against him.

"Behave," he whispered. "You have no idea what I could say, or do, in front of this crowd. I'm an unknown entity and I have absolutely no shame. I'm not easily embarrassed. Ask Mitch."

Caroline shot daggers at him from the corner of her eye. Josh chuckled.

"Baby, not everyone has your well-developed sense of right and wrong. People need a little incentive." Josh trailed his fingers up her back and into her hair. She gave him a haughty glance over her shoulder. It was intended to remind him of his place. Which, he guessed, was somewhere around the level of a subject to Queen Caroline. "You have a very low opinion of people."

"No. I'm a realist. A realist with resources. Resources that are yours to use. That's what marriage is about. We help each other."

"We're not married yet." Caroline gave him the evil eye, and the chuckle he'd been stifling erupted from him.

He leaned in closer to breathe her deeply. He slid his hand down her back until it curved comfortably on her hip.

"Two last things," Dougal was saying. "Don't hassle the happy couple—they have a right to their special day, just the same as you do. And second, there's a sale on chips at the pub after the meeting." He looked at Betty. "This one wasn't organised by Betty."

There was a whoop of laughter as people noisily cleared out of the hall. Caroline jumped to her feet and practically ran from Josh. He shook his head slowly. *You can run, but you can't hide.*

Josh watched Dougal talk to Caroline. His huge belly was wrapped in a pink shirt and green tartan waistcoat. He looked exactly the way a Christmas gift would look if a drunken Elton John was wrapping it. Caroline stepped out from behind Dougal, and her eyes caught Josh's. Josh smiled before blowing her a kiss. She stumbled, and Dougal reached out to steady her.

"I'm Caroline's best friend," a voice beside Josh said.

He turned to find a stunning redhead, flanked by the guy who was responsible for Betty. Josh stood and offered his hand.

"I'm Kirsty, and this is my fiancé, Lake." She gripped his hand tightly when he moved to let go, and leaned towards him. "If you hurt my friend, or upset her in anyway, I will eviscerate you."

Josh blinked, then smiled. "Good to know."

Lake didn't smile as he offered his hand. "Lake Benson, of Eye Spy security. Ex-special forces. Who's doing the security for the wedding?"

Josh shook his hand. "You?"

"Right answer." Lake's lips twitched.

Josh got the feeling that was this guy's version of a grin. Kirsty nodded with approval. "I'm watching you," she told Josh.

"And so am I." Betty wobbled up to them. "Now, what's my role in this wedding? And it better be a good one."

Lake's lip twitched again. "I'm putting you in charge of making sure Josh doesn't mess with Caroline."

Betty looked Josh up and down. She was clearly unimpressed. "Can I hurt him if he steps out of line?"

"We'll negotiate that on a case-by-case basis."

Her eyes glinted with glee. "I'm in."

Josh bit back a laugh. This was the most fun he'd had in years. Coming to Scotland was the best decision he'd ever made. Nope, he thought as he looked over at Caroline, it was the second best. Proposing to the ice queen was number one.

CHAPTER 13

It was less than two weeks to the wedding and the town was on lockdown. They'd made national news, and it wasn't good. Mitch grabbed the remote control and turned up the volume on the massive TV screen, which was now wedged into the much smaller office because Caroline had banished it from the grand room. The volume was almost deafening— the only way they could hear it over the building works.

"In other news this Tuesday morning," the breakfast show presenter said, "the small Scottish town of Invertary appears to have set up its own form of passport control." A photo of Josh appeared on the screen. "Grammy Award-winning singer Josh McInnes is soon to be married in this Highland town. To a local girl, Caroline Patterson." A picture of Caroline looking very severe flashed on the screen. "It's rumoured that Caroline met the singer at the library, of all places."

The screen changed to a shot of the domino boys manning a makeshift barrier on the main road into town. "Nobody with a camera is getting in here," Archie said. "We're going to keep this wedding private if it kills us." He smiled into the camera lens. "Or kills you. Don't even think about sneaking over the hills; we have people watching and we'll get you."

It cut to the woman who was interviewing the domino boys. "As you can see, the town is taking this wedding very seriously indeed. As members of the press, we haven't been allowed to go any further than this roadblock."

The camera scanned the growing crowd beside the entry point to town. There were several news crews.

"Although being stuck out here isn't so bad," the woman said. "We're getting regular food deliveries."

A face pushed into the frame with the reporters. "This little problem"—Morag McKay pointed at the roadblock —"isn't going to stop the wonderful members of the press from tasting my award-winning pies."

She beamed at the camera. It was gruesome. The reporter stepped away from Morag. "We've seen many unusual and secretive celebrity weddings over the years, but we've never seen one where a whole town shuts down. We'll keep you posted on future developments."

The screen went black. Mitch turned to Josh, who was sprawled out on the tiny two-seat sofa.

"This is a publicity nightmare. Your PR team have no idea what to tell anyone." Mitch pointed at the TV. "They're turning you into a laughing stock. There may be no coming back from this."

Josh clasped his hands behind his neck. Mitch's tension was contagious; Josh's neck was beginning to freeze on him.

"They'll get fed up and move on to something else. I don't have time to deal with this right now. Caroline will be here any minute. We're picking out a wedding dress today."

"You need to make time." Mitch sat on the arm of the chair facing Josh. "We're a three-ring circus for the entertainment press. This story is going to run every day until the wedding, and for years after it." He threw the remote onto the chair and rubbed a hand over his face. "This wedding idea of yours is blowing up in our faces. Your credibility is going down the drain. A few more weeks of this and the story will be right up there with Jacko's monkey, Mel Gibson's meltdown and just about everything that Miley Cyrus does these days. You're screwing up everything you've worked to achieve. Is it worth it?"

Josh ran his palms down his jean-clad thighs. He was beginning to feel stir crazy. The work crew were ripping apart his home, and every day it became more uncomfortable. The carpet was gone, the walls were clad in dark wood panelling and most of the ground floor was out of bounds. He'd been exiled to the tiny TV room that was overcrowded with furniture, the kitchen, which was full of his moody parents, and his bedroom, which was far too empty for his liking.

"Look." Mitch huffed out a sigh. "Maybe we should move the wedding. A resort in the Caribbean, or LA? At least there they're used to dealing with celebrities."

"I can't. It's one of Caroline's conditions. Get married in Invertary."

"Fine, at least let me call in some expert security. Guys who are trained to deal with the press and not make things worse every time they open their mouths."

"Lake Benson is handling security. You checked him out yourself. He's got a great rep. What more do you want? If we replace the domino boys with gorillas in suits, everyone will say it's overkill."

"And this isn't?" Mitch pointed at the blank screen. "Do you want to be known for your music or for this farce?"

He had a point. "No professional security on the roads. I want to keep it low key. Make sure Lake is keeping an eye on everything in case it gets out of hand. In the meantime, issue a statement letting it be known that we are very touched by the quirky locals, who feel so strongly about Caroline that they are making sure her wedding is private. Tell them I feel like a member of the family and that we're all real amused by the town."

Mitch thought about it for a minute. "Okay, that could work. Are you sure you want to go through with this?"

"Oh, yeah, I'm sure. I haven't had this much fun in years."

"It isn't about having fun. You have a future to think about."

"That's exactly what I'm doing here. Working on my future." Josh threw a cushion at Mitch. "Admit it, you like her too."

"Yeah. She's something else. But I'm not the one marrying her."

"I know. Lucky me."

"Yeah." Mitch flicked a glance at the TV. "Lucky you."

CHAPTER 14

Josh was sick to his back teeth with wedding dresses. He'd had about six cups of coffee while he waited in Harrods for Caroline to pick a dress. It was mind-numbing. Seriously? How hard could it be? They were all white. Surely *that* narrowed the choice down a little? Josh was way past his limit for shopping. In fact, he'd used up a lifetime of shopping tolerance on this one trip alone. He would never be able to shop again.

At least that was reassuring.

"I hate this." Caroline came out of the changing room.

The bodice of the dress was tight-fitting lace, the skirt layer upon layer of what looked like net curtains. She looked like she was drowning in a marshmallow pit.

Josh cringed. "It's bad."

She nodded, turned and signalled to the woman who was helping her to bring in the next dress.

Josh held up his hands in surrender, even though Caroline couldn't see him. "I can't take any more."

Caroline's head popped out from behind the cream-coloured door. "Well, go do something else."

"I did everything I came here to do."

It had only taken the morning to get to London via helicopter and private plane, which meant they'd been holed up in the wedding dress department for the whole afternoon. Unlike some people he could mention, it'd taken him a whole half-hour to fit his wedding clothes. He honestly couldn't see what was taking so long.

"I'm starving." His stomach rumbled right on cue. One measly sandwich for lunch was nowhere near enough for a full-grown man.

Her head appeared again. She was irritated. "Go get something to eat."

"And leave you alone?" He shook his head. "What if you need me?"

She blew some hair out of her eye. "Why on earth would I need you for this?"

"I'm giving opinions."

She sighed heavily. "You're right. You're invaluable." She disappeared again.

"Can I order pizza?" he asked the woman beside him.

Her horrified expression said it all.

A few minutes later, Caroline was back out in a halter-neck dress that skimmed her knees. He knew it was worth thousands, but it still looked cheap.

"No. Just no."

"I didn't think so." She disappeared back into the changing room.

"What about a sandwich? Or a banana?" He was about five minutes away from begging the assistant to have mercy on him and feed him. "Anything. I'm dying here."

"I have a cereal bar in my bag," the woman said hesitantly.

"Bring it on." He thanked her profusely, but it was gone in two bites.

"Come on, Caroline, pick a dress. How hard can this be?"

Caroline's head appeared around the changing room door. She frowned at him. "If this is so blooming easy, you pick one."

His eyes lit up. He could do this. He glanced at his watch. And there still would be time for an early dinner. "You're on."

With a long-suffering glance towards heaven, the assistant handed him an iPad, which contained a virtual showroom. He flicked through the dresses, as Caroline had done about a million years earlier. Her choices were on the rack beside him. As far as he could see, they were all ugly. At last, his hand stilled. "This one." He pointed at the dress.

The assistant raised an eyebrow, but turned on her heels to fetch it.

"You better not have picked red," Caroline called through the changing room door. "There's no way I'm wearing red."

"Would I do something like that?"

"I honestly have no idea what you're going to do next."

And that made Josh feel pretty chuffed.

At last, the sales assistant swept into the room with a dress wrapped in cellophane. Josh patted his stomach to reassure it that food was coming soon.

"There's a great steak place in here," Josh called to Caroline. There was silence. "We can eat something else if you want." His stomach protested loudly. His stomach wanted steak.

The door to the changing room swung open, and Caroline walked out. There was a look of complete shock on her face. Josh held his breath. She spread her arms wide and turned slowly. When she looked back at him, her eyes were wide and she nibbled on the spot on her bottom lip that he liked so much.

"It's perfect." He came to stand in front of her. "You're beautiful."

She blushed. "I wouldn't go that far."

He put his finger under her chin and tipped her face up to him. "I would."

"What you need with that," the assistant said, "is the most darling little pair of Charlotte Olympia shoes. I'll just fetch them." She tottered out of the room.

"Thank you," Caroline said once the assistant was gone.

And then, to Josh's surprise, she put a hand on each of his shoulders, went up on tiptoes and kissed him. His first kiss from Caroline that she'd given willingly.

Suddenly he wasn't hungry for food any longer.

CAROLINE RELEASED Josh and stepped back from him. She felt a little stunned. She hadn't meant to kiss him. It was just that the dress was perfect and she'd been overcome. Josh took a determined step towards her as the assistant sailed back into the room.

"These will go perfectly with this dress."

Josh clearly wasn't happy with the interruption. He folded his arms across today's T-shirt, Spider-Man this time, and leaned against the wall by the floor-length mirror.

"The shoes are lovely." Caroline smiled at the assistant.

They were kitten-heeled sling-backs in the same shade of white satin as the dress, only they were embroidered and embellished with beads. With the woman's help, Caroline slipped them on, and the dress fell more gracefully. She assessed herself in the mirror, but it was hard to be objective because the dress was the most beautiful thing she'd ever seen.

The boat neck skimmed across her to fasten discreetly on each shoulder. The sleeveless bodice fitted her form perfectly until it flowed out from beneath her hips to trail in a wide but simple skirt with a short train on the floor. There was no embroidery, no beading, nothing to detract from the simple elegance of the dress. It took her breath away.

"How did you know?" She smiled at Josh, who was eyeing her with the same hungry look he had when he spoke about steak.

He didn't give her the cocky smile she expected. Instead, he shrugged like it was nothing. "I kept an eye out for something Grace Kelly would have rocked."

She blinked at him. "You think I look like Grace Kelly?"

"Better." His expression was dark and loaded with promise. It made her tingle in places she wasn't usually aware of.

Caroline faced the assistant. "This is the one. I'll take the shoes too."

The woman made a note on her iPad. "We'll need to arrange for a fitting, to make sure it's perfect on you. When should I book?"

Josh answered for her: "Next week. You have the wedding dates and details, right?" The assistant nodded. "In that case, it would be best if you came to us this time."

"That won't be a problem."

Caroline skimmed her hand down the smooth silk bodice. Never in her life would she have imagined getting married in such a dress. She glanced at Josh to see if he was in as much awe of the dress as she was.

"I need to eat. Now." Nope, Josh wasn't in awe of the dress. He gave her a pleading look. "Are we done here?"

She bit back a smile. "Yes. We're done."

"About time." He turned to the sales assistant. "Don't offer her anything else. If there's something you think we need, bring it to Scotland. We're done and we're going to eat."

Caroline and the woman exchanged an amused look.

"Are you getting changed or do I need to help you?" Josh said with a growl.

Caroline laughed as she ran for the changing room.

. . .

THEY WERE SITTING IN HARRODS' Steakhouse, perched on high stools around the gleaming marble counter. Behind the counter, an army of men in chef's whites took orders for steak, and cooked it while their customers watched. The aroma was mouth-watering. Caroline swivelled on her stool. Behind her there were several counters similar to the one they were seated at. One for meat, another for seafood. She supposed this was Harrods' version of a fast-food court.

They sat at the end of the counter. On the stools at the other side of Caroline were two men in business suits, deep in discussion about the economy. Josh turned towards her, spreading his knees wide so that they sat either side of hers. The stools were fixed to the floor, so Caroline couldn't move away from him. Not that she wanted to. He rested his right hand on her thigh.

"You can't live on salad and water, baby. This is a long day. We left early. You need energy."

They'd had this discussion already, when he'd ordered the world's biggest steak with a barrel of fries. His thumb caressed her knee. Caroline found it hard to concentrate on his words when his touch was vibrating throughout her body.

"Josh, I'm getting married. I need to look my best."

"Baby, you can do that on a steak."

"I want a salad."

He frowned. "Nobody wants salad."

She rolled her eyes at him.

"Okay," he said, "how about we get some cake for dessert?"

Caroline scowled at him. "Do you want me to look fat at the wedding?"

His eyebrows shot up. "You won't look fat. You'll look perfect."

"Not if I live on steak and cake, I won't."

He threw up his hands in exasperation. Clearly he didn't understand a word she was saying. But she knew that on her wedding day, the world would be watching, wondering what kind of woman made Josh propose. There wasn't time to change her image, to become more stylish. There was nothing she could do but look exactly like what she was—a plain, mousy librarian. But she could at least try to be the best mousy librarian possible. Which meant no cake.

Josh scooted forward. His thighs pressed into her legs. His right hand moved slowly up her arm to rest at the base of her neck. "I like how you look. Even if you gorge yourself on cake, that won't change."

Caroline blinked hard at him. She was wearing her only other dress. A pretty pink linen shift that she'd bought in a sale when shopping in Glasgow years ago. She'd teamed it with cream flats and a simple silver necklace that her grandfather had given her. It had a single daisy pendant hanging from it. She didn't have any other jewellery on, and her only makeup was some mascara and a swipe of lip gloss. She was plain and under-dressed, especially for Harrods. And he liked how she looked?

He leaned towards her. His left hand stroking her knee. "I like how you look a lot." She held her breath, mesmerised by the desire in his eye. "I like how you taste even better." He growled softly before his lips touched hers.

Caroline didn't have time to panic about kissing in public. In fact, she didn't have time to think at all. One touch of Josh's lips and she sank towards him. His hands held her tight; otherwise she'd have fallen off the stool and flat on her face before him.

"Better than steak," he murmured against her lips.

She couldn't think. His tongue teased its way inside her mouth, and all she could do was sigh. He tightened his grip as flashes went off in her head.

Suddenly Josh was gone. The flashes hadn't been in her head. There was a photographer brandishing his camera at Josh. Caroline gripped the counter to steady herself.

"Get lost, McInnes. I got what I needed. I'm out of here. Get your hands off me or I'm gonna sue then watch this on E! News."

Caroline sucked in a breath as her hand went to her mouth. Josh had his fists twisted into the T-shirt of a lecherous-looking man. He was short and acne scarred, and reeked of smoke. Josh's face was thunderous. Caroline felt everything still within her. Suddenly the fact he didn't have a bodyguard made perfect sense. Josh could obviously take care of himself.

He shook the photographer. "You know the rules, Pyro. No paparazzi in Harrods."

The smaller guy sneered, making his face twist into something ugly. "I got the shot I wanted. I'll make ten times more than whatever fine I have to pay here. Kicking me out won't make any difference." Pyro poked Josh in the chest. "Thanks for the payday, bud."

Josh snarled. "Don't think I won't hurt you."

"You do and you'll be front-page news. I'm not the one assaulting someone. Everything you do is money to me. So go ahead," the photographer spat out. "Hit me. I'll live off that payday for a year."

Caroline sprang from her stool and put her hand on Josh's arm. He didn't look at her. She wasn't sure he even felt her.

"Maybe," Josh said to the worm, "that seems like a good deal to me."

At the far end of the room, Caroline could make out security uniforms running towards them.

"Josh." She held his arm tightly. "He's not worth it."

"Better listen to the little lady," the photographer sneered. "Seems like she's got the brains in this setup. You were always a grinning idiot. I mean, look at you. You could have had anyone you want, and you pick her."

Caroline went still. Josh's biceps flexed. His eyes were dark. Something in Caroline snapped. She let go of Josh, snatched the camera from the photographer's side and clicked it loose from its strap. She held it in her hands.

"Get your hands off my property, bitch!"

Josh took another step towards the photographer. Looming over the man. Itching to strike out. "Don't talk to my woman like that." His voice was thunder. "Don't look at her. Don't take pictures of her. She doesn't exist for you."

"Or what?" the idiot demanded.

Caroline had heard enough. "Is this one of those cameras that can email photos?"

The guy's glance flicked to her. She saw worry in his eyes. "What do you care?"

"I'm guessing by the look on your face that you didn't have a chance to send the photo yet."

He wet his bottom lip. Nervous.

"Good," Caroline said. "I've had enough of this discussion."

She took the memory card from the camera, dropped it on the floor and crushed it with her heel. A stream of cursing cut through the gasps. The photographer fought to get at her. "I'm going to kill you for that. Bitch!"

"Done here," Josh said.

He pulled back his right hand, made a fist and aimed.

There was a sickening crunch. Pyro bent double and held his nose. Blood dripped onto the floor.

"Well done, asshole," he spat. "That's money in my pocket."

Josh folded his arms and scanned the rapt crowd. "Anybody get a picture of what happened?" There was silence. "Anybody witness what happened?"

"Guy fell over," someone shouted. "Broke his camera. Banged his nose."

"Saw the whole thing," someone else called. "This store needs to maintain its floors better."

Josh glared at the paparazzo. "Looks like you need to find another payday."

"You'll pay for this," Pyro said. "You don't mess with the paparazzi. We have the power, man."

"This is Harrods." Josh calmly wrapped his arm around Caroline's shoulders. "They don't like the paps in here. You know that, Pyro. You lot killed the owner's son. Remember Diana, asshole? There's a reason this is a paparazzi-free zone, and you just blew it."

Two burly security guards followed by a man in a perfectly cut suit screeched to a halt beside Josh.

"Trespassing," the man in the suit said. His face was grim. He motioned to the guards.

The security team grabbed the photographer and yanked him towards the back of the shop.

"You'll regret this. You and that ugly bitch you're marrying," the guy shouted.

Caroline jerked straight. His words were a slap.

"I'm sorry about that, Mr. McInnes," the man in the suit said.

Josh tightened his hold on Caroline. "So am I."

As Caroline tried her best to become invisible, the man turned to the crowd.

"Please forgive this unseemly disturbance. If you would

all like to make your way to the bakery, you'll find complimentary snacks and drinks for everyone."

The crowd moved with excitement, abuzz with chatter. Caroline felt herself being turned in Josh's arms. She was wedged against his side and, without thinking she wrapped her arms around his waist.

"We've lost our appetite," Josh told the guy in the suit.

"Of course," he said. "I'll deal with this mess. You and your fiancée enjoy the rest of your day."

Caroline watched him go as a few people lingered to stare at them.

"What do you want to do, honey?" Josh stroked her hair.

"I want to go home."

He kissed her head, grabbed her hand and marched them towards the exit.

CHAPTER 15

Caroline got back from London to find her old-style answer machine was at capacity. It was the type where the light blinked to show a message had been recorded. The more messages, the faster the blink. It was going so fast Caroline couldn't keep track. Usually she dealt with her calls as soon as she came through the door. This time she didn't. She headed for the kitchen, flicked on the kettle and sank into a chair at the table.

The ride home from London had been tense. They'd been in the limo on their way to the airport when Josh's cell phone rang. He looked at the screen and frowned before answering.

"Who are you and how did you get this number?"

There was silence before Josh cocked an eyebrow in Caroline's direction. He handed the phone over to her. She hesitantly took it. He folded his arms and shook his head at her, as though she'd done something wrong.

"Why am I hearing about your wedding on the TV?" her sister screamed in her ear.

"Elaine," Caroline said on a sigh.

"Yes, Elaine. Your sister. Your only family. The one person

you should have called with the news. Instead I find out the whole town knows before me. Not only that but BBC entertainment news, E! News and CNN." She let out an angry growl. "I'm feeling the love here. If I wasn't the size of a beached whale I'd get on a plane and sort you out in person."

Caroline took a deep breath. "I was waiting for the right time to tell you..."

"That would have been straight after you said yes to Josh freaking McInnes!"

"Calm down," Caroline told her. "Think of the baby. I didn't want to stress you and throw you into early labour."

"So you thought hearing about my only sister marrying a famous singer from the news was going to be *less* stressful than telling me yourself?"

Caroline pinched the bridge of her nose. She so didn't need this right now.

"I'm sorry I didn't tell you. Things have been insane since we agreed to get married. I should have made time. It's no excuse."

She listened as her sister let out a deep breath. "So, what's the deal? How long have you been dating this guy? Why didn't you tell me about him?"

Caroline felt her stomach plummet. The answers to those questions weren't going to help at all. "Elaine, this isn't the best time to talk about all of that. I'm in a car on the way to London City Airport. We've been shopping for wedding dresses. I'll call you when I'm back home."

She heard a sniff. "I'm going to miss your wedding." Elaine sobbed. Caroline scrunched her eyes shut as her chest ached. "Can't you wait? I want to be there when my sister gets married."

Caroline shot a glance at Josh. "It's part of our deal to get married fast. Something to do with being a celebrity."

"I don't want to miss your wedding. You've always been there for me. I want to be there for you."

"You will be, honey. We'll come visit as soon as it's over. You need to concentrate on taking care of my new wee niece. That's more important than a wedding any day."

She listened as Elaine struggled to gain control of herself. "I love you."

"I love you too, honey." Caroline's eyes misted.

She heard her sister's sobs grow fainter.

"Hi, Aunty Caroline." It was her ten-year-old niece, Emma. "I can't believe you're marrying Josh McInnes. I've told all my friends. Can I come stay with you next school holidays? I want to meet him. Does he know One Direction? What about Katy Perry? Does he know any movie stars? Can I come to Hollywood with you?"

Caroline laughed. "I'll talk to Josh, sweetie, see what we can do."

"Cool." And then she was gone.

Caroline stared at the phone for a minute before handing it back to Josh. He took it silently before signalling to the driver to pull over. He climbed out of the limo and strode into a British Telecom shop. A few minutes later, he handed her the latest iPhone.

"We'll set it up on the plane."

Caroline eyed the box with suspicion. "I don't want a phone. I don't need a phone."

"Your sister had to call Lake to get my number so that she could talk to you. You need a phone. How are people supposed to talk to you if you don't have one?"

"They call my house and leave a message. Or call work to talk to me. Or they walk to my door. Everyone I know is in Invertary. I don't need a phone."

He turned towards her. "Elaine isn't in Invertary. Your

sister needed to talk to you. And I might like to talk to you without leaving a message for you to get back to me."

Caroline plonked the phone on the seat beside her and folded her arms. "So this is about you."

"No, this is about people being able to get hold of you. It's about you being safe. What if you're out alone and get hounded by the press? What if some crazed fan decides they want to get too close to you? You need to be able to call for help."

Caroline glared at him. "You're blowing this out of proportion. Lots of people don't have cell phones."

Even as the words came out of her mouth, she realised they were arguing about something ridiculous.

"You're keeping the phone." He clenched his jaw.

"I don't need it."

"Caroline, I just decked a photographer," he said, like that explained everything.

"You didn't have to."

"Yes. I did." He turned to her, and his demeanour was intense. "I've been living with this crap for years. It comes with the territory. I'm not an idiot. I court the press. I have to, otherwise I won't sell records and I want to sell records. But the paparazzi are something else. They don't play by the rules. They don't care what damage they cause. They don't care that something is off limits. They'll do whatever it takes to make their money. And that includes hounding the people I care about."

Caroline bit her bottom lip. Her stomach had squeezed into a tight ball.

Josh gave her a look, which she assumed meant he was the boss. "You're taking the cell phone and you're going to keep it on you at all times. On top of that, I'm going to talk to Lake about a bodyguard for you."

Caroline blustered, "You will not! I don't want some random guy following me around. I can take care of myself."

"Yeah, right." He tapped the screen on his phone before putting it to his ear. "Lake? Yeah, got a problem here. I punched a paparazzo in Harrods. I'm worried about Caroline. Can you sort out someone to watch over her?" There was silence for a moment as Caroline fumed. "Great. We're on the same page, then. See you when we get there." He hung up and gave her a smug smile.

"I can't believe you did that." Caroline wanted to punch the man. "You are so going to regret it."

The mood changed in the car. Suddenly the tension and anger was gone. Josh's eyes sparkled at her. He was amused. Again. Well, too bloody bad. Caroline was furious.

"What you going to do, honey? Call off the wedding?" He grinned widely. "You never back down on your word. Remember? Plus, if you run off now I'll get my studio and the castle restoration will stop dead. Is that what you want?"

"I might be marrying you, Josh McInnes. But I don't have to make it pleasant and I don't have to be nice to you."

The infuriating man leaned forward and touched his nose to hers. "Bring it on, honey. Give me everything you've got."

Caroline made a growling sound in the back of her throat, wrenched herself out of his grip and slid as far away from him on the seat as she could get. While she glared out at the passing streets, Josh's deep chuckle filled the car.

That was the last time she'd spoken to him. Even when he'd walked her home. She'd just opened the door, walked inside and slammed it in his face. She'd heard him laughing on the other side before she'd stalked to the kitchen. And now her answer machine was blinking with messages. Messages she planned to ignore for the first time in her life.

Caroline took her tea into the living room and threw herself into the threadbare sofa. She covered her face with her hands. Her life was unravelling. Her sister was upset. Josh was interfering with everything and bossing her around—when no one bossed her around. Ever. Celebrities were coming to town and she had no idea how to behave around them, let alone what to wear when she met them. Beth had quit her job, leaving Caroline in the lurch. The paparazzi were circling like buzzards. The town was on lockdown. The domino boys were playing soldier. And there were stolen sex books on her desk.

She grabbed a cushion from beside her and screamed loudly into it.

CHAPTER 15

At two o'clock in the morning, Caroline woke to loud music. For a minute she wasn't sure where the noise was coming from. She didn't have the sort of neighbours who threw wild parties. She had neighbours who misplaced their hearing aids and called the fire brigade to help find them.

As the fog from her brain cleared, she realised that the music was coming from outside. Close outside. Her front yard, to be exact. Caroline threw back the curtains and peered out. What the heck? Josh was standing in the middle of her tiny lawn with a stereo at his feet. He waved happily when he saw her, and then threw his arms wide. Before she could blink, he was belting out "Sweet Caroline."

Caroline stepped back from the window in shock. She rubbed her eyes. If this was a dream, it was a blooming noisy one. She pulled the curtain back again. Nope. No dream. Josh was still there. Singing. Loudly. She pushed up the old sash window and leaned out. He was mid-song now, and lights were coming on along the street. Morag McKay stood on her doorstep in pink terry robe and hairnet. You didn't need Superman's eyesight to know she had a scowl on her face.

Caroline pointed at Josh. "Stop that right now."

He grinned. Caroline froze. That wasn't a Josh grin. She stared at him in horror. It was Josh, but it wasn't Josh. Her poor sleep-deprived brain couldn't quite understand what she was seeing. He was wearing a suit, a black one with pristine white shirt and black shoelace tie. Caroline had only known him a week, but in that time she'd never seen him in anything but cartoon T-shirts. He kept singing.

"Be quiet. If this is your idea of apologising, it isn't working. I'm still mad at you."

He rocked back on his heels, did a little twirl and carried on singing.

Caroline slammed the window shut. Stormed through her bedroom and barrelled down the stairs, without stopping for a robe or shoes. She threw open her front door wearing only her pyjamas.

"Josh." She stopped dead.

That wasn't Josh. He looked a lot like him. He had the moves. He even sounded like him. But he wasn't Josh. This guy was shorter, less muscled, and his features weren't right. Close enough to mistake in the dark, but anyone who knew Josh would know this man wasn't him. Whoever it was grinned widely at her, then winked. Caroline stepped back into the house, closed the door, locked it tight and called the police.

"THIS IS a new one even for me," Officer Donaldson told her. "Thought I saw everything during my time in London, but I never came across a woman with her own personal tribute band."

Caroline pursed her lips. "He isn't my tribute band. He isn't pretending to be Caroline. He's out there pretending he's Josh. In the middle of the night. Waking up the street."

Officer Donaldson's eyes crinkled with amusement. "I know that, Caroline. I'm taking him back to the station. Do you want me to charge him with trespassing and disturbing the peace?"

Caroline chewed her lip. In her normal run-of-the-mill existence, there had never been a reason to decide whether a singing stranger should be charged by the police. "How about a warning?"

Donaldson nodded. "He seems harmless enough. Maybe a bit overenthusiastic about the wedding, though."

Caroline toed the carpet with her bare foot, vaguely wondering if she should start painting her toenails now that there was a man in her life. Her back snapped straight. A man she was mad at. A man she wasn't talking to. That sort of man didn't get painted toenails.

Donaldson smiled at her. "He came all the way here from America as soon as he heard about the wedding. Keeps telling me he's Josh's biggest fan."

"That's what Kathy Bates said right before she chopped off James Caan's foot in *Misery*."

"She didn't chop off his foot in the movie, she smashed it. You're thinking about the book, that's where her character chopped off the guy's foot."

Caroline glared at him. Really? That was relevant how? He was totally missing the point.

"Okay," Donaldson said, as he ran a hand through his short black hair, making it stand on end. He didn't seem to care. Someone said something through the radio that was strapped to the shoulder of his blue uniform. "This thing is going to get crazier before it settles down. Your wedding is attracting a lot of attention. I know you think you have the town locked down tight, what with the domino boys manning barely legal barriers that I'm turning a blind eye to, but the crazies are still going to slip through."

Caroline didn't say anything. What could she say? Her life had become entertainment for everyone she knew.

The police officer sighed. "I'll talk to Josh. See if we can sort out some security for you. Keep the nutters away until after the wedding."

"No!" Caroline took a step towards him. "He already arranged something with Lake and I told him I don't want it."

Donaldson put his hands on his lean hips and looked down at her. Not quite as tall as Josh, but not far off. He had the whole police demeanour thing going for him, so it was quite intimidating. Caroline rallied all of her skills in dealing with difficult people. "This is my business, not Josh's. You don't need to talk to him."

Officer Donaldson studied her for a moment. "Caroline, if you were my fiancée I'd be seriously cheesed off if someone was harassing you and I didn't find out."

"No one was harassing me. It's just an enthusiastic fan singing in my garden."

"The garden of a woman alone. In the middle of the night."

Caroline swallowed hard. "I don't want to tell Josh."

He leaned in towards her. "Why?"

She bit her lip.

"Caroline." His tone said he was running out of patience.

"Fine." She folded her arms and stuck her nose in the air. "Because I'm not talking to him. I don't want him to know because I don't plan to talk to him, or deal with him, until I walk down the aisle. And even then, the only words I plan to say are 'I do.' Then I may never talk to him again."

Donaldson fought a grin as Caroline surged on, her anger winning over her normally icy demeanour.

"He's annoying. He's arrogant. He's bossy. He doesn't listen to a word I say. He keeps butting in on things that are none of his business. He does what he wants when he wants

—without listening to what I tell him. In fact, I'm pretty sure he doesn't listen to me at all. He certainly doesn't do what he's told, and I've had enough. So I don't want you to tell him. Do you hear me, Officer Donaldson?"

She pointed at him then realised she was pointing. Caroline never pointed at people. It was rude. She clasped her hands together tightly but kept up the glare. Damn man was almost as annoying as Josh.

"Yeah, I hear you. You don't want me to tell him because you're giving him the silent treatment?"

She straightened her shoulders, and for the first time in her life had to work at being intimidating. "No. I'm explaining the dynamics of our arrangement. He is *not* in charge."

She didn't say that she was in charge. As far as she was concerned, that went without saying.

The police officer threw back his head and laughed. "Fine, Caroline. I'll let you handle this the way you want."

She nodded. About time.

He went out the door, shaking his head while chuckling. "This should be fun," she heard him say before the door shut behind him.

CHAPTER 16

Josh balanced carefully on the planks that were now his hall floor as he made his way to the kitchen for breakfast. It was quiet for a change. Usually the noise was overwhelming. It didn't sound like a renovation. It sounded like a demolition. Every day the castle looked worse than the day before. There were gaps in the walls, holes in the floors and dust everywhere. But it was the noise more than anything else that was getting to him. He couldn't think. Couldn't work. And couldn't get a minute to himself.

He pushed open the kitchen door and everything got worse. His mum, complete with new hairstyle and clothes, was making coffee for the workmen. There were four of them standing at the counter, each scoffing a freshly baked muffin. His mother was beaming as she fussed over the men. Josh had to blink twice to get his head around it. He hadn't seen her like that since he was in high school. Back then Josh's house was the social hub of the neighbourhood, and his mum was the centre.

But it wasn't the fact she was playing hostess to the men who were destroying his home, and his patience—it was the fact his father was hunched over at the dining room table watching her do it. And if the look on his face said anything, it was that he didn't like it one bit.

"Coffee, darling?" his mum called to Josh.

"Sure." He sauntered to the counter.

He heard his dad grunt behind him. A nonverbal comment on Josh taking his mother's side. His mother pointedly ignored his dad, and the grunt.

"You've got to have one of these muffin things." The foreman waved a muffin at him. "As far as I can tell, they're a cross between a scone and a fairy cake."

"You telling me you've never had a muffin?" One of the younger guys looked like he'd just heard Santa wasn't real.

"We don't do fancy stuff in our house. Unless the missus makes it, or gets it from Morag, we don't eat it."

"Muffins aren't fancy. You can get them in the supermarket."

The other three men looked at the young apprentice pointedly. His whole head went red. His wide eyes shot to Josh's mother. "Except your muffins, Mrs. McInnes. These are really fancy."

His mum took pity on the boy and offered him another. He wasn't too embarrassed to take one.

She smiled at Josh. "Why don't you sit down and I'll get you some breakfast?"

He shook his head. "Had some when I got back from running this morning. Coffee is good enough."

"Running?" one of the men said. His tone made it clear that Josh may as well have said ballet dancing.

"Yeah." Josh sipped his coffee.

"Why the hell do you do that, boy?" the foreman asked.

Josh tried not to laugh, but he knew he couldn't stop his face from twitching. "Keep in shape."

They all looked at him like he was mad.

"If you want to get fit take up a proper sport—rugby or football. Something men play," the foreman said. "Only the women run around here, in their wee girly outfits. Please tell me you don't wear a girly outfit."

Josh almost choked on his coffee. "No, no girly outfit."

"To be fair," one of the other men chimed in, "the women only run because Lake runs and they like following him."

"That's true." They all nodded in agreement.

"And Lake is allowed to run. He's ex-SAS. He couldn't be girly even if he tried," the foreman pointed out—at the same time implying that Josh wasn't man enough to stop from being girly.

Josh looked up to see his mother grinning at him with a twinkle in her eye. He grinned back before he went over to join his dad.

"Look at her." His dad sounded more like a growling lion than a man. "Flirting with all the workmen."

"She isn't flirting, she's being sociable. It's how she is."

"Ha! She hasn't been social for years. Why start now?"

"What do you mean? Mom's always been the centre of a crowd."

"Boy, that was before you went to college. Things calmed down when you weren't trailing that harem of girls everywhere you went."

"What about her own friends? The old crowd."

His dad looked at him like he was an idiot. "It's a long way to travel from Atlantic City to Fort Lauderdale just for a barbecue."

Josh sipped his coffee while he watched his mum. She was in her element, fussing over the men. "You two never joined any groups in Florida?" He suspected he already knew the answer.

"Not my thing."

"No, but it's Mom's thing." Josh put his mug on the table

in front of him and watched his dad. His face was twisted into a disapproving look, but his eyes were hurting. "Maybe that's your problem right there? Maybe Mom's been bored?"

His dad's eyes turned hard. "Are you saying I bore my wife?"

Josh cocked an eyebrow at him. They stared at each other for a minute. "She's social. You aren't. Where's the compromise?"

"I compromise." His father shifted uncomfortably in his seat. "I don't stop her going out."

Josh couldn't believe his ears. The man was a bigger idiot than he thought. "That's it? That's your compromise? You really don't have a clue about women, do you?"

His father sat back in his seat and folded his arms. "More than you, boy. At least I hooked mine the old-fashioned way."

"By getting her pregnant?" As soon as the words were out of his mouth, he regretted them.

His father's face turned purple. "If you weren't my son, we'd be outside right now."

Josh held up his hands in a peace-making gesture. "Women need finesse. They need romance. They need conversation. And Mom needs a social life. Not just sitting in silence with you all the time. Take her out for a nice dinner. Let her meet people. Give her some romance."

His father leaned forward. "Is that right?" His voice was a hiss. "Well, if women need romance so bloody bad, how come you're marrying one that you have an *agreement* with?"

"That's different." Josh folded his arms and frowned.

His dad sat back, triumphant. "You don't have a bloody clue either."

They glared at each other.

"Do you two want a muffin?" his mother called over to them.

From the look in her eye, she hadn't missed a thing that had gone on between them.

"I'm good," Josh told her.

"If the muffins come with flirting, then I'll have to decline," his father said.

And for the first time ever, Josh badly wanted to knock some sense into the man.

The four workmen mumbled something then fled the room. His mother folded her arms over her new pink blouse. "Did I hear you right, Andrew McInnes? Did you accuse me of flirting with those men?"

His father scowled at her. "You heard me."

"You are an idiot." His mother read Josh's mind as she slapped her palms on the counter in front of her.

"I'm just calling it how I see it." His father sounded pompous.

Josh tried to shuffle away from him in the hope that he wouldn't be tainted by association. His mother kept glaring at his father, and then she nodded as though deciding on something.

"Josh." She turned towards him. "We weren't going to tell you this until after the wedding, but your father and I are getting a divorce."

Before Josh could speak, his dad growled. "No, we're not."

His mum swung back to him. "Yes we are. I filed before we left."

The air in the room became charged. "You what?"

"We talked about this. We agreed. I filed."

"We didn't talk about it."

"I asked you if that was what you wanted. You didn't say anything. So I took that as a yes."

His father jumped to his feet. "You took that as a yes?"

"Calm down," Josh said to both of them. It was pointless.

"Well." His mother was so furious, Josh half expected to

see lightning bolts coming off her head. "As I keep telling you. I can't read your mind. If you don't talk, I have no idea what you think. Or what you want."

His father thudded a fist on the table in front of him. "I don't want a bloody divorce."

"Tough!"

Josh stood up and put up his hands between them. "Maybe we should all take a minute to calm down?"

"I am calm," his dad bellowed.

"Yeah, I can see that," Josh told him.

"See"—his mother pointed in the direction of his father —"this is exactly what I'm talking about. I tell you what I want and you ignore me. I ask what you want and I get silence. Give me one good reason why I should stay with you?"

"Because you made a vow, woman. How about that for a reason?"

"I vowed to stick with Andrew McInnes. The man who made me happy. Who made me laugh. Who talked to me and spent time with me and did things with me. That man I would stay with. Unfortunately, he's long gone and I don't have a clue who *you* are."

She stormed around the counter and headed for the door.

"Come back here," his father snapped. "We're not done."

"As I keep telling you," his mother said calmly, "I am." Then she was gone.

Josh watched his father as the anger waned. His eyes flicked between panic and pain. "What the hell am I supposed to do with that?"

Josh took a deep breath. "How about you give her some of the stuff back that she loved when she made those vows? Maybe that's a good place to start?"

All the fight went out of him. He slumped to the table. "I don't know what happened. Things used to be good."

Josh placed a reassuring hand on his dad's shoulder. "You want her back, don't you?"

The depth of pain in his father's eyes made Josh stagger. "She's the love of my life."

Josh patted his dad on the back. "Maybe she needs to feel like it?"

He wasn't sure his dad heard. The man pulled his cold cup of coffee towards him and stared into it. Josh ran a hand over his face as the drilling started. It felt like it was happening in his head. Enough was enough. It was time to deal with Caroline and her "restoration" plans.

He dug his phone out of his back pocket as he walked across the kitchen and scrolled to Caroline's cell number. He got voicemail. He gritted his teeth. The whir of the circular saw started as he pushed through the kitchen door. He found the community centre number and hit that.

"Community centre, what do you want?" barked the voice in his ear.

"Betty?" Josh stepped out into the hall.

The place actually looked worse than it had done half an hour earlier.

"Is that you, Yank? Caroline's got me manning the damn phone."

"Put her on, will you? I need a word."

Josh waved his hand in front of him to cut through the plaster dust.

"No," Betty said.

Josh stilled. "Stop screwing around, put Caroline on the phone."

"She doesn't want to talk to you. And it's my job to protect her from your stupidity."

"Did she say that?"

There was a cackle in his ear. "In as many words. She doesn't want to talk to you, or see you, until the wedding."

Josh frowned at the phone. "Did she say why?"

"No. She's got a bug up her bum about something, but she isn't sharing what."

"I'm coming over," Josh told her.

"You can come if you like, but she isn't here."

Josh stopped with his hand on the door to his office-slash-TV-room. "Where is she?"

"She said she wasn't telling me, because she knew you'd ask."

Josh growled and ended the call. Cutting off Betty's latest bout of hysterical laughter. He entered his office.

"Josh," the foreman shouted, "don't go in there—"

Josh stepped into the room as he turned to the old man—and the floor disappeared beneath him.

He felt water hit his knees as his feet sank into mud. The floorboards were now chest level. Four men skidded to a halt beside him.

"I tried to warn you, son. We have a burst pipe. Had to rip up the floor."

"I can see that. Seeing as I'm eye level with your knees. Now are you going to help me get out of here?"

"Aye." The foreman started to chuckle. "In a wee minute."

And then the four of them bent double laughing as Josh waited to be dug out of his hole.

"JOSH PHONED," Betty said as Caroline swept into the centre. "He isn't happy. I like this bodyguard gig. It's entertaining."

Caroline pursed her lips. "You are not my bodyguard."

"Whatever you say, lassie." Betty dismissed her with a smirk.

"What have you gone and done now?" Archie asked Caroline.

For some reason the domino boys had decided to hole up in Caroline's office to play their game.

"Why are you lot here?" She put her old brown briefcase on the desk.

Archie cocked his head at Betty. "You left her answering the phones. We're damage control."

"Who's manning the barricades?" There was a sentence Caroline never thought she'd say.

"The Knit Or Die women."

Caroline wasn't sure if that was good news or bad. She rubbed her temples.

"They took that life-sized cutout of Lake Benson with them so they would be more intimidating," Brian said.

Bad, Caroline decided. Definitely bad news.

"Never mind all that." Betty waved her arms for attention. "What's going on with Josh? Why aren't you talking to him?"

Caroline suddenly had the complete attention of everyone in the room. "Time for you lot to get back to the blue room. I need my office."

"Answer the question, lass," Archie said.

She stared him down. "It's none of your business."

"Same way keeping photographers away from your wedding is none of our business and acting like your secretary is none of our business?"

Caroline scowled at him. The man fought dirty. "You were the ones that blackmailed your way into helping with the wedding. Congratulations. You're helping with the wedding."

"What's going on with you and Josh?" Archie wasn't to be dissuaded.

"Fine." Caroline shooed Betty out of her chair. "If you must know, Josh and I are having some relationship dynamic difficulties and I'm making a few things clear."

The men looked blank. Betty gave Caroline an evil smile. "She means he isn't doing what he's told," Betty translated.

Caroline gave them her most haughty glare. "He's bossing me around. And I don't like it."

Suddenly all the faces had grins. Knowing grins.

"It was bound to happen," Archie said. "I just never thought it'd be in my lifetime."

Caroline ignored them as she sorted the mess Betty had made of her desk.

"It bodes well for the rest of us to know there's one who can do it," Brian said with a nod.

Caroline frowned at them. "Do what?"

They started to laugh.

"What?" Caroline was really getting annoyed.

"Caroline, love," Archie said. "Stand up to you. That's what. You've met someone you can't order around. It's priceless."

"That's it." She pointed at the door. "Thank you for helping, but now it's time to leave."

The men left, still laughing as they went.

"And for your information," she told them as they walked to the blue room, "this isn't about who's in charge, it's about making it clear to Josh that he can't tell me what to do. And if he tries, there will be consequences."

"Yep," Archie said on a grin. "I'm betting there will be consequences, all right."

Caroline shut the door on his delighted face. Men. No matter the age, they were all annoying. Including the vicar. She'd just spent an hour going over what she wanted for the wedding because he wouldn't deal with the wedding planner. She looked at the clock. An hour until she was through for the day, and first thing on her list was placing an ad for a new assistant.

Betty wandered back into Caroline's office, armed with a cup of tea and a mince pie.

"What are you doing back here?"

Betty pointed at Caroline. "Body." She pointed at herself. "Guard."

Caroline ground her teeth. Hard. Trying to ignore her eighty-six-year-old bodyguard, she reached for the phone and called the local paper. The wedding might be taking over her life, but she still had to find a replacement for Beth.

CHAPTER 17

After a long day dodging her geriatric bodyguard, Caroline was sitting down to a late dinner when the doorbell rang. With a heavy sigh, she opened the door and instantly regretted it. Josh was standing on her doorstep. His arms were folded over his Hong Kong Phooey T-shirt, and he was amused. Determined but amused.

"I'm not talking to you." Caroline started to close the door.

"Good." Josh smacked a hand on the door, stopping it mid-swing. "In that case, you can listen."

Caroline pushed the door. Josh raised an eyebrow at her that said, *Really, you think you're stronger?* She put her weight behind the door. With a shake of his head, he bent over, picked up a gym bag at his feet and walked past her into the house. Caroline slammed the door and followed him into the kitchen.

"What are you doing? I don't want you here. I'm not talking to you."

"I told you, that's fine. I'll talk." He leaned against the

counter at the sink—as usual, taking up too much room in her house. "I'm moving in."

Time stopped. There was a rushing noise in her ears—she was pretty sure it was the sound of steam trying to get out of her head. "You're what?"

"Moving in. Here. With you."

"No you are not."

He smiled at her, reached over and picked a piece of garlic bread from her plate. He ate it slowly.

"Yes," he said. "I am. The castle is a bombsite. My parents are waging World War III in what's left of it. The noise is driving me demented. So I'm moving in here. Where it will be quiet, because you're not talking."

Caroline folded her arms and tapped her toe on the linoleum. "Get a room at the pub."

"No."

"You're not staying here."

"Yes. I am. What are you going to do about it? Throw me out?"

A frustrated growl started in the pit of Caroline's stomach and worked its way up through her clenched teeth. "You have no idea who you're dealing with."

He grinned widely. "Neither do you, baby."

Frustrating. Annoying. Infuriating. Pig-headed man. She clenched her fists then reached for the phone on the wall beside the door. She dialled the police station. Josh casually pulled out a chair at her kitchen table and proceeded to eat his way through her vegetable lasagne. Caroline fought the urge to kick him. Hard.

"Invertary police station," the woman said.

"Agnes, it's Caroline Patterson. I need to speak to Officer Donaldson."

Josh quirked an eyebrow at her. She smiled thinly.

"Is this about that crazy singer the other night?" Agnes said.

"No, it's about a different one. Can you put Officer Donaldson on the line, please?"

"No problem, honey."

There was silence while Josh watched her as he casually ate her meal. He thought he was untouchable. She'd see about that.

"Caroline, what can I do for you?" the officer said.

"Josh McInnes is in my house and I want him to leave. Could you come over and escort him out, please?" She gave Josh her "so there" look. He didn't seem impressed.

"I'm a bit confused, Caroline," Donaldson said. "Do you mean the real Josh?"

"Yes, the real Josh." Honestly, she wondered if there was an IQ test for becoming a police officer. There should be.

"You want me to escort your fiancé off the premises?"

"Yes."

"Has he hurt you in any way?"

"Of course not," Caroline told him.

"Threatened you?"

"No."

"Damaged your property, stolen something, made you feel afraid in any way?"

"No."

"They why do you want me to make him leave?"

"Because…" Caroline knew her tone said she thought she was dealing with an idiot, but she was too annoyed to do anything about it. "He's here with a bag telling me that he's moving in, and I told him he isn't. He's not listening and I want him gone."

There was a heavy sigh. "Is the wedding off? Are you and Josh finished?"

"No. I just don't want the man in my house. I'm not talking to him."

There was silence. Josh had finished off her meal and was now stretched back in his chair, grinning at her. Like the idiot he was.

"Caroline." Donaldson's tone had a hint of suffering to it. "I can't make your fiancé leave your house unless there's a legal reason to do so. Turfing him out because you're giving him the silent treatment doesn't cut it."

"But I don't want him here. And he's definitely not spending the night."

There was a heavy sigh. "Put Josh on the phone."

With a smug smile, Caroline handed the phone to Josh.

"Thanks, baby."

His attitude made her want to scream. She fought the urge.

"Yeah?" he said into the phone, then there was silence. His eyes hit her. Then he was laughing. Hard. "My place is a pit," he told Officer Donaldson. "She's got a crew ripping up floors and tearing down walls." More silence. "Yeah." He looked at Caroline, something hot flashing in his eyes. "She's a handful, all right."

"That's it," Caroline snapped. "Give me that phone."

Josh handed it over with a lazy smile.

"Why aren't you telling him to go?" she demanded as soon as the phone was at her ear.

"Caroline, this is a domestic situation. You need to sort it out between the both of you. You don't need the police. My advice is that you stop giving the guy the cold shoulder and talk to him. Maybe you can deal with this before it's time for bed. In the meantime, I have proper police work to do. If he gets out of hand, or does anything threatening, give me a call. But seriously, being in a huff with your boyfriend is not a reason to call the cops."

"He's not my boyfriend." No. He was the thorn in her side.

"Sort it out," was all Donaldson said before the line went dead.

Caroline glared at Josh.

"Thanks for dinner." He stretched lazily. "It was great."

Caroline made a little strangled noise. "You can't stay here."

"I *am* staying here."

"I don't want you here."

"I'm picking up on that."

"You can't stay here if I don't want it."

He gave her a look that said differently.

They were at a standoff. Caroline honestly didn't know what to do. She had been sure that the police would have intervened and taken care of things. Maybe she should call Kirsty and get her to use her influence with Lake, then he could kick Josh out. Unfortunately, Lake was working with Josh. Traitor. There was nothing she could do. She was stuck with him.

"I'm still not talking to you. As far as I'm concerned, you're invisible."

His mouth twitched. "Want to tell me what I did to deserve the silent treatment?"

"Seriously? You don't know?"

He shook his head, amused. Caroline felt fury course through her. She counted off his transgressions on her fingers. "You ignored my wishes and organised a bodyguard for me. Which turns out to be Betty, so all that's doing is winding me up. You bossed me around. You didn't listen to me. You need a serious attitude adjustment."

Josh burst out laughing. He laughed so hard he had to wipe tears from his eyes. Caroline waited impatiently for him to calm down. "Great, now I know what I'm being punished for. Have at it. Let me know when you're done.

And Betty isn't your bodyguard. It's a guy called Gary. Betty is just hanging out with you because Lake wants her gone."

Caroline put her hands on her hips. First thing in the morning, she was going to pay a little visit to Lake Benson. In the meantime, she needed to sort out Josh's delusions.

"Telling me to have at it is not how this works. You're supposed to learn from your behaviour and change."

"Oh, I'm learning, all right." He grinned at her. "I'm learning that your control issues have control issues all of their own. We're going to be dealing with this for years. So have at it, baby. I'm sure it will make you feel better."

Caroline clenched her fists at her sides and stamped her foot like a toddler. She honestly couldn't remember the last time she was so angry. She couldn't even speak. After a minute or two trying to evaporate him with a glare, she turned on her bare feet and stomped up the stairs to her bedroom, slamming the door behind her.

JOSH GRINNED SLOWLY. It was like dealing with a teenager. He traipsed up the narrow staircase with its faded orange and cream striped wallpaper. At the top of the stairs were three doors. The middle one held a tiny bathroom. The one on the right was open, so he figured the closed door on the left was Caroline's room. He turned the handle. The door didn't budge. He shook it. Nothing.

"Caroline. Open up. Seriously, this has gone on long enough. Open the door."

There was no reply. Josh folded his arms and frowned at the door. "I want to talk."

He wanted to do a helluva lot more than talk, but he kept that to himself. Still no answer. "This is not the way to start a relationship." He gritted his teeth. "I'm going to knock down the door."

"Go ahead and try." Caroline's voice was muffled. "But I'm not taking you to the hospital when you break your shoulder."

"Open the damn door."

"No. I didn't ask you here. I don't want you here. This is exactly the problem I was talking about—you don't listen to me."

"You mean I don't follow orders?"

More silence.

Josh contemplated his options. Kick down the door, or sleep in the guest room. He looked around the postage-stamp-sized landing. There wasn't enough space to manoeuvre. She was probably right. He'd most likely bounce off the door. He thought about the noise he'd heard earlier. Had she barricaded herself in? He clenched his jaw.

"We'll deal with this in the morning," he told the door.

It was a warning. He hoped she heard it loud and clear. With tense movements, he turned to the guest room and flicked on the light. There were two small single beds made up with faded pink blankets. Equally faded pony wallpaper, a white wardrobe and dresser set and a box of well-used dolls made up the rest of the room. Josh stared at the tiny beds for a beat before picking one and lying on it. His legs hung over the end from his knees.

"You have got to be kidding me," he shouted.

Through the walls, he heard the muffled sound of Caroline's laughter.

Josh folded his arms and looked up at a poster of a horse someone had pinned to the ceiling. Caroline had backed him into a corner. He could do as she expected, which was pretty much obey her every wish. Or...

Josh grinned up at the horse. Yeah, he liked that second option a whole lot better.

CHAPTER 18

The first thing Josh did after he discovered that Caroline had snuck out the house before dawn was go shopping. He hit the Invertary high street like it was Rodeo Drive. He sorted out a new TV and satellite, paying extra to have it installed that afternoon. Then he bought a tool set from the guy at the hardware store, who made some sort of dig about singers knowing more about hair gel than hammers. The grocery store was next, where, for a price, he convinced them to deliver everything he needed later in the day. By the time lunch rolled around he was hungry, but satisfied. He'd managed to tick off all his chores and hadn't gotten accosted by a fan even once. In fact, to his delight, he discovered that no one in Invertary cared who he was. It was actually kind of cool.

As he pushed open the door to The Scottie Dog, he spotted Mitch sitting on a high stool at the long, dark wooden bar.

"Cold beer, not that warm stuff that comes from the tap. Proper ice-cold beer," he told Dougal as he slapped Mitch on the back.

"Only sissy foreigners drink their beer cold." Dougal handed over an ice-cold bottle of beer.

"Grab a table, we've got stuff to go over." Mitch folded his laptop.

"How are the wedding plans coming along?" Dougal boomed.

Josh wondered if the guy had any volume control whatsoever.

"I think it's going fine. I'm leaving it to Caroline and the wedding planner. As far as I'm concerned, my job is to turn up, not get drunk and say I do when asked."

Dougal nodded wisely. "Women's stuff."

Josh headed over to the booth Mitch had nabbed by the window. "What's up?" Josh put his beer on the table opposite Mitch.

Mitch looked tired; there were circles under his eyes. "I'm moving out of the castle. I got a room here. I can't stand the noise anymore."

"Join the club. I moved in with Caroline."

"Are you sure that's any more peaceful than the castle?"

"I'm working on it. What do you want to talk about?"

"The usual—the record company want a date for the next album. I want to know what studio to book. There's a bunch of memorabilia you need to sign off on. Some group in Norway wants to cover one of your singles. Some socialite wants to know if you'll play her birthday party—she has money to throw around and keeps upping it every time I tell her you don't do that sort of thing. We've had about a million requests for interviews. We're still one of the hot topics on E! News—they love the barricade, especially now it's being manned by a group of middle-aged women who knit and gossip. Oh, and a life-sized cutout of Lake Benson in his underpants. What else? Your accountant needs to talk to you. Stevie has a new song he wants you to hear, and *People* magazine want the rights to your wedding photos."

Josh took a slow swallow. "So not much, then?"

Mitch let out a frustrated chuckle. "The sooner we get out of Scotland and back to normal, the better."

"Caroline wants to live here permanently." Josh watched his friend's eyes bug wide. "She wants to keep working at the community centre."

Mitch looked at the ceiling. "You told her things are going to change, right? That being in the public eye can screw things up?"

"Yeah." He paused. "She said I'm not Prince William."

Mitch started to laugh. Josh turned to Dougal, who came over armed with menus. "Forgot to ask if you're hungry."

"Starving. What's good?"

Dougal stuck his nose in the air as if offended. "Everything."

Josh handed back the menu. "Surprise me, then. Just make sure it's a man-sized portion."

"Make that two," Mitch told him.

Dougal smiled as he bustled away. Josh turned to the window. They were sitting on the side of the pub that faced the loch. The rich blue water was perfectly still, while the hills on the other side of the loch seemed hazy through the warm afternoon sun. He took another drink. It wasn't LA, that was for sure, but Josh was beginning to think that was a good thing.

"I only intended to use the castle as a holiday home. But it's not so bad around here."

"No," Mitch agreed as he watched the loch. "It's not so bad."

As they stared quietly out into the distance, Josh caught sight of a familiar face and stilled. "Are you seeing what I see?"

"Yeah," Mitch said.

The two men pushed out of the booth.

"Back in a minute," Mitch called to Dougal. "Put the food on the table."

He nodded, clearly curious as to where they were going. Josh and Mitch jogged across the road towards the loch and the man in the suit.

"Josh!" The guy spread his arms wide and grinned. "I love it here, man. I'm going to add a kilt to my act." He paused. "To *our* act. You got to add a kilt, man."

Josh folded his arms tight. Out of the corner of his eye he could see Mitch scowl. "What are you doing here, Danny? You know you're not allowed within two hundred feet of me."

"I looked into it." Danny was clearly delighted at his brilliance. "Restraining orders are only valid locally. So don't worry, I'm not breaking the law. I'm okay."

Josh let out a sigh. Great. As long as his stalker was okay. "I'm not worried about you, Danny. We had a talk, remember? I told you to back off, to concentrate on your own life, but you didn't. That's why we have the restraining order. It's supposed to make you restrain yourself. You need to go home."

"I need to be here," Danny told him. "We're doing Scotland, man. We're getting married."

"No. *We're* not getting married. *I'm* getting married."

"Yeah, that's what I mean. But I need to soak up the new married Josh. Got to get the vibe right for my act."

"Danny." Josh could hear the tightness in Mitch's voice. "You don't need to get the vibe right. All you need to do is turn up wearing your suit and sing Josh's songs. That's all people expect from you."

Danny shook his head again. Josh briefly wondered if he

was overheating in a black wool suit in the middle of summer.

"You're wrong, Mr. Mitch," Danny said. "I have a reputation. I'm as close to the real thing as folk are gonna get. When I turn up they get the full Josh experience." He swung his head back to Josh. "Except for the goofy T-shirts. The general fanbase doesn't need to know about those." He seemed to think about it. "Although maybe I should get some too?"

Josh looked skyward as he searched deep for patience. "How did you get into town, anyway?"

Danny grinned widely. "I told the women at the checkpoint I was you. I sang 'Fly Me to the Moon' for them. Got a standing ovation."

Josh ground his teeth. "Were the press there?"

"Only a couple. Don't worry, man, I didn't sign any autographs this time. I did tell them that I was happy to be marrying Caroline. Said she was the best thing that had happened to me."

Josh clenched his fists. Tight. "Danny. We've been over this. You don't stand in for me with the press. You don't pretend to be me when you're not doing a gig. You don't follow me around—especially not halfway around the world."

The guy looked so crestfallen that Josh almost regretted being firm. Almost.

"I'm trying hard, man."

"You seeing that counsellor I set up for you?"

"I'm in Scotland, man, how am I supposed to do that?"

Josh counted to ten. "Before you came to Scotland?"

"Yeah." Danny grinned Josh's grin back at him. The one he'd once told Josh he'd spent four months in front of a mirror perfecting. "She says I'm fine. She liked it when I sang 'My Way' for her. Did it every session. Cool lady."

Josh gave Mitch a look and saw him nod slightly. As Josh turned back to his stalker, Mitch pulled his phone out of his back pocket.

"So, we adding a kilt to the act?" Danny said.

"No. There is no we. You need to leave Invertary."

"I can't leave. We're marrying Caroline. I like Caroline. She's pretty and smart. Got great legs. She looks like a fifties movie star. One of the girl-next-door ones, not the vamps."

Josh stilled. He felt, rather than saw, Mitch, who came back to stand close to his side.

"You've seen Caroline?" Josh's tone was a threat. Danny didn't hear it.

"Serenaded her the other night. She was sweet. Sang 'Sweet Caroline' until she called the cops." He leaned in towards Josh. "You picked good, man. We're going to like her."

Josh felt the muscle in his jaw twitch as Mitch's hand rested on his shoulder.

"Two minutes," Mitch said. "Cops on the way."

"So," Danny said, "what are we wearing to the wedding?"

Josh took a deep breath, counted to twenty this time and told himself not to punch his stalker. Well, not while the cops could catch him doing it.

CAROLINE WAS EXHAUSTED by the time she left work. Without Beth, she had to do twice the workload at the centre. The domino boys had helped out, getting the rooms cleared and ready for the people who booked them, putting away library books and even answering the phones, but it was still a lot of work to pack into a day. Not to mention the press had gotten wind of Caroline's place of work, and every second phone call was someone poking into her business. The last woman hadn't even said hello, she'd just launched right into asking

Caroline what lingerie she was taking on her honeymoon. In the end Caroline had put James on the phones. He'd forgotten his hearing aids again and spent ten minutes with each caller shouting, "Can you repeat that?" It cut down the messages by half.

Now it was almost four o'clock, and she'd ducked out of the centre an hour earlier than normal so she could get to the church for their weekly meeting with the vicar. Caroline charged into the church foyer and straight into Josh. He was leaning against the wall. His arms were folded and his ankles were crossed. He seemed perfectly relaxed, but there was nothing casual about the look in his eye. Without even thinking about it, Caroline took two steps back.

"Heard you met Danny Costanzo." He was intense. Josh didn't do intense. Did he?

"I have no idea what you're talking about."

"He was the guy singing for you in the middle of the night."

Caroline swallowed hard and took another step back. Maybe they should meet with the vicar another day? She eyed the door. Maybe she should run?

"When were you going to tell me? I had to hear it from the cop when he came to escort Danny out of town."

Caroline stopped retreating. "That was very wrong of him. He promised he wouldn't tell you."

Josh paused, and a muscle in his jaw pulsed. "He promised not to tell me?"

Caroline lifted her chin. "I handled the situation. There was no need for you to be informed."

Josh leaned away from the wall and prowled towards her, his usual lazy saunter gone. Caroline retreated and felt her back hit the wall behind her. He placed his hands on the wall either side of her head. She felt the heat from him throughout her body.

"Caroline." His voice was a husky whisper. "Any guy gets in your face in any way, you tell me. Am I clear?" Josh trailed a gentle finger across her jaw to her cheekbone. "Are you listening, baby?" He was so close she could feel the air from his words hit her mouth. Her very dry mouth. "You can call the cops, but you call me too. You *always* call me. We talked about this in London. There are some scary people out there that will try to get to me through you. I need to know you're safe."

Caroline blinked hard. She fought to clear her mind as her body registered the hard length of him. "It wasn't a big deal. I wasn't afraid or anything. I think you're overreacting."

He pressed in against her. She felt his breath against her ear. "You *always* call me."

"But..." She wasn't even sure what else she was going to say.

"Always, Caroline. Am I clear?"

She didn't trust herself to speak. Instead, she nodded. It was a mistake. Her cheek brushed against his, and she stilled. Josh's right hand worked its way into her hair at the base of her head. His touch was gentle, but firm. Caroline stood frozen. She hadn't seen Josh like this before. Sure, she'd gotten a glimpse when they were in Harrods. She knew he must be formidable to make it so far in his profession, but usually she only saw the laid-back side of him that laughed at the world. This Josh was something else entirely. She wasn't sure what to make of him. Or the intensity that came off him in waves.

His other hand slowly curved around her waist. Sensations rushed through her body like the wildest storm, leaving devastation in its wake.

"Now, to other things. I'm done with the silent treatment. You need to get used to the fact that you can't command me. We're a team. Sometimes you'll tell me what to do and I'll be okay with that." His voice was a low, murmured hum at her ear. She felt her eyes close against her will. "And sometimes I'll tell you what to do and you'll be okay with that too." His lips brushed the sensitive skin below her ear. "Are you listening to me?"

Caroline could only make a grunting noise. The floor was undulating beneath her feet, and she needed to concentrate on remaining upright.

"Good. I'm glad I have your attention." She could have sworn she heard a smile in his voice. "You are not the boss of me. Of us. And neither am I. You don't need to be in charge. Or in control. We do this together. Got it?"

Caroline nodded.

"Good," he said.

His hand tightened in her hair. She wrapped her fist into his cotton shirt at his waist. Josh pushed back slightly to look down at her. She blinked up at him, feeling slightly dazed.

He smiled slowly. "I'm glad we understand each other."

Caroline licked her lips as her gaze shot between his mouth and his eyes. Josh took the hint and pressed his lips to hers. His kiss was slow and deep and thorough. It swept her away until there was nothing left for her but the smell of him, the taste of him, the feel of him. He nibbled her bottom lip, making her gasp into his mouth. Instantly his arms tightened, his head slanted and his tongue plundered. Caroline's hands found their way to his head and wound themselves in Josh's hair. It felt lush against her sensitive fingertips. Josh spread his legs so that they were either side of Caroline. Her whole body was pressed against him and still it wasn't close enough. At last Josh pulled away. Caroline moaned in protest. He ran his thumb over her bottom lip.

"Not here, baby," he rasped. "We've got to get through this counselling thing first."

It took her a minute to understand his words. Counselling? With the vicar? She peered behind Josh. They were in the church vestibule. No. They were *making out like horny teenagers in the church vestibule.*

Josh smiled against her lips. "Take a deep breath. Don't freak out. Lightning didn't hit. Remember, in a little while I'll be kissing you here officially anyway."

Caroline took a deep, steadying breath.

"Good girl." He nodded before taking her hand and pulling her into the church proper.

As Caroline's head wrestled control from her body, she realised they hadn't had a discussion like adults. No. He'd overwhelmed her with pheromones and sex appeal until she'd agreed with him.

She narrowed her eyes at him. Sneaky American.

Josh caught her look and winked at her.

Blast it. The man knew exactly what he was doing. Caroline straightened her back, promising herself that she wouldn't fall for his manipulation again. No matter how good it felt.

With a knowing smile, Josh led them in to meet the vicar.

CHAPTER 19

Helen came home from a day exploring the Scottish country-
side to find the castle peaceful for a change. Thankfully the
floor was now back where it should be, and she didn't have
to balance on planks to get to the kitchen. She glanced down
at her new dress and smiled. It was a yellow sundress with
huge blue cabbage flowers. The sales assistant had talked her
into matching blue ballet flats and a pale blue denim jacket,
of all things. She couldn't remember the last time she'd worn
clothes that were so bright and fresh. It made her feel
younger, which was always a good thing.

When she pushed open the door to the kitchen, she
stopped dead. The dining table was set for two, a small vase
of pink carnations sat in the middle of it, alongside a bottle
of red wine. There were even two pink candles waiting to
be lit.

"Damn it to hell," Andrew muttered from the stove.

Helen turned to see her husband struggling to drain
spaghetti, without losing it down the sink. Despite herself,
she smiled. "It's easier if you dump it into a colander."

He looked at her like she was speaking Japanese.

"A thing with lots of holes," she explained. "Lets the water out. Keeps the pasta in."

"Huh. I'll do that next time."

Helen shook her head to clear it. Did she hear the words *next time*? "What's all this, then?"

"What does it look like?" He was concentrating on dishing spaghetti onto plates. "We're having dinner."

"Together? The two of us?"

"Do you see anyone else here?"

Helen hung her handbag on the back of a chair and shrugged out of the denim jacket. She saw Andrew's lips purse and knew he was fighting the urge to criticise the jacket. She almost slipped it back on.

She felt awkward as she watched her husband in the kitchen. There was nothing she wanted to say to him. Nothing either of them could say. Not to mention, this was the first time she'd seen him cook in thirty-five years. It was as though she'd slipped into another dimension.

"Nice dress," Andrew muttered as he spooned out the spaghetti sauce.

Helen almost fainted on the spot. He noticed her dress? He gave her a compliment? Who was this man?

"Sit," Andrew ordered. So she sat.

He plonked a huge plate of spaghetti bolognaise in front of her. "I don't know what the big deal is about this cooking. Seems to me you've been complaining for years about nothing."

Ah, there he was, the Andrew McInnes she knew so well. "Cooking is great if you do it now and then. Try doing it three times a day for thirty-five years and see how it feels. Then add to that the fact you're supposed to read everyone else's minds and *know* what they want to eat, so that you don't have to listen to the whining and complaints when you dish up something they don't want. Yeah, it's a blast."

Andrew glanced at her from the corner of his eye. "I suppose if you put it like that, it's not much fun."

Helen dropped her fork with a clang. Andrew McInnes had heard something she said. Actually heard it and took it in. It was a red-letter day. Someone inform the Pope.

"So where did you go today?"

Nope, she was wrong. Now was the time to inform the Pope of a miracle. He'd asked a question about her day. She stared at him.

"Well?" he prompted, sounding his usual grumpy self.

"I drove to Fort William and had a look at Glencoe."

There was silence. Helen forked the pasta. The sauce wasn't bad, considering she was sure it came out of a jar. He was cooking—yeah, right. He'd boiled water, browned off some meat, added a jar of sauce and cooked some pasta. No wonder it wasn't that big of a deal to him.

"Is that where you got the dress?"

She stared at him. "Yeah."

"They have it in any other colours?"

She nodded.

"Maybe we should go back and get you the rest."

That was it. Helen put her fork down and turned to him. "Okay, what's going on?"

He tried to look innocent. "Nothing. We're having a nice dinner."

She folded her arms. "We never have a *nice* dinner. Usually we eat in silence or you watch sports while you eat and I sit beside you. What's with the conversation?"

"Can't a man take an interest in his wife?"

"I'm sure *he* can. But *you* never do."

He glared at her. "Eat your food."

Helen stared at him for a moment, before picking up her fork. She was uneasy. She wasn't sure whom she was having a meal with. They ate in silence for a while. Now *this* she was used to.

"Did you have a word with Josh about marrying that woman?" Andrew said.

"That woman's name is Caroline."

"He's making a fool of himself."

Helen felt her back tense. "He's thirty-five, he can do what he wants, how he wants to do it."

"But marrying a woman he doesn't even know? A woman who clearly doesn't have a clue about life? What use is that going to do him?"

Helen put her fork down carefully. "I like Caroline."

"She's not for Josh. What good is a librarian going to do him when he's wheeling and dealing in Hollywood? She's never even been out of the country. All she's going to do is slow him down."

Helen felt her hackles rise. "Slow him down in regards to what?"

"His career."

She leaned towards him. "I don't know if you've noticed this, but Josh's career is already where it was supposed to be. There's nowhere else to go. Sure, he can do the same thing better, or slightly differently, but he has nothing to prove anymore. Not to anyone. So how, exactly, is a lovely girl like Caroline slowing him down?"

"She doesn't even know how to dress. How is he going to take her on the red carpet? He'll be a laughing stock. Hell, he is already. Have you seen the news? She's got the old folk manning barricades at the edge of town. There's a group of women who sit and knit while they 'screen' people."

Helen stood up. "I know. I met them this morning. I invited them for coffee."

He scoffed at her, making it clear he thought she was a fool.

"That's it, Andrew McInnes, I've had enough. You're old and mean and bitter. You don't see Caroline for the woman she is, the woman who is lovely and kind and good for Josh. You don't see me for the woman I am either. This dinner isn't about spending time with your wife. It isn't about mending bridges. It's about you trying to salve me so that you can get things back the way you want them to be. Well I don't want them like that. I don't want *you* like that." She pointed a finger in his face. "You've got fifteen minutes to pack up and get out of the castle. Fifteen minutes and then I'm calling in people to turf you out. Because unlike you, I've been making friends here in Invertary. I haven't been spending my time alone and bitter and miserable. So pack up and get out. I've had enough of you."

She spun on her heels and walked towards the door. Then she had another thought and turned back to him.

"I don't know what happened to you. You used to be strong, daring, fun. I liked that man. I *loved* that man. If that man came back, he might have a chance. This one"—she pointed at him again—"isn't worth my time."

And then she stomped up the stairs to her bedroom.

CAROLINE AND JOSH waited in the meeting room for the vicar to stop faffing about and join them. A sharp elbow hit Josh's side, making him flinch. "What was that for?"

"You can't kiss your way out of trouble, Josh McInnes." Caroline's voice was low, even though they were the only two in the room.

"That's not what I've been told." He couldn't help but smirk. His lips had gotten him out of all sorts of trouble.

"So," the vicar said as he entered the room. "How did you two get on with the homework?"

Caroline was all business again. "We did well. We're

working our way through the book. I think we have about half answered now. Right?"

She turned to Josh, who couldn't begin to express how much he didn't care about the homework. "Right." Even he could hear it lacked conviction.

The vicar didn't seem convinced, but he limited his criticism to a glare. He smiled at Caroline. "Caroline and I had a chat this week about the ceremony. She's agreed to the common vows, although she refuses to vow to obey."

Josh burst out laughing. "Sorry." He held up a finger, asking for a minute. "That's better. I'm fine now. It's passed. I'm serious. This is serious." He cleared his throat. "It would have been surprising if she *had* vowed to obey."

Caroline glowered at him. "No woman vows to obey these days."

Josh patted her knee. "Especially you, baby. I'm pretty sure you're genetically incapable."

She gave him the evil eye. "Do you *want* me to vow to obey?"

He tried to swallow the laughter that bubbled up as he held up his hand in surrender. "I want you to vow what you're happy with and then stick with it."

"That doesn't answer the question."

"No." Josh was struggling to keep it together. "No, I don't want you to vow to obey."

She stuck her little nose in the air, pleased that he'd clearly come to the correct conclusion. Josh started to laugh again as his stomach muscles began to cramp.

"Don't mind him," she told the vicar. "He's easily amused."

The vicar studied them for a moment. "So, when do you two want to start a family?"

"Straight away," Josh said as Caroline said, "In a year or so."

They looked at each other as the vicar patted his belly, obviously pleased with himself.

"You want to try for a family straight off?" Caroline seemed terrified at the thought.

"I'm not getting any younger." Josh wanted to add *and neither are you*, but thought better of it.

"You're only thirty-five; you have years ahead of you to make babies." She blushed. "I mean have children. I thought we'd spend some time getting to know each other first before we added children to the mix. Men don't have a deadline—there's no hurry for you."

Josh inclined his head and gave her a searing look through his lashes. She bit her bottom lip as she watched him. He hoped her thoughts had gone in the same direction his had gone—south. Very south. Straight to the baby-making part of this discussion. He eyed the curve of her hips and wondered how fast he could get her out of her clothes.

She nudged him. "Are you listening to me?"

He ran his palm down her thigh. It was encased in another Teflon-coated grey skirt, but it still felt sexy as hell, especially when his touch made her wriggle in her seat. "How about we start trying in six months?"

Her eyes went wide. "I can do six months."

The vicar cleared his throat to get their attention. "Have you decided where you're living yet?"

Caroline looked up at Josh. Her eyes were softer, less guarded than usual. The way they were when he was kissing her. It took his breath away. He made up his mind on the spot. "We're going to live in the castle."

Her face lit up. "Really? I thought we had to live in LA?"

"We can travel." He shrugged like it was nothing, but seeing the look on her face made him want to concede to everything. To give her everything, just so he could see that look every day.

"Of course. I keep forgetting you're rich. You can afford to travel back and forth."

Josh felt that statement sear through his chest. After all the women he'd known who had only seen his money, the fact Caroline saw everything except it, was a miracle. "*We* can afford to travel, baby," he reminded her.

She smiled up at him again. The kind of smile that made a man want to beat his chest and roar.

"Okay." The vicar stood. "This is getting a little nauseating. I think we're done with the counselling. I've got better things to do with my time. You two are free to go. See you at the wedding." He left the room, banging the door shut behind him.

They stared after him. Caroline reached for Josh's hand. Josh warmed as their fingers entwined. Her eyes were still on the door the preacher had disappeared through, and Josh wondered if she was even aware she was touching him. "Do you think that means we passed?"

Josh really couldn't care less. He winked at Caroline. "Want to practice more kissing for the big day?"

Caroline gave him a playful smack on his chest with the back of her hand. As she left the room, she stopped to look over her shoulder at him. "Maybe we could practice some more at my house." Her voice was a sexy rasp he hadn't heard before.

She batted her eyelashes at him as a blush crept up her cheeks. She was beautiful.

"Anything you say, Caroline." Josh reached for her hand. "You're the boss."

THEY WALKED HOME in the warm evening air, with the sun low in the sky. It made the whitewashed houses of Invertary gleam golden. Josh draped his arm over her shoulders,

189

and Caroline had no choice but to wrap hers around his waist. He snuggled her into his side as they walked down the hill towards her house, and she was overcome with the notion that she'd never fit anywhere so perfectly. As they walked, Josh told her tales from his music career. They turned into Muir Street, and Caroline was laughing at the story of him falling off the stage in Italy when Josh sucked in a breath.

"You have got to be kidding me. Just when I've sorted access to the bedroom."

Caroline frowned. Access to the bedroom? She followed his gaze and saw Josh's father sitting on her front stoop, and her stomach sank. Great. Josh dropped his arm from her shoulder, and she felt unreasonably cold. Ignoring the shivers, she straightened her back and prepared for the worst.

"There's no room at the inn," Josh's father said.

Josh looked around them.

Caroline followed his gaze. "What are you doing, Josh?"

"Looking for a pregnant woman and a donkey."

"That's not funny," his father said.

"Neither is you turning up on Caroline's doorstep."

"I need a place to stay. The pub is full, and all the B&Bs—the whole three of them—have guests coming in. Guests that want to ogle your farce of a wedding."

Josh folded his arms and glared down at his father. "Yep, that's exactly the right thing to say to get us to take you in."

"Helen threw me out. It's only for a night or two."

"Don't ask me." Josh cocked a thumb at Caroline. "Ask Caroline. It's her house."

Brilliant. Now he'd offloaded it on her. She bugged her eyes out at him in reproach. Then she looked back to his father. He was still as unflinching and cantankerous as he'd been when she'd first met him. Only this time there was pain in his eyes. The man was hurting.

"Of course Josh's father is welcome to stay." She hoped she sounded convinced, because she definitely didn't feel it.

Josh sighed beside her. When she looked up at him, his lips thinned and his eyebrow went up. She raised her palms in a "what could I do?" gesture. He shook his head in disgust.

Enough of this. Caroline pushed past the two of them to open the door. Two hulking men, who barely fit in her home, followed her into the kitchen.

"Got any beer?" His father dumped a heavy bag on the floor.

"Uh, no," Caroline told him.

The man's expression made it clear that he considered her lack of beer to be another failure on her part.

"Yeah, we do." Josh opened the fridge. He caught Caroline's eye and gave her a small smile. "I'm going to be here a while, so I stocked up."

Caroline bit back a snarky comment. "The bathroom is upstairs, Andrew. There's another bed in the room Josh is staying in. You can take that."

"Don't bother." Josh finished taking a swallow of his beer. "The beds are so short, half your legs hang off. Better take the couch. It's next door."

Without a word, Andrew lifted his beer, and his bag, and strode to the living room. Oh yeah, having him around was going to be delightful. Caroline rushed up the stairs to grab some bedding from the closet in her bedroom. She stopped dead—her bedroom door was gone.

"Josh!"

His face appeared at the bottom of the stairs. "I was going to mention that." He gave her a cheeky smile.

"Where is my door?" It took all of her self-control not to start throwing things at his head.

"I removed it. That way you won't lock me out again."

She ground her teeth. "Bring back my door."

"We'll talk about it tomorrow, baby. Right now we have more important things to deal with." He cocked his head towards the living room and his father.

"You're going to regret this," she promised.

"I thought I might," he mumbled as he headed back to his dad.

Caroline resisted the urge to kick the wall nearest her. What was she supposed to do without a bedroom door? There were two men in her house. Two men she hardly knew—even though she couldn't keep her hands off one of them—and she didn't even have privacy in her bedroom. She eyed the guest room. That had a door. Maybe she should sleep in there. That would serve Josh right. She looked back at her large, soft bed and let out an angry mewl. Her bedroom was the one place in the house where the décor reflected her. The one place she felt at peace. She'd be damned if she'd give it up for Josh. Let him sleep on the tiny beds. Door or no door, he wasn't getting her bedroom.

Fuming, Caroline grabbed some bedding and stomped back down the stairs. She found Andrew sitting in the middle of the sofa with a TV remote in his hand. His eyes glued to the spot above the fireplace. For a second Caroline was confused, then she turned to find a brand new flat-screen where a painting of a swan used to be.

Caroline pointed at the TV. "What's that?"

Josh was sprawled out in an armchair. His lips twitched as he lazily folded his arms. "It's a TV, Caroline."

She dumped the bedding on the couch and put her hands on her hips. "I know it's a TV. It's not *my* TV. What's it doing here? Where is my TV?"

"Sweetheart." Josh rose lazily and took a step towards her. "I know you liked your TV but it was older than my parents. It didn't even have ESPN. This one has HD, CNN and ESPN.

Plus, it hangs on the wall, so it frees up that little table for you to pile more books on."

Caroline felt her blood pressure rise. "Why are you spouting acronyms at me? How am I supposed to know what HDPSN is and why should I be excited about it? I didn't ask for this TV. I don't need it. I don't want it. I barely watch TV. Take it back."

Josh stepped into her space. He put a hand on either side of her neck. His thumbs caressed her jaw. He gently angled her face up to him. "I guessed from the state of your TV that you didn't watch it much. But I'm staying here right now. And a man needs access to football."

"Josh McInnes," Caroline said, "if you think—"

His lips covered hers. The kiss was sweet, tender and very, very sensual. Caroline felt the tension drain from her body with each touch of his lips.

"I'm sitting right here and I'm fighting the urge to vomit," his father said.

Josh moved away from her as he swept his thumb over her bottom lip. "Are we okay about the TV?"

Her brain was foggy. "Okay," Caroline whispered.

He smiled at her, kissed her on the nose and gently pushed her towards the door.

"Go get ready for bed. You're up early tomorrow."

Feeling slightly drugged, she nodded to the men and sped up the stairs. She was halfway through pulling on her favourite pink satin pyjamas when she realised that she'd followed Josh's orders without so much as blinking.

Her eyes narrowed. He was manipulating her. And using his magic lips to do it.

"So that's where I've been going wrong all these years," his father said as soon as Caroline disappeared. "I should have just kissed your mother to get her to do what I wanted."

Josh fixed him with a look. "It might have helped. Hell, anything might have helped."

He sat back down into one of the faded brown armchairs. A spring poked into his back. His father flicked channels, looking for a game to watch.

"What happened tonight?" Josh brought the beer bottle to his lips.

His father's eyes stayed on the screen. Josh had about given up on an answer when he spoke. "I made dinner for her and lit a couple of candles, thought it might help."

"And it didn't?"

His father cast him a sideways glance that made Josh steel himself for the stupidity to come. "It was going fine until the topic turned to you and your wedding."

"Ah." Josh nodded knowingly.

His father frowned. "I don't approve."

"No kidding," Josh mumbled.

"Nobody seems to care that I don't approve."

"That's because nobody does."

His father growled. "Don't I have a right to stop you from ruining your life?"

"No. You have the right to tell me you think I'm ruining my life. You exercised your right. Now you have the right to shut the hell up and let me get on with it."

"You're being a fool."

"The apple doesn't fall far from the tree."

His father glared at him. "This isn't about me and your mother."

"You're wrong, that's exactly what it's about—for you. The only problem you have to deal with is your marriage. I can handle my own life."

"Yeah, right!"

Josh ignored him. He leaned forward and put his elbows on his knees.

"What does Mom want?"

"I'll be damned if I know."

"You know. What does she want?"

There was a heavy sigh. His father's shoulders slumped, and he looked older than his sixty-seven years.

"She wants me to be the way I was when I met her."

"So, what's the problem?"

"The problem is that I'm not a young man. I've lived a life. I can't turn back the clock."

Josh stood. "Well, I suggest you find a way to convince Mom that you are the man she wants. Otherwise you're going to get that divorce whether you like it or not."

The answer was silence. With a shake of his head, Josh left him to mope, and climbed the stairs to bed.

CAROLINE LAY in the middle of her bed with the white lace fringed duvet pulled up around her neck. She was wearing her pyjamas, but she still felt naked. Vulnerable. And all because there was no door on her bedroom. She'd heard every single word Josh and his father had said. The house was small. Noise travelled. And now she could hear Josh coming up the stairs to bed.

She held her breath as he reached the landing, but instead of turning right into the guest room, he turned left into her room. For a moment she was stunned. Then she heard his shoes hit the floor.

"What are you doing?" Her voice sounded as panicked at she felt.

"Coming to bed."

She heard a zip and then jeans being pulled off. "Your bed is across the landing."

"Nope. It's in here with you. Those beds over there are made for midgets. This whole house is made for midgets. I've hit my head on the doorframes too many times to count, and the only way I can get my whole body wet in the shower is if I sit in the bath."

"You're not sleeping in here."

"Yes, I am. Your bed is big. Sure, it looks like it belongs to a fairy princess, but it's a great size."

She sat up straight. "You've seen my bed?"

"Baby, I took the door off the hinges. I've seen the whole room. I even tried out the bed. It's still a tight fit, but at least my feet don't hang off it."

"You were in my bed?"

From the dim light in the room she could see him pull his T-shirt over his head. "Have to say, I like the décor in here a whole lot better than the rest of the house. Didn't have you pinned for frills and flowers, but it suits you."

Caroline pointed at the door. "Go to the other room."

"No." He pulled back the duvet on the side of the bed nearest the door. "Move over."

"Fine!" She clambered out of bed. "You can have the bed. I'll sleep next door."

She stomped to the door, furious that the man was kicking her out of her own bedroom. A strong arm snaked around her waist, her feet left the floor and the next thing she knew she was on her back in the middle of the bed and Josh was climbing in beside her.

"Get out of my bed. I didn't ask you into it."

He pulled the duvet over them. "Actually, you did. You accepted my proposal."

"I told you I don't want to do any touching before we get married."

"Yeah, you tell me lots of things. But actions speak louder than words, and your body is saying that touching is good. In fact, I'm pretty sure it's flashing a big old neon sign that's begging for more touching." He trailed his fingers over her silky pyjamas to the curve of her hip.

Caroline tensed. "Your father is in the house."

"And I can hear everything," his father's voice came up to them.

Caroline froze in place. This was humiliating.

"We're only going to sleep," Josh said. "That's it. You think you can handle that?"

She smacked his chest. His wide, bare, warm chest. *Get a grip*, she ordered herself.

"I don't trust you," she said. "You kiss me every time you want me to agree with you."

She saw Josh's teeth flash in the dim light, and it made her shiver. "Yeah, and it works great. But we're just going to sleep. In a bed that fits me. That's it. We can hardly fool around when there's no door on the room and my dad is listening."

"Too bloody right," came the voice from downstairs.

Caroline glared at Josh as the absurdity of the situation hit her. Her anger fled. She started to shake. The laughter bubbled up inside of her, beginning in her stomach and working its way out until it exploded from her mouth.

"That's right, enjoy it while you can," Josh muttered.

Caroline gasped for air. This was too much. "You shot yourself in the foot taking off the door." She barely squeezed the words out between laughing.

"Yeah, it cracks me up too."

Caroline wiped her eyes and hiccupped. She was still grinning and trying not to giggle when Josh rolled her over and tucked her back into his front. He slid an arm under her neck and wrapped it tight around her shoulders. His other hand rested on her stomach. She was locked in tight. So tight she was surprised he didn't throw a leg over hers to keep them in place too.

"Sleep," he ordered.

"How am I supposed to do that? I'm not used to sharing a bed with anyone."

Josh stilled behind her. "You've never even shared a bed with anyone? Never slept beside anyone?"

Caroline felt her stomach clench. They were having *that* talk. The one she'd been trying to avoid. "No. I've never slept beside anyone." She swallowed hard. "Or with anyone."

The muscles in his arms tightened. "Are you telling me you're a virgin?"

She blinked hard into the darkness. Oh how she hated that word.

"I wanted to wait until I was married to be intimate. Obviously I've never been married. So I'm still waiting. I had planned on getting to know my future husband quite well before we, uh, became intimate. There was a boy in college— we were serious; I thought we'd get married. But then I came back here, to help out with my sister. And, well, since then, I haven't dated very much. There hasn't been time. Or the interest." She stared into the darkness. "From men, I mean. They aren't that interested in me. So time just went on. And here I am. Still waiting until I get married." He was tense behind her, and Caroline felt tears well in her eyes. She shouldn't have told him.

Josh's arms wrapped firmly around her. "Well, guess what. You're getting married now." His fingers brushed her breast.

She smacked his hand away. "Not today, I'm not!" Caroline chewed her lip. She had expected more of a reaction. Didn't guys think this sort of thing was a big deal? "Doesn't this bother you?"

"No. It doesn't bother me. Why would it bother me? It means I get you all to myself."

"I don't have any experience." She closed her eyes. "I don't know what I'm doing. I need you to be patient with me."

"Or"—she felt Josh grin against her temple—"we can throw caution to the wind and I'll teach you every dirty thing I know. That way you'll be a sexpert by the wedding."

He sounded so wicked it spiked Caroline's curiosity. She wriggled against him, knowing she shouldn't ask. She did anyway. "What kind of experience do you have, exactly?"

"For the love of all things holy," Josh's father shouted, "don't tell her. I don't want to listen to my son's sexcapades."

Caroline wanted to die. She groaned against Josh's arm as she felt him shake behind her. "Your father heard everything." She was never leaving the bedroom again.

"It's nothing to be ashamed of, lass," his father shouted.

"I want to die. Right now. This minute. I'm never leaving this room, ever again. Never."

Josh turned her and buried her face in his chest as he kept laughing. Caroline honestly couldn't remember ever being so humiliated. How could she look Andrew McInnes in the eye ever again? Oh no. If she married Josh she'd have years of dealing with his father. "I can't marry you," she told Josh.

"Sure you can." He was still chuckling.

"I can't face your father." Her voice was barely a whisper.

"Sure you can," his father shouted.

"This house has better acoustics than some of the venues I've played." Josh stroked her back. "Don't worry about it. It's not a big deal that he knows."

"It is to me." She pressed her face to his shoulder.

Josh held her, cooing soothing noises at her. They stayed like that for the longest time. And then they heard loud snoring coming from beneath them.

Josh raised his head to stare at the doorway. "We really need that door back."

Caroline hoped she'd see the funny side of this—one day. She looked up at Josh, but could barely make him out in the dark. "You don't think I'm a freak?"

"No, baby. A control freak, yeah. A freaky virgin, no. I told you, I like it. I have you all to myself."

Now she wanted to kiss him. Instead she wriggled in place. A sense of relief flooded through her as a small smile curved her lips. Josh's fingers traced a lazy circle on her hip.

"Great PJs, babe," he said into her hair.

Caroline settled in closer and fell asleep with a smile on her face.

CHAPTER 20

Caroline was dreaming of Josh's kisses. Something she'd been doing since the first time he'd kissed her. Only this one was different. This one felt real.

"Time to wake up, baby."

Another kiss on her lips. Her hand slid across wide shoulders and held him in place. Her legs stretched long on her bed. Oh, this felt good.

"Are you awake, Caroline?" His voice was an amused tease against her lips.

"No. I'm dreaming."

He chuckled before running his tongue over her bottom lip. "Is it a good dream?"

"Oh, yes." She ran her hand down the bare rippling muscles of his back. "It's delicious."

Another chuckle. "Good to know."

"Stop talking and kiss me. You're ruining my dream."

Smiling lips found hers and did as they were told. Caroline groaned into his mouth as he held her tighter. Wonderful. Her brain wasn't quite awake, or quite asleep. But better than that, her body was on fire. Every single inch of her skin was tingling.

"My skin is on fire," she told him.

"What can I do to help?"

She didn't know. Her tongue touched his lips and he kissed her again. Deeper. Harder. She pressed up into his chest, trying to make the ache in her breasts go away. It didn't help.

"Do you want me to touch you?" he whispered.

"You are touching me."

His hand slowly slid from her waist to her breast. The heat of his touch seared through her pyjamas and straight to her heart. She pressed into him.

"Do you want me to touch you here?"

"Yes, please."

Josh chuckled again as his hand stroked her feverish skin.

"You like this?"

"More," she moaned.

His thumb flicked over her nipple. She gasped. Josh caught the end of her gasp with his mouth. She clung on to the ridges on his back as sensations overwhelmed her. Slowly his hand slid down from her breast. She moaned her complaint and felt him smile against her lips. A second later he stole under her top. Skin on skin. Perfect. His tongue swept lazy patterns inside her mouth as his fingers found her nipple and circled it slowly.

"Beautiful," he told her.

"Need more," she breathed.

"Your wish is my command."

His knee worked between her legs until his thigh was touching her. *There.* Without thinking about it, she ground into him. Josh pushed the edge of her pyjama top upwards. The feel of the satin sliding over her skin was almost more than she could take.

"More?" he said.

She moaned her agreement.

His lips moved to her breast. Caroline would have come straight off the bed if it wasn't for Josh holding her in place. Her breathing was fast; her head was spinning. Her fingers dug into warm muscle as his tongue did wonderful things to her nipple. She widened her legs so she could move closer to him. She wrapped her leg around his hip, arching into him. He grunted his approval against her skin. He blew cold air across her nipple, making her moan. He took her in his mouth and sucked. Hard. Her hips pushed upwards. Desperate. So desperate. Her nails dug into his back. She needed more. She needed all of him.

"You're killing me here," Josh said against her skin.

Caroline couldn't reply. She felt his teeth brush her sensitive skin, and before she knew it, her hand was in his hair and she was pulling his mouth back to hers. Her tongue pushed in as soon as he was close enough to taste. She couldn't get enough of him. His palm on her breast, his thigh between her legs, the taste of him, the smell of him. She was drowning in him.

"You have no idea how much I want you," Josh told her.

Caroline's head was fog. The words were lost in it. He pushed away from her, just enough so she could see the heat in his eyes.

"Oh," she whispered.

"Yeah, oh," Josh whispered back.

There was a loud yawn from downstairs. "I'm awake and I'm coming up to use the facilities. You two better be decent," came the roar from beneath them.

Josh put his forehead to hers. He ran his thumb over her throbbing nipple one more time before pulling her top back down. "Sometimes, I hate my dad."

Caroline fought for control of her body. She didn't want

to stop. Part of her didn't even care that there wasn't a door on her room. Let his father see. Let everyone see. Just don't let Josh stop.

"You don't think he heard, do you?" She worried her lip.

Josh shook his head. "He was snoring until a minute ago."

"I'm at the bottom of the stairs," bellowed his dad.

Josh sighed heavily. "I'll put the door back on today."

"That would make us all thankful," his father grumbled as he thumped up the stairs.

A giggle erupted from Caroline. She wasn't sure if it was from the absurdity of the situation or the humiliation of it. Josh gave her one last hard, but short, kiss before rolling over to the edge of the bed. He picked up his jeans and pulled them on. Caroline watched in fascination as the muscles in his back and thighs rippled. Suddenly she wished his briefs were gone so she could watch all of him ripple. Josh turned to her as his dad passed their room and slammed into the bathroom.

"We're not done here," he promised.

With a wink, he disappeared down the stairs.

JOSH LEFT Caroline in bed while he dealt with his father. After his trip to the bathroom, the man glued himself to the TV. He was methodically working his way through the snacks Josh had bought.

"Are you going to sit there all day watching TV?"

His father grunted.

"Don't you want to sort out your marriage?"

Silence.

"How about getting lost so I can spend some time with my fiancée?"

"Not going to happen, son."

Josh pulled out the big guns. "I'm calling Mom."

"Yeah, good luck with that." He went back to eating potato chips.

"At least put on some pants. No one wants to see you sitting around in your underwear."

Josh resisted the urge to knock some sense into his father. Instead he went into the kitchen, refilled his coffee mug and called his mother. It was another pointless exercise in parental intervention.

"He acts like we should be in an old folks' home," she told him. "He doesn't want to do anything. Go anywhere. Socialise with anyone. He barely talks to me, and when I talk to him he doesn't hear me. I can't keep living like this. I'm sorry, Josh, but I can't."

"What can he do to fix it?" *Please. Let there be something.*

"I don't know if there is anything he can do. This is who he is. He can't change just for me. It isn't possible."

"Maybe there's something else behind his behaviour? He's always been moody, but this is overboard. Maybe we should get him to a doctor? He isn't behaving rationally. And he's a pain in the backside."

"I thought of that. I had a quiet word with our doctor before his yearly check-up. There's nothing wrong with him."

"Nothing a good psychiatrist wouldn't sort," Josh mumbled.

His mother sighed. "Some people mellow as they get older. He isn't one of them."

"Mom, he needs to come back to the castle. Caroline and I need privacy and Dad barely tolerates her."

"I'm sorry, Josh. You'll have to find somewhere else for him to go. I can't have him here."

And that was the end of that. Between his mother's stubborn streak, Caroline's obsession with historical restoration and the gung-ho attitude of the work crew that had taken over the place, the castle was now out of bounds for the McInnes men. With a sense of doom, Josh started calling around the accommodation in Invertary. He was prepared to beg, or bribe, to get his father a room. Whatever it took to get some time alone with his fiancée. He was on his third failed attempt at finding his dad somewhere to go when Caroline rushed into the room.

"You let me sleep late. I'm never late." She grabbed her briefcase from beside the kitchen table. Her hair was slightly ruffled and she still had that sleepy-eyed look. Cute.

"I didn't let you do anything. You were the one who rolled over and snuggled in."

"If you hadn't been in my bed, I'd have been up hours ago."

Josh came up behind her and wrapped his arms around her waist. He kissed her neck and felt her shiver. "If I hadn't been in your bed you wouldn't have woken with a smile on your face."

"Enough of that." She playfully smacked him away. "I need to run."

She turned to the door. Josh grabbed her arm. "Not without a goodbye kiss you don't."

She opened her mouth to protest, a cute little frown on her brow. Josh clasped her cheek in his hand and touched his lips to hers. With a gentle sigh, she leaned in to him. Delicious. When he freed her, her eyes were heavy-lidded with desire. The perfect look on her.

"I really have to go."

"Yes. Please. Go. You two are making me sick," came the shout from the living room.

"Are you dealing with that?" Caroline pointed in the direction of his father.

Josh let out an exasperated sigh. "Trying to."

With a look that said he'd better deal with it, and fast, she ran for the door. Josh went in to see his dad. "This is her house you're camped in. You could try to be nicer. Otherwise you'll be sitting in your underpants out on the street."

As usual, there was no reply.

Ten minutes later, Josh's day got even worse—Caroline's bedroom door had been taken away with the trash.

CHAPTER 21

After three nights sleeping beside Josh and waking with him touching her, Caroline was pretty sure she was going to lose her mind. She was suffering. Dying from frustration. It was a delicious feeling to be eased awake by the man's skilful fingers and tongue. That morning his fingers had drifted beneath the waistband of her pyjama trousers. He had her so wound up from his teasing touch and sinful lips that she was desperate for him to ease the ache she constantly felt. But his father woke up and that was the end of that. She shifted on her office chair and wondered if it was possible to die from sexual frustration.

Although it was entertaining watching Josh's great plan backfire, she really wanted the door back on her bedroom. Thankfully, Josh was at the hardware store as soon as it had opened, ordering a new one. A door was good. A door would help. Having Josh's dad out of the house would help even more.

Caroline frowned at her computer screen. She should never have let the local paper advertise the vacancy on their website. Now she had to wade her way through 15,427 applications for the position of her assistant.

"Don't take this the wrong way, lass," Archie said when he heard about the applications. "But I don't think these people are interested in working with you so much as getting to Josh."

"Really? You think?" She was busy deleting emails from anyone who didn't live within a fifty-mile radius.

"Sarcasm, Caroline?" Archie patted her head, as though she was a dog. "I'm so proud. I didn't know you had it in you."

"I keep forgetting he's famous," Caroline grumbled.

Archie took his cap off his head and scratched his thinning hair. "I'm not sure how that's possible, lass. Haven't you noticed the town is fit to bursting? There are a lot of lookie-loos here to catch a glimpse of him. Not to mention there's a road barricade at the edge of town, which now has a camp set up beside it full of media folk. Every time you turn on the TV you see something about you and Josh. Which reminds me, you really need to smile more. You look glum in every picture."

"Thanks. I'll make that a priority."

"You do that." Archie dunked a biscuit in his tea, then cursed when it broke.

"Delivery for you," Findlay announced as he waltzed into the room.

He plonked a brown paper package on the desk in front of her. James looked through the window from the library, where he was manning the phones. "Is it something good?"

"I haven't opened it yet."

"Get on with it, then," James said.

Caroline slit the paper and pulled out a plain brown box. She took off the lid and her jaw fell open. She jerked to her feet.

"What is it?" James demanded. "I can't see anything."

"You don't want to see," Findlay said with disgust.

Archie bustled around to peer in the box. "Bloody hell. That's just sick. Maybe you shouldn't look at this, lass."

Caroline stared at the contents. Her mind reeling. Who would do something like this?

"Better call the police station," Archie told James. "We'll be needing them."

"Tell me what it is," James said.

"Just call the police."

James grumbled, though he did as he was told.

"I'll make tea; you need a good cup of tea. A strong one." Findlay headed to the kitchen.

"Sit down, Caroline, love." Archie put his hands on Caroline's shoulders and pressed her towards the chair.

Caroline sat. She reached for the box, but Archie moved it out of the way. "I watch a lot of crime programmes. The police will want to fingerprint that."

She nodded. She felt a little dazed. "We need to call Josh. He made me promise to call if anything happens."

"What's his mobile phone number?"

She looked at him blankly. "I don't know."

"I'll try the castle."

"Try my house too; he might be there."

Archie nodded as he reached for the phone. Against her better judgement, Caroline peered into the box. There was a small cloth doll wearing a grey suit. The doll had pins stuck into it, one through the eye, and someone had painted on red dye for blood. In a clear plastic bag beside the doll was what looked like a heart. It was bloody and horrible. Lying on top of it was a note. It said: *Caroline Patterson, you don't love him. You can't love him. Your heart is as dead as this one.*

She sank back into her chair and wondered what to do

next. Deep inside she was convinced that there was a way to gain control of the situation.

She just had to find it.

"I CAME AS SOON as I heard." Helen bustled into Caroline's office ten minutes later. "You poor dear, you must be devastated."

Caroline gave her future mother-in-law a bewildered smile. "That was fast. The package only arrived ten minutes ago."

"Package?" It was Helen's turn to look bewildered.

"The police are here," Archie said from his position by the front door.

"Police?" Helen sat down on the only other chair in Caroline's office and looked around as though the answer to her question was somewhere in the room. "I'm not sure this is something the police can sort out."

Caroline frowned at her. "This is definitely something for the police."

She heard voices, masculine voices, in the vestibule.

"I think you're taking this a bit far," Helen said. "I understand how you feel. I was upset too. But it's nothing a little shopping won't fix."

Caroline didn't have time to deal with Helen, or her bizarre reaction to the box, because Officer Donaldson strode into the room.

"We need to stop meeting like this," he told Caroline. She attempted a smile, but didn't quite pull it off. "Archie gave me the basics. Where is it?" Caroline pointed to the box on the edge of the desk. "Who handled it?" He held the box lid by the corners and lifted it up.

"Findlay, Archie maybe, I can't really say. I touched the outside of the box, but not the contents."

"Caroline?" Helen was worried. "What's going on?"

She turned to explain it to her when Kirsty, followed by Lake, burst through her door.

"Caroline, honey." Kirsty rushed over to give her a hug. "I'm so sorry. We were in the newsagent when we saw it. Don't let it get to you. I'll help you and it won't be an issue anymore. I promise."

Caroline squeezed her friend back, but shot a questioning look to Lake, who seemed amused. She pulled herself out of Kirsty's arms. "I'm not sure what you're talking about. How could you see the box in the newsagent? Did they get one too?"

"Box?" Kirsty looked at Lake. "I'm talking about the newspapers."

"What newspapers?"

Helen shook her head stiffly at Kirsty, who seemed to get the message. "You haven't seen them?" Kirsty said. "Well, don't worry about it. It's nothing we can't fix."

Caroline shook her head to clear it. Had everyone around her gone insane?

"Holy guacamole." Betty stomped into the room. "You're more famous than Kate Middleton."

She pushed everyone out of her way and thumped a pile of newspapers and magazines in the middle of Caroline's desk.

"Oh no," Helen groaned.

"You don't need to see those." Kirsty made a grab for the pile.

"Hands off, they're mine," Betty warned.

Kirsty looked pointedly at Lake.

"I can remove you or the magazines," he told Betty. "Your choice."

She grinned a toothless grin at him. "You're like a son to me."

Caroline reached for the newspaper on top of the pile while everyone was arguing. She turned it over to see the front. The headline screamed, *Is this the most boring woman in Britain?* And there she was, dressed in a grey suit, looking severe.

"What on earth?" She grabbed another one.

This one had *The grey lady of the north* as its headline. The subheading asked why sexiest man alive Josh McInnes could marry someone like her. Caroline swallowed hard.

Kirsty and Helen came up beside her. Each of them tried to take the bundle out of her hands.

"No, I want to see."

Woman's Weekly had a double-page spread dedicated to her. It showed six photos of her all in different grey suits. All with makeup-free faces. And all without a smile. The article demanded that Caroline burn the suits and hire an image consultant. It said she was letting the country down.

The front cover of *Francine Magazine* showed a picture of her alongside headshots of the presenters from *What Not to Wear*. The duo had decided that she needed their help. They were campaigning to get people to put pressure on her to take them up on an offer of a full makeover.

"How did they get all of these photos?" She stared at the double-page spread. "Some of these are years old."

"Caroline." Officer Donaldson cut into her thoughts. "We need to talk about the box."

Kirsty spun on him. "Can't you see she's upset? The country thinks she looks terrible. Talk about a box some other time."

He looked at the ceiling for a moment before answering her. "As important as Caroline's clothes are, someone sent her a box with a threatening letter and an animal heart. I think that takes precedence."

"What the hell?" Lake pushed through the women to get to the desk. "When did this arrive?"

"This morning," Officer Donaldson said.

"Postmark?"

"Fort William."

"Where's Josh?" Lake said. All eyes turned to Caroline. "Did anyone call Josh?"

"I asked Archie to call the houses. I don't have his mobile phone number. He programmed it into the phone he gave me, but the phone is in my kitchen drawer."

Lake sighed before reaching for his cell phone. "Get to the community centre. Caroline got a package you need to see, and she's made national news."

Everyone looked at Caroline. There was silence. The men were stony-faced. Archie's cheeks were red and he looked like he could hit someone. All the women's faces, except Betty's, were hugely sympathetic. Helen had tears in her eyes.

"Let me see that box. I can help." Betty tried to elbow past Lake. He grabbed a handful of tartan dress at the back of her neck to stop her. "I watch *CSI*. I know what I'm doing."

Lake stepped in front of her, his arms folded.

"Kirsty," Lake said. "You and Helen sort out tea for everyone. Take Betty with you. Everyone waits in the blue room. Nobody talks about this until they've spoken with us. Got it?"

Kirsty nodded, and with Helen's help, she manhandled a grumpy Betty out of the room.

"Archie," Lake continued, "close up the centre. Get everyone except the domino boys out of here."

Archie nodded and bustled out of the room. Caroline was left with Lake, Officer Donaldson, a pile of offensive articles and a box with a heart in it. They stared at each other.

"Everything will be okay," she told them. "I'll sort this out."

The window to the library opened.

"Got a woman on the line," James said. "She's from the BBC and wants you to come on her programme. She says you'll get a makeover and they'll give you free clothes. Sounds like a good deal to me."

Lake reached over and slid the window shut. James stared through it for a moment before he disappeared.

"Now about this box..." Officer Donaldson said.

Caroline sat in her chair and tried to focus on his words. She needed to get the chaos under control. She'd learned the hard way as a child that when people lost control, terrible things happened. Her parents had lost control of their car. Caroline couldn't lose control of her life. She straightened her back. No. She needed to get on top of this situation. And fast.

CHAPTER 22

As soon as Josh got Lake's message, he dropped his sandwich on the bar at The Scottie Dog and ran for the door—with Mitch hard on his heels. They sped up the high street to the community centre, attracting curious glances as they went.

Josh's mouth thinned when he saw the notice pinned to the door: *Temporarily closed. We'll let you know when we open up again. Don't worry about library fines in the meantime, we're post-poning them.*

He pushed past the notice and into the library. He spotted his mum and Kirsty sipping cups of tea with the domino boys, and an irate Betty stomping around at the back of the blue room. Ignoring them, he pushed open the door to the office.

Caroline stood behind her desk, her hands clasped tightly in front of her. She looked calm, in control and perfectly fine. If it weren't for the slight hint of panic in her eyes and the tick on the edge of her jaw, he wouldn't have worried. Josh went straight to her, holding her close, and relaxing slightly now that he had her in his arms.

"You okay?"

She nodded against his chest before pulling back to look up at him. "I tried to call, but I forgot your number."

"It's programmed into your phone, baby. Give it to me and I'll show you."

"It's in a drawer in the kitchen."

Josh stared at her for a beat. "It's called a *mobile* phone, Caroline. The idea is that it's *mobile*. It goes where you go."

"I know that." She stepped away from him. "I didn't think I needed it with me at the community centre."

"Well, now you know you do."

She frowned at him, folding her arms tight against her chest. Josh left her to sulk. He turned to the men in the room. "What's going on?"

The cop cocked his head towards the box. Josh leaned across the desk to peer in. There was thunder in his ears. "Who sent it?" His voice was tight.

"We don't know yet."

"Postmark, Fort William. Could be a local. Could be a visitor," Lake said.

"Fingerprints?" Josh clenched his fists to stop from hitting something. Or someone.

"I'll send it off," the cop said, shrugging, "but the lab can take weeks."

"Was there an outright threat with it?"

His eyes were on Lake and Donaldson, but it was Caroline who spoke. "Apart from the note, I'm taking the fact someone stuck a needle through a doll's eye as a threat. The doll is supposed to be me. She has the same fashion sense." Her voice was brittle, making Josh think he was missing something.

"What's the rest of this story?" he asked Lake.

Lake nudged some tabloids and magazines towards him. "Caroline has made national news, and it isn't good. Same story in all of them. Some are sympathetic, some aren't. The photos were taken over the past few years. Looks like someone local fed the press."

Josh felt pain in his jaw as his teeth clenched hard. He handed the pile of papers to Mitch, who let out a grunt of disgust as he sifted through them.

"This is why your mum and Kirsty are here. They saw the papers and came to offer support." Lake smiled slightly. "We were in the newsagent when Kirsty went ballistic. She tried to buy every copy until I pointed out that even if Caroline was in the shop, she probably wouldn't notice. Romance novels and Scottish heritage magazines, yes, tabloids and fashion mags, no."

Caroline beamed at Lake. Josh stepped towards Caroline, threw an arm around her shoulders and tugged her to his side. Sure, it was a possessive move. But he was too annoyed to care.

"I think you should ask the butcher if he's sold any hearts recently," Caroline told Donaldson.

"Aye, I thought of that, Caroline," the local cop said.

"And you should also ask at the newsagent if anyone bought a big parcel box."

The cop just stared at her. Josh squeezed her shoulders. "I think Officer Donaldson knows what he's doing, baby."

She wasn't listening. "Another question is why did the package come here instead of to my home address? Maybe it was sent by someone who only knew where I work? I know!" She shrugged out from under Josh's arm and bent over her computer. She pressed some keys, and a minute later a list of email addresses began printing out. "All of these people applied for the job as my assistant based on the fact I'm marrying Josh. Most of them aren't from town, so they would only have the community centre address. Maybe one of them doesn't want me to marry Josh."

The cop accepted the list. "That's a good idea, Caroline, but I know what I'm doing."

She snapped her back straight and stuck her nose in the air. "I'm not saying you don't. I'm only trying to help. To coordinate this situation." She didn't wait for a reply. Instead, she looked at the magazines. "As for this. We'll organise some people to check where the photos were taken; that should narrow down who took them and lead us to whoever sold the story."

"Or"—Josh nudged her away from the magazines—"I can have Lake and Mitch deal with that, while you get fitted for your wedding dress."

Her eyes snapped to the clock high on the wall. "I forgot all about the fitting."

"I know. They called me three times because they kept getting the voice mail on your cell. *Mobile* phone, babe, *mobile* phone."

"Right." Caroline bent down and picked up her ugly briefcase. "I better get to the castle."

Josh stopped her before she could escape. "Do me a favour, make sure Mom and Kirsty go with you."

"Why?" She looked genuinely confused.

He bent and kissed her nose. "They're upset. It will be a good diversion for them. Plus Kirsty has to try on the bridesmaid dresses they brought for her."

"Right. Of course she has a fitting too." Caroline strode to the door. "If I think of anything else you should do," she said to Officer Donaldson, "I'll call."

"You do that," he said with a smile.

Once Caroline was gone, Josh felt his rage build. "Your guy is still with her, right?"

"You don't need to worry. I told him to wait outside. He won't let her out of his sight."

Josh took a deep breath then looked to Mitch. "The

tabloids and mags...I need you on damage control. They know Caroline doesn't have a team behind her or they wouldn't have tried this garbage. Now she has my team. Make this go away. Do everything you can think of to turn this around for her. Okay?"

Mitch gave a tight nod. His disgust was clear. "Half of this is slander. I'll throw the book at them. While I'm at it, I'll pull strings, get the name of the person who fed them the story and the photos."

Josh nodded, feeling slightly relieved. He could always depend on Mitch.

The cop gathered up the box. "I'll follow up on the box and keep an eye on the mail. I'll have the domino boys run interference in case anything else turns up. It would probably be for the best if Caroline didn't open any more packages." He ran a hand over his face. "We all know she thinks she can handle anything, but that girl doesn't have a clue about her own limitations. We need to save her from herself."

Josh couldn't agree more. "I'll talk to the domino boys about keeping the centre closed until after the wedding. That will make it harder to get anywhere near Caroline."

"Good idea." The cop pointed at Josh and Lake. "Keep her safe. I don't know what this means—it could just be someone screwing around, but we don't take any chances." They nodded. "Josh, I'll need a list of anyone who's been overfamiliar, issued threats, that sort of thing. They could be targeting Caroline to get to you."

"I'll get it to you," Mitch said.

The men stood grimly silent for a moment.

"Right, we're done here. This used to be a nice, quiet job," Donaldson grumbled. "Then all you foreigners started coming to town and now I'm dealing with crazy ex-boyfriends, buildings burning down, voodoo dolls and sheep hearts, crazed reporters and road blockades. I need a vacation."

"What's he talking about?" Mitch asked Lake.

"Kirsty's ex burned down her shop. He's making a big deal out of nothing."

"Yeah, right," the cop said.

"It's not us," Lake told him. "It's the women. Wait until you get one of your own, then you'll see."

Donaldson's grey eyes went wide. "This commitment thing isn't for me. I have plans."

"Yeah." Lake's grin was wide. "That's what we all say."

Josh left the men to their argument and went in search of the domino boys. The sooner they shut down the centre, the better. In fact, if he could have locked Caroline away to keep her safe, he would have done exactly that. He snorted. He could just imagine how well that would go over with his little control freak.

CHAPTER 23

"I love, love, *love* your dress," Kirsty cooed.

"I know. You said."

Caroline stood still on a stool while the dressmaker pinned and marked the gown. They were in Helen's bedroom, which had the only full-length mirror in the castle. It was also one of the few rooms where the dress wouldn't get covered in restoration debris. She turned to see the dress from the back. It was gorgeous.

"Champagne." Helen waved the bottle as she entered the room. Her eyes went misty at the sight of Caroline. "Oh, darling, you look wonderful." She held Caroline's hand in hers. "If your parents were here, they would think that they'd never seen anyone more beautiful."

Caroline saw Kirsty suddenly turn towards the window as she wiped her cheek.

"Thank you," Caroline told Helen.

Helen's eyes softened before she took a deep breath. "Now, champagne for everyone. Including you," she told the woman at Caroline's hem.

"Not for me." Caroline smiled at Helen's enthusiasm. She could see where Josh got his. "I don't drink."

"With everything that's going on in your life, now's a great time to start." Helen put a glass in her hand.

Caroline gave Kirsty a stunned look, and Kirsty laughed.

Helen held her glass high in the air. "To Caroline, the perfect daughter-in-law. I couldn't have picked better if I'd done it myself."

As everyone sipped, Caroline blinked back tears. She dared a sip too. It didn't taste anything like the terrible wines she'd tried over the years. It was sweet, bubbly and delicious. She took another sip and decided she did drink after all—but only champagne.

JOSH WAS in the mood for a fight. Unfortunately, seeing as none of the people he wanted to hit were available—namely, all of the UK tabloid press, every paparazzi photographer he'd ever met and whoever was behind Caroline's sick gift—he'd have to settle with the only thing he did have access to that was driving him nuts. He went back to Caroline's place to deal with his dad.

He found his father sitting in his underpants, surrounded by the debris of constant snacking. He was watching the trashiest talk show Josh had ever seen. Some guy was undergoing a polygraph because his girlfriend didn't believe he hadn't slept with her two sisters. Josh shuddered and snatched the remote up from beside his father. He clicked off the TV.

"Hey, I was watching that!"

"As thrilling as that show must have been, it's time to quit watching TV. It's time to step up and behave like a man."

Darkness swept over his father's face. "Watch what you're saying, son." It was a low, rumbling warning.

Josh didn't care. "I'm done with this. You look like a hobo and you smell worse. You're making everyone miserable and you're screwing up your life. It has to end."

"Or what?"

Josh felt a muscle in his jaw throb. "You don't want to know what."

"Are you threatening me?"

"If that's what it takes."

His father threw up his hands, making empty chip bags flutter to the floor. "This has nothing to do with you."

"I'm your son and I'm fed up watching you screw up your marriage, blaming everyone except yourself. You need to sort this out."

His father surged to his feet with a roar. "How? How can I sort this? You're so bloody brilliant, you tell me."

Josh resisted the urge to negotiate with his fists. He had to remind himself this was his father.

"Suck it up and be what Mom wants. That's how. You were that guy once. You can do it again. Let go of whatever is making you a mean-tempered son of a bitch and show the woman you love her."

His father stepped into Josh's space. His nose inches from Josh's. Fury emanated from him.

"I can't be the man she wants me to be. That man is gone. All that's left is an old man. I've always been too old for her, but now there's no hiding it." His face went purple. "I've been waiting for this day to come. The day when she decided she was too young for me and went off to find another man."

Josh took a step back. "Is this what this is about?" Josh shook his head. "Mom isn't looking for another man."

"She spent eight hours on the flight over here chatting up a guy in his forties. I saw it. Flirting like I didn't exist. It was just a matter of time."

"If that's what you think, why don't you stop fighting her on the divorce and cut her loose."

"Because I love her!" The bellow was so loud it made the photo frames on the wall shake.

Life seemed to seep from his father, and he sagged back onto the couch.

"I can't be the man I once was. I'm sixty-seven, son. I'll never be that man. Your mum is only fifty-five and she looks years younger. She deserves better. She deserves someone who won't keel over and die at any minute. I should let her go. I know that. It's all I think about. I tried. I moved out of our bedroom in the hopes it would be easier to let her go. I saw the writing on the wall years ago. The day I woke up sixty and your mum was still in her forties, I knew the end was coming. I looked at her then, full of life, barely middle-aged and married to an old retired man." He looked up at Josh, his eyes glassy. "I thought with some distance I could let her go, but I can't. I can't let her go and I can't be what she needs, either."

The anger evaporated from Josh as he slumped into an armchair. "Mom doesn't want a younger man. She wants you. She doesn't care how old you are. She loves you."

"We don't want the same things anymore."

"No, you've convinced yourself that you don't want the same things anymore. Somewhere along the way you've talked yourself into thinking that you're old and you can't do the things you want to do. It's a load of crap." Josh rubbed a hand over his face. "You guys should never have sold up the business and retired. You haven't done any of the things you said you'd do when you weren't working. All you've done is sit in the house and wait for the end. I should never have bought you the place in Florida."

His dad smiled sadly. "We thought it was what we wanted. House on a golf course, days in the sun. It was the dream."

"Obviously it was the wrong dream."

They sat in silence for a while. Each of them deep in thought.

"Mom loves you, Dad," Josh said at last. "She doesn't want someone else, she wants you. You need to stop acting like you're at death's door and live life with her. You might be in your sixties, but you're healthy and fit. You don't look half bad, either. Give her a chance. She'll compromise. She doesn't care what you do as long as you do something together. You've got to listen to me on this. I know it's the truth."

His dad gave a faltering smile. "How come you know so much about women?"

"I learned at the feet of the best." His dad's eyes shot up. Josh barked out a laugh. "Not you. Hell, really not you. I'm talking about Sinatra, Dean Martin, Harry Connick, Jr., Sammy Davis…"

His dad inclined his head in agreement. "I still think you're making a mistake marrying Caroline."

"Maybe if you stopped being such a bastard and made an effort to get to know her you would think otherwise."

"Maybe," his father conceded. "You know, it may be too late with your mother. I'm not even sure what to do, and if I did, I'm not sure it would work."

"You've got to try, right? Maybe you should talk to someone about your age issues?" Josh said.

"You mean like a shrink?" His dad chuckled. "I don't think so. I don't need anyone screwing around in this head." He tapped his temple. "No, what I need are some ideas on how to win your mother back. I tried flowers, I tried cooking for her. I'm out of ideas."

He looked around as though an idea would present itself to him, and then he grinned slowly. "I think I know just the place to start." He gave Josh a look filled with glee.

Josh shook his head as he pulled himself out of his chair. "How about you start by putting your pants back on? That would do us all a favour."

THE DRESS FITTING at the castle had morphed into an impromptu hen night. Kirsty had called her mother so that she could see Caroline in her dress. Her mother came to the castle bearing cake. She then called the rest of the women in her knitting group, and they all descended on the castle. Helen was in her element—she kept saying how much she loved entertaining, and to prove it she unearthed music, made snacks and had Kirsty run to the pub to get more champagne and supplies for cocktails.

By eight o'clock, Caroline was buzzing. She wasn't sure how much champagne she'd had, because it was like drinking lemonade, and she was thirsty.

"Take a look around," Kirsty said in her ear as the group of predominately older women fought over where to serve the food. "This is us in twenty or thirty years."

Caroline put her head on her friend's shoulder. "If that's the case, I need to make more friends. You need a large group to cause this much chaos."

"Don't put the ice cream there," Kirsty's mum wailed.

Caroline and Kirsty burst out laughing.

"Thanks for agreeing to be my maid of honour," Caroline said.

"I'd have broken both your legs if you asked anyone else."

"Even Elaine?"

"Elaine is nearly nine months pregnant. I'd like to see her in a bridesmaid's dress."

"There is that." Caroline took another gulp of her champagne, and her head began to swim.

"Right," Helen announced, "everyone eat and then we'll sort out Caroline."

"What?" Caroline said as Kirsty grabbed her arm and led her to the kitchen table. "What do you mean sort me out?"

"The pictures in the magazines." Kirsty's mum rolled her eyes.

"I don't understand." Caroline's head was filled with candyfloss. Lovely, fluffy candyfloss. "How can we fix it?"

"Well..." Heather was wearing her Knit Or Die T-shirt, and the words swam in front of Caroline's eyes. "The first thing we can do is get rid of all of those grey suits you wear and buy you some decent clothes."

"We need a shopping trip!" Jean squealed with delight. "Let's go to Glasgow. Tomorrow. Kirsty can show us the good places to shop. We can have lunch. It will be great."

Everyone except Caroline cheered. "I have clothes. I don't need more."

Although there was plenty of food on the table—mini-pies, finger sandwiches, cheese balls, amongst other things—Caroline decided to start with cake. She piled her plate with a slice of each of the cakes available. Usually she watched how much cake she ate. She was always telling herself that discipline was important. That there was such a thing as too much of a good thing. Control. It was all about control. As she reached for her champagne to wash down a mouthful of decadent chocolate fudge cake, she began to think control was seriously overrated.

"What we need to do"—Shona pointed a fork at Caroline —"is burn your wardrobe. That way you won't be tempted to wear that stuff again."

"That's not a bad idea," Kirsty said through a mouthful of cake.

"What's wrong with my clothes?" Caroline demanded.

Everyone stopped eating and stared at her. If it wasn't for

the compassion in their eyes, the looks she was getting would have been offensive.

Kirsty's mother leaned over the table and patted her hand. "Caroline, we all know that you didn't have a lot of money to spend on clothes over the years, and you've done brilliantly. But now it's time to splash out and get some new clothes. The magazines are being mean about you, but they do have a point. A pretty girl like you shouldn't be wearing grey all the time. You need a new look."

"But I don't want to be different." Caroline felt slightly panicked.

"Not different." Kirsty hugged her. "Still you, only with some pretty dresses and a splash of colour. Don't worry. I'll make sure you get things that suit you. It isn't a makeover; you don't need to panic. It's just shopping."

"And lunch," Jean reminded everyone.

"I *am* beginning to hate the grey suits," Caroline confessed as the women grinned at her. "The domino boys tried to convince the wedding planner that the colour scheme for my wedding should be naval grey."

The women laughed so hard they had to hold on to the table to stop from flopping over. Caroline grinned at them. "Fine, we'll burn my suits."

A cheer went up.

Caroline got into the spirit of things. "We'll burn all of it. I have money. I've only had myself to look after these past few years. I can afford a new look." She surged to her feet. "Let's start a bonfire."

Kirsty tugged her sleeve. "Aren't you forgetting something?"

Caroline stared at her blankly.

"The clothes, honey?" Kirsty said.

"Oh yeah." She brightened. "I'll get Josh to bring them over. Who's got a cell phone with Josh's number in it?"

Helen dug hers out of her bag and dialled the number. Then she handed it over.

"HEY, MOM." Josh answered the phone in the middle of rustling up some sandwiches for him and his dad.

"I am not your mother," Caroline said in his ear, making him smile.

"Caroline, baby, what's up?"

"I need you to bring all of my clothes to the castle."

Josh's heart skipped a beat, maybe two. "Are we moving in?" He almost did the Snoopy dance at the thought of a room with a door.

"No. We're having a bonfire."

He looked at his phone as a cheer went up in the background. "What's going on?"

"Give me that," someone said. "Josh, this is Kirsty. I invited my mum and her knitting group to the castle—we're eating and drinking cocktails, and as soon as you get here we're going to set fire to Caroline's clothes. Got it?"

"Yeah," Josh said, because he wasn't sure what else to say.

"And tomorrow we're all going to Glasgow to go shopping."

"Girl trip," someone shouted.

Now it was beginning to make more sense. "Has Caroline been drinking cocktails?"

"No," Kirsty said.

Josh's eyes narrowed. "Has Caroline been drinking at all?"

"What does he want to know?" Caroline said.

"He wants to know if you're drinking," Kirsty whispered loudly.

"Is it bad if I am?" Caroline whispered back—equally loudly. "Tell him it's none of his business."

The phone was passed again. Josh leaned against the kitchen counter as he waited to see whom he'd talk to next.

"Caroline may have had a glass or two of champagne," his mother said. There was a pause. "Maybe three or four."

"I'll be there in half an hour," Josh said through a grin.

He dug a couple of bin liners out from under the sink and headed for the stairs. If Caroline was drunk, this was something he wanted to see. He glanced into the living room to find his dad had, thankfully, put his pants back on. He took two more steps before he backtracked. His father was lying on his back on the couch reading a romance novel.

"You've lost your mind, haven't you?" Josh asked with resignation.

"Go away. I'm doing research."

"Research?"

His father scowled at him. "These books are full of how women expect men to behave. I'm getting ideas for winning your mother back. Now go away."

Josh shook his head and climbed the stairs. Once in Caroline's room, he set about putting her clothes in the bags. She hadn't been specific about what clothes she wanted to burn, so Josh loaded up everything except the two dresses he liked and one set of lavender lingerie that he thought was cute. Then he went back downstairs, fished Caroline's phone out of the kitchen drawer and called the only cab in town to take him to the castle.

WHEN THE DOORBELL RANG, everyone expected it to be Josh. Which, now that Caroline thought about it, was stupid, because Josh had a key.

"There's a guy at the door who isn't Josh," Heather said with some confusion.

Caroline elbowed her way past the women to find herself face to face with fake Josh. "What are you doing here?"

She was aiming for prim, but her words didn't come out properly. They were slightly slow and took a long time to form in her mouth. She felt like she was chewing the words rather than speaking them.

"I'm looking for you," Danny said. "We need to talk about the wedding."

"Why would I talk about the wedding with you?"

"I thought as a wedding present I'd offer to sing at the reception."

"I know you," Helen said. "You're that boy who thinks he's Josh."

"I make a living being Josh," Danny pointed out.

"Can you sing?" Jean demanded.

"He's actually very good," Caroline said. "He sang in my garden the other night."

Danny beamed at her.

"It's nine o'clock on a Friday night. Don't you think it's a bit late to come offering to sing?" Heather said.

"I'm on American time," he informed them, and the women nodded as though that made perfect sense.

"If you're going to sing at the wedding, we should hear you to make sure you're good enough," Shona said.

"I can do that." Danny straightened his tie.

"I'm not supposed to let him in the house. He's a stalker." She winced. "Sorry, Danny."

"No offence taken."

"What about the marquee?" Helen said.

There was a round of delighted squeals.

"Everyone to the back of the house," Kirsty's mother ordered.

The women poured out of the front door and around to the back of the house, taking fake Josh with them.

Caroline trailed behind them. "I'm not sure this is a good idea. Josh was pretty clear about keeping away from him. In fact, he said the police had escorted him out of town."

Kirsty hooked her arm in Caroline's. "He seems harmless. Plus, what can happen to you surrounded by the rest of us?"

Caroline nodded her agreement and suddenly felt dizzy. "You're right. He's come all this way to sing. It would be impolite not to let him."

"And we wouldn't want to be impolite."

"Somebody sort out the music," someone shouted.

"Let's party," shouted someone else.

"Looks like we're partying." Kirsty picked up the pace, dragging Caroline along with her.

"Wait." Caroline pulled her friend to a stop. "My champagne." She ran through to the kitchen and nabbed a bottle, then ran back to Kirsty. "It's just like lemonade, only it makes me feel bubbly and yummy inside."

"Mmm, not quite like lemonade, then."

They followed the music back to the marquee behind the castle.

CHAPTER 24

The front door to the castle was ajar and there was no sound coming from inside. Josh dropped the black garbage bags full of clothes on the top step and quietly pushed open the door. The hairs on the back of his neck stood to attention as he silently stepped through into the hall. Room after room was empty. He slid his phone out of the back pocket of his jeans and dialled Lake.

"I'm at the castle. The door is open and I can't see the women."

Josh walked to the kitchen, noticing the debris of a meal half finished. Had someone taken them? Was that even possible?

"I'm on my way."

Josh heard a car door slam on the other end of the phone. "Where's the guy you had watching Caroline? I don't see him."

"I'll check on that."

Josh heard a car start. Lake was a couple of minutes away at most. He looked out the kitchen window. The marquee for the wedding peeked out from behind the trees at the far end of the formal garden. And it was lit up like a Christmas tree.

"I think they're in the marquee. I'm going to check it out. I don't like the fact that the castle is wide open."

"Don't do anything stupid," Lake said before Josh ended the call.

Josh slipped out the back door and jogged across the grass to the marquee. Halfway there he heard the music—and the giggling. His stomach uncoiled slightly. It wouldn't relax completely until he saw Caroline.

The marquee was a series of white satin peaks over a wooden frame. It had several sets of stained glass panelled doors. Josh inched open the set closest to him and stopped dead.

He recognised the music as one of his background tracks. Two bars into it and he knew it was the intro for "Stuck in the Middle with You." He spotted Caroline's trademark grey skirt the instant he'd entered the room, and his heart seized with the knowledge she was fine. Josh folded his arms and watched the sight in front of him. Most of the women were in a row with their backs to him, all bent over slightly. Behind the row of women, another woman stood watching their backsides and shouting instructions. It took Josh a minute to figure out that she was teaching them to twerk.

"You're doing it all wrong," the short blond shouted. "Your bums are supposed to jiggle up and down, not side to side. No, Shona, not like that. You don't bend your knees. You look like you're doing squats. Haven't any of you seen Miley Cyrus doing this on TV?"

"Who is Miley Cyrus?" one of the women shouted.

"She's a singer. Young. Trashy. Making bad decisions she'll regret when she's older."

Josh followed the answer to his mother and groaned. He wished he'd never looked. The last thing he wanted was an image of his mother shaking her ass in the air. It would be stuck in his brain forever. Like a landmine in his mind, ready to go off any time he stumbled onto it.

"I don't understand," Caroline said. "Why am I doing this?"

Josh started to grin. She sounded confused and totally blitzed.

"For fun," said the backside beside Caroline. With its tight jeans and long legs, it could only belong to Kirsty.

Josh felt the air shift as someone came up beside him. He glanced over to see Lake relax his grip on the revolver in his hand.

"Tell me I'm not seeing this," Lake said. "I'll never be able to un-see it."

"I know exactly what you mean."

"That's it," the commandant instructor shouted. "Jiggle those behinds."

There was lots of giggling as someone started singing. Josh's eyes shot to the raised stage where the band would play. His smile disappeared. "You have got to be kidding me."

"Crap," Lake said beside him as Danny launched into song.

Josh clenched his fists tight. "I thought he was gone. I thought you had a man watching her. This garbage isn't supposed to happen."

"I rang my guy. He said you were here with the women and he'd gone home. I didn't realise he meant your double was here. I thought he meant you. I was just pissed he'd up and gone without checking it was okay to leave."

"I'm not happy."

"No shit," Lake said.

"Time to shut this down."

Josh headed for the stereo someone had dragged into the room, while Lake headed for the singing stalker. Josh pulled the plug from the socket and there was silence—for about a second.

"Hey," shouted the instructor. "Put the music back on, we're twerking here."

The other women straightened and turned around as Josh strode towards Caroline. She was flushed, bewildered and clutching a bottle of champagne. He took the bottle off her and handed it to Kirsty, who looked a little annoyed until she spotted the death grip Lake had on Danny's upper arm. "Oh hell," she muttered.

"Did you bring my clothes?" Caroline leaned in to him.

She was trying to stand tall, no doubt aiming for that intimidating posture she loved so much. Unfortunately, the fact she was swaying meant she couldn't pull it off.

"They're at the front door." Josh held on to her arm. "The wide open front door."

Caroline looked at Kirsty. "We forgot to shut the door." She didn't seem bothered.

Kirsty shrugged; she wasn't bothered either. Josh resisted the urge to knock their heads together.

"You let in a stalker." Josh put his hands on his hips and waited for an explanation.

The rest of the women moved towards Caroline as though to rally around her. He narrowed his eyes at them. Caroline's gaze swept the room, looking for the stalker. When it hit Danny, she made a little O shape with her lips.

"We didn't let him in. We kept him to the garden. Danny wants to sing at the wedding. We were auditioning him."

The women nodded.

"With your butts in the air?" Josh said.

Kirsty bit back a laugh, and he glared at her.

Caroline leaned towards him as though she was imparting a grave secret. "He's not really a stalker. He's more like a pet."

Kirsty nodded. "Like a puppy who wants to please us."

"And he's not a bad singer," one of the women said.

"Although not as good as you are," another said.

"I'm not sure about that," the first said. Her face lit up. "Maybe we should have a sing-off—get them both going and judge who's the best?"

There was a cheer of enthusiasm from a group of tipsy middle-aged women. Josh heard a cough and looked over to Lake. "Are you dealing with that?" Josh pointed at Danny.

"I called the local cop. He's on his way."

"I didn't mean to upset you, dude," Danny called out to him. "I just want to be part of the festivities. This is a big day for us. We're getting married. It'll change the whole act."

Josh counted to ten and gritted his teeth. Caroline caught the action and turned to Danny.

"Sh!" she said in a stage whisper. "Josh doesn't like it when you think you're part of his life."

Lake coughed again. Danny's shoulders slumped, and he practically pouted. All the women melted.

"Oh, the poor wee thing," one of them said. "Don't be so hard on the boy. He only wants to be like his idol."

"See?" Kirsty said. "Just like a puppy."

Josh worked at keeping a tight rein on his temper. He was counting to ten in Spanish when he heard a car roll up. A minute later, Officer Donaldson strolled into the room.

"You." He pointed at Danny. "Back of the car." Lake pushed Danny in Donaldson's direction. "Put these on and lock yourself in." The cop handed Danny a set of cuffs as he passed him.

Danny's shoulders slumped even further as he took the cuffs, his feet dragging across the newly laid wooden dance floor.

Caroline pouted. "Are the cuffs really necessary?"

Donaldson gave her an even look. "Last time I drove him

out of town, he gave an impromptu concert in the back of the car and smacked me on the head twice while performing. He's getting cuffed this time."

The women glared at the cop before following Danny with pity in their eyes.

"Your singing was great," one of the women shouted.

"I'd hire you in a minute," another called.

Danny gave a small smile and a little bow, then cuffed himself and walked to the car.

"Idiot. He should have cuffed himself after he opened the door. I hope he can get in the car like that." Donaldson shook his head.

Lake came up to stand beside Josh and the cop. As though they'd been trained to do it, the three men folded their arms across their chests and glared at the women. One or two of them shuffled on the spot. Caroline pushed her shoulders back and looked ready to fight. Kirsty bit her bottom lip, and it looked like his mother was about to make a break for it. There was a long silence.

"Does anyone else's bum hurt from all that exercise?" one of the women said.

And they all burst out laughing. They were holding each other up and wiping their eyes. Caroline was giggling but trying hard not to, which made Kirsty laugh even louder. Josh turned to the men beside him. "No point lecturing them tonight."

"Nope," Lake said with a grin.

"I'll talk to you tomorrow about security. Especially Caroline's bodyguard," Josh said.

"That guy is gone. He can kiss his security career goodbye. I'll put someone else on her tomorrow."

Josh nodded. They were still going to talk.

Donaldson turned to Lake. "How many you got room for?"

"Four."

"I'll take the rest." He turned to Josh. "I assume you're taking care of Caroline."

Oh yeah, he was going to take care of Caroline, all right.

Lake grinned again. "Okay," he said. "Let's round them up."

They walked towards the hysterical women. Josh cupped the back of Caroline's head, and she stopped laughing long enough to look up at him. "How much have you had to drink?"

She frowned as though concentrating really hard. "I don't know."

"Have you had anything to eat?"

"Cake." She smiled proudly.

Josh sighed. "I'm taking Caroline and my mother into the kitchen; the rest of you are being escorted home."

"Can I go in the police car?" someone shouted.

"No, I want to go in the police car with officer hotpot," Kirsty's mum said.

"It's not hotpot, it's hotshot. Hotpot is a casserole," Kirsty told her.

Josh watched as an argument broke out amongst the women.

"It's not fair," his mother mumbled. "I don't get to go in the police car."

Josh rolled his eyes, grabbed his mum and Caroline by the elbows and marched them towards the house. He wasn't sure the other two could cope with the rest of the women, but they were on their own. He had enough to deal with.

CAROLINE'S HEAD WAS SWIMMING. Everything seemed interesting and fresh. The stars were so sparkly. The grass crisp beneath her feet. The air brisk against her skin. What little skin was on show. She was overdressed. What she really wanted was to feel the cool night air all over her body. She reached up and popped open a couple of buttons on her blouse. That was better. Vaguely, she wondered if there was a pool at the castle. She didn't think there was. They needed a pool. When she was queen of the castle, she'd put in a pool. She started to giggle again.

Josh looked down at her. He wasn't smiling, but he didn't seem angry, either. His eyes dropped briefly to her blouse, and he shook his head with a resigned smile. Caroline suddenly felt even warmer. She reached up and popped another button open. Josh's eyes went dark.

When they reached the kitchen door, Josh ushered his mother inside.

Caroline stopped dead outside the door. "I don't want to go in there. I want to stay out here with all this lovely fresh air."

Josh frowned at her. "You need to eat."

"I'll eat here. Get me some food." Caroline plopped onto one of the reclining wooden chairs on the patio, grateful that no one had taken the thick blue cushions in for the night.

"Yes, ma'am, right away, ma'am," Josh muttered as he disappeared into the kitchen.

Caroline tugged her blouse off. She still felt too stuffy. So she removed her skirt too. That was better. With a sigh, she lost herself in the vista overhead, unaware of just how long she'd spent staring at the sky until Josh appeared beside her again. He crouched down and held out a plate with crackers, cheese and grapes.

"I see you lost your clothes."

"I was too hot."

His lips twitched. "Nice underpants."

Caroline lifted her head to look down her body. Minnie

Mouse stared up at her. "They were on sale. There's nothing wrong with Minnie Mouse."

"Nothing at all," he said solemnly.

It was so unfair that his lips were fuller than hers. She wanted to reach out and trace his upper lip, feel the curve of the bow dip against her finger. Feel his breath on her skin. Her gaze skimmed along the strong line of his jaw, over cheekbones most models would kill for and up to those electric eyes. They crinkled at the edges, letting her know that she was amusing him again. She sighed heavily. Just when had she become so darned funny?

"Do you wear coloured contacts?"

He blinked hard before giving her a lazy grin. "No, baby, my eyes are real. Like the rest of me."

She was pretty sure that there was innuendo in there somewhere, but it went over her head. Her hand reached out and skimmed over his shoulder. She felt the muscles ripple and tense under her fingertips. It made her shift restlessly in her seat.

"Eat." He pressed a grape to her lips.

She did as she was told, opening her mouth for him to feed her. She ran the tip of her tongue over his thumb before he released the grape. Josh let out a low groan. Caroline's breath quickened. "Would you take off your T-shirt if I asked you to?"

Josh chuckled.

"I won't do anything to offend you," she said haughtily. "I only want to look at your muscles. You have more than you deserve, seeing as you live on burgers and only run when you're being chased."

Another chuckle. "I'm not stripping for you, Caroline."

She pouted, pulling herself up from her reclining position to sit on the edge of the chair. Her knees bumped Josh's, and he put the plate he was holding down on the tile beneath them.

"Why not?"

"Because stripping will lead to touching, and you're in no state for touching."

She poked him in the chest. Ooh, it felt good. She flattened her palm against him and smoothed it over his pecs and down to his stomach. The frustration of the past few days grew within her. "Touching is a good idea. I like it. Let's touch some more."

Her other hand joined the one that was on Josh's stomach. She watched as the two of them made their way up to his shoulders. How was it possible to get so excited about shoulders? She'd read almost all the sex books she'd stolen— sorry, borrowed—from the library, and not one of them mentioned shoulders. Mainly they mentioned...

Her gaze dropped to the front of Josh's jeans, which were looking very tight. She'd slept beside him for three nights now and she still hadn't seen him out of his underwear. Maybe he didn't want her to see him? Maybe something was wrong?

Josh's shoulders started to shake under her fingertips. She looked up to find he was silently laughing at her. She frowned. "It's not nice to laugh at me."

"Baby," he said in that deep voice of his. The one that rumbled through her body. "You're staring at my—"

She pressed a finger to his lips. "Don't say that word. It's a rude word."

He laughed against her finger. Caroline ignored him, once again distracted by the bulge at the front of his jeans. She'd felt it against her, but she hadn't seen it. Or touched it. Surely if there wasn't a problem he'd want to show it to her?

"Is there something wrong with you? Something you don't want me to know?"

Her eyes went wide. She'd read the chapters on sexual dysfunction, so she knew what could go wrong. She leaned closer to him so she could whisper. "Are you having problems *down there?*" She took one hand off his shoulder and pointed at his crotch. She blushed. "I read about this. There are things you can do if your, um, uh, *equipment* isn't working properly. I can lend you the books." She cringed. "Once I've taken them back to the library."

She felt inordinately proud of herself. There. She'd done it. She'd talked about sex. She beamed at Josh. He shook his head slowly as a huge grin lit up his face. "I don't have any problems with my *equipment*. It's functioning perfectly fine."

"Then what are you worried about?" She took a deep breath. "Are you worried I won't like it? I have to tell you, Josh, I haven't seen any real...equipment. Only the ones in books. So you don't have to worry; my expectations are really low in that department."

Josh threw back his head and roared with laughter. She smacked him on the chest.

"I'm thrilled to hear you have low expectations, baby." He wiped his eyes.

Caroline didn't see what was so funny. She thought she was bending over backwards to be understanding and considerate. "If there isn't a problem, why don't you take off your T-shirt." She licked her lips. "In fact, why don't you take off everything."

He put his hand softly on her cheek, and she rested into it. "I'd love to get naked with you. But now isn't the right time. You're plastered, baby."

"I am not." Caroline shot to her feet, making Josh wobble before landing on his backside. "I only had a few glasses of champagne. There's nothing wrong with me." She swayed slightly, her head suddenly full of the stars in the sky. It was distracting. And then a thought occurred to her. "Unless there is something wrong with me?" Horrified, she looked down at Josh. "There's something wrong with me, isn't there? That's why you don't want to touch me. I thought you liked touching me. You had your hand down my pyjamas this morning."

Josh shook his head slowly as he stood up. "There's nothing wrong with you."

"Is it because I'm so inexperienced? Or is it because I'm so plain? I thought you liked my breasts." She cupped herself, trying to decide what she thought of them. "They're not that big, but they stay where they're supposed to. I thought they were okay. They're not big enough, are they?"

She looked up to find Josh staring at her chest, a pained expression on his face. She was right—she wasn't good enough. She let her hands drop and started to turn away.

"Baby." Josh's hand shot out and wrapped around her upper arm. "There is nothing wrong with your breasts. You are beautiful."

She looked up at him. Oh, but he made her giddy. His height and width seemed to engulf her. It should have over-whelmed her, but instead it made her feel precious.

"Then take off your shirt and let me touch you."

Josh swore under his breath before he reached over his shoulder, grabbed a handful of T-shirt and yanked it over his head.

"I'm all yours."

Caroline ran the flat palms of her hands down his chest, tracing muscle, feeling him respond to her touch until she met the waistband of his jeans. For a second she frowned, before she solved her problem by delving under the fabric.

"Caroline, you keep exploring like that and things are going to take a turn you're not ready for."

Caroline felt her need morph to anger. "But I am ready. I'm ready for all of it. I'm thirty-one. I've been ready for a very long time. I know I said we should wait until the wedding. At least, I think I said that. It doesn't matter, because I've changed my mind." She pointed at his jeans. "Get them off now."

"I don't want to make love to you for the first time when you're drunk. I want you to be in the moment with me. And I don't want you to regret it afterwards."

"I won't regret it."

He ran a hand through his silky, dark hair. The sight of him, in the soft night light, made her ache in places she couldn't even name.

"Baby, we're getting married in a week. We're going to do this. We're going to have sex. Trust me. It doesn't have to happen tonight."

She stamped her foot like a child, because that was exactly what she felt like. That was what he was treating her like. Wasn't she a woman? Didn't she know what she wanted? Didn't she have a right to ask for what she wanted? Damn right she did. She pointed at the big lout, momentarily distracted by the way the moonlight rippled over his chest and caught in the dip at his stomach. "I demand that you get naked right now, Josh McInnes."

"Not tonight, baby."

She strode towards him. He backed up, a huge grin on his face.

"If you won't take them off, then I will."

Josh started to laugh. He held out his hands in front of him. "Caroline, you need to sit down and eat something. Then we'll talk about this."

She marched towards him. He retreated faster than she could move. It was annoying.

"Stop running away. Man up. I demand we have sex."

Josh's laughter made his shoulders shake, which in turn

made the muscles move. Caroline was momentarily distracted.

"Let's wait until you're sober," he said through his laughter.

"Josh McInnes, you are a big fat coward." She pushed him on his chest.

She'd only expected him to take a step back. Instead his legs caught on the back of the low wall behind him, and Josh toppled head first into the garden. Caroline was left staring at his feet, which were now pointing up to the sky.

"Oh my goodness, Josh." She ran for the steps that led down into the garden.

She couldn't see Josh's body. It had been swallowed by a lavender bush.

"Help. Somebody help," she shouted.

"I'm fine." Josh didn't sound fine. "Just give me a hand to get out of this bush."

Caroline reached for the hand that had appeared through the lavender. She yanked hard, but nothing happened. "Help," she shouted again.

She almost sank to the ground in relief when Mitch ran around the corner of the building. He came up short when he saw Caroline standing in her underwear.

"Is that Josh's feet?" He pointed at the shoes in the air.

Caroline nodded. "We had a little accident. Josh was too scared to have sex so he ran away and fell into a bush."

"Don't say a word," the bush warned Mitch. "Just get me out of here."

"I think he has concussion," Caroline told Mitch.

Mitch dissolved into hysterics. He wiped his eyes as he pulled his cell phone from his pockets. He aimed it at Josh. "This is one for Facebook."

"You better not be taking photos." The bush shook as it threatened Mitch.

"Would I do that?" Mitch grinned at her.

"Get me out of here." Josh didn't sound happy.

Caroline suddenly ran out of steam. She sat down on the grass beside Josh's bush. It was lovely and cool on her skin, so she lay out flat on it. Josh and Mitch were a dull noise in her head while she looked up at the stars. *Perfect*, she thought as she drifted off to sleep.

BY THE TIME Josh was freed from the bush, Caroline was out cold. Spread-eagle on the grass.

"Don't even think about taking a photo of this," he warned Mitch.

"You don't want it for the family album?"

"What are you doing back here, anyway? I thought you'd be tucked up in bed at the pub."

"I came back to see if you needed help. Good job I did, isn't it?"

Josh couldn't help a grin forming on his lips. "She was trying to seduce me."

Mitch grinned back. "By shoving you into the lavender?"

They smiled at Caroline as she gently snored.

"I better get her to bed. She's going to have a serious hangover tomorrow."

He crouched beside her. Her creamy skin shone in the moonlight. Her lips were parted slightly and her hair was spread out around her. Man, but she was beautiful.

"I'll leave you to it." Mitch thumped him on the shoulder before he disappeared.

Caroline looked so peaceful that part of him wanted to lie beside her and wait for the dawn. Instead he scooped her up and held her tight. Caroline opened drowsy eyes and smiled at him, then curled her arms around his neck.

"I love how you feel," she told him.

His stomach knotted.

"You're always so warm." She rubbed her cheek on his chest. "You feel strong, yet soft and smooth." She kissed the spot she'd rubbed as he carried her to the back door. "I want to lick you all over." Her tongue traced along his skin.

Josh bit back a groan. If she'd been sober. If she hadn't polished off so much champagne that she'd become someone else, he'd had taken her at her word. Then he would have taken her. Instead he turned towards the hallway and started the long climb to the fourth floor and his bedroom. Typical. He eventually got Caroline into a room with a door and she was too sloshed to care.

"I feel so dizzy," she moaned as her head hit his chest.

"You're drunk, baby." He smiled down at her.

"I've never been drunk before."

"No kidding." He turned the corner to start the next flight of stairs.

"I keep doing all these things with you I've never done before. Drinking. Lying. Stealing sex books." She looked up at him, beautiful wide eyes through dark lashes. It made his chest tighten. "You're corrupting me."

He laughed, feeling it bounce off her body. She huffed as her head fell back to his chest. She was limp in his arms. "I don't know why you picked me," she whispered.

Josh's arms tightened.

"Anyone can see that you're out of my league. I have no idea how to behave in your world. I don't know what I'd even do there." She sighed. "You should have picked one of those socialite women—they know how to have parties and talk to people who are famous or rich. Half the time I don't even know what to say to the domino boys." She looked up at him. "I won't blame you if you change your mind, Josh. There's still time. You can marry someone better. I would understand."

Josh clenched his jaw tight. How could she not see how special she was? He opened his mouth to tell her as she snuggled closer to him. Her breathing evened out, and Josh glanced down to find her fast asleep. He held her tightly against him as he opened the door to his bedroom. For a minute he just stood there. He didn't want to let her go. Not even for a second. At last he bent over and put her where she was meant to be—in his bed.

He traced a finger down over her cheek. Beautiful, crazy girl. He pulled off his jeans and climbed into bed beside her. He wrapped her tightly to his chest and held her there.

Where she belonged.

CHAPTER 25

Caroline's head was inside out. Not only that, but someone had taken sandpaper to her brain. Her eyeballs were dry. Her eyelids didn't work. The light was too bright. Her mouth was full of fur. And every single muscle in her body ached. It was hell. She was in hell. A place where her brain hurt and someone left all the bloody lights on.

She heard chuckling. It was too damn loud. She pressed her palms to her ears and groaned before burrowing her head under the pillow. She'd come out later. Maybe. If it was silent. And dark. And she could move without a limb falling off.

"Come on, baby." Josh's voice was muffled through the pillow. "I've got some water and pills for you. It'll help."

Caroline thought about telling him to go away, but it took too much effort. There was more chuckling. The man was a sadist. The pillow disappeared. The light was back. She wasn't sure what to cover first—her eyes or her ears.

Strong hands lifted her, turned her and propped her against the headboard. She'd seen people do this with sheep —pose them for their own amusement. Caroline covered her eyes with her forearm. It kept out the light but did nothing for the thumping—someone was playing bongo drums behind her eyeballs. A cold glass hit her lips.

"Drink," was the rumbled command.

She drank. It tripped over the fur in her mouth and soothed her throat.

"Pills," he ordered. "Open up."

She opened up. Two pills. More water. She kept her hand over her eyes as she heard Josh walk away. She heard curtains being pulled. Suddenly it was much darker.

"Better?"

She groaned in reply.

"Guess we're not going to be *touching* this morning." Josh sounded amused.

If she had any energy she would have thrown something at him. Instead she just toppled to the side and let her face hit the pillow beside her.

"Okay, I can see you're no use at all. I'll come back later."

He gently traced his fingers over her cheek, then her neck, shoulder and hip before she felt them disappear. She heard his footsteps and a door close.

It took her another ten minutes at least to realise she was naked.

With a long, guttural groan, she pressed into the bed and hoped the whole thing was a nightmare.

Because she did *not* want to deal with reality.

"How's Sleeping Beauty?" Mitch asked when Josh wandered into the kitchen.

"Suffering."

Suffering and stunning. Her skin felt like satin. During the night Caroline had gotten out of bed, complained loudly about her clothes being too heavy, stripped out of her underwear and climbed back in with him. If she hadn't been four sheets to the wind, he'd have been in heaven. As it was, he spent the night holding her naked body and trying not to let his hands wander—well, wander too much. He thought he deserved a medal.

"First hangover?" Mitch grinned.

"According to her it's her first everything." Josh reached for the coffee pot. "She says I'm corrupting her."

They clinked coffee cups in a toast to a job well done.

"Must you two be so loud?" Josh's mum complained as she came into the kitchen.

One side of her hair was spiked out from her head, and the other side was mashed flat against it. Her yellow robe was wrapped tight around her and she hunched over as though standing was almost too difficult.

"Somebody needs coffee," Mitch said out of the side of his mouth.

Josh tried not to laugh. It was tempting to give his mother the same lecture she'd always given him when he'd tied one on when he was younger. She never showed any sympathy for self-inflicted illness—especially illness of the hangover variety.

"Coffee, yes." She walked gingerly to the dining table, assuming someone would bring her a cup.

"I'll get it, will I?" Josh poured her a cup.

"What was it you used to tell us about restraint, Mrs. Mac?" Mitch was definitely in an evil mood. "Oh, yeah, that it was a sign of maturity." He hid behind his coffee mug.

"Obviously I'm regressing." Helen reached greedily for the coffee mug Josh held out. "I was mature. I don't have a clue what I am now." She tried to smile up at Josh. It looked like a grimace. "Do we have painkillers? Lots of them. Strong ones."

"I'll get you some."

"Bless you," she muttered before sipping the coffee.

Josh came back with a bottle of pills. "We need to talk about Dad."

"This is not the best time." Helen lunged for the painkillers.

"There's never a good time. At least right now you can't argue back, or run away. I'm taking the advantage."

He pulled out a chair beside her at the table.

Mitch headed to the door. "That's my cue to go. I've got a couple of leads on the photos of Caroline that went viral. I'll run them down today and let you know what I come up with."

As soon as Mitch was gone, Josh turned to his mother. "What's it going to take to make you reunite with Dad?"

Helen hugged her coffee mug to her chest and scrunched her eyes against the light. "I don't want to take him back. He's on his own now."

"You can't throw away thirty-five years of marriage."

"Watch me."

Josh pinched the bridge of his nose. "This is me Mom, you can be honest. We both know you don't want a divorce. You want Dad back the way he was when you first met him."

Her eyes became glassy with unshed tears. Her shoulders slumped. "He's the only man I've ever loved. The only one I want to love. But he hurts me every day. I can't live like that. I could have forty years ahead of me, and I don't want to spend it watching daytime TV and eating in silence. I want to live. I want him to live. But he doesn't want that. He's done. Ask him. As far as he's concerned, sixty-seven is the age to quit living. It doesn't matter to him that we could have years and years ahead of us to enjoy. To live." The look in her eyes was heartbreaking. "So I'm done. I want to live, and I can't do it with him."

Josh took his mother's hand in his. "What if he made an effort to change?"

She looked so dejected. "Honestly? I don't think I'd believe it. He's stubborn, cantankerous and set in his ways. Your dad hasn't been anything but predictable for the past few years. I don't see that changing."

"He might surprise you yet."

"No. He won't." His mother gave him a brave smile. "I know this is the last thing you need to deal with right now, what with the wedding and starting a new life with Caroline. So don't think about us. We're adults; we can deal with this by ourselves."

Josh took a deep breath. "Neither one of you is behaving like an adult, Mom."

His mother sat away from him. "Well, you only have another week to put up with us, then you'll be off on honeymoon and we'll deal with our marriage mess by ourselves."

Josh smacked his forehead. Hard. "Honeymoon! Shit."

"Josh McInnes. Language."

He rolled his eyes at her. "I forgot about a honeymoon."

"Seriously?" Caroline's voice came from the doorway. "You only had one job."

He couldn't help but grin at the way Caroline was standing. It was as though she was afraid to move any part of her body. She was dressed in the same clothes as yesterday, although now they were crushed. Her face was pale. Her hair was ruffled and her feet were bare. She was adorable.

"The one job I had was to get the rings." Josh resisted the urge to smack himself on the forehead again. Then he made a mental note to get the damn rings.

"Yes. You're right." She still hadn't moved from the doorway. The look on her face told him that she thought taking another step would be akin to climbing a mountain. "I'll sort out the honeymoon."

"You will not," Helen said loudly, then flinched. "That's the groom's job. It's tradition."

Caroline smiled wanly at her. "Nothing else about this wedding is traditional. Why start now?"

"I can sort the honeymoon," Josh told them both. How hard could it be? He'd call someone and get them to make arrangements. "Where do you want to go?"

Caroline put one hand on the wall beside her, while the other rubbed her temple. "Surprise me. I've never been anywhere."

"You've never been out of the country?" His mum seemed surprised.

"I went to London with Josh last week."

"I don't think that counts, baby," Josh told her softly.

In his head he put Paris and Venice to the top of his list. He couldn't think of two more romantic locations. Perfect for a honeymoon. He stopped short. Why was he thinking about romance? This wedding wasn't about romance. It was about commitment. He gave himself a mental kick in the behind. Still. Paris was always nice. He looked at Caroline. She'd like Paris. And he'd like showing it to her.

"I'll sort out the honeymoon. And the rings."

Her eyebrows shot up her forehead. "Tell me you already have the rings."

"Of course I have." He tried to cover his gaff with a fake laugh.

The two women glared at him, making it clear that no one was fooled by his declaration. "Okay, I forgot. But I'll get them. There's plenty of time. The wedding is a week away."

"Yeah," his mum said with heavy sarcasm. "Loads of time."

Josh ignored her. "Do you want coffee, baby?"

"No. I don't like it. I just came in to tell you that I'm going home." She looked down at her feet. "As soon as I find my shoes." She looked back up at him, the effort in making every movement clear on her face. "Do you think they'll come if I call for them?"

Josh grinned. "I'll get them. Then I'll walk you home."

She shook her head, then her hands flew up to hold it on. "I'll walk home alone. I need some time by myself. I'll call you tomorrow."

Josh didn't like that one bit. "I'm coming with you."

"Please. I need some time alone. Just tonight. Okay?"

Josh growled before relenting. "I'll stay here tonight, but I'm coming back to your place tomorrow."

"Okay." She was clearly relieved.

"But I'll get your new bodyguard to drive you home."

"New bodyguard? What happened to Gary?"

"Turns out he was an idiot."

As Caroline swayed in place, he went to find her shoes.

When he returned to the kitchen, Caroline was explaining her problem with champagne to his mother. "I thought it was like lemonade. So easy to drink. You forget there's alcohol in it."

"Champagne is like that," his mother commiserated. "Whatever you do, don't try any of those chocolate liqueurs. It's like drinking candy. One minute you're thinking, this is delicious, next minute you're face down in your own vomit wondering what the heck happened."

Caroline shuddered. "Thank you. I'll steer clear of those."

"Here's your bag and shoes." He knelt down before her and helped her step into her shoes.

"Thank you." Even with a hangover, her manners were impeccable. She patted him on the cheek. "I'll see you tomorrow. Bye, Helen." She turned to go.

"Oh, hell no." Josh grabbed her arm and swung her back round towards him. She squealed. "That is not how you say goodbye to your man."

His lips clamped down on hers as he threaded his fingers into the hair at the back of her head. After a thorough kissing, he released her. She wobbled on her feet.

"Bye, Caroline." His mum's tone was heavy with amusement.

Caroline touched her lips, then blinked hard as though to clear her head. Josh smiled knowingly. Maybe now she would regret this desire to be away from him. She mumbled something about needing time alone as she wobbled to the front door.

CHAPTER 26

Caroline had forgotten that Josh's father was camping out in her living room. Her tiny house was full of brooding, grumpy man. She couldn't even hide in her bedroom and pretend that her life hadn't been invaded, because there was still no door to her room. Instead she'd taken a bottle of water, a strip of aspirin and a box of chocolate chip cookies to bed and spent the night listening to Andrew McInnes snore and fart.

It was delightful.

Since the centre had been shut for the rest of the week, Caroline found herself without a purpose. She'd wanted to curl up on her couch and read some trashy romance novels in the hope of forgetting about her life, but Andrew had beaten her to it. The man had been going through her books, sticking notes to the pages and jotting down anything he thought was important in one of her notebooks. Every now and then he'd grunt or bark a laugh. Once he shouted, "You've got to be kidding me! These women are sick! Who writes this crap?" Then there was silence again.

By mid-afternoon Caroline had had enough of being

overrun by McInnes men, and was on her way into the living room to tell Josh's father that he'd overstayed his welcome. Instead the back door opened and Josh walked in like he owned the place.

"Go away," Caroline told him. "But not before you take him with you." She pointed in the direction of the living room, in case there was any confusion.

Josh walked straight over to her and wrapped her in his arms. Caroline froze for a minute.

"Hey." He looked down at her. "What did I do to get the freeze-out?"

"I don't know. I haven't decided why I'm mad at you yet. I'm pretty sure everything is your fault, but I need to put it together logically."

She felt him shake as he silently laughed at her. Against her better judgement, she rubbed her cheek on the cotton of his blue T-shirt and gave in to a sigh.

Josh's dad came rushing out of the living room and ruined the moment. Thankfully, he was fully dressed. The man might be in great shape for his age—heck, for any age— but he was going to be her father-in-law, and watching him trot around half naked was just yuck. She shuddered at the thought.

"Get in here, you two. I've figured everything out."

He disappeared. Josh looked as confused as Caroline felt.

"Do you think this means he's ready to leave?" Caroline whispered.

"We can only hope," Josh said.

"Hurry up," his father yelled.

Josh dragged Caroline into the living room. There were three pieces of paper taped to the wall beside the TV. Andrew stood in front of them as though ready to give a presentation. There was a pile of romance novels on the table beside him.

"Sit on the couch." They did as they were told. "Right. I've been reading through all this crap that Caroline has been stockpiling."

"Hey!" Caroline said.

"Sorry." It looked like he was struggling not to roll his eyes. "What do you want me to call it?"

"Romantic literature."

"Yeah, right, whatever." Andrew turned to the wall with a board marker in his hand. He wrote the words "What women want" on the paper behind him.

Josh pointed at the paper. "Wasn't that a movie? Didn't Mel Gibson already figure this out?"

Caroline elbowed him to shut him up. The sooner his father got this over with, the closer they were to him leaving.

Andrew tapped the paper. "After doing some research, I've got the answer to this. The real answer. Not some Hollywood version of it." He looked at them as though he was waiting for something. Caroline wondered if it was applause.

"Okay," Josh said. "I'll bite. What do women want?"

"According to all of these books—" Andrew swept his hand towards the piles he'd been skim-reading—"women want three things from their men." He turned to the first piece of paper. "They want big romantic gestures." He wrote the words down. "The kind of thing that makes most men gag—writing in the sky, stadiums full of flowers, that sort of rubbish. The bigger, and more public, the better. And if that isn't enough, they need the man to explain why he's doing it. In detail. He has to tell her why he loves her and why she's special at the same time." He pointed his pen at them. "We're talking all the things men would rather vomit than say—you know, things like 'you're so pretty, you have dainty feet, you make great apple cake.' Whatever gets them to tear up and go all mushy is perfect. Apparently women can't figure out for themselves why a man wants to be with them, so they need to hear it from the horse's mouth."

Caroline gaped at the man. Josh seemed highly entertained. Caroline wondered if he was going to put his father on pause and fetch some popcorn.

"Second." Andrew turned back to the wall and started to write again. "They want a man who's forceful and in charge —like a caveman, but wearing a suit. The suit is important. It needs to be tailored to fit, and it helps if there's a six-pack under it." He lifted his T-shirt to show off his stomach. For a guy of his age, he was definitely toned. It gave Caroline high hopes for Josh in the future. "What do you think? Do I need to do some sit-ups?"

They looked at him blankly.

"Never mind." Andrew dropped his shirt. "Anyway, the books call this caveman stuff being 'alpha.'" He made air quotes. "Basically, he's a bastard who does what he wants but is sexy while he's doing it, so he gets away with it."

Caroline closed her eyes briefly as Josh's shoulders began to shake beside her. At least he kept his hysterics quiet.

"I wish I was filming this," Josh whispered. "We should get him to run seminars."

"Lastly"—Andrew frowned as his mouth pursed —"women want kinky sex."

Caroline almost choked. Josh reached behind her and thumped her back.

"Sorry," Andrew said. "This isn't really a discussion for mixed company, but I figured you'd be fine with it seeing as you read this crap. Sorry. *Romantic literature.*"

There were tears trailing down Josh's face from his silent laughter. She narrowed her eyes at him. He shrugged helplessly. "Don't let this worry you. I take after my mom."

Andrew wrote "kinky sex" on the last piece of paper pinned to the wall.

"Women want to be tied up and tortured. But not in a malicious way. It's supposed to be sexy torture. I can't go into detail"—he nodded in Caroline's direction, implying he was being circumspect for her benefit—"but let's just say that there are things in those books that made me blush—and I used to work in the shipyards."

Josh shot Caroline a heated look. "I think I need to read these books."

Her cheeks burned.

"Anyway," Josh's father continued. "Apparently spanking is the in thing." He consulted his notes, making Josh laugh again. "Sensual spanking," he corrected. "And blindfolds are popular too. And you're supposed to make the woman call you 'sir.'" He blinked hard. "I don't see that one flying with your mother, but what the hell, I'll give it a try." He studied the pieces of paper on the wall. "So there you have it. Women want romantic gestures, arrogant cavemen and kinky sex."

He folded his arms, incredibly pleased with himself. "What do you think?" Andrew gestured to his list. "Caroline. You're a woman. I'm right about this, aren't I?"

Josh turned towards her with mischief in his eyes. "Yes, Caroline, tell us. Is he right? Is this what women want?"

Caroline blustered. "Um, well, you've definitely done a lot of work."

Andrew stood there proudly. Caroline almost didn't want to burst his bubble.

"But these books are fiction." She glanced at Josh, hoping for help. She didn't get any. "If you railroaded a woman in real life, the same way some of the heroes do in the books, you'd get smacked on the head, or shown the door."

Andrew frowned, clearly unconvinced.

"And, um, not every woman wants to be tied up, or um, spanked."

Andrew started to say something, but Caroline beat him to it.

"Romantic gestures are always welcome, though, especially if they're genuine."

Andrew pointed at her with the pen. "You're being politically correct, aren't you? Modern women can't admit that they want a caveman, in and out of the bedroom."

"No. I'm trying to remind you that these books are fiction." She walked to the shelf behind her. "This one is all about a hero who turns into a werewolf. Does that mean all women want a werewolf for a husband?"

"Is he alpha? Into kinky sex? Does he tell her how much he loves her to the point where you want to vomit?"

Caroline couldn't argue with that. The hero in the book did do those things.

"See?" Andrew fist-pumped the air. "I'm right. I know exactly what to do to win Helen back. Now if you'll excuse me, I need to go to Glasgow and buy a new suit. And some kinky gear." He stopped in front of Caroline. "Do you know where to buy that stuff? It's been a while since I've been to Glasgow."

"No! I don't know where the sex shops are." She gave Josh a "please help me" look. He held up his hands. "Listen, Andrew, you don't need to dress in a suit, or t-t-tie Helen up"—she flushed as she stuttered over the words—"to win her back. You only need to spend time with her, enjoy doing stuff together, talk to her, have fun. It's that simple. That's what women want. They want attention. They want to feel important to their husbands. They want to feel attractive and sexy. They want to feel loved. You don't need the other stuff."

Andrew snorted. "No offence, pet, but I'd rather take the advice of a bunch of freaky books than listen to a woman who had to make a deal with a stranger to get married."

Josh shot to his feet. "Apologise now. We talked about how you treat my fiancée. This isn't it."

Caroline found it hard to look anywhere but the carpet. He was right. She didn't know anything about men, romance or relationships. She'd had to bargain to get a chance at marriage. She was the last person he should listen to. She was pathetic. A hand rested on her shoulder. She expected Josh, but looked up to find his father staring at her. It took a minute to realise there was compassion in his eyes.

"I am sorry, that came out wrong. I might not agree with this arranged wedding, but I've learned some things these past few weeks. You're a good woman, Caroline. I'll admit that I wish my son was marrying the love of his life, but I don't think for a minute that you won't do your best by him." Andrew cleared his throat, obviously embarrassed. "Okay, enough of this mushy stuff. I'm going to Glasgow. See you in a couple of days. Try to stop your mother from running off with another man while I'm gone."

With that, he picked up his bag and strode out of the room. They listened to the door bang shut.

"That little presentation of his was more than I've heard the man say in years. Pity most of it was complete and utter garbage." Josh grinned down at her. "Think we should warn my mom?"

"What would you say? 'Your husband is coming for you, he's armed with fluffy handcuffs and he won't take no for an answer'?"

Josh chuckled. "Yeah, let them sort it out themselves." He turned her towards him. His eyes glinted with delight. "In the meantime, we have other things to deal with. My father is gone and we have the whole house to ourselves. Now"—he waggled his eyebrows at her—"what do you think we should do with our time?"

CHAPTER 27

Whatever Josh's plans, they went up in smoke about two seconds after the words were out of his mouth. Caroline's front door swung open and a voice shouted, "Josh, get out here."

Josh hung his head. "It's Mitch. What does a guy have to do in this town to get a little privacy?"

He squeezed Caroline, kissed her hair and lumbered off at his usual laid-back pace to see what his best friend wanted. Caroline sighed and followed. The men were in her garden, staring at her house. They had identical poses—legs apart, arms folded. And identical looks on their faces—angry.

"What is it?" Caroline stepped out to join them.

"Have you called the cops?" Mitch said.

"I came in the back door. This is the first I've seen it."

"I'll call." Mitch pulled out his phone. "With everything that's happening, I've got the guy on speed dial."

Caroline turned to see what the men were staring at, and sucked in a breath. Paint-splattered words decorated the wall of her house. The words were a stark reminder of a truth Caroline already knew. *You're not good enough for Josh.*

"At least they can spell." Her hand fluttered to her throat. "Lots of people miss the apostrophe in *you're*."

Josh raised an eyebrow at her, but it disappeared as soon as he spotted the quivering lips she was trying to hide. "Don't let it get to you. We'll sort it."

He hugged her to him, and for a moment Caroline let herself absorb his heat and strength. Somehow she felt as though the words were written on her skin, rather than her home.

"Oh crap," Mitch muttered from behind them.

Caroline and Josh spun towards him. She couldn't miss the pointed look the two men shared. Josh placed his hands on Caroline's shoulders. "You know, I could really use a cup of coffee." He smiled. "Any chance you could make us one?"

Caroline straightened her back. Whatever Mitch had found, it wasn't good.

"Of course I will. As soon as you show me whatever it is you don't want me to see."

Mitch sighed and nodded at the gate. Josh took her hand and led her to it. Caroline felt the blood drain from her cheeks as she spotted the little cloth doll. It was dressed in a grey suit and had a noose around its neck. Josh snarled beside her as Caroline's stomach twisted violently.

"Well, I think it's safe to say someone doesn't like me."

The looks of anger and pity on the faces of the men made her want to run.

"We'll get to the bottom of this," Josh promised.

"I know." Although she felt far from certain that they would. "I'll make coffee."

She walked past the nasty words that marred the home her grandfather had left her and, feeling slightly dazed, headed for the kitchen.

. . .

"I WAS on my way to see Caroline when I got the call." Officer Donaldson was talking before he got out of his police car.

"It's the same guy who sent the package to her office," Mitch told him.

"What makes you think that?" Donaldson was all business.

Mitch pointed to the doll on the fence. Donaldson looked as disgusted as Josh felt.

"Aye, that would narrow it down."

Without another word, he walked over to examine the wall. He traced a letter with his finger. "Dry. Must have happened late last night. Did you hear or see anything suspicious?"

"I wasn't here." Josh wanted to kick himself for letting Caroline sleep without him. "But my dad was in the front room." He pointed at the window above the words. "He would have mentioned if he'd heard something."

Donaldson nodded. "I'll need to speak with him."

Josh rubbed a hand over his face. "He's gone to Glasgow to buy a suit and sex toys." They stared at him. "Long story."

"Fine." Donaldson sighed heavily. "We'll deal with him later. In the meantime, I need Caroline to write a list of women she thinks might be particularly upset about this wedding. It's obviously someone she knows."

Josh took a step towards the man. "What makes you think it's a woman?"

Mitch and Donaldson both gave him identical "are you an idiot" looks. He shrugged. They were involved with the law. Josh wasn't. What did he know about this stuff? He sang songs for a living. He bet they wouldn't know what G-major looked like if it was painted on the wall.

"Josh." Mitch sounded like he was speaking to a slow child. "The dolls are handmade—do you see a guy doing that? Or even knowing how to do that?" He gestured to the words on the wall. "The paint is sparkly purple. How many guys would have that around, or would buy it to graffiti a wall?"

"Has Caroline seen this?" Donaldson said.

"Yeah." Mitch gestured towards the house. "She's inside making coffee. She didn't seem too upset."

Josh glared at his best friend. How could he have missed how upset Caroline was? She'd gone into Ice Queen mode. Her back was so straight it looked like she was strapped to a board. Her skin was pale and her heart had been beating fast. She was freaked. Donaldson cast a wary glance towards the house. At least he seemed to be sceptical that Caroline was coping well. It put the guy up a notch in his estimation.

Donaldson rubbed his chin. "Maybe she doesn't need to hear this right now."

Josh nodded. Damn right she didn't need to hear any more bad news. "Spit it out."

The guy let out a long breath. "The roadblocks are coming down as we speak. One of the TV stations got their lawyers involved and they're being given access to the town." Mitch cursed, and Donaldson cast him a glance. "Let's face it, they were barely legal anyway. We've been pushing our luck keeping people out of town. I'm surprised we got away with it this long."

Josh felt as though he'd been kicked in the stomach. "We're going to be overrun with press."

"You've got about an hour before the town is flooded," Donaldson said grimly. "We can keep them off private land, but that's about it."

Josh eyed the house. Caroline's place was far too open to hide from the press. He made a decision. "I'll move her to the castle. She's safer there."

Mitch agreed. "I'll call Lake and sort out security."

Josh threw back his head and studied the clear blue sky. "She's not going to like this."

"Worse than that," Donaldson said, "she'll want to sort it."

"Any chance we can deal with this before the cameras get here?" Josh pointed to the wall.

"I'll get what I need as fast as I can," Donaldson said.

"And I'll work on hiding the message until it's painted over," Mitch said. "We're going to have to paint the whole house. A patch job would stand out too much. I'll sort it out."

"I guess that leaves me to deal with Caroline." Josh paused on his way into the house.

Donaldson and Mitch shared a grin.

"Aw, poor Joshy boy," Mitch said. "He's scared of the big bad Scottish lassie."

Donaldson laughed.

Josh ignored them. He wasn't scared of Caroline. He was wisely cautious. It was a completely different thing. He called out for Caroline as he strode to the kitchen. It was empty.

"Caroline?" he shouted up the stairs.

Nothing.

"Caroline?" He peered out the back window, then checked the living room.

She wasn't in the house. He rushed back to the front door. "Caroline is gone."

The smile disappeared from the cop's face. His eyes narrowed. "Is there sign of a struggle? Did it look like she left on her own?"

"No sign of a struggle, but her handbag and keys are still here."

"Let's make some calls," Donaldson said. "It's probably nothing, but best we locate her before the press do it for us."

Josh wanted to hit his head against the wall. Instead he turned on his heels back to the kitchen. He pulled open Caroline's junk drawer. Her cell phone was still inside. He slammed the drawer shut.

Damn impossible woman.

CHAPTER 28

They were out of coffee. Caroline had been tempted to serve tea—she didn't like coffee anyway, but she knew Josh hated tea and couldn't do it to him. She nabbed her wallet from her bag, let herself out the back door and walked the short distance through the lane to the high street shops. It would only take her ten minutes to fetch what she needed.

She was studying the chocolate biscuit selection when she felt a presence behind her.

"Hey, sweetheart."

Caroline jumped, placing a hand on her heart. Danny grinned at her. As usual, he was dressed in a black suit.

"You gave me a fright. And don't call me sweetheart." What was it with Americans and pet names?

"Whatever you say, *darling*." He winked at her.

Caroline stifled a smile. There was something about Danny that was delightfully adorable.

"Not long till the big day." Danny picked a pack of cookies off the shelf and handed them to her. "These are my favourites. I don't know about you, but I'm getting nervous."

It took Caroline a minute to realise he was talking about the wedding. "Why are you nervous? I'm the one getting married."

"Caroline, Caroline, Caroline." He brushed his knuckles down her cheek in a way that was far too familiar. "It isn't only you. *We're* getting married. It takes two, remember?"

Caroline took a step away from him and frowned. "We're not getting married, Danny. I'm marrying Josh."

For a second he seemed confused. "That's what I mean. You and Josh." He didn't sound convinced.

Caroline opened her mouth to ask him if he was okay, but his gaze snapped to the window behind her. Lights flashed. People shouted.

"The press are here." Danny grabbed her arm and swung her away from the front of the store. The coffee pack she'd been holding fell to the floor.

"Out the back," shouted Agnes Stewart from behind the counter. "I'll delay them."

"Thanks, Agnes." Danny yanked on Caroline's arm and pulled her towards the back of the shop.

"What are you doing?" His grip was too tight to break. "Let me go."

"I can't do that, sweetheart." Danny led her through the stock room and out the back door. "We can't let the jackals get you."

Caroline tripped over the doorstep and out into the alley. "You don't have to help. I'm fine."

"Look, do you want to stay here and answer questions, or do you want to get some privacy?"

Caroline heard the shouts of the press behind her. The thought of being stuck in that mob, with people thrusting cameras in her face, made her feel ill.

"I want out of here."

"Well hold on, sweetheart. I'll take care of you."

They ran down the alley towards the cemetery. Danny helped her to climb the fence into the park. Once inside, he took her hand again and rushed her towards Macgregor's folly.

He yanked open the door to the small cylindrical building. "We should be fine in here for a while. We'll head back home to the castle when the press have gone."

Caroline separated herself from the man and peeked out of the door. She could hear voices shouting her name, but no one had come in to the cemetery. She closed the door again and slid down the stone wall to sit on the floor. Her life was insane. She couldn't make sense of it anymore.

"Hey." Danny crouched in front of her. "Don't panic. Everything is going to be fine."

Caroline looked up at him sceptically. He grinned as though he was enjoying himself.

"I've been thinking." Danny seemed almost abashed. "This is all getting a bit much. How about we skip town and get married in Vegas? Just the two of us. What do you say?"

Caroline stared at him. He was perfectly serious.

"Danny"—Caroline deliberately used his name—"we're not getting married. I'm marrying Josh."

He frowned as though concentrating hard. "Yeah, yeah." He nodded to himself. "That's what I mean. Why don't you and Josh elope? Put an end to this circus."

Caroline looked up at the circular window in the peak of the dome. Why indeed? "I always dreamed about getting married here."

Danny held her hand, and she let him, taking comfort from the wrong man. "And is it how you thought it would be?"

She couldn't help herself. She started to giggle.

Danny grinned as he gave her hand a squeeze. "Vegas is looking good now, huh?"

He wasn't wrong.

There was a lot of noise from outside the building. Danny peeked out of the door. Flashes went off. "We're surrounded, sweetheart."

Caroline groaned. "I need to call for help, but I left my phone in the kitchen." Josh was going to kill her. How many times had he stressed taking the phone with her? Yep. She was a dead woman.

Danny pulled his cell phone from his pocket and handed it to her. "I'd call Josh, but I'm not allowed. Although that might just be an American rule."

Caroline rolled her eyes as she took the phone. She couldn't call Josh anyway—she couldn't remember his number.

"Come out, Caroline," the voices outside called. "We only want a photo."

"Josh, Caroline, what are you doing in there?" someone else called.

"What is this place?" a guy's voice said. "It looks like a giant penis."

"It's a folly," Danny shouted through the door. "It's supposed to look like a penis."

"Josh? Is that you?" a guy's eager voice shouted. "Why won't you come out and do an interview?"

Danny adjusted his tie as though he was about to step outside.

"Don't you dare," Caroline warned. "Josh told you no more standing in for him."

He was so crestfallen she almost felt sorry for him.

"If we can get them out, we can take a picture of them in front of this giant dick. That will sell," someone said.

"Give me a boost up to that window and I'll see what I can do," another voice said.

Caroline was out of time, and there was only one number, apart from her own, that she knew by heart. She opened the phone and dialled the community centre. It was time to call in the domino boys.

CHAPTER 29

"Where the hell is she?" Josh spat. They'd called the castle, the pub, Kirsty's shop and the community centre. No one had seen Caroline. "Invertary is not that big. Why can't we find her?"

"Calm down," Mitch told him.

It made Josh want to punch him. "Has anyone ever in the history of the world actually felt calmer when someone ordered them to?"

He could have sworn he heard Mitch mutter, "Smartass."

Josh stopped pacing in the middle of Caroline's living room floor. "You don't think she was taken, do you? I've seen the movie. It didn't end well. Liam Neeson went all ninja on the kidnappers. I don't have those kind of skills."

Mitch ran a hand down his face. "We've been over this. There's no sign of a struggle."

"Her bag is still here. Her keys. Why would she leave without her keys?"

"The back door was open. We were here. It's not like she'd get locked out if she left. She's probably gone for a walk. It's a small town. Someone will have seen her."

"Got her," Donaldson shouted from the front of the house.

Josh and Mitch ran out. There was a decorating crew setting up scaffolding, but no Caroline.

"Where is she?" Josh demanded.

The cop ran a hand through his hair. It was obvious the job was getting to him. Josh didn't need to be a shrink to recognise burnout when he saw it. "She's stuck in Macgregor's folly with your singing clone."

Josh blinked hard as the words registered. "He took her?"

The cop shook his head. "He was rescuing her. The press cornered them at the local supermarket and they ran."

"Great." Mitch threw up his hands in disgust. "I bet they have some fantastic shots of your fiancée running with your doppelganger. People will think it's you."

Although Josh sympathised that his best friend had one more press relations nightmare to deal with, now wasn't the time. "Focus on that later. Right now we need to go get Caroline."

Mitch spun to face him. "Are you nuts? You can't go. That will make things worse. It'll be a paparazzi feeding frenzy if you turn up."

Josh went toe to toe with his best friend. "Don't even try to stop me."

Caroline may think she could deal with everything, but being trapped by a screaming horde of photographers was scary as hell, even for the most seasoned celebrity. There was no way Josh wasn't going to rescue his woman.

"Fine." Mitch poked Josh in the chest. "I warned you. It's your career. Your suicide."

"Exactly." Josh took another step towards Mitch.

There was a high-pitched whistle. Mitch and Josh turned towards the cop. "Boys," Donaldson said. "Focus."

Josh ripped his angry gaze from his best friend.

"We'll follow you," Mitch told the cop.

Donaldson sped away in his police car as Mitch and Josh climbed into Mitch's SUV. The drive was short. As they pulled through the gates to the cemetery, Josh could see the rounded top of the phallic brick building above the trees.

"They should have knocked that monstrosity down, not restored it." Mitch spoke Josh's mind.

The noisy crowd of photographers and cameramen came into view. Amongst the paparazzi were a few reputable TV stations. They were riled up, acting with a pack mentality. They were out for blood. Preferably Caroline's, but Josh's would do just the same.

Mitch was grim-faced. "How we going to handle this?"

Josh studied the crowd. "I'm hoping they'll see me and it'll take their attention away from the folly long enough to get Caroline out."

"I don't like it."

"I didn't ask you."

"You never do, but I'm always the one cleaning up after you."

Josh ignored Mitch's grumbling and climbed out of the car. He walked over to Donaldson's cop car. The cop fell into step beside him. The two of them moved towards the crowd. Josh knew it was a matter of seconds before he was spotted. Except no one even turned in their direction. The crowd's attention was firmly fixed on the building in front of them.

"Step away from the folly!" A loud voice, clearly shouting through a bullhorn, was aimed at the crowd.

Josh turned to the cop with a questioning look.

Donaldson shook his head. "It's not one of my staff. Maybe it's one of Lake's guys?"

"What guys?" Lake jogged up beside them. "I heard and came right over."

Josh pointed towards the building. "Is that one of your guys on the horn?"

Lake shook his head, his lips pursed into a tight line. "The only guys I have here are the ones I brought with me. Maybe it's her bodyguard?"

"Can't be." Mitch stared at his feet as he spoke. "I sent him for a break when I arrived."

The rest of the men glared at him, and he had the good sense to look apologetic.

"I said, step away from the folly," the voice shouted again. "Right now, you bampots!"

Lake shook his head, seeming almost resigned.

"Oh no," the cop groaned at the same time.

"What?" Josh demanded.

Lake cocked his head towards the crowd. "I know that voice. It isn't a guy. It's Betty."

Josh pointed at the folly. "You said Danny was in there with Caroline, not Betty. What's going on?"

Lake pointed at the parting crowd. "I think it's a rescue attempt. Look."

Mitch grunted with disgust. "No amount of PR will fix this."

"Back off, you bunch of bloodsucking vampires," Betty's voice boomed out over the noise of the crowd.

Cameras flashed. People called out, hoping it would make Betty turn towards them as she parted the sea of reporters in front of her.

"Touch anyone and I'll break you in two," she threatened.

Behind her were two figures hidden under white bed sheets. They were flanked by the domino boys, who were armed with golf clubs. Josh could make out Caroline's sensible cream-coloured pumps under the sheet the first person wore.

"Oh hell no, do you hear that?" Mitch said.

And sure enough, under the noise of the crowd they could hear singing. Danny was belting out "My Way" from under his sheet. Beside Josh, Lake struggled to hide his grin.

"This isn't funny," Josh told him.

Josh watched as the group of armed geriatrics, and two ghost people, made their way slowly through the graveyard.

"Take a good look." Mitch pointed to the sheet-cloaked figures. "It's the ghost of Christmas future. And it's heralding the death of your career."

"Do you think they plan to walk like that all the way home?" Donaldson took his hat off and ran his hand through his hair, making it stand on end. "I don't see any cars waiting."

"Maybe they plan to use their old folks' discount and take the bus?" Lake started laughing again.

"Keep your filthy hands to yourself," Betty shouted.

"Okay, enough of this." Donaldson sounded resigned to his fate. "Time to intervene." He spoke to Lake: "You round up the rescue squad and I'll get *Casper* and her little friend."

Josh moved to follow the cop. Donaldson stopped him in his tracks. "Back in the car, Josh. This is enough of a mess without you making it worse."

He gritted his teeth, but did as he was told.

"So now you listen," Mitch moaned before going to help Lake with the old folk.

Josh climbed into the SUV and watched through the heavily tinted windows as Donaldson grabbed hold of Caroline and Danny. He marched their sheet-covered bodies towards the waiting cars. Lake and two of his men herded the crowd of reporters to stop them following. Betty helped by shouting at everyone through her bullhorn. Mitch worked his way up the line of domino boys, disarming them. Once Caroline was in the police car, Mitch jogged over to the SUV and climbed into the driver's seat.

"Half of those guys think it was you under the sheet. How are we supposed to fix this?"

"We don't. We tell them it was a stunt put on by the crazy locals to draw attention from the castle and from us."

Mitch pursed his lips. "How much more of this are we going to have to fend off?"

"The wedding is Saturday. Then this will all be over." Josh resisted the urge to cross his fingers.

"Yeah, right," Mitch scoffed.

They sat in silence as they followed the cop car to the castle.

CHAPTER 30

Josh was mad. He just wasn't sure whom he was mad at. Caroline for calling the domino boys to rescue her instead of calling him? Danny for turning his fiancée into a spectacle? The press for hounding them? Mitch for sending away the bodyguard? There were too many options to choose from. Unfortunately, the only one available to shout at was Caroline.

"I've had it." Josh pointed at Caroline. "No more going out on your own. No going to work this week. No going anywhere without your damn cell phone. Even if I have to glue it to your hand."

Caroline sat tall and proud on one of his kitchen chairs. His mother pottered about in the background, pretending she was invisible while making emergency tea.

Caroline's shoulders snapped back. "I'm sorry, but for a minute there I thought you were telling me what to do. I think I was mistaken, because you can't possibly think that it's okay to lay down the law with me."

Josh stopped pacing in front of her. He folded his arms and glared down at her. He had the height advantage, but somehow Caroline seemed to have more power. He considered sitting at the table beside her, but he was too keyed up to stay still.

"You'll do what I say. Your life is in danger. There's a nutter out there sending you bleeding hearts and voodoo dolls. The town is overrun with paparazzi, who don't care what damage they cause as long as they get their payday. You're too available for people. You walk everywhere and you work in a public building. I'm not having it. How are we supposed to keep you safe until the wedding? You're staying here, in this castle, where I can protect you."

"No." Caroline folded her hands in her lap. Her chin rose. "I don't need you to look after me. What is this, the fifteenth century? I'm perfectly capable of looking after myself."

"Yeah, right. That's why you ended up stuck in that penis building with a guy I have a restraining order out against."

Caroline shot to her feet. "That building is *not* a penis. It's a folly."

"Yeah, way to focus on the most important part here."

"You are not my keeper, Josh McInnes. I can leave my house to walk around town any time I like. All I did was go to buy coffee. For you, I might add. I don't even drink the stuff. I'm sure I could have handled the press. They just caught me by surprise."

"So you ended up running through the streets hand in hand with my stalker."

"He's a nice man." Caroline's voice began to rise. "A bit deluded, but nice."

"Great. A nice stalker. That makes it okay, then. There are photos of you both all over the internet." Josh took a step towards her. He could feel the heat coming off her as her anger visibly grew. "There's one of him with his hands all over your ass, while you climb a fence. Tasteful."

"He was helping me!"

"He was groping you!"

Caroline's hands fell to her sides and clenched into fists. "I don't care about the stupid photos."

"Well, I do. This is my career we're talking about here. Half the world thinks it was me in the suit shoving my fiancée over a fence into a graveyard, the other half thinks you're having it on with my stalker. And don't even get me started on the old folks' rescue. What the hell was that?" Josh threw up his hands in disgust. "You called the domino boys instead of me. Instead of Lake. Hell, instead of the cops. You called three geriatric old men, who came armed with golf clubs and an eighty-six-year-old psycho carrying a bullhorn. You're turning our wedding into a pantomime."

"Since when do you care about the press?"

"Since it started to affect my reputation."

She scoffed. "Your womanising reputation or your care-free idiot reputation?"

There was a gasp from the direction of his mother. Josh had forgotten she was there. He lowered his voice and had to work to get the words past his clenched jaw.

"Look." Josh was trying to remain reasonable. It was hard, hard work. "I told you what you were getting into when I proposed. I told you again when the minister asked if you were keeping your job. I don't live in the same world you live in. In my world you have to fight for privacy. In my world there are people who can cause you harm, just because they think they know you. In my world you need to think twice before you do things, because everything you do can attract the wrong sort of attention. The dangerous sort. You are now in my world. You don't have the same freedom you did before, because that freedom will put you at risk. And I won't have that."

She put her hands on her hips and glared. "Well, what if I don't want to be in your world?"

Josh felt the wind go out of him. There was silence. He could hear Caroline's breathing. Her eyes flashed at him. Her skin vibrated with anger.

"Are you saying you want out?" Josh kept his tone carefully even. "Are you saying you don't want to marry me?"

"I'm thinking about it." Her words were like a kick to the gut. "When I said yes, I didn't realise I was agreeing to marry a man who wanted to be in charge of me. Who thinks he has the right to order me around."

"So what?" Josh scowled. "I'm not supposed to give a crap about your safety? If you decided to jump out of a plane without a parachute, because you 'can take care of yourself,' am I supposed to wave you off with a smile? Get real. You're behaving like a baby. You could have been hurt today. I won't allow it to happen again. Not while I can do something about it."

Her nostrils flared and her chin flew up. "How about you do something about this!" Then she kicked him in the shin. Hard.

"What the hell?" Josh rubbed his leg, grateful her shoes didn't have steel toecaps.

She pointed in his face. "And don't think you're coming anywhere near my bed. Ever again. That boat has sailed. Any kids we have will be made with a turkey baster." She stormed past him, slamming the kitchen door behind her.

"At least she's still talking about kids." Josh groaned as he plopped into a chair.

He listened for the sound of her stomping up the stairs, and was relieved when he heard it. For a minute he thought he'd hear the front door slam as she left him. The fact there were photographers parked at the gates might have factored into her decision to stay. Although, knowing Caroline, he wouldn't have put it past her to climb the garden wall if she was that determined to get away.

"You're going to have to fix this," his mum said.

Josh shot her a "you have got to be kidding me" look. "I'm right and you know it. She could really get hurt. There are all sorts of lunatics out there, and marrying me puts her on their radar. I need her to be safe. Even if it means handcuffing her to the bed until the wedding."

His mum sat down on the chair beside him. "You need to be patient with her. This is out of her comfort zone. Caroline is used to being in control of everything. She can't do that with the life you're offering her. She must be terrified."

"Yeah, she looked it," Josh scoffed.

But he wondered. He'd had all of his adult life to get used to being famous. It had happened gradually for him, so there'd been time to adapt. Caroline had been thrown in at the deep end, with barely three weeks to adjust.

He suddenly felt guilty. Maybe he'd been a bit harsh. "I better go talk to her."

"Are you sure? Perhaps leaving it to the morning is better."

"No." Josh sighed. "I'll do it now."

He dragged himself off the chair and headed for the stairs, wondering if Caroline had gone to his bedroom or taken one of the empty ones. Ten minutes later, he had his answer: Caroline hadn't taken any bedroom. Instead she'd opened the window on the first floor beside the oak tree and climbed down it. Josh felt steam come out of his ears. Damn impossible woman. She'd gone over the wall after all.

Josh pulled his phone out and called Mitch. He needed a lift past the reporters to Caroline's house.

CHAPTER 31

Caroline woke up in her bedroom on Thursday morning with a splitting sore head and her wrist handcuffed to her headboard. She stared at the silver cuff for a minute in disbelief then took a deep breath.

"Josh!" she screamed at the top of her lungs.

She heard his slow stomp as he came up the stairs to her bedroom. She should never have given him a key to her house. Oh, but wait. She didn't give him one. He stole it.

"You rang." Josh leaned against her bedroom doorframe.

He was dressed in romance novel classic, as Caroline liked to think of it: faded blue jeans and nothing else. He folded his arms across his bare chest and crossed his bare feet at the ankles. He was the image of relaxed sadist.

"Get this thing off me." Caroline jangled the cuffs.

"Nope. You can't be trusted. You're a danger to yourself and you don't listen to me."

Caroline pushed her hair out of her eyes and glared at him. "You mean I won't do what I'm told."

The idiot actually had to think about that. "That too," he said.

She took a deep breath. It didn't help, so she took some more. After about half a dozen she felt able to talk to him without her head rotating 360 degrees, like something from a horror movie.

"Josh"—she used her best "let's be reasonable" tone—"you need to take these off me. I need to go to the bathroom."

There, he couldn't argue with that.

"I can bring you a bucket." His smile was wicked.

Caroline knelt up on the bed and pointed at him. "I'm being serious. You can't handcuff me to the bed. What are you? A barbarian? Take these off this minute or I'll call the police." She eyed the phone on her bedside table.

"Where do you think I got the handcuffs? I explained to Officer Donaldson that you wouldn't listen to me and I couldn't trust you to stay where you were put. I made it clear that this was a safety issue. He was happy to help. He wants you safe too."

Caroline felt the top blow off her head. "Stay where I'm put? Stay where I'm put?" Her voice rose to that scary high-pitched level that only dogs could hear. "When I get out of here, Josh McInnes, you are going to be so sorry. I'll give you one last chance to do the right thing, otherwise you are really going to regret this."

Josh shrugged like her threat meant nothing. "I'm making eggs. I'll come back when you're more reasonable."

With that he thumped back down the stairs. Caroline stared after him mutely. She couldn't believe he'd left her. She couldn't believe he hadn't done what he was told. Furious, she reached for the phone beside her bed. There was no dial tone. She screeched in frustration before slamming the phone back down.

"Now, if you'd kept your cell phone with you like I told you to, you could call someone right now," Josh called from downstairs.

Caroline wanted to hit him so badly it actually caused her physical pain. He was so dead when she got loose. She'd never been one to hit people, preferring mental torture to physical, but Josh brought out her violent side. She planned his punishment while she fumed.

"And another thing." Josh's voice interrupted her planning. "I found your stolen sex books. We're going to have a nice long chat about that later."

Caroline screamed in frustration and threw the useless phone through the open door.

"She is going to kill you when she gets free." Mitch sipped coffee at Caroline's tiny kitchen table.

Josh shrugged. "I should have done this weeks ago. Her 'ruler of the world' mentality is going to get us all in trouble. If she'd been contained we wouldn't have needed the roadblocks, or the domino boys. We wouldn't have Danny bouncing back into town to chat with her. There wouldn't be any crazy gifts being sent to her work—well, not that she knew about, anyway. It would have all gone a lot smoother."

"You've lost your mind, you know that, right?"

"You're not telling me anything new. You said that to me when I proposed."

"Yeah, but this is further proof."

Josh concentrated on the omelette he was making. In a little while he'd go back upstairs for round two with Caroline. Maybe by then she'd be so desperate for the toilet that it'd make her more reasonable.

Josh eyed his best friend. "You didn't send Lake's guy away when you came inside, did you?"

Mitch looked at the ceiling for a beat. "Don't worry, I won't do that again."

Josh grunted. Lake had a guy at the front door of Caroline's house and one at the back. There wasn't much space between her doors and the public footpaths, but at least the bodyguards were keeping the press back. Josh had also closed all the curtains in the house. It was as private as a tiny terrace house could be. Thankfully, Lake's men were also dealing with the neighbours, who had come either to find out what was going on or complain about what was going on. That left Josh with one responsibility—Caroline.

"I snuck out of the castle to get away from you," Caroline shouted. "Can't you take the hint?"

"So"—Mitch leaned over to grab the coffee pot for a refill —"what exactly is the plan here? I'm assuming you have a plan. Right?"

"Absolutely." *Kind of. Maybe.*

"You want to share the plan with your best friend, lawyer and manager?"

Josh plonked two plates full of food on the table. It was man food. Meat. Eggs. None of that vegetable or bran garbage. Nothing you would feed a gerbil. He sat in the chair beside Mitch.

"The plan is to convince Caroline that her life can't go on as usual. She has to make changes. She has to take her safety seriously. And she has to realise that her choices affect more than her—they affect me and my career as well."

"That sounds great," Mitch drawled. "I'm sure she'll be eager to change everything about her life."

"She needs to see reason."

"And how are you going to get her to do that? Tickle her until she submits?"

Unfortunately, that was the part of the plan he wasn't so clear on.

"Look"—Josh put his fork down and took a gulp of his coffee—"she could have been hurt yesterday. She can't go out alone. Even if her crazy voodoo stalker doesn't go after her, there's still the press. You know as well as I do that dealing with them can be terrifying. The paparazzi want her to crack under the pressure. It's exactly the kind of picture they could auction off."

"Hey"—Mitch held up his hands in surrender—"you're preaching to the choir."

"You've got a visitor," the guy on the door called through.

"Who is it?" Josh shouted back.

"Archie McPherson."

"Archie?" Caroline shouted. "Archie, I'm being held prisoner. I need help."

Josh ignored her as he sauntered to the front door. Archie was shutting it behind him. He cast a curious glance in the direction of the stairs.

"I came to check on the lass," he said.

"Archie, get up here and set me free. Josh has me handcuffed to the bed."

Archie grinned at Josh. "You're a kinky son of a monkey, aren't you?"

Josh grinned back.

"This has nothing to do with sex," Caroline shouted. "He's trying to inflict his will on me. He won't let me have a mind of my own. He's locked me up because I won't do what I'm told." They heard the cuffs rattling as she banged about. "Archie McPherson, get up here right now and set me free, or I swear on Granddad's grave I will hurt you along with Josh once I get out of these things."

Archie's eyebrows rose so far up his forehead they disappeared under his grey cap. "She's furious." He was awestruck.

"Spitting mad," Josh agreed.

The old man leaned in towards Josh and lowered his voice. "She never loses her temper. She usually gets all icy and freezes your balls off with something she says." He removed his cap and scratched his head. "I've known her since she was a wee girl, and I've never seen her angry."

"Welcome to my world—in it she's mad all the time."

"Archie McPherson," Caroline shouted. "I'm going to count to three, and if you aren't up here by then there's going to be trouble. One."

The two men looked up the staircase.

Josh shook his head in wonder. "I'm not sure what she thinks she's going to do to us."

"Aye." Archie sounded bewildered.

"Two!" Caroline's voice rose an octave.

Archie shuffled his feet. "Well, I can see you have everything in hand here. I'd best be getting on. I'm guessing Donaldson knows about the cuffs."

"That's where I got them."

A slow, wicked smile lit up Archie's face. "Tell Caroline I dropped by and I'm glad she's well." He put his hat back on his head. "And tell her not to forget about the boiler that went kablooey." With a laugh, he opened the door.

"Three!" Caroline screamed. "That's it, Archie McPherson. You are on my list. You are number two on my list."

"Good luck, son." Archie slipped out the door.

Josh sauntered back into the kitchen to finish his breakfast, only to discover Mitch had already eaten it.

Josh swatted him on the back of the head. "Don't you have somewhere to go?"

"Nope." Mitch reached for the coffee again.

"Someone needs to deal with the wedding planner now that Caroline is indisposed."

Mitch's eyes lit up. "Now that you mention it, the delectable Millicent could probably use a hand." He put the coffee pot back in its stand. "Don't you just love an English accent?"

Josh smiled knowingly. "I'm partial to Scottish, myself."

"I need to use the bathroom," Caroline shouted. "If you don't release me, there will be an accident."

"Okay, I'm out of here." Mitch headed for the front door. "Don't worry about the wedding. I'll deal with Millicent. I'll tell her Caroline is tied up at the moment." With a grin, he put on his sunglasses and left.

"I can't hold it much longer. Josh, get your backside up here right now."

With a chuckle, Josh trotted up the stairs to his fiancée.

CHAPTER 32

Caroline sat on the sofa facing Josh, and fumed. He'd *graciously* allowed her to use the facilities and get dressed. Before he let her leave the bedroom she'd had to swear a vow, hand held high, that she wouldn't run. Now she was on house arrest and currently engaged in a staring contest with the insane American she'd promised to marry.

"Could you at least put a shirt on?" Caroline snapped.

Josh looked down at his bare abs. "What? I thought you liked my chest. I thought you wanted to, and I'm quoting here, lick it like an ice lolly."

She felt her face burn. "That was before."

"Before what?"

"Before I realised how much of a bully you are. It's a decidedly unattractive quality in a man."

He smiled like he knew better.

"You can't keep me here as a prisoner." Although Caroline sounded convinced, inside she wasn't so sure. "This is my town. I have responsibilities here. A life here."

Josh ran a hand over his face, sighed and then leaned forward to perch his elbows on his knees. He took a deep breath before pinning her with those stunning blue eyes of his.

"I might have said some things yesterday that I regret."

"Really? You think?" Caroline wasn't ready to let go of her anger quite yet. The man had chained her to a bed! That might be entertaining in a romance novel, but in real life, not so much.

"I'm trying to apologise here, Caroline." His tone said he was running out of patience with her.

"Is that what you're trying to do? It wasn't clear."

His jaw clenched tightly before he took another deep breath. "I'm worried about you. Worried about your safety. Worried that your trusting nature will lead you to give time to people who don't deserve it." He hung his head before looking at her again. "I'm worried you'll get hurt."

The wind went out of Caroline. He was worried? She couldn't remember the last time someone was concerned about her. For as long as she could remember, it was her job to look out for everyone else. "You don't need to worry, Josh. I really can take care of myself. Honestly. I'm thirty-one. I'm not a child."

"Don't you think I know that? But this is a different world you're in now, baby." The muscles in his shoulders clenched and unclenched, causing a chain reaction in Caroline's stomach. For someone who was always so easy-going, he oozed tension. "I've had a long time to get used to being a celebrity. It started slowly for me—getting recognised locally, then nationally, now globally. I've had time to develop strategies to cope. I've also had time to get to know what that world is like. To recognise the danger in it." The concern in his eyes made her heart beat faster. "But you have only had a couple of weeks."

Caroline leaned forward on the sofa. "I keep telling you. That's your life. Not mine. I don't need time to get used to it."

"Yeah. It's my life. It's got nothing to do with you." He snorted. "So how come the photographers are hounding you? Why are magazines running spreads on what you wear? Why did thousands apply to be your assistant?" He let out a long breath. "I wish it were different. I really do. But you're in this along with me now. My fans want to know all about you. The paparazzi want to take your picture. People want to use you to get to me. That's your reality."

Caroline wanted to argue that he was wrong. She wanted to believe she was separate from everything his celebrity brought about, but she was only fooling herself. There was no separation. As soon as she'd agreed to marry him, she'd kissed her privacy goodbye. The knowledge came crashing down on her. She studied the ugly faded carpet her grandfather had picked out decades earlier, as she chewed on her bottom lip. No matter which way she looked at it, the situation didn't change.

"I can't keep working at the centre, can I?"

Josh pulled his chair forward so that he was within touching distance. He reached for her hand, his hold strong and sure. "I'm sorry, baby."

Caroline looked around her living room. The photos of her as a child smiled back at her. The walls of books she'd poured herself into seemed to close in around her.

"Everything has to change, doesn't it?"

"Yeah." His voice was soft. He threaded his fingers with hers.

Caroline looked up into his eyes. There was genuine compassion in them. "I don't like it."

He chuckled lightly. "Who does? I know you didn't ask for this. I chased fame. I knew what I was getting into right from the start. I'm sorry that it's part of being with me. I can't change that now."

"Would you want to change it?"

"If it kept you safe, then yeah."

They sat in silence for a moment as Josh rubbed circles in the centre of her palm with his thumb. Caroline didn't know what to say. Really, what could she say? Her life was about to change forever.

Josh took a deep breath. His smile was small and sad. "I was scared, baby." His voice was barely a whisper. "I can't remember ever feeling like that before. I don't want anything to happen to you, and my world can be crazy. I need to be able to keep you safe. And to do that, I need you to work with me. Will you do that? For me?"

The last barriers Caroline held against the man crumbled. "You sound so serious. I didn't think you took anything seriously."

"Some things are worth getting serious about. This is one of them."

Caroline felt a surge in her chest. Her heart was swelling. There was so much more to this man than most people saw. And the more she saw, the more she lo—liked. The more she liked.

"Okay, Josh. I can work with you on this."

The smile he gave her was dazzling. He trailed a fingertip along her jaw.

"That means a lot to me, baby. Can we agree that you'll take your bodyguard with you no matter where you go?"

Caroline didn't like that one bit. She swallowed a sigh. "Fine. If it makes you happy, we can agree on that."

"Oh, yeah. It makes me happy." He brushed his thumb over her bottom lip, and a tingling sensation travelled throughout her body. "And you'll remember to take your phone with you when you leave the house?"

She did sigh this time. "Yes. I'll take the phone." She thought about it. "Maybe I can get a cord and hang it around my neck. You know, like old people do with their glasses."

He brought her hand to his mouth and smiled against her palm. "Yeah, you can do that. I don't care what you do as long as it's with you. You had to use my stalker's phone to call for help. There are so many ways that could have gone wrong. What if he was dangerous? What if he didn't have a phone? Maybe a cord won't work. Maybe we should superglue it to you."

Caroline trembled at the sensation of his lips against her palm. She swallowed hard. It had become increasingly difficult to follow the conversation. Josh studied her, a small smile on his lips that told her he knew exactly what affect he had on her.

"Enough," Caroline grumbled, but it sounded half-hearted. Her mind was on other things. "I said I'll take the phone with me. But we decide everything regarding my safety together. You can't go all caveman and order me around."

He pressed a kiss to the inside of her wrist. "You order me around."

"That's how it should be."

Josh barked out a laugh. "I don't think I'll win this argument."

Caroline didn't comment on that. Mainly because he was right. "And no more handcuffs."

"But I kind of like the idea of you handcuffed to our bed and at my mercy." His voice lowered. "The things I could do to your helpless body. The sounds you would make. I definitely think we should keep the handcuffs."

Caroline shifted in her seat to assuage the ache between her legs at the thought of being at Josh's mercy. Josh raised an eyebrow at her wriggling. Annoying man.

His face softened. "Are we okay? Do you still want to marry me?"

Caroline's stomach clenched. He was gorgeous. All angles

and planes. Muscled perfection with full lips and glittering blue eyes. She wanted to lose herself in his eyes. She wanted to have him wrapped around her. The urge to hide in him was almost overwhelming. The need to give herself to Josh, to let him carry her for a while, was one she'd never felt before. What would it be like to let someone else take care of things for a little while? Could she trust him not to hurt her?

She looked into his beautiful eyes and saw an uncertainty there that shocked her. Under his carefree, cocky attitude, Josh was perhaps as vulnerable as she was.

"Do *you* still want to marry me?" She was almost scared of the answer.

He stared at her for a minute before a slow grin lit his face. His eyes sparkled with mischief. It took her breath away. "Hell yes, I want to marry you."

He yanked on her hand. She flew off the sofa to land in his lap.

Caroline felt relief from his answer buoy her spirits. She tried not to think too hard about the nausea she'd felt when she'd feared things would end between them.

"You would probably be better off with someone who is used to the whole celebrity thing." She briefly wondered why she was trying to talk him out of his commitment.

"Probably"—he grinned wickedly—"but where's the fun in that?"

"Yes, but—"

"No buts. I'm done talking. Now we get to the good part about fighting." He waggled his eyebrows at her. "It's time to make up."

Before Caroline could utter a word of protest, not that she could think of any, Josh threaded his hand in the back of her hair and pulled her mouth to his. The touch of his lips against hers was perfect. His kiss was powerful and gentle at the same time. She opened her lips for him, moving closer into his embrace. His arms tightened around her and his kiss became more demanding. It felt like there was something more to it. It was as though all his worries about her were in the kiss. There was a desperation in his touch that melted her defences. He was telling her that he cared about her safety. That he cared about her. He was kissing her like she belonged to him. And it was wonderful.

JOSH LOVED the way Caroline went molten in his arms. He ran his hands over her soft curves and tried to forget what could have happened to her. Tried to put thoughts of her being hurt out of his mind. She let out a tiny sigh of pleasure as his tongue languidly caressed hers. If anything had happened to her, he didn't know what he would do. There would be no holding him back. There would be no need to worry about his career, because he would trample over it to get to the people who hurt his fiancée. It was all that mattered.

She was all the mattered.

Josh didn't want to look too closely at what that meant. He didn't want any more talking, examining, analysing. He only wanted to feel. To touch Caroline and to reassure himself that everything was fine. That she was fine.

He trailed his lips across her jaw and down the column of her throat. She moved her head to give him access. Her fingernails bit into his shoulders as she held on tightly. He doubted that she even knew she was marking him, but he loved the sensation. He gently bit the curve where her neck met her shoulder, and she moaned, pulling him closer to her.

"I need you."

"Yes." Her answer a shuddering whisper.

Josh ran his hand down her back to the edge of her pink dress and found the bare skin of her thigh. Her skin was like silk that rippled under his touch. His mouth moved back to hers as he trailed his hand along her thigh to the curve of her behind. Caroline pressed her breasts against his chest. She moaned into his mouth. Josh grasped her tighter. The dress had to go.

He reached for the zip at the back of her neck and tugged. Caroline pulled away from him. He stilled. One hand on the zip, another on the curve of her behind. Caroline's breath was laboured. Her pulse was beating a tattoo at the bottom of her throat. Her eyes were heavy-lidded, drowsy with the same passion he felt. She placed a palm on each of his cheeks and stared into his eyes. Josh was afraid to move. Afraid to shatter the moment. He couldn't name what he saw in her eyes as she looked at him. The depth of it made him feel awe. After the longest time, she nodded as though making a decision. An important decision. He held his breath. She smiled softly.

"Take me upstairs, Josh," she whispered.

Josh felt something within him shift. He clenched his jaw and closed his eyes briefly. Everything fell into place and nothing had ever felt more right.

He grasped her hips and placed her on her bare feet before him. He brushed her lips gently with his and then stroked his hand through her hair. Her hand folded into his. Without saying another word, Josh led her out of the living room and up the stairs to her bedroom.

CHAPTER 33

There was no doubt in Caroline's mind that she had fallen in love with Josh McInnes. She wasn't sure when it had happened, but as she'd looked into his eyes, she'd known without a doubt that she had. She'd nodded to herself as she accepted the knowledge as truth. This man. Her man. She'd waited her whole life to love someone completely. And he was the one.

She watched his back muscles move as he led her up the stairs. His jeans clung to his backside, making her mouth water at the sight. She had never wanted anything more than to be in Josh's arms. Than to belong to him completely.

As he gently led her through her open doorway to her bed, she expected to feel nervous. The sum of her experience with men was so small as to be negligible. But she didn't feel anxious or afraid. She felt sure. This was what she wanted. It was going to happen anyway—their wedding was days away and Josh had been clear that he wanted children. But it felt right to Caroline that she wasn't going to make love to Josh because it was part of her agreement. She was doing it because she loved him.

"I kind of wish I'd left the door now. I keep expecting that any minute, someone will wander into your house and ruin this." His smile was cheeky, but his gaze was hot and seductive. It made her quiver.

"You're the only one with a key."

He traced a finger down her cheek. "Are you sure about this? I can wait." He paused. "If I have to."

She smiled. Poor, suffering man. *Yeah, right.* "I'm sure. I want this."

"Last chance to change your mind," he teased.

"You can't get out of it that easily."

His eyes darkened with a passion that smouldered. "I don't want out, baby."

With one step, he closed the distance between them. His fingers wound around the back of her neck. He angled her head. And then his mouth plundered hers. She hooked her hands into his jeans and hung on tightly. The room swayed around her. His scent, masculine and spicy, filled her senses. He tasted like a cross between chocolate and coffee. For someone who never liked coffee, it could make a convert out of her. She pushed herself up on tiptoes to get closer. Josh's palm flattened at the small of her back, crushing her against him.

After an eternity, his mouth left hers. They were both panting. Out of breath from passion and need.

"Turn around." His hands were on her hips, turning her before the words had left his mouth.

Caroline was unsteady as she put her back to him. Softly, he swept her hair away from her neck, and she heard the zip of her dress as it slowly lowered. All of her clothes were at the castle waiting to be burned. All she had was this dress and the lavender lace lingerie set beneath it.

"So soft," he whispered.

He trailed his lips down her neck and across her shoulder,

before returning to her spine. She heard him lower to his knees as he slowly removed her dress. His kisses followed the path of the dress until it crumpled at her feet on the floor.

"Beautiful." His hands gripped her hips as he swirled his tongue in the small of her back.

Caroline's eyes fluttered shut as she swayed in place. What was he doing to her? How was it possible that a kiss on her back made her insides tilt? His strong hands turned her.

He groaned at the sight of her. "We need to get you more lingerie." He smiled up at her. Making her painfully aware that his mouth was level with her breasts. And she knew exactly how good that mouth felt on her. "When we're at home in the castle, you should only ever wear lingerie and nothing else."

Before she could answer, he leaned forward and sucked a nipple into his mouth, right through the lace of her bra. She gasped. Her hands flew to his head. Her fingers tangled in his hair.

"Delicious." The word was a rumble against her skin that sent tingles to her core.

Caroline clutched him, like an anchor in a storm, as Josh kissed and bit and sucked. Her mind soared. Nothing existed except the sensation of Josh's touch. Gasps and moans punctuated the air. Her head fell back as her knees weakened. Josh's hand caressed its way up her back, and she felt the clasp of her bra give way. A second later, the bra was gone. His breath was hot against her skin.

"You are perfect." He sucked her into his mouth so hard that it made her scream. Her knees gave way. Josh caught her and placed her on the bed. Her hips rested on the edge, her legs dangling over the end. All thought was lost in the fog of desire that had overtaken her mind. Before she could catch her breath, Josh had stripped her of her underwear. He pushed her knees apart. Caroline struggled to think through what he was doing. Her brain wasn't fast enough. His mouth was on her before she figured it out. And then all thought was gone. All she was aware of was his tongue tasting her. Teasing her. Touching her.

Caroline felt pressure tingle and build within her stomach. Her breath came in desperate pants. She clawed at the bedspread beneath her. Unconsciously, she pushed closer to his wicked, wicked lips.

"Josh," she moaned.

He didn't answer. Instead he growled against her, sending vibrations throughout her body.

"Josh!"

Her head spun. Or maybe it was the room.

"Baby," he rumbled. "So good."

Her toes curled. Her thighs tensed. Her head arched back. And she was flying. A word fought its way from her throat. A long, aching moan of a word. "Josh."

As she slowly came back to herself, she felt Josh crawl over her body. He moved her boneless body further up the bed. Her limbs were too heavy to help. She was at his mercy.

Josh nibbled his way up her throat until his mouth met hers. His kiss was deep and sensual. Caroline curled her arms around his neck and hooked a leg over his thigh. Bare flesh met bare flesh. At some point Josh had taken off his jeans. Caroline's heart pounded so loudly at the thought of a naked Josh. Part of her wanted to push him back and look her fill. But she couldn't. She was lost in the weight of his body against hers. The sensation of firm muscles rippling over her softer form. She clasped her hands tightly around his upper arms. His biceps tensed. The power in his muscles made her body shudder.

"I'll go slow, baby," he whispered against her lips. "Tell me if you need to stop."

It wasn't until she felt him press against her that she realised what he meant. She held her breath as Josh slowly, steadily filled her.

"You are perfect. You feel so good."

Caroline arched up into him. At last, he settled his frame flush against her. His fingers stroked her face. Caroline's gaze met his. The blue had been swallowed by black. Her internal muscles clenched at the sight, making him groan. It was wonderful. Nothing had ever felt so right to her. It was on the tip of her tongue to tell him that she'd fallen in love with him. Only the certainty that anything romantic would ruin the moment made her stop. Josh didn't want romance.

But he did want her.

"Are you okay?" He placed a soft kiss on the corner of her mouth.

"Amazing. I never knew..." She let out a shuddering sigh. "It's amazing."

He smiled against her mouth. "It's about to get better."

She wasn't sure it could get better. And then his hips started to move. Every nerve in her body came alive in the same instant. Her world narrowed to only Josh. There was nothing else in the cocoon they had made. His musky scent filled her senses. His strength surrounded her. Everything within her began to climb. She was losing her sense of self. Josh and Caroline didn't exist anymore. They weren't two. They were one.

"Faster." Caroline ordered.

"Bossy." He chuckled tightly. "I should have known you would be bossy here too."

Caroline slammed her hips up into him. He groaned, and it was her turn to smile. Josh moved faster. Deeper. Caroline lost her place entirely. She clawed at him. Her senses were overloaded. There was too much to feel, to hear, to touch. It was a tsunami of sensation, swallowing her whole.

"Josh. Josh." His name was a chant. A desperate, pleading chant.

She felt him tense above her as lights flickered in front of her eyes. Her muscles clenched. She sucked in a breath. Her heart stuttered. Every muscle spasmed. A long, desperate moan. Everything within her crashed to a halt. Time stopped. A beat. Two. And then she gasped for air. Her fingers tingled. Her heart started to thud again, loudly. Her muscles became jelly. Josh fell to her side. His fingers threaded through her hair as he nuzzled her throat.

"Are you okay?"

Caroline let out a sigh. "Better than okay."

"Good." He kissed her gently, making her tremble.

He pushed back from her and searched her eyes. Seeking confirmation that she was okay with things. A slow smile lit his face. He rolled onto his back and pulled her into his side, tucking her tight against him. Caroline listened to his rushing heartbeat as it slowed to normal. She traced lazy circles on his abdomen. For the first time since she'd agreed to marry Josh, she questioned the wisdom of her decision. She was in love with the man. But he didn't want that. No. He wanted a solid commitment without romantic love. He wanted the kind of love that good friends shared. Her heart stuttered within her. What if Josh never felt anything more for her than he did right now? Would she be able to live with that? Knowing that the man she was madly, desperately in love with only felt affection for her?

She tried to tell herself to be practical. To stop wanting more than she already had. Goodness knows, what Josh offered her was far more than she ever expected she'd have. But still. A tiny, niggling part of her wondered if she would live a lifetime heartbroken that the man she married didn't love her the way she loved him.

CHAPTER 34

Andrew McInnes was as nervous as a boy on his first date. He'd spent the past few days in Glasgow being fitted for the all-important suit. He'd visited a sex shop. It wasn't what he'd expected. He'd thought he'd have to skulk through an unmarked door and buy things in brown paper bags. Instead, the vast front window was full of kinky lingerie and there were women serving behind the counter.

He'd been embarrassed at first, especially as he had no idea what to buy—except handcuffs, that is. Eventually, one of the women had taken pity on him and offered to help. He'd explained that he was trying to seduce his wife of thirty-five years. Then he'd explained his theory on what women wanted. She seemed impressed with the amount of research he'd done on the topic. Twenty minutes later, he'd left the shop armed with a beginner's kit for kinky sex. He hadn't known such a thing existed, but it did. It was all boxed up in a pink candy-striped package.

Bewildered, Andrew had spent the rest of his time in Glasgow getting a haircut and buying chocolate. If all else failed, he'd ply Helen with the biggest damn box of gourmet chocolates that money could buy.

He didn't even want to think what he would do if the chocolate didn't do the trick.

Now it was Friday and he was back in Invertary. The town was full of reporters, and Josh was holed up in Caroline's house until the wedding. Which meant Helen was in the castle. Alone.

As Andrew stood outside the castle door, he reminded himself of what women wanted. Domineering guy in a suit? He looked down at himself. Check. Over-the-top romantic gestures? He eyed the pamphlet tucked into his pocket. Check. Kinky sex? He flexed his grasp on the bag full of purchases from the sex shop. Check. He took a deep breath. This was as good as it got.

Then he rang the doorbell.

Nerves assaulted him. His palms were wet. His mouth was dry. Damn it all to hell. This was too much for a sixty-seven-year-old heart to handle. He was going to have a stroke right here on the doorstep. Helen would open the door, look out over his prone dead body and wonder why she'd ever married him. *Breathe. Damn it. Breathe.*

He was on the verge of running when the door swung open.

Helen was wearing the yellow flowered sundress that was so pretty on her. Her feet were bare and her makeup had worn off some during the day. She was stunning. Her mouth opened and shut a couple of times as her wide eyes travelled the length of him. A flush hit her cheeks, and Andrew couldn't help but puff out his chest with pride. He might be old, but he still had it going on.

"Andrew? What do you—"

He didn't let her finish. In two long strides, he grabbed

her round the waist, clutched the back of her head and pressed his mouth to hers. Operation Win Helen Back had officially started. And damn, but it felt good to have his wife in his arms again.

She smelled of peppermint and lilacs. A smell that was unique to her and made his heart shudder. Whether she liked it or not, she belonged to him. She'd always belonged to him. He might have been lax in showing it, but Helen was the only woman he had ever loved. The only one he *would* ever love. And he was never letting her go.

Helen didn't kiss him back. She didn't do much of anything. He knew she was stunned, but he kept on kissing her until she caught up with him. At last, he felt her lips move and her arms slowly wrap around his waist. He wanted to stop and fist-pump the air. But he didn't. Instead, he backed her into the wall and kissed her like she'd never been kissed before. A small moan escaped her lips, and he swallowed it down greedily. He pulled her tight against him, noticing again how perfectly she fit. Briefly he wondered if he should lift her up so that her legs would wrap around his waist. He would take her in the hall, up against the wall. Just like the heroes in all those books liked to do. Sadly, he didn't think his back could take it, and the last thing he wanted was for the both of them to land on the floor and him to writhe in agony.

No. He needed a bed for what he had planned. He mentally cursed that the beds were all upstairs. He was worried that by the time he got her there, he would have lost his advantage. That left the kitchen. He reluctantly pulled away from her kiss. He stroked his hand over her new short hair. It didn't bother him much anymore. In fact, it was even kind of sexy. He was pleased to see that Helen's breathing was fast and shallow.

"What are you doing?" It'd been a long time since he'd heard that breathless whisper. He'd missed it.

He leaned over and snatched the bag from where he'd dropped it outside the front door. Kicking the door shut behind him, he grabbed Helen's hand and strode towards the kitchen, dragging her along with him.

"Andrew, are you listening to me? You can't just come in here and kiss me like this."

"The hell I can. You're my wife."

She tugged against his grip. He didn't release her. "We're getting a divorce."

"We'll see about that." He kicked the kitchen door open and tugged her inside.

Now, where would be a good spot to get all kinky? He eyed the table. Didn't he see a scene like that once? What was the movie? Oh yeah. *The Postman Always Rings Twice.* He wasn't sure he'd liked that film. But the scene he remembered gave him ideas.

He dragged her towards the table.

"Andrew. You're acting like a madman. Stop this at once."

"No."

In a dramatic display of his masculinity, he swept the dishes off the table. He grinned at the sound of them smashing on the floor.

"Andrew. You're scaring me."

"Don't be daft." He dropped the bag beside the table. Picked Helen up and sat her on the edge. Just the right height. He stepped between her legs, cupped her head with his hands and settled his mouth on hers. This time she wasn't numb. She responded straight away. So much for her complaining. He growled with satisfaction.

Her hands slid into his suit jacket and around to his back. She clung to his shirt. Her nails digging into his back. Andrew wanted to grin. The suit worked a charm.

Slowly, he eased her back until she was lying on the table.

"What are you going?" She was breathless.

"I'm doing what I should have done a year ago when you said you needed space."

He kept a hand on her stomach as he reached into the bag. He brought out a set of black fluffy handcuffs. They looked a bit cheesy to him, but what the heck. Helen eyed the handcuffs with worry.

"Are those handcuffs?" She struggled to get up. "Stop it right now."

He snapped the cuff around her wrist, then shackled the other end to the leg of the table.

"Free me right now, Andrew McInnes. Have you lost your mind?"

He ignored her. Instead he brought out the other set of cuffs and secured her other arm. Once he'd finished, he took a step back to survey his work. He couldn't help the sense of satisfaction that welled within him. The books were right. Everything was going to plan.

Helen thinned her red and swollen lips. "What do you think you're doing?"

"We're going to have kinky sex." He rummaged around in his bag until he found the black silk blindfold.

"We're what?" Helen was screeching now.

He walked around the table until he was at her head. "No more shouting. It's ruining the mood."

Her mouth fell open. "I'm ruining the mood? What mood would that be, Andrew? The mood where my soon-to-be ex-husband snaps, takes me hostage and ties me to the table? Is that even a mood?"

He was regretting his decision not to buy one of the gags he'd seen in the shop. "I'm trying to be romantic, woman."

Her eyebrows shot up her head. "By tying me up and

threatening kinky sex? I don't want kinky sex. I don't even know what kinky sex is. I want you to leave."

"Damn it," Andrew mumbled, "I thought all women read the same books." He patted his wife's head to reassure her. "Don't worry. I studied up on this. I'll show you what to do."

Helen dropped her head to the table with a loud thump. She didn't seem to be in the mood for sex. Andrew decided to plod on anyway. He had a plan. It was a good plan. He was wearing the suit to prove it.

"Right, lift your head. I need to get this blindfold on."

Helen glared at him, but lifted her head. "I'm doing this because I don't have a choice. But as soon as I'm free, I'm calling a psychiatrist for you."

"Whatever." Andrew tied the blindfold tight over her eyes. "Can you see anything?"

"No. I'm wearing a blindfold."

Andrew studied her for a moment before he decided he'd better check. "How many fingers am I holding up?"

She ignored him and ground her teeth together. Fine. He'd just assume she couldn't see. He stomped back to the bag. Where were his note cards? They weren't in the bag. He patted his pockets and found them in the inside of his jacket. He read the first one. Cuffs? Check. Blindfold? Check.

He cleared his throat. "You need to pick a safe word."

"What on earth is a safe word?"

He smothered a sigh. This was proving to be more work than he thought it'd be. "It's a word you use when you want things to stop."

"How about I use the word 'stop'?" She sounded sarcastic.

"That's not how it works. You need a word that you wouldn't normally use during sex."

"Fine. How about 'dumbass'?"

"I don't think you're getting into the spirit of this."

"Really? You think?"

"Fine. Dumbass it is." There was no dealing with her when she was in this mood. "If you use your safe word, everything stops."

"Good." She took a deep breath. "Dumbass," she shouted.

Andrew wasn't sure what to do next. This was not going the way it did in the books. He consulted his note cards. There wasn't anything on there about her saying her safe word before things started. Should he just stop?

"Why aren't you releasing me, *dumbass?*"

He wasn't sure what to say. This didn't happen in any of the books he'd read. "I've decided that you don't need a safe word."

"That's a surprise." She didn't sound surprised.

Andrew threw the card with the advice on safe words over his shoulder. What was next? Oh yeah. Delayed orgasm.

"Okay." He eyed his wife. She didn't look turned on. She looked tense and resigned. He got the distinct impression she was enduring this. "I'm going to play with you for a while. You are mine to enjoy and you will not have an orgasm. If you do, you will be punished." He paused and read his card. He was supposed to deepen his voice and sound more commanding. He did just that. "Do you hear me, Helen? You will not have an orgasm unless I give you permission."

He held his breath while he waited to see what she would do. Her shoulders started to shake. Her lips tightened. Oh no. She was crying. He sprang forward to release her when her lips tipped into a grin and she burst out laughing.

Andrew glared at her. "You will not laugh at your master."

The laughing got louder. Tears started to roll down her cheeks. What the hell was he supposed to do about this?

"This is insubordination. You will be punished."

"Oh, stop it. You're making my stomach hurt."

"That's it. I warned you." He lifted her ankles high in the air and swatted her backside.

Helen laughed so hard she started to wheeze.

"I'm serious here." He smacked her again.

According to the books, this sort of thing was supposed to turn them both on. His wife was in hysterics, and he could honestly say swatting her ass like she was a two-year-old was doing nothing for him. He let her legs drop. Pulled out a chair and sat down to wait out her hysterics.

After several minutes, the laughter tapered off. Helen's cheeks were flushed and wet. She was still grinning, and she'd brought her heels up to rest on the table, because she'd been complaining that her stomach muscles were aching.

"Andrew, are you still here?"

He grunted.

"I guess that means you are. And you're back to your old grunting self." She giggled again, then worked to get it under control. "What now, *dumbass*?"

Andrew leaned forward and crossed his arms on the table beside her. "I'm damned if I know."

"Aren't you supposed to torture me until I beg for an orgasm?" She was mocking him. With a grin on her face.

Andrew couldn't help but smile at her. She was stunning, lying there all flushed and happy.

"I have a bag full of sex toys to torment you with."

Her eyebrows went up and peeked out from under the blindfold. "What kind of toys?" He could tell she was trying not to come across as too eager.

He grinned. He trailed his fingers up her arm to her shoulder. Pretty. She was so pretty.

"I'm not telling you now. You ruined the mood."

She pretended to pout. "So I don't get my orgasm, then?"

"I didn't say that."

She sucked in a breath, but tried to cover her reaction with a fake light-hearted laugh. Andrew felt hopeful for the first time in months. He leaned over and popped the top button on her dress.

"What are you doing?"

"Seeing what's mine." He'd stolen that line from a book. From several books, in fact. It seemed to crop up a lot. And damn if it wasn't a line that actually worked. He could feel her pulse pick up speed under his fingertips. He popped another button.

"I don't think this is a good idea." Her words were saying one thing, but the way she moved into his touch was saying something else entirely.

"I want to get a few things straight." Andrew popped another button. Her underwear came into view. She was wearing a pale yellow lace bra that he'd never seen before. He traced the edge of the cup with his finger. Pretty.

Helen let out a breath that shuddered slightly. She was working at keeping her breathing even. At trying to hide her reaction to his touch. His shoulders relaxed. It'd been too long since he'd had fun with his wife. Too long since he'd spent time studying her every reaction to him. He'd forgotten how wonderful it was to watch what he did to her. How she reacted to him. He slowly worked his way down the rest of the buttons until her dress fell open at her sides.

Goosebumps made a pattern on her skin as the cold air caressed her. He ran his palm over her stomach, feeling it clench beneath his touch. He wasn't worried about her being cold. He planned to warm her up.

"You need to release me." Her voice was shaky. "We shouldn't be doing this."

He liked that she said "we."

"I want to talk about some stuff." Her underpants were the same colour as her bra. They had a tiny satin bow on each hip. He wondered if they were there for decoration or if he could untie them.

He shifted in his chair as his trousers became constricting.

"You want to talk?" she said. He could imagine her rolling her eyes. He smiled. "You *never* want to talk. It's part of the problem. I might as well be living with a blow-up doll. You don't talk. You don't do anything at all. You just sit around waiting to die. Well, I don't want a life like that. I want to live my life. I want to squeeze as much out of it as I can."

He sighed. How many ways had he screwed things up? How many ways had he hurt his wife?

"You should have told me." It was the wrong thing to say.

"I did tell you, *dumbass*. Over and over again. That's another problem we have. You don't listen. You're too busy brooding about being old."

It was a slap to the face. He couldn't deny she was right. "I'm listening now. Tell me what you want."

She didn't say anything. Andrew waited for his wife while he toyed with the bows on her underwear. He tugged at one. Nothing happened. They were decoration. Typical.

"I told you what I need. I need to live." She turned her face away from him. Andrew didn't like that one bit.

"So we live."

"Yeah," she scoffed. "Like you'll change."

Damn right he was changing. He'd bought a suit. He had sex toys. He'd booked an over-the-top romantic trip for two. What was that if it wasn't changing? He felt a bit miffed that he wasn't getting the credit he deserved.

He'd tried the kinky sex route, and that was a failure. It was time to put the suit to its proper use and go all arrogant bastard on her. He whipped off her blindfold and watched as she blinked at the light.

"Now you listen to me, woman. There will be no divorce. There will be no argument. We're selling the house in Florida and moving somewhere else. I haven't figured out where yet, but Florida isn't working for us. You will let me back in to your bed. You will not flirt with any other men. Ever. And there will be no more talk about divorce."

Her eyes narrowed. He'd seen that look before. It didn't bode well. "Is that right? Will I do all of those things? Let me think." She pretended to consider it when it was obvious that she already had the answer. "I think not." She glared at him. "Where do you get off telling me what to do? Am I your slave? Your employee? Your child? Who told you that you know better than I do? I'll get a divorce if I damn well want to. And I'll live where I want to. And you're not getting back into my bed. Ever."

Crap. This wasn't going as planned. According to the books, she would crumble in the face of his masculine power and gratefully accept his word as law. He was beginning to doubt the books. He rubbed his jaw. It was time to try the last weapon in his arsenal—the big romantic gesture.

He reached into his suit pocket and came out with the brochure he'd gotten from the travel agent. "I booked a trip for us." He handed it to her, then realised she was still cuffed to the table. He considered letting her loose, but decided it was best to keep her there. Otherwise she might run away and he wouldn't get to tell her about the trip. He held the brochure in front of her nose and flipped the pages for her. "See? It's a three-month tour of Europe. We go to all the romantic spots you've always wanted to visit. We probably won't see much because they'll be crowded with tourists, but what the hell? Look, Venice, Rome, Prague, Paris. We'll need to deal with the French, but you can't have everything." He waved the brochure. "What do you think?"

She sighed heavily. "Let me loose. I won't run." It was as though she could read his mind.

Reluctantly, he freed his wife. Helen rubbed her wrists before swivelling on the table to sit facing him. She started to pull her dress together and button it. He put up a hand to stop her.

"Please don't. You're beautiful."

She stilled. "Andrew. I'm a fifty-five-year-old woman who's overweight. I have lines and cellulite. My boobs sag. I'm not beautiful."

Oh, the stupid woman. He placed a hand on the table on either side of her and stared deep into her eyes. "You are the most beautiful woman in the world to me."

She scoffed. "Don't be daft—"

He pressed a finger against her lips. "Don't. Don't say it. I mean it. You are perfection to me. You always have been and you always will be."

Her eyes glistened with unshed tears, and Andrew's heart shattered. What had he done? Had he really let her go for so long without letting her know what he saw? He was the fool.

At least he could change that now. "I'm sorry I haven't told you this enough over the years. I mean it. I'm not saying it because I'm scared of being old and alone. I'd rather be alone than have any other woman. You're it for me, Helen. And you are beautiful."

A single tear fell down her cheek.

"I don't need all of this." Her voice was soft. "I don't need the grand gestures, the kinky sex or the personality change you're sporting." She looked up at him as the tears fell. "I just need you. I can't stay with you if you're only going to grunt at me and hide in our house. I can't live like that."

"I won't do it anymore." He wiped the tears from her cheeks with his thumbs. "I'll talk. I'll go out. I might complain about it. But I'll try."

She didn't look like she believed him.

"Give it a chance," he said. "Give us a chance. I love you so much, honey. Don't walk away."

With a sob, she wrapped herself around him and buried

her face in his new silk shirt. Andrew held on to her, rubbing her back and cooing nonsense to comfort her. His heart was aching. He'd been a fool. An old fool. Hiding from the world and hurting his wife. He had a lot to make up for. A lot of damage to fix. He just hoped it wasn't too late.

He kissed her hair. "Please give me another chance. I might still be the grumpy arse you married, but I'll try. I'm already trying. Look at my suit."

She let out a strangled laugh.

"I really don't want to live in Florida anymore." He was sure of that, at least.

"I don't either." Her voice was muffled against his chest.

"Maybe we should move back to Atlantic City?"

"I like it here."

It was on the tip of his tongue to tell her that he wasn't going to move country. That Atlantic City was change enough. But he stopped himself in time. She needed this. And he needed her.

"We can try living here. At least we'll be close to Josh."

She sniffed loudly then leaned back to study him. She didn't let go of her grip on him, and he took that as a positive sign.

"Really?" The look in her eyes was so hopeful.

"Sure. What the heck. It isn't so bad here."

"I thought you never wanted to come back to Scotland?"

"I never want to lose you, either. Guess which is more important to me."

She thought about it. "I want to go on the trip you booked. But you can't spend the whole time complaining about crowds, foreign food and the price of everything."

"Where's the fun in that?"

She stared at him, and his heart soared. The damn trip worked! He was getting his wife back.

"Fine." He pretended to sigh. "I can do that." He thought about it. "I can try, anyway."

She took a deep breath. "We can try." Her words made him want to dance. He didn't. He kept his serious face on and hoped there wasn't a "but" coming. "But"-his heart sank-"you have to keep trying. You can't do this for a few weeks to appease me and then go back to your antisocial grunting self."

"Done." He grabbed her hand and pulled her from the table.

"Done? Just like that?"

"Not just like that. I've put a lot of effort into this. I'm committed."

She smiled at him. She still wasn't as relaxed and confident as he would have liked, but she was getting there. "So, you're the man with the plan." She shrugged nervously. "What now?"

Andrew grinned widely. "Now, gorgeous, we go upstairs to bed together and I show you exactly how beautiful you are to me."

The blush that coloured her cheeks made him feel ten feet tall. She was still his girl. "Do we have to go upstairs?"

"Damn straight we do. You're half naked and I want to find a bed. My back can't handle sex standing up and the table is too hard for you."

"I meant, can't we talk some more?"

He must have looked as crestfallen as he felt, because Helen started to laugh again. "Fine. We can find a bed." She batted her eyelashes at him, and he felt like he'd travelled back in time thirty years.

He growled and hauled her towards the hallway.

"Wait." She pulled from his grip and ran back to the table, where she gathered up the handcuffs and blindfold. She paused then snatched the bag with the rest of his booty. With a wicked smile, she rushed back to him. "We might as well see what these things can do."

Andrew kissed his wife thoroughly before taking her to bed.

They weren't out of the woods yet. But it was a damn good start.

CHAPTER 35

The day of the wedding dawned bright and sunny. The hills closest to Invertary were a lush green; the ones in the distance faded to purple. The sky was that perfect luminous blue poets wrote about, with just the odd fluffy cloud to break up the expanse. The water of the loch sparkled aquamarine and lapped idly at the shore. A soft sun reflected off the crooked white buildings that lined the high street. Birds sang. People laughed. Yadda, yadda, yadda...

It wasn't like Caroline could see this perfect summer's day. Oh no. She had to imagine it. Because she was under house arrest until the ceremony. She'd been woken by Josh at some ungodly dark o'clock and whisked away to the castle before the press got wind that she'd moved. Now all she could see was the grey stone of the castle walls, the white of the huge marquee taking up most of the garden and the destruction the renovation crew had left in its wake.

She stepped back from the tiny bathroom window, where she'd been watching the mass of people prepare for the day.

"I can't do this." She held on to the porcelain sink and stared at her reflection. "No. I can do this. Of course I can do this. I promised to do this." She rested her forehead on the cool glass of the mirror. "No. I can't do this."

There was a knock at the door. "Caroline, are you coming out of there sometime today? I've still got your makeup and hair to do. It's only five hours to the wedding. We have to hurry."

Caroline groaned. And not the good kind of groan she'd taken to making any time she was around Josh. That man had turned her into a sex addict. She'd even consulted her stolen books to see if there was a chapter on the subject. There wasn't. She'd tried investigating it on the internet while Josh was asleep, but the sites her search brought up made her unplug the computer from the web and pray for forgiveness.

"Caroline?"

Any minute now, Kirsty would fetch Lake to kick down the door.

"I'll be out in a minute. I'm just..." Her mind went blank. She'd already showered. There was no other reason to spend twenty minutes in the bathroom. At least, none she wanted to use as an excuse.

Kirsty sighed loud enough to be heard through the solid wooden door.

"Something is wrong. If you don't come out and tell me what this minute, I'm going to fetch Lake."

"You are so predictable." Caroline took a deep breath and opened the door.

She was wearing a new lingerie set that Kirsty had brought over for her. A white satin corset with lavender velvet bows and matching thong. Caroline tugged at the corset. She couldn't breathe. It must be too tight. She needed air. There wasn't enough air in the room. She walked past a worried Kirsty to open one of the turret's windows.

"What on earth?"

Kirsty came over to stand beside her.

Caroline pointed. "There are tartan sheep all around the marquee. Where the heck did they come from?" She looked closer. "Oh for goodness' sake, they're pooping everywhere. I'm going to talk to the wedding planner. This was not on the list I made for her."

She marched towards the door.

Kirsty ran to stand in front of her. "You are not going anywhere. Not until you tell me what's going on in that head of yours."

Caroline folded her arms. "I'll tell you once I get back. I need to sort out the sheep problem first."

"No you don't. The sheep are a gift from the domino boys. They had the Donaldson twins dye them."

"Did they buy the sheep?"

Kirsty sported her best innocent look. It wasn't good enough.

"We can't have stolen sheep at our wedding. I need to deal with this."

Kirsty stepped in front of her. "In your underwear?"

Caroline looked down at herself. The wind went out of her. She turned and flopped onto the armchair nestled into the bay window. Kirsty crouched in front of her.

"What's wrong, honey? Please tell me so that I can help you."

The concern in her best friend's eyes made Caroline's heart ache. She chewed her bottom lip.

"I'm not sure if I'm making a mistake or not." The words were out of her mouth before she could stop them.

"It's not too late to stop the wedding." Kirsty's eyes were sympathetic, but the set of her mouth was determined. Caroline was in no doubt her friend would wade out into the crowd to put an end to this day—if that was what Caroline wanted.

"No. I need to go through with it. I promised." She threw back her head and covered her face with her hands. "It's just...I've fallen in love with him and I'm afraid I'll spend my life married to a man who doesn't love me back."

There was silence for a minute. "I don't understand, sweetie. You didn't seem to mind that this was a loveless arrangement when you made it."

"That was before I fell in love. Now I think it might break me to spend a lifetime wanting his love back." She groaned. "Oh my goodness." Caroline sat up straight. "I just had a thought. What if he falls in love with someone else?"

Kirsty scoffed. "I wouldn't panic yet. I thought the whole point of this wedding was that he didn't believe in romantic love."

"Just because you don't believe in something, doesn't mean it isn't real."

Kirsty sat on the arm of the chair and patted Caroline's shoulder. "Don't go through with it. Call it off. You deserve someone who loves you back."

"Do I really? Does anyone? None of us deserve to be loved. That's why it's so special. We don't do anything to earn it. The people who love us give it freely."

"Fine, you deserve romance, then. You deserve hearts and flowers. After the way you've spent your life taking care of everyone around you and making things special for everyone else, you deserve a man who'll do that for you."

Caroline let out a long, heavy breath. "I don't need that stuff." She clenched her fists with determination. "Ignore my moaning. This is a case of pre-wedding jitters. Everyone gets them. Heck, Josh is probably going through exactly the same thing right now." She stood up and tugged at the corset. The window was open, but where was the air? "I need to be realistic. I'm thirty-one. I want a family. Josh is promising me one. He's promising a glamorous life. Not that I want a glamorous life, but it was nice of him to offer. At the very least, I'll never have to worry about paying bills. It's a good deal. He'll be kind to me. And he's great in bed." Caroline flushed. "I didn't mean to say that out loud." She stopped dead. "What if he goes off me? I'm a novelty right now, but what if he decides he wants other women? If he doesn't love me, what's to stop him?"

She bent over and gasped for air. Why, oh why, was she getting married on the hottest day Scotland had seen in a hundred years? There was no blooming air!

Kirsty rubbed her back. "Take slow breaths. Everything is going to be okay."

"I need to get out of this corset. It's strangling me."

"I don't think it's the corset, sweetie, but I have other lingerie sets for you to try. We'll find something that feels comfortable."

"Yes. Different underwear. That will fix everything." Caroline gave her best friend a grateful smile.

"Normally, I would totally agree with you, but in this case, I'm thinking not so much."

Caroline frowned. "Just get me out of this thing. I need to get ready. I'm getting married in less than five hours."

"I'm not so sure about that," Kirsty mumbled as she dug around in the huge bag full of lingerie she'd brought with her.

JOSH WAS ROCKING HIS TUX—EVEN if he did say so himself. He looked around the packed church and felt smug. He was getting married. Not only that, he was getting married to Caroline Patterson. He'd hit the jackpot. He was a walking advertisement for why you should get your best friend to find you a wife. It was the best idea he'd ever had. He was a damn genius.

As he stood at the front of the church, he eyed the packed pews. His side of the building was full of friends and distant family members. There were a few famous faces, but nothing along the lines of some celebrity weddings. Josh liked to think he'd invited only those he actually considered friends, and not just anyone he thought should be there.

He wished he could say the same of Caroline. She'd felt it was her obligation to invite practically everyone in town. While his side of the room sat in a dignified manner, quietly chatting. Caroline's side of the room was raucous. Not only that, but he could see folk pointing at his more famous friends, and he could have sworn at least one person was sneaking photos.

Caroline had given Lake strict instructions about confiscating cameras and phones. Josh signalled to Lake, who was dressed in a black suit and shades. He had a wire tucked discreetly around the back of his ear, and Josh saw him talk into his wrist once or twice. You would have thought he was guarding the president.

Lake strode over to Josh like a man on a mission. "What?"

"Some of the Invertary mob have cameras."

"Who?" He was a man of few words.

"The one in tartan."

Lake hitched one eyebrow. "Is that supposed to be funny? Point out one person on that side of the church who *isn't* wearing something tartan."

Yeah, he had a point. "Four rows in, three people along."

"Better." He strode off.

"Nervous?" Mitch came up beside Josh.

"Nope."

"Second thoughts?"

"No way."

"Any worries about your future at all?" Josh eyed his

friend. Mitch shrugged. "You wouldn't let me organise a bachelor party. I'm trying to be a good best man here."

Josh looked at the ceiling of the church, asking quietly for patience. "I am absolutely convinced I'm doing the right thing. Is that what you want to hear?"

"Fine." Mitch sighed. "Ten minutes to showtime. You'd better give me the rings."

Everything within Josh stilled.

Mitch sucked in a breath. "Seriously, tell me you have the rings."

Josh smiled nervously.

"Holy crap, you didn't even order the damn things, did you?" Mitch's voice was gaining volume.

"Shh!" Josh hissed. "And stop cursing. We're in a church and I'd rather not get struck by lightning on my wedding day."

"You're gonna get struck with a lot more than that if you don't have a ring when Caroline gets here. She is going to be seriously pissed. It was your one job. How could you forget your one job?"

"It wasn't one job. I organised the honeymoon."

"Technically your PA organised the honeymoon. You spent all of twenty seconds on the phone telling her where you want to go."

He had a point. "What are we going to do?"

Mitch cast a glance at the altar. "Pray?"

"Yeah, smartass, apart from that?"

"We have to borrow some. Come on, let's talk to your parents."

They strode over to Josh's parents with smiles plastered to their faces. No need for anyone to suspect a problem.

"We need to borrow your rings," Josh whispered.

His mum stared at him for a minute before swatting him on the arm. Hard. "You forgot the rings? How could you forget the rings? Send someone to the castle for them. We'll wait. It shouldn't take long."

Josh looked at his shoes. "I forgot to buy them. I need to borrow yours."

His mum looked like she wanted to hit him again. His dad stopped her, but started laughing at the same time, which didn't help.

"You can't borrow mine," his mum hissed. "I haven't been able to get them off for years."

"And I don't have one." His dad wiggled his bare ring finger. "Never did like rings."

Josh eyed his parents. They were very cosy. His father had his arm wrapped around his mom's shoulders. He pointed at them. "Is this for show or is the divorce off?"

"It's off." His dad looked pretty pleased with himself.

His mother scowled up at him. "No it isn't. I'm keeping it in reserve in case you slack off and go back to your boring old ways."

"We'll talk about this later, woman." He gave her a look that made his mum blush.

"I like our talks," she said coyly.

His father grinned, and Josh had a sudden urge to vomit.

Lake stepped into Josh's peripheral vision. "Caroline has arrived. Time to take your position."

Josh shared a look with Mitch. "I am so screwed. Can you even get married without rings?"

Mitch held up his hands helplessly. "How should I know?"

Yep. Josh was screwed.

CHAPTER 36

Kirsty fussed with the back of Caroline's wedding gown. "You are stunning. Perfect in every way."

Caroline looked down at the beautiful dress and matching designer shoes—*they* were stunning. She was just along for the ride. All she'd added to the ensemble was a pair of pearl earrings that had belonged to her mother, and a comb with heather in her hair. Plain. Simple. Just like her. The music started. A string quartet shipped in from Edinburgh played the traditional Pachelbel's Canon in D. Josh got a say in the rest of the music for their wedding, but Caroline wanted something traditional to start.

"Okay." Kirsty stared at her. "Are you sure?"

"Yes."

"We can still make a run for it."

"I know. I'm doing this."

Kirsty chewed her bottom lip. At last, she nodded, turned and walked down the aisle. Caroline waited the allotted time to follow. Her mind wasn't on her actions, and she was grateful that the wedding planner had insisted that they have a rehearsal the evening before. She took a deep breath as faces turned to look at her. People smiled and stood. Caroline kept her eyes forward. She clutched her bouquet of flowers tightly. Her mind was so blocked she couldn't even name the flowers in it. Heather. There was definitely heather.

In fact, there was purple heather everywhere. The wedding planner had done a wonderful job decorating the old church. There were bunches of heather and white roses attached to the end of each pew. Two huge displays of purple and white flowers bracketed the front of the church. Soft purple lighting had been added to the columns that held up the balcony, making them glow in a dreamlike way. It was beautiful. Pity she couldn't concentrate enough to admire any of it.

She spotted Helen, who was standing in the aisle. Andrew gripped her and pulled her back. Helen smiled while she dabbed at her eyes. And then Caroline saw Josh. The air left her lungs in a whoosh. She tripped over her dress, but righted herself quickly. Josh pinned her with his translucent blue gaze. His smile was wide and confident. His broad shoulders were perfectly accentuated by the cut of his suit. He was stunning.

And she was going to marry him.

Breathe. Just. Breathe. The church was as stuffy as the castle had been. If Caroline could have dragged her eyes away from Josh, she would have checked to see if any windows were open. She wanted to tug at her dress, but instead clenched her bouquet until her fingers ached.

A lifetime later, she made it to the front of the church. Josh reached for her hand.

"You are beautiful, baby," he whispered against her cheek. "I could eat you all up." She looked up at him. "Later," he promised, making her stomach spin.

She was doing the right thing. She'd promised. She always kept her promises. *Breathe. Just breathe.*

The minister cleared his throat. "Dearly beloved, we are gathered here, in the sight of God..."

Caroline didn't hear anything else. Josh squeezed her hand. His smile was warm and reassuring. Her heart beat so hard within her chest she felt like it was trying to escape. Josh seemed calm and unaffected. Caroline's palms began to sweat. She'd been to plenty of weddings. She didn't remember any of them taking this long. And where the heck was all the air?

The minister's voice broke into her thoughts. "...If any person can show just cause why they may not be joined together—let them speak now or forever hold their peace."

Josh looked over his shoulder and grinned cheekily at their guests. There was a smattering of laughter.

Then a voice rang out. "I have just cause."

Caroline's heart actually stopped. Josh made a growling sound beside her. Mitch shot Josh a worried look. They all turned towards the voice at the back of the church. Danny stepped out from behind a pillar.

"What the hell?" Josh said.

"Language!" the minister snapped at him. "You're in the house of God."

Josh gave him a scathing look. "That is my stalker. He shouldn't be here, let alone making an objection."

Caroline watched as Danny strode towards the front of the church. He was wearing his ever-present black suit and tie. Lake and his men started jogging towards the man.

"You can't marry him." Danny's voice wavered, as though he wasn't quite in control of it. "He's an impostor, Caroline. He has you all fooled. I'm Josh McInnes. I'm the one who loves you. You need to get rid of him and marry me before it's too late."

There was a ripple of murmured shock and amusement.

"Oh, man, he's finally lost the plot." Mitch patted Josh on the back.

Lake grabbed Danny's arm and spoke quietly into his ear.

Danny shook his head violently. He struggled in Lake's hold. His arms flailing wildly.

"Don't let them take me," Danny shouted. "I love you, Caroline. I want to marry you. You belong to me."

Caroline watched in horror as the tribute singer was dragged away, one man on each side of him, his heels squeaking on the wooden floor. Some people were smiling after him, as though it was a show put on for the crowd. Other people seemed shocked and upset for the man. Caroline found that she was shaking slightly.

"It's okay." Josh wrapped an arm around her shoulder. "I'll make sure he gets the treatment he needs. This has been a long time coming."

As reassuring as that was, Caroline couldn't stop the words repeating in her head. Danny, a man who didn't know her, was shouting that he loved her. Words she'd never heard from Josh. Nausea assaulted her. Everything was off kilter. Nothing made sense.

I made a promise. Everything will be okay.

The vicar cleared his throat. "Anybody else got an objection?" The crowd laughed along with him. It was all good-natured fun.

Until another voice piped up. "I object. Anybody with a brain would object to this farce."

Caroline closed her eyes. This was not happening. She opened them to find her ex-assistant Beth making her way along a pew, stepping on people's toes as she went.

"Sit down and stop making a fool of yourself," Betty called to her.

Beth ignored the woman. Josh turned to the minister. "Do we have to allow this? I don't even know that woman."

"She has to have her say, son." From the way the vicar shook his head, it was clear he wasn't impressed either.

Beth was in the aisle now. She stormed towards the platform they were standing on. Stopping right in front of Caroline. She was dressed in a red glittering mini-dress that was far too sexy for a wedding and had an over-large red handbag slung over her shoulder. She tottered in heels Caroline couldn't have even stood in.

"You." Beth pointed at Caroline with clear abhorrence. "You don't deserve Josh."

Warning bells went off in Caroline's head. Those were the words painted on her wall. She took a step back from Beth.

Beth took a step forward. "You are a horrible person. And Josh needs someone nicer."

"That's enough," the minister barked. "That is not a valid objection. Get back to your seat. Better yet. Get out. You obviously aren't in the spirit of the occasion."

Beth smirked at him. "Like I care what you think." She turned back to Caroline. "You don't deserve Josh. You shouldn't get to marry someone like him. You're boring and grey. Everything about you is grey. There's nothing there to attract a man like Josh. You're just like your dull, old-fashioned clothes."

"That's more than enough." Josh stepped towards her. Lake was still dealing with Danny. Josh turned to Mitch. "Deal with this."

Mitch shot Beth a look filled with disgust. "My pleasure." He took a step towards the woman.

"You're wearing the wrong colour," Beth spat at Caroline. "It should be grey. Like you."

She reached into her oversized bag and came out with a bottle.

Caroline's mouth fell open as everything happened at once. Josh and Mitch lunged at Beth. Helen screamed. Beth

335

smiled the nastiest smile Caroline had ever seen. The crowd gasped in unison.

And then the bottle exploded. Grey paint shot out. All over Caroline's beautiful dress.

"Fantastic!" a man shouted. There were flashes. Caroline looked in the direction of Beth's date. Pyro? The paparazzi photographer from London was at her wedding? With Beth? And he was taking photos? Photos of the most humiliating day Caroline had ever had. Caroline felt the room sway. A hand held her arm. Kirsty. Kirsty was there.

Lake came rushing into the church, followed closely by Officer Donaldson.

"Marry me," Beth was screaming as Mitch held her hands tight behind her back. She fought against him. Fought to get to Josh. "Marry me. I'll be good to you. I won't bitch at you. I won't boss you around. I won't be all stiff and formal. You don't want to marry her. It'll be like sleeping beside an old wooden plank. I'll treat you right. Marry me."

Josh shouted at the police, "The guy with her, her date, he's paparazzi."

Pyro laughed loudly. "Suck it up, Joshy boy. These pictures are going to finance my holiday home in the Riviera."

Caroline watched as Josh's fists clenched. He took a step towards the laughing photographer. The minister put a hand on his shoulder to stop him. "You're needed elsewhere, son." The two men gave her a look she couldn't decipher.

Pyro jumped over the pews, pushing people out of his way. He ran for the back of the church. The police followed. Lake handed a still-screaming Beth over to some of his men before chasing after the photographer. They disappeared out of the door that led to the church hall.

"Marry me!" Beth looked feral as she fought against the men holding her. "Don't marry that bitch. She's unlovable.

Everybody knows that. Her heart is a stone. You can't love her. It's not possible. Marry me!"

Everyone watched in stunned shock as a sobbing and screaming Beth was removed from the church.

Suddenly there was silence.

And then every eye in the room turned to Caroline.

CHAPTER 37

Josh sucked in a breath. He ran a hand over his face. Caroline was rooted to the spot on the platform beside him. Her back was straight. Her shoulders back. Her eyes were wide. And her skin was so pale it was practically blue. Kirsty stood beside her, patting her arm, murmuring words that he doubted Caroline could hear.

Her white dress was spattered with grey paint. It dripped from the skirt, making a puddle on the floor. Caroline just stood there. Staring at nothing.

Josh moved to her. "It's okay." He softened his voice even though he wanted to throw back his head and roar. "It's okay." He put his hands on her shoulders and stepped in closer to hold her.

"Don't." Her lips were trembling. "You'll get paint on you."

"It's okay," Josh whispered.

She was stiff in his arms. Even though her feet stayed rooted to the spot, she tried to lean away from him.

"It's okay." He wrapped his arms around her, threading one hand into her hair, while the other tightened around her waist. "It's okay."

He felt her body shiver. Her posture didn't change, but she turned her face into his chest.

Mitch was standing behind Caroline. His arms folded. His face like thunder.

Josh caught his friend's eye. "Clear this place out. This day is over."

Mitch nodded firmly. He tugged at a weeping Kirsty, letting her know that she should help get the guests out. She gave Caroline one last desperate, heart-breaking look before she went to help.

"It's okay. Don't worry. It's all being sorted," Josh murmured against Caroline's ear as he rubbed her back.

She didn't move. She just stood in his arms. Trembling. He gritted his teeth and forced himself to calm down, for Caroline's sake. She needed him. What he really wanted to do was slay everyone who had upset her. He wanted to wipe the slate clean for her. Make everything right. He wanted to take away every last bit of her pain. He wanted her happy again. Safe again.

He felt a hand on his shoulder. The vicar. "You can use my office."

Josh nodded his thanks, but he knew Caroline wouldn't move. The best he could do to give them privacy was to clear the room. In the meantime, he used his body to shelter her from the crowd. Hiding her from curious gazes and prying eyes. It was his fault. All of this. He'd turned Caroline into a public spectacle—simply by asking her to marry him. He should have realised how devastating public scrutiny could be to those who weren't used to it. She'd been right all along. He did need a woman who was used to the celebrity life. Someone hardened to the scrutiny. Someone who could deal with the press.

But he only wanted Caroline.

"It's done." Mitch appeared in front of him. "The room is

clear. I'll wait outside by the limo. Let me know when you want to go back."

Josh nodded. "The reception?"

"It's being taken care of. Millicent's cancelling it."

"Thanks."

Mitch shook his head sadly as he turned away. Josh listened as Mitch's footsteps echoed through the now-empty church. The heavy wooden doors closed with a dull thud after him. Josh kissed Caroline's temple.

"Everyone is gone, baby. It's just us."

They stood like that for the longest time. Caroline was stiff and silent in his arms. Josh was beginning to think he should call for a doctor when Caroline's shoulders suddenly slumped. She started shaking. He heard one tiny sob, but the rest of her tears fell in silence. Josh held her close. He wanted to kill the bastards who had hurt his woman.

"It's okay, baby. Don't cry. We'll fix everything."

She pulled away from him. Her eyes were red, swollen and owl-like.

"How are we going to fix this, Josh? I don't think it's possible."

He ran his thumb over her trembling bottom lip. "Of course it is. We'll wait a few days then try again. I'll get you a new dress and we'll be more careful about who we invite."

She shook her head. "No." She pushed away from him. Now they were both covered in paint. "We obviously weren't meant to do this. We weren't meant to be together." Her big green eyes implored him to understand. He didn't. Not one bit.

"Weddings get ruined all the time." Josh tucked a strand of her hair behind her ear. "Some get hit with hurricanes, or earthquakes, or dodgy relatives. Ours isn't any different. We can't call it quits just because some things went wrong."

Caroline barked a fake laugh. "*Some* things went wrong?"

She stared down at her dress, and another tear rolled down her cheek. Josh felt his chest ache. She looked back up at him. "Beth was right." She bit her lip as she fought for her precious control. "You're too good for me. I am unlovable. That's why you picked me, so that there wouldn't be any danger of you falling in love with me. I am bossy. And cold. And—"

He stepped into her space and cradled her face in his hands. "Stop. Don't listen to a word that crazy witch said. There is nothing wrong with you. You're good and kind. You're funny and loving. You're beautiful, and moral, and oh-so-sexily innocent." He kissed her nose. "You are too good for *me*, baby. Not the other way around. I keep wondering when you're going to figure out that you could do so much better than me."

Caroline closed her eyes. "Oh, Josh. You can't mean that. I don't even know how to dress. The country is calling out for my makeover. I embarrass you at every turn. My personality is as grey as my wardrobe."

"No." He shook his head. Wishing he could strangle the crazy woman who poisoned Caroline's mind. "No. It's not true. You're wonderful the way you are. You never embarrass me. Never. Why would you even think that?"

Caroline pushed away from him. She took a deep breath. Her shoulders went back. Josh's stomach turned at the sight. It was her fighting stance.

"I think we should call this marriage off."

Josh put his hands on his hips. He summoned his patience as stared down at the floor. He shook his head. No. There was no way that was happening. He knew she was upset. She deserved to be upset. But call off the wedding? No. Just. No.

"We made an agreement. We're getting married."

"I don't want to marry you." Her voice cracked. She was lying. He knew it.

"Don't say that, Caroline. You don't mean it. We have a deal. We agreed."

"It won't work out for us." She backed away from him. "I'm not the kind of person people love."

"You aren't thinking straight. This isn't about love. It's about commitment." Josh almost choked on the words. They felt like a lie. His shirt was too tight. He loosened his purple tie and popped the top two buttons. He should have put his foot down and gotten married in a T-shirt. "We made a deal. I'm holding you to it."

"I can't." She looked like she was about to run. "I can't marry you. It hurts too much."

What the hell? Josh ran his fingers through his hair.

"You're not making any sense." He reached for her, but she stepped away from him. "We'll go back to the castle. We'll get cleaned up." He tried to grin at her, but it felt forced. "I'll show you the delights of showering together. Once we're clean, things will be clearer."

"Josh." She held her flowers in front of her, as though they were a shield. "I was thinking about backing out long before everyone intervened."

Josh felt like he'd taken a kick to the gut. He actually started to bend over before he thought to stop himself.

"You were going to call it off?"

"It's the right thing to do." Her shoulders slumped. She looked defeated. Silent tears ran down her cheeks. "You don't want me. You want a business arrangement. Which was fine. It was great when we both wanted the same thing." Her voice shook. "But things changed." The pain in her eyes made every part of him ache. She took a shaky breath. "I fell in love with you, Josh."

The ground shifted beneath him. Josh looked around for something to hold on to. There wasn't anything.

Caroline gave him a sad little smile. "You see why it won't

work? You don't want to be in love. You picked me because you know you'll never love me like that. It's safe for you. Beth was right about that. I'm not the kind of woman men fall in love with. Which means I would spend my life loving you and watching as you never loved me back. I can't do that. It's soul destroying. Waiting for you to find the woman you will fall in love with. Waiting for you to leave me."

She wasn't making any sense. Why would he leave her? Why would he want another woman? He only wanted her. "You love me?"

"And you don't love me." It wasn't a question.

Josh's throat was closing up. "Caroline," was all he could get out.

"It's okay, Josh. I understand. Thank you for giving me a chance at a family. Thanks for trying to give me the wedding I thought I wanted. Thanks for making me feel special for a while."

Josh was paralysed. His power of speech had fled. He felt like his insides were being ripped out and displayed. He couldn't get his head around anything she said. None of it made sense.

With a trembling smile, Caroline turned and stepped down from the platform. Josh struggled to breathe. She was walking away from him. He tried to stop her, but he couldn't move. He kept his eyes on her until the heavy doors of the church swung shut behind her. Suddenly his legs wouldn't hold him anymore. He flopped to sit on the platform steps. His head fell into his hands. He struggled to breathe.

She was gone.

His Caroline was gone.

CHAPTER 38

"You're an idiot."

Josh looked up to find his father standing in front of him. "I can't deal with you right now."

"Do I look like I care?" He sat down on the edge of the platform beside Josh. "Why did you let that girl go?"

"What are you talking about?" Josh felt his anger rise again. He wanted to punch someone, and if his dad didn't get lost, it might be him. "You don't like Caroline. You don't want me to marry her. You've been nothing but clear about your opinion since you turned up in Scotland."

His dad huffed. "I may have been wrong."

Josh looked at the ceiling. Wishing a science fiction portal would open and suck him into another universe. One without any of the crap he had to deal with. "You *may* have been wrong?"

"Fine." His dad grunted with disgust. "I *was* wrong. Happy now? I may be wrong, but you're a bloody fool if you let that girl go. She's a keeper. And she loves you."

He really didn't need to explain his life to his father right now. "That's the problem. I don't love her." The words were harder to get out than he thought they would be. "I proposed to her because I don't believe in that romantic love stuff. I want a partnership. That's it."

"I can't believe I raised such an idiot. Where did I go wrong?"

Josh stood and glared down at the man. This conversation was icing on the cake from hell that was his day. "I'm just doing what you did. You got married because Mom was pregnant with me. It's not like you fell in love and desperately wanted to be together. But look at you now. You've been married thirty-five years and you're committed to each other. You've grown to love each other. And now that you've sorted out your problems with Mom, everything is fine. I want that. It worked for you. It should work for me."

"You don't know anything." His father stood, anger twisting his face. "I didn't marry your mother because she was knocked up. I married her because she was my world. I was crazy about that woman from the moment I set eyes on her. When I wasn't in the same room as her, I felt like my arm or leg was missing. I lived for every smile she gave me. I still bloody do. I didn't marry her because she was pregnant, you fool. I married her because I loved her. I was just grateful that she had to marry me because she was carrying you. I didn't want to take any chance that she'd get away from me."

"You were in love?"

"Head over heels."

"How come I never knew?"

"There's a lot you don't know, son. But don't worry. I'm here to sort you out." He wrapped an arm around Josh's shoulders. "And the first thing you need to do is go after the woman you're in love with. Fix this mess. Marry her. Put babies in her belly as fast as you can. That's what you need to do."

"You are nowhere near a modern man, are you?"

"As Popeye would say, I am what I am."

Josh shook his head. Oh how he loved these little father-son chats.

"I'm not in love with Caroline." He pulled away from his father. "I just care about her. A lot." He sighed at the thought of her out there, hurting, alone. He should be with her. He should be holding her. Everything was all mixed up. "I worry about her. You've seen what she's like. Her world is black and white; she expects everyone to be moral and do the right thing just because it's the right thing to do. People use her. They treat her badly. They say things that hurt her because her personality is so forceful they think they can say anything they like to her. But she's soft underneath. She cares about everyone. And she gets hurt. She needs someone to look out for her. To translate the world around her. To make people see how great she is and to stop them from hurting her. That's all this is. I wanted to marry her and be that person."

"Son"—his father clasped a hand on Josh's shoulder —"you're talking about love."

Josh shook his head. "No. It's mutual respect. And attraction. Serious attraction. She's so damn beautiful. The first time I saw her, I thought, 'I get to marry Grace Kelly.'" He looked at his dad. "She looks like Grace Kelly, doesn't she?"

"Exactly like her." His father smiled. "Son. You're in love."

"I can't be. I don't believe in it."

His father threw back his head and roared with laughter. "Fine. You're not in love. It was purely an arrangement. So I guess you'll chalk this up to experience and go find yourself another bride." He seemed to think about it. "If you hurry, you can slot someone else into the wedding you've already organised."

Josh felt a wave of nausea rush through him.

"There was a woman at the post office around your age."

His father would not shut up. Years he spent grunting, and now all he did was talk. "She doesn't look like Grace Kelly, but she has good child-bearing hips. And that's what this is about, right? Get a woman. Start a family. She's got a good reputation as a solid and reliable person. I can send Mitch over to check her out for you, if you like?"

"No." Josh felt anger claw at him. "I don't want that."

"Why not? It doesn't matter who you marry, right? As long as she's young enough and isn't chasing your fame. When I spoke to this woman, she wasn't impressed that you were a singer. She isn't into music that much. She sounds perfect. Doesn't she?"

"No. I don't want her." Josh bit back the rage he was feeling.

"You could at least check her out. If you go over there now, we can still get the vicar back here before it gets too late. Your mother and I are off on a three-month trip in a couple of days. It would be good to get your wedding out of the way before we go. Come on." He grabbed Josh's arm. "Let's go see her now."

"No!" Josh roared. He yanked his arm from his father's grasp. "Stop pushing me to check this woman out. I don't want another woman. I only want Caroline."

His father smiled. "And there it is."

Josh was breathing hard. His fists clenched and unclenched. Caroline. He only wanted Caroline. No one else would do. He wanted her soft body under his. He wanted to laugh at her bossing him around. He wanted to plan a future with her and fight over who got to decide what happened. He wanted to kiss her every morning and hold her every night. He wanted to protect her from the world. And give her the world at the same time. He thought of a life without Caroline in it and saw something ugly. He needed her. She was perfect for him.

He loved her.

Josh closed his eyes and took his first calm breath since the wedding was interrupted. The words settled in his soul as truth. He loved Caroline Patterson. Madly. Deeply. Completely. He was in love with her. Crazy, cheesy romantic love. The kind he'd avoided. The kind he'd mocked. The kind that now didn't seem that stupid after all. A deep tranquillity overcame him. Everything slotted into place. He couldn't believe it had taken so long to see the truth. He looked at his dad.

His dad grinned like an idiot. "What are you waiting for? Go get the woman you love."

This time Josh didn't correct him. But he couldn't run after Caroline. He'd screwed this up big time. He'd hurt her when he'd let her walk away. No. He'd destroyed her. She'd told him she loved him and he'd said nothing. She would never believe him if he declared his love now. No. Words weren't enough. He needed to do something else. Something bigger. With a shake of his head, he turned to his dad.

"About this newfound knowledge of yours—what women want. I might need some input with planning an over-the-top romantic gesture." He couldn't believe he'd been reduced to asking his dad for help.

His dad thumped him on the back. "That's my boy. But don't forget the caveman act and kinky sex. It worked for me."

"Now I'm going to vomit."

Laughing, his dad followed him out of the church. Josh felt the weight of the day lift from him. He would fix this. He would marry the woman he was meant to marry. Caroline loved him, and he was going to show her that he loved her too. Everything was going to be fine.

. . .

IT WAS mid-afternoon the following day before Caroline got out of bed. And she only did it then because someone knocked at her door. She dragged herself down the stairs in her pink satin pyjamas, not even stopping to brush her hair. The domino boys had been standing guard outside her house since the wedding fiasco, and Caroline knew they would only let someone get to her door if it was important. Sadly, nothing was important enough to get dressed for. It was Kirsty and Officer Donaldson who were interrupting her pity party. She swung the door wide and led them into the living room.

"Oh, sweetie," Kirsty cooed at her. Her sympathy was overwhelming as she crushed Caroline in a hug. This was why Caroline had insisted on being alone the night before. She could barely cope with her own emotions, other peoples' were a step too far.

"I'm sorry to bother you, Caroline." Officer Donaldson stood in the middle of the room, taking up far too much space. Just like Josh did.

She forced herself not to think about him. She was already suffering from one emotional hangover—she didn't need to start crying again.

"I wanted to tell you that we've charged Beth. She's the one who sent you the package and painted your house." Donaldson was grim with his news.

Caroline had already figured out that Beth was behind her problems. Well, not all of them. He who shall not be named was behind the rest.

"Sit down, sweetie." Kirsty tugged her into the sofa and patted her hand.

Donaldson took a deep breath. "She was also the one who sent the photos of you in your suits to the magazines and newspapers. And she's been letting the paparazzi guy, Pyro, live with her. She snuck him into your wedding as her date."

That was what Caroline got for being polite and inviting her in the first place.

"As for Pyro." Donaldson shifted his feet on the spot, and Caroline knew the news wasn't good. "We caught him, but not before he'd sent the pictures to his publisher. I'm afraid photos of your wedding, and what Beth did, are all over the media."

Caroline supposed she should be upset at the news, but she couldn't work up the energy. The photos didn't matter. In a few days, no one would be interested in the woman who almost married Josh McInnes. Whoever Josh chose next would get the attention. No doubt he'd learned his lesson and would go back to dating celebrities.

"Don't worry," Kirsty told her. "It will all be fine. The photos will be old news in a day or two. Some other celebrity will do something more interesting and the media will turn their attention to them. You only have to hold on until this passes."

Caroline wanted to tell her friend that she honestly didn't care about the photos. She wasn't sure she cared about anything. Instead, she nodded her agreement and left it at that.

"Okay." The police officer seemed to have given up waiting for a response from her. "I'll be in touch."

With that, he strode out of the house. Caroline was relieved to see him go. One less person to deal with. Unfortunately, he let someone in when he left. Mitch entered the living room with an apologetic look on his face.

"How are you doing?" His smile was gentle. With one look at Caroline's red, swollen eyes, he nodded. "About how I expected." He sighed. "I'm sorry to add to things for you, but Josh wants you to come to the castle tonight to sign some papers."

Kirsty jumped to her feet. "Can't that wait? Doesn't he

have a heart at all? Surely he realises Caroline isn't up to this right now."

"I'm sorry. I know the timing isn't great. But I'm sure Caroline wants to resolve this as much as Josh. It won't take long." He turned to Caroline. "Can you be there at eight o'clock?"

"Can we make it another day?" Caroline knew she sounded pathetic.

"Sorry." Mitch gave her an apologetic shrug. "He's leaving the country tonight. So it has to be this evening."

Caroline felt a sharp jab in her side. He was leaving already. She'd never see him again. She ignored the pain that twisted her insides, and told herself that this was a good thing.

"Fine. I'll be there."

"Thanks. That's great." He turned to Kirsty. "Can you walk me out? I'd like a word."

Kirsty frowned, but followed Mitch. Caroline was glad that they were gone. She loved Kirsty, but she hoped her friend would follow Mitch out the door and come back in a year or two. She slid over to lie on the couch, curling her knees tight into her chest. Tomorrow, she promised herself, she would stop wallowing in self-pity and get on with her life. The centre needed her. She still had things to do. She would feel better staying busy. It was a good plan. That left her with today to mourn what might have been with Josh.

When Kirsty came back into the room, she had a strange look on her face. As though she was excited about something, but loath to show it.

"This won't do." Kirsty grabbed Caroline's arm and yanked her into a seated position. "Enough of this. If you're going to deal with Josh tonight, we need to get some work done. You can't turn up in your PJs. We need to get you cleaned up and do something about those eyes. Do you have cucumber? Never mind. I'll send one of the boys to fetch some. They're just sitting out front playing dominoes anyway. Since the press left town there's really no need for them to be there." She tugged Caroline to her feet. "Shower," she ordered. "I brought new lingerie to cheer you up. You can wear that, and that pretty lavender dress of yours. There's no way I'm letting you go to the castle looking anything but stunning. One look at you and Josh will regret that he ever let you walk away."

Caroline thought it would take more than an old dress and new underwear to make Josh regret anything. But Kirsty was right about one thing. There was no way she could confront Josh with red, swollen eyes, wearing pink pyjamas. As she dragged herself up the stairs to the shower, part of her wished she still had her grey suits. They were like armour. And armour sounded perfect for saying goodbye to the man she loved.

CHAPTER 39

Caroline arrived at the castle at exactly eight o'clock, flanked by Kirsty and Archie. Archie had demanded to attend, saying she needed all the moral support she could get. Caroline couldn't say no. She was ill with the thought of facing Josh again. If there had been any way to avoid it, she would have. Instead she'd given herself a pep talk on the fact that being an adult meant facing difficult situations. She needed to be mature. She needed to be calm. She needed to hide in a closet until she was sure Josh was out of the country.

Caroline felt battered. Her insides were raw with the emotional beating she'd endured—most of it caused by her own stupidity. What made her think that she could marry Josh McInnes? She was silly idiot of a woman. At least she'd had the sense to realise in time that he would never love her. He'd obviously recognised that she was unlovable as soon as he'd set eyes on her. There was no other explanation as to why he'd picked her, out of the millions of women who would have jumped at the chance, to be his wife.

She placed a hand on her stomach and tried to calm the chaos inside her. It was humiliating to have to face the man again. For them to both be reminded of the reasons why their marriage plans had been such a joke. People like her didn't marry people like Josh. It was one of the laws of the universe. She'd been stupid to challenge it. And as soon as she got this awful evening over with, she'd slink back to her place in the scheme of things and give up on her hopes of having a family. It wasn't for her. She was sure of it.

Caroline's head ached as Kirsty drove them to the castle in Lake's car. She'd been worried that there were still some press lingering. There were none. Caroline and Josh were old news.

"It will be okay," Kirsty said as she reached over to pat Caroline's hand.

She didn't have the heart to contradict her friend. It wouldn't be okay. It would be torture. She would be ripped open after this visit. And she would spend days, months, years, putting herself back together.

The castle looked deserted, which was a relief to Caroline. When they got to the front door, they found a note pinned to it.

"It says we're to go round the back. Josh is in the garden," Archie told them, even though they could all read it for themselves.

Caroline licked her dry lips. "That's a strange place to deal with paperwork." Why couldn't he just have been waiting for her in his office? She wanted to get this over with as fast as possible.

"He's American." Kirsty led Caroline to the back of the house. "Strange is a way of life for them."

They walked around to the back of the house and Caroline was relieved to see that there was no trace of the marquee. Or the tartan sheep.

"You returned the sheep to their owner, didn't you?"

Archie shot her a look that clearly said she was mad.

"What else would we do with a bunch of hand-painted sheep?"

There was no sign of Josh at the back of the house, but they spotted Mitch coming down the path that wound its way through the old orchard.

"Caroline." He smiled at her. "Glad you could make it. Josh is this way. Follow me."

He ushered her on in front of him.

Her stomach fluttered. She felt faint and wanted to retreat. Maybe he could mail the papers to her for her signature? Now why hadn't she thought of that before coming to the castle? Caroline eyed Mitch nervously over her shoulder. "Why am I meeting Josh in the garden? I thought he wanted me to sign some papers."

"He does. It's better if he explains."

Caroline clenched and unclenched her hands. A cold sweat broke out in the small of her back. She wanted to go home and crawl into a box of chocolates. And stay there until she vomited or passed out.

"What are these papers for, anyway? Is it something that can wait? Maybe Josh could mail them to me?"

"They're mainly to do with the renovation and really should be signed straight away. You're here now. Why not get this over with?"

Caroline's stomach rolled. She'd forgotten all about the castle restoration. She guessed that was something else that wouldn't go ahead. One more thing she'd screwed up. And one more thing she'd deal with after this meeting was over. The workmen would be so disappointed. It was a look she was getting used to seeing on the faces of the people around her.

Her feet dragged as she rounded a bend in the path. If Kirsty and Mitch hadn't been behind her, she would have turned and fled. This was a mistake. Seeing Josh again would be too painful. Being anywhere near him would be agonising. Why was she doing this to herself? Didn't she deserve some time to heal? To hide?

She tripped over something on the path and jerked to a halt. Her hand fluttered to her mouth. "What on earth?" Thousands of bubbles floated towards her. They covered the path and danced around the trees. She gave Kirsty a questioning glance and became even more confused when her friend beamed widely.

"Keep going, Caroline." Mitch urged her forward. "Not far now."

Kirsty squeezed her hand. "It's okay, sweetie. You'll see."

Archie smiled and nodded.

Caroline's brain was frozen. The scene in front of her didn't make sense. Gingerly, she stepped through the bubbles and slowly followed the path. Her palms were clammy. Her mouth was dry. A part of her mind was screaming hysterically. She felt like she was walking into a dream. Or worse, a psychotic hallucination.

"Have I had a breakdown and I'm lying in a hospital bed?" she whispered to Kirsty.

"No, silly. You're actually here."

"So there really are bubbles?"

Kirsty gave her a one-armed hug as they walked. "Just like you planned when you were a girl. Remember?"

Caroline felt her knees weaken. She couldn't mean...? No. Kirsty didn't mean the wedding she'd planned. Her mind stuttered. This was not happening.

The path turned one last time. Caroline stopped dead. Before her was a small white gazebo decorated in thick bunches of purple heather. There was so much of it you could barely make out the wooden structure. The path before her was covered in white rose petals. Rainbow coloured bubbles floated everywhere.

And under the gazebo, standing tall was Josh.

Caroline stopped breathing. Her feet wouldn't move. There were no thoughts in her mind. It was as though time had hiccupped and she was in the void.

Josh was dressed in his jeans and a plain pale blue T-shirt. And he was smiling at her. Nervously.

Beside Josh stood the vicar. In front of the gazebo were some chairs. Not many. Enough for Josh's parents, the domino boys, Betty, Mitch and Kirsty. Caroline spotted Lake standing to the side, monitoring events closely. Kirsty nudged Caroline forward. She couldn't move. She wasn't sure what was going on, but she couldn't deal with any more humiliation. She'd reached her limit.

Josh seemed to realise that she wasn't going any further, so he slowly moved towards her. His usual saunter had turned into something far more predatory. He prowled forward. The look in his eye made it clear that she was his prey. Caroline swallowed hard, aware that it was too late to run. He would just chase her.

Josh stopped in front of her. "Hi." The soft rumble reminded her of other times they'd had together. More intimate times. Her cheeks warmed at the thought.

"What's going on?" She hated that the words came out hesitantly. "I thought you wanted me to sign some papers."

"I do, baby. I want you to sign a marriage certificate."

Caroline blinked at him until her brain caught up. "A marriage certificate?"

Josh reached for her hand. Tingles ran up her arm and straight to her heart. "We're getting married tonight."

She shook her head. "I told you. I can't."

He stepped towards her. "You told me you couldn't because you love me. Do you still love me, baby?"

Caroline felt the tears she'd been fighting all day. They flooded her eyes, ready to spill. She blinked furiously. Josh stepped into her space. One hand wrapped around her to press against the small of her back, closing the distance between them. She should have protested. She should have moved away from him. But it felt so good to have his hands on her again. To have him hold her again.

He leaned down to nuzzle her ear. "Do you still love me, Caroline?"

She sucked in a sob. "Yes."

"Good." Josh kissed her neck below her ear. "Because I love you, baby."

Caroline felt every muscle within her tense. "You don't mean it." Could he? It didn't make sense. "You don't believe in falling in love."

"Yeah." He spoke against her neck. "About that. I was wrong. I fell in love with you." He wrapped both arms around her, bringing his clasped hands to rest in the small of her back. His blue eyes captured hers. "I fell in love with you the minute I opened the door and found Grace Kelly staring up at me. I fell even deeper when you wouldn't let me make a sound studio in the castle. I fell in deeper still when you got drunk on champagne and propositioned me in the garden. And I fell all the way when you took me to your bed and let me make love to you."

Caroline's head was spinning. "You don't mean this. You're only saying this to get me to marry you."

He chuckled. "Hell yeah, I'm saying this to get you to marry me. I want the woman I love to be my wife."

"What about the arrangement? What about a life of committed friendship and mutual respect?"

"Baby." He kissed her softly on the lips, stealing the air from her. "We can have that too. But we'll also have romantic love and seriously hot sex."

Caroline couldn't think straight. Her whole body vibrated with hope. But she didn't believe him. "Yesterday, I told you I love you and you let me walk away because you didn't love me. How could that change overnight? You don't love me one day, but you love me the next. It isn't possible."

He pressed his forehead to hers. "I get that you don't believe me, baby. But I do love you. It took you walking away for me to realise that I can't let that happen again. If you leave me, you take my heart along with you. I'll never love anyone else. You're it for me, Caroline Patterson. And I would really like to turn you into Caroline McInnes. Say yes. Don't make me suffer. I deserve it. But don't do it. Marry me tonight."

Caroline's thoughts stumbled over each other. "I thought you were leaving the country tonight."

"*We're* leaving the country tonight. I booked a honeymoon. I wouldn't leave without you."

Caroline was terrified to believe him. Her heart was too fragile. She stared at him for the longest time. Josh seemed happy to let her think things through.

"Prove it," she said at last. "Prove you love me."

He gave her a long, slow grin. "That's easy." He turned towards the gazebo, took her hand tight in his and pulled her along with him. Their family and friends smiled their encouragement. Even Josh's dad seemed pleased. When they got to the gazebo, Josh turned to her.

"I took a leaf out of my dad's book." There was a noise behind him as his band appeared from the bushes. "Women want big romantic gestures. Right? Well, the boys are going to help me with that."

Caroline was confused. "You don't believe in romance."

"I believe in it where you're concerned. You deserve some romance. And I'm only too happy to give it to you." He turned to the band. "Let's go, boys."

The secluded area was filled with music. And Josh began

to sing. To her. For her. The words of Etta James's "At Last" floated around them.

There was no mistaking the depth of feeling in Josh's face as he sang to her. He let all of his emotions show in his eyes. Caroline's heart stuttered as tears slid down her cheeks. He gently and lovingly wiped them away for her. When the song ended, he pulled her close and whispered in her ear. "Remember my dad's little talk? The big romantic gesture is only part of what women want. I've got a suit and handcuffs on standby, just in case this doesn't work."

A laugh erupted from Caroline. "You really mean it. You love me?" She stared into his eyes, searching for confirmation. And gasped when she found it.

"I really mean it. I love you, Caroline Patterson. All of you. Even the bossy bits."

She laughed some more as she wiped her face. "Then marry me, Josh McInnes."

"Damn right I'm going to marry you."

They turned to face the preacher. He grinned at them. "I hope you don't mind, but I've adapted the wording of the service. I'm not asking for any objections this time."

The group behind her laughed. The preacher's words were a blur until Josh was asked if he took Caroline to be his wife. His answer was loud and clear. "I really do." There was a cheer.

The minister turned to Caroline and asked if she took Josh as her husband. Caroline stared into Josh's eyes and saw anxiety there. He was worried she'd refuse him. She touched his cheek with her palm and took a deep breath. "I do."

Josh grabbed her around the waist and kissed her hard.

"Hey," the minister shouted. "We aren't at that part yet."

With a grin that made her giddy, Josh put her back on her feet. Their friends were whooping loudly.

"It's time for the rings," the vicar said.

Mitch handed them to Josh. He turned back to Caroline. "They're not what you expected because I thought we could pick them out together on our honeymoon."

She looked down at the two plastic toy rings in Josh's palm. She cocked an eyebrow at him.

"You forgot to get the rings, didn't you?"

Mitch covered his mouth as he struggled not to laugh.

"I might have let it slip." For once Josh was the one who turned a nice shade of red.

Caroline put her hands on her hips. "I gave you one job to do, Josh McInnes."

He rolled his eyes. "Is this really the time and place for that discussion?"

She looked over her shoulder at their grinning friends and family. "Probably not, but don't think it isn't going to happen."

He winked at her. "I wouldn't expect anything less."

He placed the pink plastic ring on her finger and grinned like he'd won the lottery. "We can pick out the one you want in Paris. Along with some new clothes." He thought about it for a minute. "And lots of lingerie."

She smacked him on the chest. He nabbed her hand and held it tight above his heart.

"Okay," the vicar interrupted. "It's Sunday night and I usually spend it watching *Strictly Come Dancing*. So how about we wrap this up?"

Josh squeezed Caroline's hand tight.

"By the power vested in me, I now pronounce you husband and wife. Have at it. Kiss the woman."

"With pleasure." Josh's lips descended on Caroline.

It wasn't a polite kiss. It was a long, deep plundering kiss that stole the air from her lungs and the strength from her legs. When Josh pulled away from her, his look was knowing. "We're having a short reception. In the kitchen." He quirked an eyebrow at her, but did it with a smile. "Because the kitchen is the only room in the house with a floor." Caroline grinned at him. "Then we're heading to Paris. You and me. No people. No houseguests. No press. I'll have you all to myself."

He leaned down and kissed her again as the band began to play. Josh wrapped his arms around her, tucked his face in the crook of her neck and swayed to the music. Caroline gripped his shoulders. She wasn't entirely sure that this wasn't all a dream.

"Well, Mrs. McInnes." She felt the words against her skin. "Any regrets?"

"Give me a week to answer that," Caroline told him with a cheeky grin. "I'm sure I'll come up with something."

EPILOGUE

Nine Months Later—Invertary Castle

When Josh McInnes realised that his wife had gone into labour, he did what any self-respecting celebrity would do and called his manager.

"Caroline is having the baby. Right now. And we need to get the midwife." Josh had him on speakerphone while he pulled on his shoes.

"Then why are you calling me?"

"He's got a point." Caroline was calmly checking the battery on her e-reader. Josh was pretty sure that there wouldn't be time during labour to read a book, but he wasn't going to tell her that. Since she'd given up her work at the community centre, she'd filled her time with researching Invertary history and reading dodgy romance novels. Well, that and running the town.

He turned his attention back to Mitch. "Pyro and a bunch

of his paparazzi mates are camped at the gate. I'm worried the midwife won't be able to get into the castle."

"Then why not call, Lake? What am I supposed to do about it?"

Caroline doubled over the bed as another contraction hit her. How could she be so calm? When the pain passed, she shouted at the speakerphone, "Don't worry, Mitch—it's his automatic reaction to call you when anything happens. We're hanging up now to call the midwife."

"We are?" Josh wasn't sure the midwife could deal with Pyro.

"Hang up, Josh. See you later, Mitch."

Josh pressed the end button before Mitch could reply.

Caroline smiled at him. She was even more beautiful than the day he'd met her. "Call the midwife. And call Betty. She knows what to do about Pyro."

"Betty?"

"Lake's on another job. I made arrangements with Betty."

"But Betty?" Josh stared at her.

His wife was in labour. The baby was coming. And he wanted her to call an eighty-seven-year-old woman with an attitude problem?

"Josh. Dial the phone now or you'll be delivering this baby."

He dialled the midwife. "I'll be right there," she promised before hanging up on him.

"We should be in a hospital." Josh knew there was no point bringing it up, but he couldn't help himself. They'd been arguing about this for nine months.

"The nearest hospital is an hour's drive from here. Plus I want to have our baby at home."

"What if something goes wrong?"

"Calm down, Josh. It's just a baby. Women have been having them for a very long time."

"They haven't been having *my* baby!"

Caroline waddled over to him and pulled him down for a kiss. "You need to call Betty."

"Damn it." He dialled the wicked witch of Invertary and put her on speaker. "Betty, it's Josh. The baby is coming."

"Say no more. Operation Stork is good to go."

"Operation Stork?" He could feel his blood pressure rise as he asked the question.

Betty cackled before he heard a dial tone.

"It'll be okay." Caroline bent over the bed again. "Rub my back. The midwife will be here soon."

Josh wanted to run screaming around the building until someone who knew what they were doing turned up. Instead, he rubbed his wife's back.

"This is the last child we're having." He'd get a vasectomy if that was what it took. He wasn't going through this again.

Caroline laughed. Man, but he loved her laugh. "You used to be so easygoing. I had to fight to make you take anything seriously."

"You've been a bad influence on me."

She laughed some more.

A horn honked outside. The front door slammed. A few minutes later, the midwife barrelled in. "Has he freaked out completely yet?" She grinned at Josh. He glared at her.

Caroline smiled at him. "Better call for backup. Any minute now he's going to need medical attention."

How she could joke at a time like this, he didn't know.

"Saw Betty and the old folk downstairs. They're lobbing eggs at the paparazzi."

"Eggs?" Josh knew he was screeching. He couldn't seem to stop it. "That's the big plan."

Caroline patted his hand. "That's phase one." She turned to the midwife. "Maybe you should give him something to calm him down."

As the two women chuckled, Caroline suddenly stopped still.

"What is it?" He knew they should have gone to the hospital. It was a mistake letting Caroline get her own way on a home birth. He should have laid down the law. He scoffed to himself. Like that ever worked. He glared at his wedding ring. Even though he'd had it engraved with the words from The Lord of the Rings: *one ring to rule them all*. The damn thing had no power at all.

Caroline pointed downward. "My water broke."

Josh saw the first signs of an actual birth, and it was too much for him. The room spun and the last thing he felt was his head hitting the floor.

"WAKE UP, DADDY."

Josh could have sworn that was Mitch.

His eyes flickered open to see Mitch grinning down at him. He had his iPhone in his hand. "This is definitely going on YouTube."

"Leave him alone." Caroline sounded amused.

Caroline! The baby!

Josh struggled to his feet to find his wife propped up in bed, a little bundle of pink wrapped in her arms. "Is that the baby?"

"Come meet your daughter." Caroline smiled at him. Her face was flushed and her hair was dishevelled, but she had never been more magnificent.

Stunned, he walked over to her. "How long was I out?"

She laughed. "A while. But you fainted several times. You kept coming to and then you'd see something you didn't like and you'd drop again. Don't worry, Mitch filmed it. Your passing out, I mean, not the birth."

He glared at his friend, who shrugged. Josh took a deep breath and pulled back the pink blanket. The most beautiful little face appeared. It was a tiny Caroline. He stopped breathing.

"Our daughter," he said with awe.

He dragged his attention away from his perfect little person to kiss his wife. "Man, I love you."

She gave him the same smile that got them in this position in the first place. "I know." Her voice was smug.

Josh brushed her hair back from her face. "Are you okay? Was it tough?"

She laughed. "It was fast and painful. But I still think I had an easier time than you did."

"Let's not do it again." Josh reached for his daughter, and Caroline handed her over. As soon as he held her in his arms, his heart melted. He didn't think it was possible to love someone as much as he loved Caroline. Now there were two women who owned him. "Well, maybe not for a couple of years, anyway."

Caroline reached for his hand as she grinned at him. "You promised me three babies."

He sighed. It was no use arguing. Caroline always got her way. "Fine. But the next time we go to the hospital."

"Yeah," Mitch said. "Let them deal with Josh when he passes out."

Caroline shut her eyes and snuggled back against the pillows. She had a very self-satisfied smile on her face. Josh watched his new-born sleep. He had it all. Wife. Daughter. Home. Life was pretty damn good.

"See?" He confronted his best friend. "And you thought that whole arranged marriage idea was dumb. Bet you regret that now."

"Yes. I am in awe of your genius."

"Damn right. The plan was brilliant."

Mitch rolled his eyes, and Josh thought he heard Caroline giggle. Let them think what they liked. No one could convince him that his wedding plan didn't turn out perfectly.

FIRST CHAPTER OF MAGENTA MINE

Harry Boyle fell in love with Magenta when he was eight years old. It happened in the sandpit of the local primary school. The five-year-old girl had been building the biggest sandcastle Harry had ever seen. He'd paused beside her, wondering if he should give her tips on how to make it more structurally sound, but he'd learned the hard way to keep his super brain to himself.

"Hairy Boil," one of the class bullies shouted behind him. "You going to play with the wee girls now?"

There was laughter.

Magenta looked up at him with huge golden eyes, her honey-coloured pigtails askew and full of sand. She blinked several times as she studied him. "That's a funny name. You don't look hairy."

Harry took her comment seriously, as he did most things. "They're making fun of my name. It's Harry Boyle."

She scowled. "That's mean." She studied him a bit more before nodding to herself. "Do you want me to punch them for you?"

Harry's mouth fell open at her words. He looked over his

shoulder at the group of boys who were still pointing at him and laughing, then he looked back at the fairy in the sandpit. He would have laughed too if she hadn't been so serious. The bullying had gotten worse since his brother Flynn had gone to secondary school, and as much as he would like someone to stand up for him, he didn't think a five-year-old girl was the best protector to pick.

"They'll get fed up soon and annoy someone else," he said.

"I don't mind hitting them." She shrugged and turned back to her castle.

Harry couldn't take it anymore. "You need to reinforce it, or it will collapse."

She eyed him thoughtfully. "How?"

Harry sank to his knees beside her and showed her how to make the castle stable.

And that's how his friendship with Magenta started. Of course, back then she was still called Maggie Fraser. It wasn't until she was thirteen, and Harry was in university, that she dyed her hair black, bought a giant tub of eyeliner and started calling herself Magenta. Harry had come back to Invertary for the holidays to find his friend replaced by a sullen Goth who'd looked him up and down slowly, smirked and turned away from him. She'd never turned back.

And Harry had never stopped loving her.

"*She's* the reason you're making us pack up and relocate to the middle of nowhere?" Rachel didn't make any effort to hide her disgust as she pointed at the lingerie shop. Magenta could be clearly seen through the shop window.

Harry looked at his business manager. He'd met Rachel in the university cafeteria when he was sixteen. His big brain had meant that he was years younger than his fellow students and socially out of his depth. Rachel had felt sorry for him and had pretty much adopted him as her pet—at least, that's what it had always felt like to Harry. She'd been

370

older and wiser at nineteen, not to mention she was studying the much more socially savvy business studies course. The friendship had stuck, and eight years later, Rachel was the face of Harry's programming business. And he was grateful for it.

"Her name is Magenta, and she's not the only reason we're moving to Invertary." He glanced around his hometown, with its rows of quirky white and grey crooked houses and cobblestone roads. Heather-covered hills cradled the town, while the cool loch sparkled beside it. "Look around, Rach—this is much nicer than London."

She stuck her tiny nose in the air and folded her arms over her designer blue business suit. Everything about Rachel was polished and expensive. She'd once told him her shoes cost more than his car. Every time he looked at them, he wondered why.

"You know how I feel about this," she said. "It might be pretty up here in the Highlands, but our business contacts are in London and Europe."

"We can conference call. Skype. Fly in for face to face. I don't see the problem. This isn't Outer Mongolia. It's Scotland."

"You can't network over the phone. You do that face to face, over lunch or a casual drink after work. None of which we can do here."

"I don't do that stuff anyway," Harry pointed out.

"No, but I do." She flicked her manicured fingers in the direction of the town. "What am I supposed to do here while you're communing with your laptop? This town is stuck in the fifties. It doesn't even have a decent clothes shop. And you want to drag everyone up here. The team will go insane inside of a week."

"No they won't." Harry sighed. "As long as they have internet access, they won't care. It's only you who'll miss the

London scene. I told you. You can stay there. We'll work it out."

"Who will you bounce ideas off if I'm not here?"

"I can call."

"It won't be the same." She patted the tight bun that held her auburn hair.

He couldn't argue with that. For eight years she'd been his sounding board, and he wasn't sure how he'd function without her. Rachel let out a dramatic sigh.

"Why this girl? I don't see anything special about her. I mean, she works in a lingerie shop and she obviously has no idea how to dress. She didn't even finish school. How are you supposed to have a conversation with her?"

Harry shook his head. Rachel's issues were for Rachel to deal with.

He cocked his head at the shop behind them. Eye Spy was a security company run by ex-SAS member Lake Benson. It was no secret that Harry specialised in security programming, and Lake thought there might be some benefits in a working relationship. So far their meetings had gone well.

"You go in," he told Rachel. "Tell Lake I'll be in in a minute. I'm going to talk to Magenta."

"Fine. I hope it goes better than the last three times you've tried."

"Couldn't be worse," Harry mumbled as he walked over the street to Kirsty's lingerie shop.

"Here he comes again," Kirsty said from her spot at the window. The ex-model turned to Magenta, who was unpacking a new line in thongs at the back of the shop. "How about this time you let him talk to you instead of doing your best to scare him off?"

Magenta rolled her eyes. "I don't want to talk to him. Just

because we were friends when we were kids, doesn't mean I owe him anything now."

"That's harsh. Even you can be more polite than that. I've seen it. I know it can happen."

"I'm busy," Magenta said. "Tell him to come back later."

"You tell him. I can't. It's like kicking a puppy."

Only if the puppy was over six feet tall, muscled in a lean way and had sexy silver eyes. Magenta clamped down on her thoughts. So Harry had grown up pretty. So what? She still didn't want to deal with him. She heard the bell over the door and felt her body tense. Why the heck didn't he go back to London, where he belonged?

"Hi, Magenta." His deep voice seemed to rumble and vibrate throughout her body.

Taking a steadying breath, she turned towards him. "What can I do for you, Harry?"

She kept her face expressionless, and was grateful that she'd opted for her thigh-high platform boots this morning. She needed the extra height to stop from gazing up at him.

"I thought we could get together tonight. Eat. Talk about old times." He wore a grey T-shirt with Einstein's head on it, and Magenta wondered if Einstein would be proud that he adorned T-shirts and bobblehead dolls.

"Sorry, Harry, I'm busy." She took a step back towards the box of thongs she'd been unpacking.

Out of the corner of her eye she could see Kirsty scowling as she wagged a finger. Magenta ignored her.

"Tomorrow, then." He thrust his hands into the pockets of his faded blue jeans. Magenta knew he was worth a lot of money. It'd been the talk of the town that Harry had sold a program he'd developed to the UK government for millions. It almost made her smile to see he was still wearing his old, tatty jeans. Clothes were never something Harry had noticed as a kid. Not like the designer-clad sidekick he'd dragged to town with him. Everything about her screamed money and class. Magenta frowned at yet another reminder that she would never travel in the same circles as Harry.

"I'm busy for the foreseeable future," she told him.

"Is there a way you can get un-busy?" His smile almost made her crumble. He somehow managed to pull off sexy and sweet at the same time.

"Harry," she said on a sigh. "I don't want to get together and rehash our childhood. I don't want to get together full stop. I know this isn't what you want to hear, but you just need to suck it up."

Any other man would have tucked tail and run at such a blunt rejection. Not Harry. Bloody stupid man. Harry smiled and took a step towards her.

"Well, I would suck it up, if I believed you. But I don't. So how about you clear some time in your busy schedule for me?"

"Not going to happen." She swallowed hard and thrust a handful of pink underwear at him. "You might as well make yourself useful while you annoy me. Sort these into sizes."

Harry looked down at the silky thongs then gave her a wicked smile. "See, this is why we need to spend time getting to know each other again." He moved forwards, crowding her space. "You think handing me lingerie is going to make me turn red, stutter and run. But I keep telling you. I've grown up. I'm not the kid you knew." He took another step towards her, making her breath hitch and her body vibrate at his nearness. "Lingerie doesn't scare me, Magenta. Neither do you." His voice was a low, sexy rumble that woke up her erogenous zones. "I like lingerie." He held up a thong. "These would look good on you."

Magenta sucked in a breath. "Time for you to go, Harry." She was pleased that her voice sounded as sharp as usual.

He placed the underwear on the counter beside her. "I'm not giving up. You and I have unfinished business."

With that, he turned and sauntered out of the shop. Magenta let out a long, slow breath.

"What is wrong with you?" Kirsty flicked her russet-coloured hair out of her eyes before glaring at Magenta. Kirsty had cut it after her accident years ago, but now she was letting it grow out. "You two used to be inseparable. Now you won't even talk to the guy."

"That was a long time ago. People change." Magenta turned her focus back to the underwear as she quietly worked at getting her body back under control.

"Yep, they do. And Harry has changed for the better. You may as well give in and meet with him. See what he wants. You might actually enjoy hanging out with him again."

"Yeah, right. And pigs might fly over Invertary dropping free bacon on everyone."

Magenta turned her back on her boss and concentrated on her work. She didn't know why Harry was so interested in spending time with her. She'd made sure to burn the bridges between them when she was thirteen. It had ripped her apart, but she'd known that it was the right thing to do. For both their sakes.

"How did it go?" Lake asked as Harry let himself into the security shop.

Harry used his hand to mime a plane flying, crashing and exploding.

"That good, huh?" Lake's mouth twitched as it tried to smile.

"Isn't it time you gave up?" Rachel said. "It's obvious she isn't interested in you."

They were sitting at a round conference table in Lake's back room. Harry pulled out a chair, flipped it, straddled it and leaned on the backrest. "She's interested. When I bumped into her sister a few months ago, she told me Magenta used to write our names together in hearts all over her books. She said Magenta still keeps a scrapbook about me. She's interested, all right. She's just scared."

There was cackling from the corner. "Not a lot scares that lassie," Betty said.

Harry grinned at the eighty-seven-year-old. Betty had always fascinated him. She was known for her lies, her sick sense of humour and her willingness to meddle for entertainment's sake—and she didn't give a damn who knew it. Lake had inherited Betty when he'd bought her shop, and seemed to treat her like some sort of mascot. She was currently installed in her tatty old armchair, feet on a stool, reading a magazine. Harry cocked his eye at the magazine title—*Survivalist Now*. He gave Lake a questioning look.

Lake's lip twitched. "She saw that movie with Will Smith, the one where zombies take over the world. Now she's preparing for a zombie apocalypse."

"Aye, you laugh now, son, but you'll tell a different story when they're out to eat your brains, and the only thing between you and being somebody's snack is the preparation I put in."

Harry stifled a grin as Betty turned her attention back to him. "You need to stop trying to talk to that girl in the shop. You need to get her alone somewhere. A lingerie shop is no place for a heavy discussion."

"Getting her alone is hard. She's either at the shop or in the house she shares with the twins." He shuddered. Dealing with his twin cousins was worse than dealing with the UK government. "Plus, I asked her out to dinner tonight and she turned me down flat."

Betty shifted in her chair, then tugged her hairnet down over her mostly bald head. "That's where you're going wrong. You don't ask her to go out with you. You surprise her when she's alone, preferably in a place where she can't run away."

"Please tell me you aren't taking relationship advice from Lake's Hobbit," Rachel said.

"Hey," Betty snapped. "Lake's the only one allowed to call me that."

Rachel rolled her eyes dramatically. "Can we please go back to London, where we belong?"

"Aye." Betty gave Rachel the evil eye. "Send her back. She's too stuck up to fit in here."

"So," Harry said loudly to ward off a counterattack from his business manager. "Got any suggestions on how to get her alone?"

"Well, it just so happens that I do." The look on Betty's face was pure mischief. She was clearly up to something, but Harry was too desperate to let it worry him. "Saturday afternoon, Magenta is going into the old mine to take some pictures. She'll be alone. I reckon you should make a picnic and surprise her there."

Huh. That wasn't a bad plan. He looked at Lake, who shrugged. "I wouldn't take relationship advice from Betty either," he said, making Betty grin with pride.

"That's my boy," she told him.

"So where in the mine is she taking photos?" Harry asked.

Betty gave him a toothless grin. "I can't rightly explain it. Best if you pick me up on Saturday and I'll show you the way. There are a lot of mine entrances; it'd be easy for you to go to the wrong one."

"It's a deal," he told her.

"Idiot," Rachel said.

Lake just grinned.

Get Magenta Mine now and keep on reading!

ABOUT THE AUTHOR

I'm a Scot, living in New Zealand and married to a Dutch man. I write contemporary romance with a humorous bent – this is mainly due to the fact I have an odd sense of humour and can't keep it out of anything I do! If I wasn't a writer, I'd like to be Buffy the Vampire Slayer, or Indiana Jones. Unfortunately, both these roles have already been filled. Which may be a good thing as I have no fighting skills, wouldn't know a precious relic if it hit me in the face and have an aversion to blood. When I'm not living in my head, I'm a mother to two kids, several pet sheep, one dog, four cats, three alpacas, two miniature horses, eight guinea pigs and an escape artist chicken.

9 780473 461300